Winnie and Wolf

A. N. WILSON

arrow books

Published by Arrow Books in 2008

1 3 5 7 9 10 8 6 4 2

First published in the United Kingdom in 2007 by Hutchinson

Arrow Books
The Random House Group Limited
20 Vauxhall Bridge Road, London, SW1V 2SA

www.rbooks.co.uk

Addresses for companies within The Random House Group Limited can be found at:
www.randomhouse.co.uk/offices.htm

The Random House Group Limited Reg. No. 954009

A CIP catalogue record for this book is available from the British Library

ISBN 9780099492474

The Ran   )
Council (FSC   ll our
titles that are prin   ¬SC logo.

Typeset in Fourni   irlingshire

Winnie and Wolf

A. N. Wilson was born in 1950 and educated at Rugby and New College, Oxford. A Fellow of the Royal Society of Literature, he holds a prominent position in the world of literature and journalism. He is a celebrated biographer and novelist, winning prizes for much of his work. He lives in North London. *Winnie and Wolf* was longlisted for the 2007 Man Booker Prize.

'An outstanding novel, brilliantly imaginative and hypnotically readable' Selina Hastings, Books of the Year, *Sunday Telegraph*

'Superb . . . In this tour de force of imagination and historical reconstruction, Wilson makes a credible human being out of a monster . . . Unlike any other novel this year, and as well written as you would expect, it's a novel with substance' Susan Hill, Books of the Year, *Independent*

'A moving and disturbing narrative, whose climactic scene . . . is unforgettable' Rowan Williams, Books of the Year, *Times Literary Supplement*

'A deliciously irreverent portrait of Hitler, Wagner and 19th century philosophy that will have you laughing out loud' Cristina Odone, Books of the Year, *Sunday Telegraph*

'Readers and critics alike loved this account of the relationship between Adolf Hitler and Winifred Wagner. Operatic in scale and emotion' Alex Clark, Books of the Year, *Observer*

'Wilson's achievement is startling . . . Most contemporary English fiction looks rather etiolated and pointless by comparison' Hywel Williams, *Guardian*

'A thoroughly engrossing read . . . A.N. Wilson offers a plethora of fascinating ideas on politics, philosophy and, above all, the music of Wagner . . . *Winnie and Wolf* vividly brings to life a place, a time and an extraordinary family' *Mail on Sunday*

'Wilson ha[s] . . . superbly well' *Litera[ry Review]*

To
Beryl Bainbridge

I received the typescript of this book from a woman I truly believe to be the daughter of Adolf Hitler.

Winifred Hiedler died at the Raymond and Rubie Kranz Seniors' Home for Retired Musicians on 27 October 2006. I had been visiting Ms Hiedler for some years, since I joined our Lutheran congregation in South Heath as junior pastor. She had lived either in our neighbourhood (which is, as you may know, a suburb of Seattle) or in downtown Seattle itself.

It is perhaps worth saying a word about her name. The former Mrs Senta Cristiansen, she came to the United States in 1968 with her husband. They had no children. They were both professional musicians, he a violinist, she a cellist, playing in one of the larger orchestras in Stockholm before applying to work in the United States. Shortly after she received her naturalization papers, Mrs Cristiansen, as she was then, reverted to her former name of Senta N———. (She made it a condition of this book being made public that her adopted family name be kept secret.)

She joined our congregation at South Heath before I arrived as a pastor in the mid 1990s. Anyone from 97th St Lutheran Church, South Heath, will remember her as a courteous, bright-eyed, white-haired woman, with a brisk walk and perfect manners. She always wore the same beige-coloured mackintoshes, and the only variation in her wardrobe of a Sunday morning appeared to be her wide choice of berets, in pink, pale-blue, green etc. etc. She spoke perfect English, with an only slightly foreign intonation, which many took to be Scandinavian. She was a regular supporter of all our church work; she was always available, until infirmity made this impossible, to help with any of our charitable undertakings, including taking food to the down-and-outs, AIDS awareness, and baking for our annual Christmas socials with deprived children. Also, she took an especially keen interest in the choral singing, though she was occasionally critical both of our choice of music and of its execution. She would attend church socials, but only if they were in our social centre. She did not accept personal hospitality, never came to the homes of any member of our congregation, and never invited any of them into her home. I was the only person, apart from medical personnel, who ever visited her at the Seniors' Home.

While she was still active, she vacated her small apartment in downtown Seattle and took the room which she occupied until her death at Kranz Seniors'. She was more than eligible for her place there, having spent most of her professional life as a poorly paid and highly skilled musician, and having limited resources. (Her hip replacement operation in 1995, for which she insisted on paying herself rather than claiming from Medicare, left her with next to no assets.)

In all the time I knew her she was named Winifred Hiedler. I did not know that she had chosen legally to assume both the first name and the second name in 1982, when she was fifty years old, after she received through the mail the text of which this book is composed. Nor did she ever speak to me about this book. After her second hip began to cause difficulties, her churchgoing became less frequent and I took to visiting her on a regular basis. We spoke very largely of generalities – the news, television programmes (she was particularly keen on staying up for *Larry King Live*!). But she also liked a comedy show called *Bewitched!* and, of course, music. It was in the course of these conversations that I was told that although her husband had been Swedish, and she came to the United States from Sweden, she had in fact been born in Germany. At first this information was thrown out quite casually, but in time I came to see that this deeply reserved woman who had, as I came to realize, no living friends or family, had a secret, or a story, or something which she wished to communicate.

It was some five years before she died that she gave me a stout parcel. As I discovered after her death, it contained the typescript of this book. She asked me not to open, still less to read, it until after she had died. I have kept to this promise.

I have myself translated it into English. If the pages are to be trusted, they purport to be what amounts to an extended letter, or meditation, or memoir, addressed to Ms Hiedler from her adopted father, a Herr N——, born in Bayreuth, Franconia, in 1902 and dying in East Germany some time in 1979–80. He lived in the industrial town of —— for the last decades of his life.

These pages contain the astounding claim that Senta Schmidt, of Germany, later Mrs Cristiansen of Stockholm, later Seattle, and the Winifred Hiedler who was such a devoted member of our church congregation, was none other than the daughter of Winifred Wagner, the composer's daughter-in-law, and Adolf Hitler.

The fact that my old friend legally changed her name from Senta Cristiansen to Winifred Hiedler twenty-six years before she died is a token of the fact that she herself clearly believed the contents of this book. Hitler's father Alois was the illegitimate son of a woman called Maria Anna Schicklgruber. When the child was five years old, Maria married an itinerant millworker called Johann Georg Hiedler, and the boy Alois adopted this name, only later spelling it Hitler. Evidently my old friend believed that it was possible, even in a Lutheran congregation where many German émigrés worshipped, to adopt the surname Hiedler without appearing too conspicuous, and evidently she was right, since I never heard any member of the church make the fantastic suggestion that this mild-mannered, reclusive and polite woman might be the daughter of a mass murderer. As a serious-minded and truthful person, she clearly chose to change her name so as to . . . so as to what? To tell the truth?

That she was the adopted daughter of Herr N——, the author of these pages, there seems no reason to doubt. As for the rest, it is difficult to see how some of this story can be true. Though Ms Hiedler believed it enough to go to the trouble of changing her name, there is more than sufficient evidence in the text itself (for example, when the author actually meets Winifred Wagner's son Wieland in 1960 and is barely recognized) to suggest that it is, just possibly, a work, not of fraud, but of fantasy. It seems to have been the case that Ms Hiedler was indeed an adopted child and, as anyone with pastoral experience can tell you, the need to find a birth parent can lead down the most bizarre avenues of speculation. Another possibility is that this is a work of fiction, penned by Ms Hiedler herself. If so, it would certainly suggest very deep mental unbalance; but, as I have emphasized, I only knew her on a superficial level and she was always careful to keep herself to herself.

Hermann Muller, Assistant Pastor, South Heath Lutheran Church, Seattle, WA 153977

Easter 2007

The Flying Dutchman

Die düst're Glut, die hier ich fühle brennen
Sollt' ich, Unseliger, die Liebe nennen?
Ach nein! Die Sehnsucht ist es nach dem Heil:
Würd' es durch solchen Engel mir ʒu Teil!
                    The Flying Dutchman

'Are you a policeman?'

It was a disconcerting question, coming as it did from the shadows behind a life-size bust of the goddess Athene, which stood on the occasional table on the upstairs landing.

'Only,' the goddess continued, 'you keep following Uncle Wolf about.'

'Do I?' I asked edgily.

'I haven't told anyone,' said Athene.

'Why not?'

'It could be our secret. If you'd like.'

Friedelind, aged seven, stepped into the chiaroscuro.

'That would be good,' I conceded.

She was a substantial child, much larger than most seven-year-olds. Her fleshiness was disconcertingly adult and she entirely lacked shyness. When I had arrived in the household the previous year, the children had very naturally shrunk back. Time had been necessary before I got their confidence. I had been employed as a general assistant to their father, Siegfried Wagner, himself a composer, an inspired conductor, as well as the director of the Festival Opera at Bayreuth. My business was chiefly with him. I helped him with his correspondence, organized his diary and was a general dogsbody about the house, taking telephone calls and in effect acting as an unofficial valet to Siegfried and butler to the rest of them when the need arose. Siegfried needed, a fact which caused the predictable raising of eyebrows, a young man at his side. When they had asked me to do the job, Siegfried and his wife Winnie had alluded, as tactfully as possible, to the great age of his mother, Cosima, the composer's widow. It was suggested to me that when the day came of her departure from this planet, there would be a wealth of papers for me to study. I would be given the first glimpse of such treasures as her correspondence with her great husband and be allowed to read her diaries.

One of the great perks of my humdrum employment was that it allowed me to breathe in so much information about Richard Wagner and permitted me to quiz the older members of the household – the composer's surviving daughters. Occasionally, very occasionally, I was allowed to accompany the Mistress (that is, Wagner's widow Cosima) on her stately progress into the Hofgarten, or even to sit with her and listen to her daughter Eva read aloud to her. In Cosima's presence, however, my questions were strictly forbidden.

It was my hope, one day, to write a book about Wagner and philosophy. All these dazzling operas, even the apprentice work in *Rienzi*, but certainly *The Flying Dutchman* and everything he had written subsequently, did not merely seem to me the most wonderful music that had ever been composed. They were also the most fascinating examples of philosophy transposed into art. They were dramatized ideas.

So, the answer to the seven-year-old Friedelind's intrusive question was yes, I was an investigator and I did want to solve a mystery, or series of mysteries. How was it that the young revolutionary Richard Wagner who had been expelled from Dresden in 1848 for being a political subversive came, after his death, to be the hero of the most reactionary figures in Germany? Why did the grand duchesses, and margraves and lieutenant-generals resplendent in their uniform come up the Green Hill outside Bayreuth to sit through hour upon hour of subversive operas which, if seriously considered, would have caused them all to evaporate? How did it come about that Wagner who, even in his more conservative old age, despised any political parties and was unimpressed by Bismarck himself, how did it come about that he was seen as the great hope of all these bizarre '*völkisch*' parties who were making such headway in our poor confused Germany in those post-First World War years?

Is it possible to be apolitical? Wagner was left-wing. Then he stopped being left-wing largely because he read a philosopher called Schopenhauer. He read Schopenhauer over and over again. Schopenhauer came to believe that the only way to wisdom was by a denial of the will. He read the Upanishads and believed that Western thought (apart from Plato and Kant) had been misguided altogether. He was against Christianity, systems, tyranny, but above all the tyranny of the mob. He had once allowed soldiers into his room so that they could get a better aim at rioting students. This anecdote always haunted me. I too loved Schopenhauer, but could one want to shoot enthusiastic young people who merely desired to demonstrate against injustice or the folly of things?

Wagner had in him this need to renounce the will, but did he also have in him something of that violence? That understanding of violence? Was that partly what appealed to some of the nastier *völkisch* types with their desire to beat up Jews or have pub brawls with the Reds?

Was I a policeman?

'Uncle Wolf is only staying one night,' the child persisted.

'Really?'

'He has really, really, important work to do back in Munich. Partly he's written a book which is going to save Germany. Mummy gave him the paper and pencils to do it. While he was in prison. Do only bad people go to prison?'

'Not invariably, but on the whole, yes.'

'That's not an answer.'

'Most of the people who get sent to prison are bad.'

'Uncle Wolf is good, though?'

'He went to prison for trying to start a thing called a revolution. He and some other men tried to throw out the government, that's

9

the people who rule over us, the people we had elected to rule over us. Uncle – your friend – shot men. People got killed. That is why he went to prison.'

'Mummy says that there have been three really great Germans – Martin Luther, Frederick Grossman and Uncle Wolf.'

I forbore to wonder aloud whether Goethe, Beethoven, Hegel or Einstein deserved consideration. Instead I asked, 'Who's Frederick Grossman?'

'No.' She giggled and corrected herself: 'Frederick . . .'

'Friedrich der Grosse?'

'That's him.'

'He was the cleverest king Prussia ever had, but very ruthless. He had lots of wars. Lots of people got killed.'

'He is a great – is it philatelist?'

'Philosopher.'

'That's it. He's a philosopher, he has really, really clever thoughts. And he is wise, and good and he's going to save us all from the Reds and the Jews.'

'Frederick the Great? He *read* philosophers. He wasn't one himself.'

'No, Uncle Wolf.'

'Oh, I see.'

'Are you teasing?'

'No.'

'You don't sound as if you think Uncle Wolf will save us from the Jews.'

'I don't think we necessarily need saving from the Jews.'

'Luther and Frederick the Great hated them too, you know.'

'I haven't really thought about it much, Friedelind.'

'Only Mummy says Uncle Wolf has a bit of a bee in his bonnet and the yids we know are all right, the ones in the orchestra and dear Dr Liebermann.'

'Of course.'

'I like Dr Liebermann. When I had that cold last year? When it was really, really bad and Mummy said it was all in my imagination and I had to go out for my walk as usual in the Hofgarten? And Dr Liebermann came and said "I prescribe three days in bed with hot drinks and Grimm's fairy tales".'

'That was kind of him.'

'Too kind, Mummy says. But are you?'

'Go to bed, Friedelind. You're meant to be having your afternoon rest.'

'I wouldn't tell anyone. If you were a policeman. It could be our secret.'

Later that afternoon, coming back through the large entrance hall of the Wagners' house, I could hear Wolf's voice, rasping and blaring from behind the closed doors of the salon. It was a very carrying voice at the best of times, but during one of his recitations for the children it rose to an extraordinary volume.

I had just walked out to the little kiosk halfway down Richard Wagnerstrasse with a haversack of paper money, hoping to buy myself the *Völkischer Beobachter* and a packet of cigarettes – but I did not, as it happens, possess enough for the newspaper, which was selling at thirteen billion marks. By the time I had paid the twenty billion for cigarettes there was no cash left over for the nationalist newspaper we all liked to read (it was 1925) and whose aspirations during that period – a recovered German economy, the undoing of the Versailles Treaty, the restitution of the German lands in the Ruhr region at present occupied by the French – seemed even less realistic than the ambitions of the fisherman's wife in the Grimms' story, which Wolf was enacting (more than reading) for the children.

You remember the folk tale, no doubt. A fisherman lives with his wife in a pisspot beside the sea – and every day the fisherman fishes and fishes. One day he catches a flounder, but the fish explains to him that he is not truly a fish. He is a prince under an enchantment, and if the fisherman will only spare his life he will grant him his wish. The fisherman goes home and talks to his wife. The fisherman's wife is in a state of perpetual discontent. She tells him to go to the flounder and to ask for a little cottage to live in. So off he goes, chanting over the water in the Pomeranian dialect,

Flow-undurr, flow-undurr, where be ye?
Come up out of that thar bubblin' zee!
Moy woyf Ilsebill won't be content
As oi'd 've wished and oi'd 've meant.

The wife's discontent grows and grows. Unhappy with the cottage, she wants a palace; discontented with the palace, she won't be satisfied until she has occupied all the land round about it. Disgruntled with owning huge estates, she wishes to be king – then emperor – then pope. With each crazy request to the flounder, and with each recitation of the fisherman's rhyme, the sea boils more angrily and the skies darken. By the time I had slipped into the salon the wife had become pope and the poor husband was hoping to creep out of the bedroom unobserved by his ever more ambitious companion.

The three children at Wolf's feet were Wolfgang, aged six, Friedelind, seven, and Wieland, eight. Little Verena, aged five, sat a bit apart from them on the knee of her mother Winifred. I forget who else was present – perhaps Lieselotte the governess, perhaps not. What I chiefly recollect of the scene was the wide-eyed wonder with which the children hung upon the words of this master storyteller. Though remaining in his chair, Wolf conveyed, by stealthy movements of his shoulders and comical screwings-up of his features, that he was the hen-pecked fisherman trying to escape his wife, now transformed into the pope. But His Holiness had woken up.

'"Not so faarst!" said the fisherman's wife.' Little Verena looked alarmed at the wife's sternness but the other children wriggled with ecstatic amusement. '"You mus' go back to thar that flow-undurr un' you mus' zay"' – he paused. His extraordinary eyes flashed. I have never seen such eyes. It was the utter luminosity of a very bright moonlight night sky. He looked to each child in turn. Two of them were giggling, two were a little fearful. After all, the wife had been a king, an emperor, a pope – how much further could her ambition take her? Hitherto, in speaking the wife's words, the great orator had rasped out her demands.

'Now she whispered, "Oi want tew be – as *Gard*."'

Absolute silence followed. Then came a giggle from the eight-year-old Wieland. 'But she *can't* be God!'

Uncle Wolf put a finger to his moustachioed upper lip and continued, '"Oi'm *toired* with a-watchin ur the zun a-comin' un the moon a-roisin' – *oi* warnts to *make* the zun cum up uv a marnin' un the moon tew cum up ut noights."

'"Oh woify, woify, oi beg yew"' – for the husband's voice Wolf took on a mincing effeminate tone, which bore perhaps an uncomfortable resemblance to my employer, Winnie's husband, Herr Wagner. Maybe I was merely imagining this for surely Wolf, with his profound courtesy and with a reverence bordering on sycophancy for the Wagner family, would never be so ill-mannered as to mock, of all people, the son of his greatest hero? '"Please be content," lisped the feeble husband, "please be content to stay as the pope."'

'And at this', continued Wolf, 'the wife became *extremely* angry. Her hair flew wildly around her head and she ripped at her corsets and she gave the fisherman a great *kick* and she screamed and she yelled, "Oi won't *stand* for this any more! Oi want to be Gard"' – and then Wolf really bellowed. '"Oi want to be Gard."'

Another long silence and everyone in the room, including myself, was spellbound, solemn.

He continued the story, not in the Pomeranian dialect in which it is preserved by the Brothers Grimm but in his own southern Bavarian voice, a voice that possessed an extraordinary range, both of tone and of pitch. 'Outside, the storm raged on, as the fisherman made his way back to the seashore. And the houses and the trees were falling all around him, and the mountains, they shook, and the great boulders were rolling into the sea. The skies had darkened so they were black as pitch . . .'

If he had cleverly impersonated the fisherman and his wife, he did more than convey the storm. He became it. I think everyone in that room sensed Wolf's tempest, his elemental powerfulness. When the fisherman had to shout against the noise of the billowing ocean, Wolf himself bellowed, and it was as if we heard in that cry, not only the noise of the man, but of the elements themselves against which he contended. For, of course, this time the flounder cannot answer the wife Ilsebill's outrageous request, and replies, '"Go home, man! She is back sitting on her pisspot . . ." And there they sit to this very day!'

All the privileges the wife had won for herself had been withdrawn; she and the fisherman were back in the same abject squalor as before. The story was over and with something of the air of a great conductor who comes to the final bars of a symphony Wolf bowed his neck – as it were over the score – and then threw back his head. His face was gleaming with sweat. For a few seconds he stared at the ceiling with an expression of such solemnity that I thought he was on the verge of tears. Then he looked around at his company and smiled at each child in turn.

Those who never met him suppose that Wolf, like Napoleon or Stalin, was noticeably small. This was not the case. He was an average sort of height. Winifred Wagner by contrast was tall, large-boned, with beautiful clear skin, high cheekbones, an aquiline nose and a well-developed chin. She invariably wore her blonde hair wound round her head in a loose bun reminiscent of pre-war, really of pre-twentieth-century, fashion.

Wolf's friends in the Party, when they came to know Winnie, eulogized her Teutonic good looks, but she did not to my mind look remotely like a German. Archaeologists and anthropologists observe among the Celts two quite distinct physiological types. There are the short, squat brachycephalic Celts, usually dark-haired and recognisable in the Basque country, in Brittany and Ireland. There is also a quite different physiognomy, dolichocephalic, noticeably tall and usually with fair or light-brown hair. I imagine that it was to this body type that King Arthur's Guinevere belonged, and if you think me fanciful you will at least concede that I had spent a very long time contemplating Winnie's appearance. Even now, over twenty years after we last met, she fills my head. Perhaps one should not put down such thoughts on paper. The comrades have taught us all that the movements of the human heart are no more than the twitches of the bourgeois corpse in its death throes. For me, however, Winnie, whose father's name had been Williams, was the embodiment of romance in its fullest sense. Her passion for Wolf caused me agonies of jealousy at the time, as did her other liaisons – of which we shall no doubt hear in the course of this narrative. But I reckoned that the pain of watching her devote so much intense emotional energy to the worship of another man, Wolf, was just about requited by the chance, almost daily, to be in her presence.

He sat bolt upright in the modern square-backed upholstered chair with which Winnie and Siegfried had lately furnished their wing of the house. You might consider it superfluous to describe his appearance. It was that, I should say, of a kindly soldier. The fine hair was as always immaculately combed and brushed with the parting on the right of his head. He wore a cheap navy-blue serge suit, shiny at the arse and frayed at the cuffs; a white shirt and a silk tie which must have been the gift of an admirer. His shoes were always highly polished and I used to wonder at what stage of his career he found someone else to shine them for him. At this date he was a mere thirty-six years old and although he had an entourage of followers, some of whom seemed sinister, some of whom were merely crackpots, we hardly ever saw or heard of them. His visits to our small town, certainly at this stage, were made alone and he was never to my knowledge anything but courteous and friendly to his company, preferring when he was among us to discuss music rather than politics, and enjoying – at the Villa Wahnfried, Richard Wagner's house – the company of Winnie and her children or, when at the Golden Anchor Hotel in Market Place or one of the restaurants in the town, sitting around with the performers and members of the orchestra from the Festival Theatre discussing the finer points of Wagner's musicology.

She was twenty-eight on that afternoon when Wolf told the story of the fisherman and his wife – and a very youthful twenty-eight, no more corpulent than suited a woman who had given birth to four children, all still quite young, in quick succession and who liked her food. She sat with little Verena on her lap and held the five-year-old's hands in hers as she clapped and said rhythmically, 'Bra-vo! Bra-vo!' She lightly kissed the top of the child's head.

It had been a truly bravura performance.

Of course, one of the great difficulties which faces me in setting down my recollections of these events is the knowledge brought from hindsight, in a divided, twice-defeated Germany. I live in D—— in the Communist East, where I have lately retired as a schoolmaster. I am in my mid-sixties. I would not be writing these words to you if I did not want them to survive.

I call him Wolf, since that is what Winnie and the children called him. In other parts of this narrative, which will relate perhaps to his more public persona, I suppose I shall revert to the polite German convention of referring to him merely by the initial letter of his surname. I believe, even at the time in 1925, that I noted what a very distinctive interpretation Wolf had given of the famous Grimm tale. Is it a story about avarice, or about ambition, lust for power? One version, printed in 1814, two years after the Grimms printed it in their incomparable collection, sees it as an allegory of Napoleon's ambitions and fall. Wolf was right to see it as something more than a misogynistic comedy about a man giving in to a nagging wife. Had I been reading the story – and I would prosaically have read it to the children, rather than appearing to recite it, as Wolf did – I should, in common with almost all other readers or narrators, have made the fisherman and the flounder have reasonable voices; and I should have given to the wife an even more shrewish and irrational tone, as she played for ever bigger stakes and as the skies grew ever blacker. But the wife's demands, culminating in her wish to displace the Godhead, were invested with something like heroism by Wolf's rasping baritone. His smile was most triumphant when she had so overplayed her hand that the fisherman's wife had lost everything – the lands, the castles, the imperial titles – and ended up back on the pisspot. Wolf made you feel that the struggle would not have been worth it *unless* it had gone too far. You sensed that he thought the wife a greater being than her husband for the very reason that she was prepared to stake all and to lose.

The sea storm provoked by the greed of the fisherman's wife led my day-dreamy and instinctual mind to other wrecks and tempests, not least those evoked by Richard Wagner himself. As you may imagine, although he had been dead for a long time before I was born (eighteen years to be precise), his ghost haunted our town. I lived and breathed (much to my father's scorn) Richard Wagner's music. And now I was working in his house, and living among his books and pianos. His children, now grown-ups, and grandchildren still filled the place. His tall widow, now powdery, papery, wispy and vague, was still alive in her apartments at the top of the Villa Wahnfried, and Wagnerian ghosts and spirits were never far from us, not least when that most ardent of Wagnerians, Wolf, was among us.

Wolf supposedly told his Viennese flatmate (as far as we can tell the only friend of his youth) that it was while attending a performance of *Rienzi* at the Linz opera house that 'it' began – whatever 'it' was. His power mania, one must assume. Yet *Rienzi* is poor stuff compared with the opera composed only a year or so later, *The Flying Dutchman*. *Rienzi*, which tells the story of a medieval demagogue being swept to power by a wave of popular support, would have an obvious appeal to our friend, but the music is pastiche, mingling Weber and Donizetti. It is in *The Dutchman* that you first hear the authentic Wagnerian noise. In this piece for the first time we have the winning formula of mythologized autobiography translated into tormented musical language of tragic intensity.

Richard Wagner was twenty-four when he was engaged as a conductor in Riga. He had lately married the leading actress at the theatre in Königsberg – Immanuel Kant's home town – Minna Planer, a woman older than himself. From the start it was a difficult marriage. Wagner, considerably shorter than his long-haired beautiful wife, feared, with every justification, that she was unfaithful to him. She found his attitude to money intolerable – from the earliest days together they were always on the run from creditors. In Germany it was bad enough, but in Riga, then in the Russian Empire as it is once more today, heavy penalties awaited anyone arrested for debt. Wagner's passport was confiscated and he was told that his contract as conductor at the Riga theatre would not be renewed.

How much of the catastrophe of the nineteenth century can be measured in terms of its attitude to debt. For Karl Marx it was the capitalist's ultimate whip hand over the debt-laden bourgeoisie, ultimately to be withdrawn when capital itself imploded. For hundreds of nineteenth-century families the ignominy of debt shaped the whole character of life itself. It was a world without state support or state benefits. If you fell out of work and into debt you were a non-person: if you were proletarian you were fit only for the workhouse; if bourgeois for the gaol.

And in my time, the time which I am describing and in which I first met Wolf, our country itself was a debtor. Germany had become like one of those grotesques in the novels of Dostoevsky or Dickens, like the Marmeladovs in *Crime and Punishment* reduced to any level of indignity by sheer inability to pay for food, beer, coal, clothing. We felt ourselves, we the impeccably respectable and provident middle-class Germans, free-falling with the giddy improvidence of paupers. Money in the bank is more than the ability to buy a new suit of clothes or a leg of pork for dinner. It creates, or at any rate confirms, a solid attitude of mind, a belief in family, the Ten Commandments, cleanliness, order. You put your solid handmade leather shoe in front of you and knew you trod on solid German ground.

When, lo and behold – after the Versailles Treaty and our betrayal by the November criminals – that political sole trod not earth but air. France had insisted upon war reparations. Our economy was in ruins. Inflation had soared to surreal levels. The life savings in the bank, which before the war would have been enough to maintain an entire Buddenbrook household of respectability, were no longer enough to buy a box of matches. We fell, fell, fell all of us, Icaruses, bits of papery ash falling through dusk after the German Reich had been bonfired out of existence by French and Bolshevist guile.

No wonder, in 1925, we heard the youthful Wagner of 1839 speaking to us. Minna had returned to her young husband from one of her amorous escapades and he persuaded her that the only way out of the present crisis was flight. A friend from Königsberg offered to whizz the Wagners across the Russian border to East Prussia in his coach. It was a tight squeeze since Wagner, ever the obsessive dog lover, could not be parted from Robber, his Newfoundland, which was the size of a small donkey: almost taller than he was.

Wagner was naturally accident prone. At the Prussian port of Pillau the coach overturned, hurling him out into a pile of manure. Eventually, Minna, Robber and Wagner got on board the *Thetis*, a small package sailing boat whose captain agreed to let them make the eight-day voyage to London without passports. The weather in the Baltic was fine when they set out on their voyage westward, but squalls soon broke out and a journey that should have lasted a little over a week took three times as long. The dog was half-starved. Richard and Minna Wagner were devastated by seasickness. The weather became so bad that the captain eventually decided to put in to a Norwegian harbour.

'And how relieved I was,' Wagner tells us,

to behold that far-reaching rocky coast, towards which we were being driven at such speed! A Norwegian pilot came to meet us in a small boat and, with experienced hand, assumed control of the *Thetis*, whereupon in a very short time I was to have one of the most marvellous and most beautiful impressions of my life. What I had taken to be a continuous line of cliffs turned out on our approach to be a series of separate rocks projecting from the sea. Having sailed past them, we perceived that we were surrounded, not only in front and at the sides, but also at our back by these reefs, which closed in behind us near together that they seemed to form a single chain of rocks. At the same time the hurricane was so broken by the rocks in our rear that the further we sailed through this ever-changing labyrinth of projecting rocks, the calmer the sea became, until at last the vessel's progress was perfectly smooth and quiet as we entered one of those long sea-roads running through a giant ravine – for such the Norwegian Fjords appeared to me. A feeling of indescribable content came over me when the enormous granite walls echoed the hail of the crew as they cast anchor and furled the sails. The sharp rhythm of this call clung to me like an omen of good cheer, and shaped itself presently into the theme of the seaman's song in my *Flying Dutchman*.

Here he is before us, Richard, and I dare say that his ghost will often visit these pages, as they visited Wahnfried in those days when I observed its day-to-day life, and as he visits this earth each time one of his music dramas is once again performed on the stage. He came to our little town of Bayreuth when his career as a composer was all but over. He had endured exile, poverty, vilification; but the worst torment of all was that he had been unable to find any theatre suitable for the performance of his *Ring* cycle. Eventually, the means came to build a theatre and a stage to his own specification. But this was in the 1870s when Wagner was tired, prematurely old and married to the much younger Cosima.

The Flying Dutchman is the work of a young man. A child of the theatre, a man of the theatre, he was born into a family where money was always uncertain. He was in exile from the solid commercial middle class. If we were being loyal comrades we should no doubt see the exiles who people his works as economic projections. He knew what it was to be a wandering Jew, an accused outcast. Like all great artists his life was an allegory of his time so that his actual exile from Germany post-1848 – his life as a political revolutionary – is mirrored by the extraordinary mythological projection of his own socio-economic exclusion. Shaw – foolish old bearded Irishman – and the comrades here see Wagner's allegories as to be explained in terms of capital and class struggle. When he went on to rewrite the medieval legends of *The Ring of the Nibelung* Wagner was, as they would think, drawing an allegory of the rise of capitalism – the gods, that is the old aristocratic order of Europe – making spurious contracts with capital – Alberich the dwarf who will exploit the masses, the Nibelungs, for the enrichment of both. The struggle between Old Order and New Money will ultimately lead to the destruction of both. Yet if this was all Wagner's music dramas were about, why did he go to the immense labour of orchestrating them, why not simply write a political pamphlet? Do not these 'political' readings of Wagner get things precisely the wrong way around? Is he not a great artist precisely because he sees so clearly what all the revolutions and changes of his time had done to the soul – are we allowed to use that word these days? – of humanity itself?

One of the things which, in those days (when I still thought of myself as a philosopher) interested me about *The Flying Dutchman* was Wagner's extraordinary dramatization of something, as far as I know, not represented on the stage since Shakespeare wrote *Hamlet*. It is actually a very simple and daily observable fact, about which philosophy has never really made up its mind, namely that there is a gulf fixed between our interior world – our psychological history, our daydreams, our preoccupations – and the world *out there* – the world of that elusive concept, an objectivity, a reality. Most, but by no means all, philosophers have taken it for granted that the world *out there* – matter etc. – has a reality. One of the problems of philosophy, known as epistemology, was to ask how what is going on inside our head – our thoughts, perceptions, ideas – relates to that reality: how we can be said to know that the table or the garden exist. My friend from university days, who had helped me with my own thesis and was about to become a philosopher of fame, Martin H——, thought that the problems of knowledge were not 'problems' at all; that the 'problem' stemmed from the Plato who had set the whole of Western philosophy on a wild-goose chase with the observer, the human mind or eye or senses as subject taking in the object – the external reality. The Greek philosophers who were earlier than Plato, the pre-Socratics, had in common with some of the great texts of Hinduism and Buddhism not made this distinction. The real mystery was Being itself and we were all, observers and observed, part of this 'Being'. (I think Martin H—— derived some of his earliest thoughts about all this from Schopenhauer whom Richard Wagner claimed to be the guide of his second phase of life.)

Anyway, coming in my early twenties to the realization that I was never going to get very far with philosophy, I came to believe more and more that very many of the problems confronting philosophers in the twentieth century had already been addressed by Wagner in the nineteenth century. And that process began, really, with *The Dutchman*. The story is a very simple one. Into a small Norwegian seaport comes a ship. The strange, pale, dark-clad captain approaches Daland, the captain of another ship, and makes him an offer. Daland can have all the treasures on the stranger's ship – gold, pearls, precious trinkets – in exchange for a night in Daland's house. Has Daland a daughter? He has. Then in exchange for Daland's daughter, Senta, in marriage, the greedy sailor can have a shipload of treasure. Daland can't believe his luck.

Senta, a dreamy maiden notionally the girlfriend of a dullard sailor called Erik, is obsessed by a picture on her father's wall of a pale, dark figure, the legendary Flying Dutchman. While the other girls merrily sing a chorus over their spinning wheel, Senta wants to sing the 'Ballad of the Flying Dutchman'. This is the story of a man who has made a pact with Satan that he could achieve immortality and be able to sail and sail around the world. The privilege is of course a curse since he sails on and on unable to die. Every seven years he comes ashore to seek a faithful wife. Were he to find one his curse would end – but he never does so.

When Senta has finished the song she tells the other maidens that she would like to *be* that maiden. Needless to say, the stranger who has struck the bargain with Daland *is* the Dutchman. Although at the end he says he cannot involve his cursed life with that of the innocent Senta, she sacrifices herself voluntarily and hurls herself into the sea.

Until he wrote *The Dutchman* Wagner was still an apprentice, learning from the Italian bel canto composers and from Weber. Operas were dramatized stories, often very silly stories, interrupted by musical 'numbers'. The heroine could sing a long aria while dying of stab wounds, fall to the stage, receive a round of applause, get up and sing her dying song as an encore. Wagner, compelled to earn his bread and butter conducting such absurdities in Leipzig, Riga, later Dresden, where he'd been to school, was to pioneer something quite new, the music drama in which the opera was seen as a whole and the music itself expressed the inner lives of the characters. In *The Dutchman*, the choruses of Norwegian sailors and their maidens with spinning wheels, and the raucous tenor Erik are all production line operatic types – they could have been dreamed up by Weber or Meyerbeer, a second-rate operatic composer whose success ate into Wagner's soul. Senta and the Dutchman, doomed from the beginning to their fatal union – redemptive in her eyes, destructive in his – inhabit a new musical world and communicate their inner lives to and through us and themselves by a completely new music.

It is a strange fact that when my lovely Winnie, when Winifred Wagner first arrived in Germany, at the age of nine, her adoptive parents immediately changed her name and called her . . . Senta, Senta Klindworth. When they had journeyed over to England, the child they picked up at the orphanage door in East Grinstead was named Winifred Williams. Knowing no German, and no family affection or happiness either, Winnie discovered both in the company of this strange old couple, Henriette, who was also an English-speaker and some sort of cousin, then aged seventy, and her ancient, white-bearded husband, Karl Klindworth, then aged seventy-seven.

I remember once walking up the Green Hill in Bayreuth towards the Festival Theatre, alone with Winnie at my side. Visitors to our town will remember that at the foot of the gentle 'Green Hill', a little way out of the town centre, is a row of sedate villas, built shortly after the Wagners had established themselves here and set on the sloping Franconian hillside on which stands the opera house where his works might, at last, adequately be performed. One of these villas bears an inscription,

> *Deutches Haus im Deutschen Land*
> *Schirm dich Gott mit starker Hand. 1900.*

Standing beside the gate and lighting up yet another cigarette, Winnie declaimed the little prayer to me and then, with a theatrical swing of the arm, she giggled.

> May God protect with Mighty hand
> A German house in German land.

'It's just what I felt about Germany, almost the moment I arrived,' she said. 'Safe. No more cruelty. No more nuns' – the orphanage was run by a Church of England sisterhood – 'devising punishments simply for being alive. In this country I found safety. Security. Kindliness. That was what I found.' Looking up at the house again: 'Seven years after that was built.'

On another occasion, during a rehearsal for *The Dutchman* in the Festival Theatre, she told me, 'They called me Senta because old Grandpa Klindworth was transcribing the opera for the piano when I arrived in the house. Was he preparing to offer me up as a sacrifice, a ransom, to a dark stranger?'

Questions like this from Winnie's lips were always answered by chesty laughs interrupted by coughing.

One of my earliest jobs had been playing the piano at the old Electric Odeon, the first cinema to open in our small town. Naturally, the early Wagner films were shown there. It might strike the modern reader as paradoxical that silent movies were made of Wagner's operas, and there would no doubt be those, my father among them, who considered the silence an improvement on the music. My father was shocked by my earning my living in a cinema, a place he considered on the edges of seediness; not completely respectable if not actually immoral. He minded even more that when I might have been perfecting Beethoven's sonatas for piano, or mastering another piece by Haydn, I was working up Karl Klindworth's piano version of the *Ring* cycle for regurgitation in the cinema.

Karl Klindworth was one of the star pupils of the Abbé Liszt and he had founded the Karl Klindworth Music Conservatory in Berlin. My father, with his intense fastidiousness, had been aware of the group during his own upbringing and education in Berlin, and viewed their ideas, both about politics and about music (the two intermingled) with shuddering disdain.

At the time they adopted Winnie, Karl and Henriette Klindworth lived in a cranks' commune where they could devote themselves to fruit-growing, vegetarianism, extreme nationalism and anti-Semitism. Each member of the group lived in his or her own little house, but the fruit-growing was communal, and the different members of the group came together in the evenings for music and conversation. Klindworth was a star among them, not only because he had been taught by Liszt, but also because he had been part of Wagner's inner circle, and he was still in close epistolary touch with the widow of their hero, Cosima. It was this tall, beaky-nosed, strong-minded woman, Liszt's daughter and Wagner's second wife, who was regarded as the High Priestess of the Wagner shrine.

Winnie, or Senta, as she had now become, learnt German at Klindworth's piano stool. He read to her from Grimm's fairy tales. Among her very first German words were those drawn from the Grimms' magical folkloric compilations. She learnt of witches, wicked stepmothers, magic forests and talking animals before she knew the German for train or hatpin. Sword, wolf, curse and gold were more serviceable words than living room, table lamp or left luggage office. Whereas most foreigners learning a language might master as their first sentence 'My luggage is at the main station. Please have it brought to this hotel,' Senta could say, 'Though I have the appearance of a Swan, I am really an enchanted Prince.' Klindworth also taught her folk songs and ballads. The ballad, says Hegel in his *Ästhetik*, comprises 'the entirety of a complete event'. Wagner used to say that the whole of *The Flying Dutchman* was encapsulated in Senta's Ballad sung in Act Two:

> *Traft ihr das Schiff im Meere an,*
> *blutrot die Segel, schwarz der Mast?*

When Senta sings this ballad about the legendary Dutchman, condemned to endless wandering unless he can find the love of a faithful wife, does she *know* that she is singing her own story? Does she know that the stranger who has offered her father money in exchange for her hand *is* the Dutchman? Did Senta Klindworth know, as the ancient pianist began to unfold to her the story of the Master, of his long years of exile from Germany, of his second marriage and eventual settling in the small Franconian town of Bayreuth, did she know then that it was her destiny to become the matriarch of the new generation of Wagners, she the stranger, she the orphan of East Grinstead?

When it was felt that she spoke good enough German, the old people denied themselves their rural idyll in Oranienburg and returned to the city, where they took a flat and sent her to school.

'Grandpa, when are you going to take me to the opera?' she would plead. Or, 'Grandpa, they are performing *Lohengrin* at the opera – please take me.'

'You must wait, Senta. Your first experience of the opera must be in Bayreuth. That is where the Master intended his operas to be heard.'

'But Grandpa . . .'

'No buts. What is on display in the Berlin opera house is not real opera. These so-called opera companies, they are just the Jewish Appreciation Society. They pretend to admire the Master but ultimately they try to undermine him.'

'How?'

'By promoting so-called modern tripe, meretricious stuff which is subversive of music itself. These operas by Richard Strauss, for example. People maintain he is the heir to the Master. But they are terrible works, infected by Judaism, so are the so-called symphonies of Mahler.'

'Are all the bad people Jews, Grandpapa?'

'Strauss isn't a Jew, but he is promoted by the fan club. These modernists and the international Hebrews who finance them are undermining all that makes Germany German. The Master long ago wrote a pamphlet called "Judaism in Music" and they will never forgive him for it. But he was right – the Jews are not a creative race, they are parasites, they sponge off other cultures, they suck them for what they can get out of them.'

'So, Mahler is . . .'

'Don't even think about such unhappy things, my child.'

She was trained up, first at a local school and then, when Henriette Klindworth fell ill, at a boarding school, where she was disruptive and rebellious. (Shades of the orphanage.) She grew fast and by thirteen she had reached her full height. As she came and went, between school and the Klindworths, she began to hear, like the distant chorus of pilgrims drifting over the morning air in *Tannhäuser*, the story of the Wagner family. To the child Senta, who heard their names at almost every meal, the Wagners were the stuff of Story. As the old man talked on and on, only shadowy distinctions existed in her mind between the stories of the operas, which were already part of her inner life, and the inhabitants of Wahnfried. Indeed, for a long time she supposed that Wahnfried was a separate realm, such as Nibelheim or Klingsor's Castle of Enchantment, rather than being the name the composer had given to his house (with a typical coinage meaning what? Peace after madness? Rest after chaos? Or mad chaos leading in the end to a sort of peace? Passion-Peace).

When the maid brought in the letters on the small silver salver to the Berlin apartment there would always be a particular happiness in his expression as old Klindworth said quietly, 'Ah! A letter from Wahnfried.'

A letter from Wahnfried inevitably meant a letter from Cosima Wagner. Her letters to Klindworth concerned the crises and problems inescapable for anyone trying to run an opera house. She asked Klindworth's advice about the music school she had set up in Bayreuth in the 1890s – a place where the Master's opposition to the 'false' singing traditions of bel canto could be imparted to any young person prepared to endure a daily diet of physical jerks and readings from the Master's prose works. Even this place, however, bred up its traitors. Alois Burgstaller, a former farmworker trained at Cosima's school, sang the role of Siegfried in 1896 – when he was only twenty-five – but he committed a doubly unforgivable sin: he sang in New York. Since Cosima regarded Wagner's works and the singers at the Festival Theatre and the members of the orchestra as her property, it was intolerable to her that a protégé should sing anywhere else. Worse, and this compounded the offence, he sang in an opera so sacred that until 1913, when the copyright ran out, Cosima would allow it to be performed only in Bayreuth – *Parsifal*.

The 'treachery' of Burgstaller happened when Senta was a little child, before her arrival in Germany, but it must have entered the canon of Wagner stories since she could afterwards remember Klindworth saying later, as he sat at the table reading the epistle (my father's daily reading in Martin Luther's translation of the Scriptures could not have been more reverent), 'Ah! A letter from Wahnfried – they have reinstated Burgstaller!' In other households in Germany comparable remarks might have been made about shifts in the Cabinet or scandals at the court of our beloved Emperor Wilhelm II.

Mention of the word scandal will naturally, for readers who know anything about such matters, prompt the question of what passed between Cosima and Klindworth over the matter of her son? Scandals at the court of the Emperor, although they obsessed the newspapers, would never have been mentioned at the unworldly table of Karl and Henriette Klindworth. If, for example, in 1902 they had even been aware of the malicious exposé by the journalist Maximilian Harden about Prince Philipp von Eulenberg they would almost certainly have dismissed the filth as lies put about by Jewish republicans. Eulenberg was one of the closest friends and courtiers of the Emperor. It was Eulenberg who had introduced the Emperor to the works of Wagner's son-in-law Houston Stewart Chamberlain from whose learned pages Wilhelm II had imbibed the comforting intelligence that Our Saviour had not been Jewish at all – the Galilee in Roman times being a largely Jew-free and Hellenized place. When the scandal burst and the Emperor was at last told he was totally incredulous: 144 allegations of improper conduct, mainly with fishermen and peasants from the Starnberger See! Some said Wilhelm passed out when told what Eulenberg and the peasants had actually done, unable to believe that anyone, still less any of his own circle, could indulge in such filthiness. One can be certain that Henriette Klindworth and her snowy-bearded husband had never discussed such matters with the growing 'Senta'.

Certainly, my own strait-laced parents in Bayreuth, who neither liked Wagner's music nor approved his cult, would never have spoken openly about what they would have deemed unnatural vice. Yet somehow, to those of us who grew up in that town, there was nothing very surprising about the stories that eventually became common knowledge about 'Fidi', as he was always known in the family. When at the age of twenty-four, after a number of false starts in my career, I told my friends that I had been engaged as Siegfried Wagner's secretary, there was no need for them to explain the raised eyebrows or the smiles. Needless to say, being uncertain at this date where my own emotional preferences might come to be directed, I found such unspoken assumptions about Siegfried – hence any young man in his employ – to be deeply offensive. Yet who, seeing him in the town in the early years of our century, could fail to have the amused thoughts which my engagement as his secretary (in 1924) evidently provoked in the minds of my friends?

Long before I ever met a member of the Wagner family, and even longer before the thought crossed my mind that my destiny might be entwined with theirs, I remember, when quite a little child, being taken by my nurse to play with my wooden hoop in the Hofgarten, the gardens of the splendid baroque palace laid out by Wilhelmine the Margravine of Bayreuth-Brandenburg in the eighteenth century when that intelligent sister of Frederick the Great chose, rather than marrying her pudding cousin George and becoming the Queen of England, to come south to this charming little town and to live a civilized life. The Palace Gardens had for a couple of generations been a public park, around which the elegant streets of our town are arranged. The Wahnfried villa backs on to the gardens, and I must often have seen Cosima and Siegfried taking their constitutional down the central *Allée* of chestnut trees or crossing one of the small ornamental bridges in their ... well, in their *ornamental* fashion. Siegfried and his mother were immediately conspicuous for their clothes, as well as for the strange figure they cut, the old lady so noticeably taller than her son. If they walked in bright sunshine he might be delegated to hold a parasol over her veiled and bonneted head. If a light drizzle threatened, he would be the bearer of an umbrella. But these solicitudes on his mother's behalf were always in danger of injuring her as the spokes of either covering device threatened her eyes rather than reaching above her stately head.

Cosima carried with her as an accompaniment to her expensive clothes of a thirty-year outmoded fashion an air of immense stateliness. If you had been told she was our now dethroned, then still regnant Queen of Bavaria you would have believed it. The train of her skirts swept behind her, gathering all the dust of the gravel walks but she showed no consciousness of this on her very long, very pale, very bony face whose nose in old age was a beak, to my child's eyes, of almost incredible size. Whereas old Cosima's costumes were of a consistency of style, her son's were suggestive of a variety of roles, not always convincingly played. Sometimes he would be the dapper figure of a boulevardier, with grey Homburg, matching grey calf gloves, frock-coat and striped trousers. At other times he would appear, equally incongruously in a small town where a certain small-town respectability made any deviation from the sartorial norm conspicuous, in waisted hunting coat, with striped jodhpurs or breeches and stockings to the knee. The hats he wore when out with his mother were as various as the other clothes, straw boaters and panamas favoured in the summer months, and a curly bowler, even a silk top hat not being unknown as he tiptoed – I would almost say minced – along.

The first time any member of the family addressed a word to me I was, I suppose, about seven years old (my birthday is on 24 August 1902) and I was, as I say, playing with my hoop. My nurse was seated on a bench watching me play, when she cried out, 'Look out!'

Two wolfhounds, much bigger than I was, liked the look of my hoop as it rolled in front of me and came galloping after me. I do not fear dogs, though I did not share the dog worship which was the common characteristic of Richard Wagner, both his wives and his only son. (I was astounded, years later, when mine became the first eyes apart from their author's to read through the diaries of Cosima, by the extent of canomania revealed – but that is to leap ahead.) The dogs only wanted to play. One knocked my hoop off course, the other would have bowled me over had I not got out of the way, but the encounter was sufficiently alarming for the nurse to elicit an apology from Siegfried. 'Watch out! Watch out!' my nurse called to me hysterically. 'The dogs are going to ...'

'Wolfy, Donner, come *here*. Heel!' called their owner, on that occasion wearing green stockings over his mustard-yellow breeches with a matching hunting coat. I was struck by his enormous stiff collar and by the abundance of yellow silk that formed his bow tie. 'Are you all right, little boy?'

'Come back – come away from the dogs,' shrieked the nurse.

As I was reassuring the colourfully dressed gentleman that I was quite all right, that the playfulness of the dogs had amused rather than scared me, his mother, standing some ten yards away from him on the gravel and looking not at me but into the middle distance, said, 'Fidi, tell them the dogs are harmless.'

These words were undoubtedly true. What struck the child who heard them was the fact that they were delivered in a 'funny voice' – later identified as a French accent, although I did not know about such things at the time. Whereas the man was kind, and smiled and laughed at me, his mother did not engage at all. Her haughtiness was chilling. Even though I was far from being a spoilt child and certainly did not expect to be the centre of the grown-ups' attention, Cosima's failure to meet my gaze and her need to communicate entirely through her son – well, they put one firmly in one's place.

Later – when my parents had finished playing what they considered some proper music, my father at the cello, my mother at the piano performing a very accurate but not especially inspired rendition of a piece by Haydn – I was able to blurt out, 'We met the most famous composer in the world.'

'Debussy, in the Hofgarten?' asked my father, with some interest, but not with incredulity, since one of the most remarkable things about Bayreuth was the fact that famous musicians, composers, conductors and performers flocked to the place.

My seven-year-old perception of these things was still a little vague, as my garbled version of nurse's garbled explanation was unfolded. When the narrative was unravelled and rolled backwards and we got to the dogs my mother said, 'Oh, you met old Frau Wagner.'

'And is that man not the most famous . . .'

'His father wrote operas and so does he,' said my father.

I was probably too young to see what a put-down (not to me but to the Wagners) this was.

Over the years, if we passed them in the street or the Hofgarten, the Wagners would acknowledge us, Siegfried by touching the rim of his hat, his mother by a little nod of the head, since although she 'looked through me' the first time I met her, she would not have displayed such lack of courtesy to my father, being a respecter of the cloth.

Clearly I had not managed to master much Wagner lore, however, when, at least a year after I'd first become aware of the couple, she so tall and stately, he so mincing on tiptoe, I'd made the mistake of referring to 'that lady' as 'that man's wife' and my mother had corrected me, 'not wife, darling, *mother*.'

One of the things that made Winnie such a very apt recruit as Cosima's daughter-in-law was her – how are we to define this? – her essential, most necessary, most maddening quality? One paradoxical word for it would be her *discretion*, though this would not be everyone's word for a woman best known to history for her reckless and seemingly unvaried admiration for the most demonized of all villains in the political rogues' gallery. But there was a sort of – perhaps Welsh – *reserve* about Winnie. Cosima fought off, sometimes with belligerent insult, sometimes with aristocratic *froideur*, those who threatened the guardianship of her husband's memory, ideas, opera house and Festival. But she possessed an extraordinary willingness to wash dirty linen in public. Winnie, by contrast, when her time came to become the Defender of the Faith, could often baffle the anti-Wagnerians, or those who wanted to bring about unwanted innovations in Wagner productions, or those who wished to stop innovations of which she disapproved, by this strange Welsh wall of mystery. Had she simply failed to see the world as her enemy or rival or enquirer saw it?

That is the central mystery of Winnie – did she or did she not *see* Wolf as others saw him? And knowing how others saw him, did this act as a spur to defend him? But after Auschwitz? She *knew* about the camps, the millions deliberately killed, the further millions who died in the war, the cities wrecked, the lives destroyed. Is our capacity to love another person often (always) accompanied by an inability to notice what it is that prevents the majority of other people loving them? (In the case of Wolf there are many complicated factors at work, of course, since he *was* extremely popular, the most popular political leader our country had ever had – so were we *all* suffering from the same delusion as Winnie?)

It goes without saying that my mind, even more than the minds of most Germans of my generation, is haunted and monopolized by the question. But we are leaping ahead – the young Senta Klindworth had an innate capacity not to 'notice', which was a vital characteristic in anyone being selected as a bride of Siegfried Wagner.

And when one says 'being selected' it is, of course, clear that the person making that selection was not Fidi but his mother.

It was in 1914, when Senta Klindworth was sixteen and seventeen years old, that she became aware of a looming crisis, which threatened the peace and stability of everything. This was not the imminent conflagration of that mysterious and, by the Klindworths, seldom-discussed phenomenon, the world, nor the collapse of civilization brought about by the World War. The Klindworths, in common with all their friends, believed that war, when it came, would invigorate rather than undermine our country. The threat was posed, rather, by the court case brought by Siegfried's sister Isolde against her mother and brother.

In 1914, not yet quite turned to the papery old lady whom I knew when I worked in her house, Cosima Wagner was an in all senses lofty old survival of a vanished world. When one saw her, as one often did in the streets of our small town, she seemed like a visitant from a lost world – the long trailing dresses, the bonnets tied with chiffon, the elaborate Parisian parasols trimmed with lace. Her long melancholy face suggested that time itself had been defied and that this illegitimate daughter of a French aristocrat and of the Hungarian Abbé Liszt was in fact someone who had escaped the guillotine, possibly escaped the condition of mortality itself, in 1789. Her long nose, birdlike hooded eyes, high cheekbones and very pronounced, thin lips conformed to no convention of beauty but there was nevertheless something breathtakingly beautiful about her. She seemed ethereal, an emblem of eternal tragedy just as her son, Siegfried, so often at her side and holding her arm, with his pale Homburg hats slightly too small for him, his large, stiff, high choirboy's collars, his pale suits and vaguely absurd spats, always gave off an air of inescapable comedy.

This, incidentally, is one reason I am putting pen to paper. I want to answer a question for you about the Wagner women – or rather the non-Wagner women, the women the Wagner men married. The composer himself ... we'll come to that: by any standards one of the great geniuses of the nineteenth century but entirely lacking in dignity and giving off all the air of Vaudeville theatre into which he was born. Yet his second wife Cosima, guardian of his shrine, was all dignity. Likewise, while it was hard to take Siegfried Wagner quite seriously, Winnie his wife was a person of mysterious integrity. For all her mischievousness, she was totally dignified. I am not just saying this because ... because of her relationship with *you*. Was Wolf a worthy hero for her or did he conform to the pattern of Wagnerian buffoonery?

Anyhow, the scandal of 1914. This must be mentioned here. In 1913 the copyright in Richard Wagner's opera ran out. It was a hundred years since the baby of questionable parentage had been born over an inn in Leipzig and it was thirty years since the great man had expired on a pink sofa in Venice (after a furious row with his wife about a young singer with whom he was trying to have an affair) and he had never been more popular. All of a sudden, however, it was no longer necessary for opera houses in New York, London, Milan, Munich, Berlin to pay the Wagner family a royalty every time they staged a production of *Tannhäuser* or *Lohengrin*.

In the year in which I chose to begin my story, 1925, a year when Germany was enjoying the benefits of a liberal republican democracy, a million marks would scarcely buy you a cup of cheap coffee which was why, when I knew them, the Wagners kept all their money in Swiss bank accounts. In the year when the copyright ran out, however, the last year of peace under the Emperor Wilhelm II, the million marks brought in by annual royalties to the Wagner family were able to sustain four or five grown-ups in some state: the composer's seventy-six-year-old widow; her daughters Isolde and Eva, with their husbands. (Eva was married to the increasingly infirm Houston Stewart Chamberlain.) And there was Siegfried. The family income must now derive from the Bayreuth Festival, and from Siegfried's own operas which, surprising as this might today appear, were sufficiently popular in the German-speaking world to generate a goodish return.

Cosima had first been married to the conductor Hans von Bülow, a passionate Wagnerian by whom she bore two children (Daniela and Blandine) and with whom she had been very unhappy. In the latter years of her brief marriage to Bülow she began her affair with Wagner. With Wagner she had Isolde, born 1865, Eva, 1867, and Siegfried, 1869. Isolde was certainly born while Cosima was still married to (and living with) von Bülow. Isolde was Wagner's favourite child. By 1913, Isolde, the mother of the only Wagner grandchild born to date, the twelve-year-old Franz Wilhelm Beidler, and herself tubercular, challenged her mother and Siegfried in the Bayreuth local court since they were trying to reduce her 8,000-mark annual allowance. Cosima played an extraordinary card. Isolde, she declared to the court, was not Wagner's child at all. Cosima claimed that she had slept with both her first and second husbands during the crucial month of Isolde's conception but that she was certain von Bülow and not Wagner was the father. The claim, if true, would disinherit Isolde and prevent the only Wagner grandson from one day becoming the director of the Bayreuth Festival. It was an astounding move of Cosima's in those puritanical times and her declaration, reported in all the newspapers, certainly confirmed the views of middle-class respectable people such as my parents that the Wagners were beyond the pale.

Isolde's claims were dismissed by the court in June 1914. She even had to pay costs. She had been born when her mother was still legally married to Hans von Bülow. Her mother had sworn an affidavit that she was the legitimate daughter of von Bülow. Case dismissed. But in the course of it some dreadful words had been exchanged, perhaps not the least of them Isolde's dig that her forty-four-year-old brother had been the subject of 'complaints'. In vain did he splutter back that such vile calumnies had been visited in his day upon the greatest king of all time, Frederick the Great, and that Prussia had expanded and grown strong by *his* hand. These were different times. Maximilian Harden, the Jewish journalist who had 'exposed' Philipp von Eulenberg and caused such scandals at the Imperial Court in Berlin, was now making innuendoes against the illustrious court of art in the Villa Wahnfried. Harden, with the skill of a blackmailer – or, as the word is sometimes rendered, investigative reporter – had uncovered many of Siegfried's same-sex indiscretions and in the Berlin newspaper *Future* he wrote his bombshell under the headline SIEGFRIED AND ISOLDE, in which his snide little innuendoes were made, just before the Bayreuth Festival.

Klindworth wrote consolingly to the mistress – *die Meisterin* – 'You have lived through a terribly painful time. Yet again the frenzied mob of the Jewish Press and Race have raged against the godly and are even now rejoicing, sure of the Extermination of their prey!' How chilling it is to read that word extermination – *Vernichtung* – used of mere scandalmongers in 1914. *The Flying Dutchman* longs for it. *Ew'ge Vernichtung, nimm mich auf* – Take me, eternal extermination. Pass thirty years and there would be *Vernichtungslager* in Eastern Europe.

And all our hands, all our German hands ... are we guilty, did we collude, willingly, unwillingly, through deliberate ignorance? Did we all acquire Winnie-like blinkers, so that we did not *see* what was before our very eyes? In the case of Wahnfried and its circle, I would contend the truth was stranger. You would say I was bound to say that? That I colluded in the toxic little circle round H, flattering his vanity and hanging on his every word while he prosed on about the music of Richard Wagner?

You decide – and condemn me if you will. These pages are not about me. They are for you, to see and to understand where you come from.

In 1914, faced with extermination by their enemy, the Wagnerian enthusiasts presented Cosima with a solution for her difficulties. Siegfried could squash the rumour mongers by getting married. Clearly he could not marry a 'normal' person. Cosima herself had been the illegitimate daughter of a famous composer. Wagner came from 'nowhere'. They could not have married their son to any normal German. To marry into the prosperous middle class would have been beneath them. To marry into the aristocracy would have revealed their own lack of real pedigree, their outsider status. A foreign woman was ideal and even more ideal would be the choice of a bride who did not lift an eyebrow at the allegations placing Siegfried in the company of Frederick the Great or Oscar Wilde.

In the summer of 1914 Karl Klindworth produced the magical solution. Clad in his travelling cloak, his dark suit and his Homburg hat the old gentleman emerged from a fly, which had conducted him from the station to the Festival Theatre on the Green Hill. On his arm, wearing a large-brimmed hat trimmed with flowers, a tightly waisted white dress reaching to her ankles, white stockings and white ballet shoes (slightly to diminish her height? she towered over her guardian), was the seventeen-year-old girl he called Senta. And he was taking her to her first-ever Wagnerian production.

Memory makes narratives. To herself, and to others, she came to repeat the story of the first few days in Bayreuth so often that it ceased to be a memory. She was coming to her destiny, her new family, her life's work – for it was to be she, and she only, who was ordained to save the Bayreuth Festival from extinction. How could she distinguish the countless hours she was to spend in the Festival House from those first impressions? Many were the summers and many the hours when she would climb the little Green Hill and, in a variety of evening costumes, greet the grandees as they came to hear operas composed by her father-in-law. Fifty and more times would she hear the fanfares of steerhorns from *Götterdämmerung* blare out to warn the audiences to take their seats.

At seventeen Winnie had been untainted by any theatrical experiences. She did not know how unusual this particular theatre was. She knew nothing then, as she was soon to learn, of the extraordinary story of how it came to be built and why it was built as it was. At the time, before the experiences became memories, the first day at Bayreuth was a jumble of impressions, none confused, but all so acute that they were in danger of cancelling one another out. There was the anxiety about her foster-mother's health. Henriette stayed behind in Berlin and Winnie was frightened travelling without her. In the train, old Klindworth had been unstoppable in his flow about whom they would meet – he named conductors, composers, the Chamberlains. It was as if you'd told a clever child that she was about to meet the characters of the Brothers Grimm. She could not quite absorb the fact that these names of whom she had heard so much belonged to real people with whom she was expected to hold conversations. Conversations! How did one conduct them? What did one say? The jokes and shared confidences of the dormitory first of the orphanage, latterly at a boarding school were no preparation for knowing what to say to Hans Richter or Houston Stewart Chamberlain.

But – too excited quite to think rather than to feel these fears – she experienced an extraordinary day: the train pulling through gently undulating countryside as they came into Franconia; Bayreuth appearing on the horizon, with its twin-towered City Church, its two royal palaces, its red-tiled roofs, its other church spires and steeples all clustered round hill and river; while at the other end of town – visible only when the bustle of arrival was half complete (porters paid, trunks dispatched in a fly to the hotel, reticule lost, found again, walking stick, spectacles ditto, ditto) – was the Festival Theatre on the hill, a building unlike any other and which had been ... disappointing? All the other buildings in this baroque town in their honey-coloured stone were lovely and of the old world, as their fly rattled over cobbles past a theatre, a church, a palace, seemly old shops with sunshade awnings over their windows. The engine shed of a building Karl Klindworth had pointed out was striking a defiant attitude of difference, which told her something at the time she was unable to take in. The hotel – they stayed at the Golden Anchor of course – was a revelation: the warm old panels of the hall and the welcoming dining room; the old-fashioned comfort and pure German cleanliness of her small bedroom at the back, the pristine lavender-scented sheets. She had no evening clothes as such. The old man had retreated to his room, she to hers and they had emerged, with faces splashed with soap and water. Had they eaten? Was it that day, or another, when he showed her the town? Was it then that she had her first walk in the Hofgarten, or took a carriage ride beyond the station to the Eremitage to see the shell-encrusted grottoes and sunken gardens and mysterious carvings? Was it that day or another that old Klindworth told for the dozenth time how Richard Wagner had alighted on this place and built the Festival Theatre for the sole and (as he thought temporary) purpose of staging *The Ring*? His talk, when not of music or of the world being taken to hell by the Jews, was always of the Wagners, so it was not possible for memory to say whether on that day of days he had said thus or thus.

But after the shaking hands, and bobbing to numbers of new people, Winnie had been led into the darkened amphitheatre. No aisles – but that did not strike her as odd since she had no theatrical experience with which to compare it. No orchestra. Where was the orchestra? There had been the thump, thump of doom decreeing the beginning of the drama, then the rustling closure of door curtains; still there was no sign of any players. Then the storm of *The Flying*

Dutchman began. She knew it by heart as a piece for piano transcribed by Klindworth but nothing had prepared her for the effect the overture would have when played by an orchestra. It was transport. She, Senta Klindworth, *was* the Senta before her. When the curtain went up, over the invisible orchestra there was a direct and uninterrupted engagement between the audience and the drama. The noise, the sheer volume of the singing! Barbara Kemp was the soprano who played *her*. The music made the experience. No other music quite did this. When the Dutchman – Bennet Challis – began his bass-baritone offer to Daland – the purchase of his daughter with a shipload of treasure – Senta Klindworth knew the beginnings of surrender. No words were given – certainly not by the Klindworths! – for this particular swooning, but here was a hint of it, a weakness, a delicious sense of falling, a moisture. Whatever magic Wagner himself had possessed to convert his own sense of exile, his own self-hatred, his own self-awareness into musical myths, it now had a life of its own that possessed the audience. The applause at the end of each act testified to its power all right, but Senta Klindworth had a deeper sense that the mystery enacted before them all that afternoon on stage was the story of her own inner life. She had no beau like the boring Erik, who begs the stage Senta not to throw herself away on the Dutchman; but Senta Klindworth felt a no less passionate desire to cast away dull normality. The attraction for her was not the trivial jolly world of the Norwegian sailors and their spinning girlfriends – rather was she drawn to the great spectral ship. When it first appeared in Act One the wind instruments struck up a ghostly threatening chord, a harbinger of the 'Valkyrie' themes in *The Ring*. The ship is inhabited not so much by ghosts as by the undead; Senta is vulnerable youth about to be enmeshed in the spidery tyrannies of the very old.

> *Sie sind schon alt und bleich, statt rot,*
> *und ihre Liebsten, ach! sind tot!*

Snowy-haired white-bearded Klindworth bends over the veiny

old fingers heavy with gold and amethyst rings of the divine Cosima, and Senta finds herself surveyed by the very sharp dark eyes of the old lady. The face is summing up the value of goods in a market. The old eyes run shamelessly up and down her future daughter-in-law's face, bosom, legs. There is something enraging but also thrilling in this as beautiful youth stands with all its advantages before crumbling old age. And at some point – that evening? next morning? – youth is brought to Wahnfried, a Flying Dutchman of a house positively peopled with ghosts and with the old: pasty, grey-complexioned servants; ashen-faced old Mr Chamberlain, already an invalid, with his uncompromisingly indoor pallor and indoor clothes – slippers, velvet smoking cap – his wife Eva – only forty-something but old to Senta – and her sister Isolde. And then – making her laugh almost at once with a joke and holding an ignited cigarette in one hand – Siegfried.

'This is the child,' says Cosima.

And, first among all these people, Siegfried says, 'How awful for you, meeting us lunatics all at once,' and he laughs and gently touches her right hand with smooth lips. The mingled smell of Senoussi cigarettes and Cologne water, always the Fidi smell.

She called it 'love at first sight' when she had made it all, the whole experience, into a story about herself.

Saying things could make them come true? Saying the right thing was better than experiencing it? Her façade of smiles was so very difficult to get behind. In love with Winnie, I wanted to tell myself that every word of enthusiasm about the man in her life was a brave carapace, that she did not love her husband, that her schoolgirl enthusiasm for Wolf was a pathetic substitute for 'the real thing' – whatever that would be. But I know now that what she said was true or as true as anything is – sort of true. Was not the trouble with Anglo-Saxon philosophy that it drove itself into the buffers with the all-out scepticism of David Hume? How can we *know* anything? Then Hume awoke Immanuel Kant from his dogmatic slumbers and our great German puzzled out the fascinating question for the length of his uneventful days in Königsberg, Prussia, now Soviet Kalinin. We Germans were off on our spiritual intellectual helter-skelter, with Fichte paving the way for Hegel's Great Schemes, with their idealism creating the modern world with our mysterious selves at the centre of it all – inventing our world as much as absorbing its mystery.

Richard Wagner was one of the most interesting manifestations of this great revolution in perceiving the world. Reality is not, as the empiricists and realists wanted to say, a fixed given. Reality is a perceived truth, about life itself. Our perspective on the world remakes it every time we see it.

Winnie was too stylish ever to complain about her lot, though later years, the years of her widowhood, would cause her some tears. She found Fidi's incurable quest for boys, throughout their marriage, a menace and an embarrassment. The endless behind-the-scenes gossip in the Festival Theatre, who had or hadn't, among orchestra or chorus boys, granted him a little favour continued all the time. Because these players and singers became Winnie's life, her extended family, she could not fail to have been irritated. It hardly ever showed, in any of my observations. Coming to Bayreuth was love at first sight for her and that was certainly true. Becoming part of the Wagner family was daunting. She found her sisters-in-law forbidding and jealous, her beaky old mother-in-law, who taught her French and made her do the dusting, an object of amused terror. None of them could have known, when they brought in 'the child' as Cosima called her, what an extraordinary stroke of luck was coming their way. Not only did she provide the family with a future – four children born either during or just after the Great War. Not only did she supply Fidi with loving, good-humoured companionship, which silenced the newspaper scandal mongers. She possessed what neither old Klindworth nor Cosima could possibly have seen in her seventeen-year-old self: the extraordinary skills required to run an opera company and keep Bayreuth alive. Cosima, who had preserved Bayreuth as a shrine to her husband's memory, thereby destroying the spirit of his injunction – *Kinder, schafft neues!* – was too old to do it. Fidi had struggled until he met Winnie. To run an opera house you do not merely need to love music and to have a good ear. You need to be able to co-ordinate an enormous assembly of often highly temperamental people – conductors, stage designers, producers, singers, musicians. When one of them goes off sick or quarrels with you, you need to know whom to ring up as a replacement. You need to know how to do auditions and how to arrange the complicated timetables of rehearsals and rehearsal rooms. You need the self-confidence to be able to hire the big stars as singers and conductors, and the strength to stand up to their grotesque egos. You need to be patient, imaginative and greedy enough to be a good fund-raiser. Go to any opera house in Germany today – or go to New York or Milan if, unlike me, you are allowed to travel – and you will find one variety or another of chaos. You would not find anyone, at the Met or the Berlin State Opera or La Scala, with quite Winnie's preternatural range of abilities. Wotan or whatever god smiles on the Wagners assuredly brought her to Bayreuth.

In that first experience of the Festival Theatre, a couple of weeks before war broke out in 1914, she had her vision, and remained for ever true to it. And I sometimes ask myself whether even Wolf himself was not simply yet another of the army of helpers enlisted by Winnie to keep the show on the road. That first experience of *The Flying Dutchman* was an enchantment, an epiphany. Senta Klindworth was led into the dark ship to lift its curse and to live among the spectral old crew who inhabited it. But if it was Senta who was led into the drawing room at Wahnfried, a timeless spectacle in her bridal costume, incomprehensively innocent, it was Winifred Williams who drew back the bridal veil. Fidi did not persist in old Klindworth's 'Senta' nonsense. (They'd died, the Klindworths, they'd done their task in the Divine Scheme and could sing their *Nunc Dimittis* – old Karl went to Valhalla in 1916 and neither lived to see the miracle they had enabled: the four children.) Fidi called her Winnie and so she remained.

The last Wagner Festival at Bayreuth was in 1915 and thereafter the stage Richard Wagner built fell silent. There was talk of reviving it after the war, but with what? As fast as they tried to save money raised in Germany by Fidi's operas, the faster did inflation destroy it. It was Winnie who urged Fidi on and Winnie who accompanied him to America in 1924 to raise the necessary six or seven million marks needed.

Shortly after getting to know the Wagner family, H was passing through Bayreuth with a rich young American admirer of his called Putzi Hanfstaengl. I came to know Putzi quite well a little later and it was from him I heard this story. Winnie and Fidi were away, so H did not go to Wahnfried to pay his respects. Rather he asked Putzi, an enormously tall, suave, musical young man, to drive his sports car to the other end of town to look at the opera house. H, you realize, had by now become an acquaintance of the Wagners but in all his time there had been no operas at Bayreuth. He'd only known the place post-war.

The two men drove up the Green Hill and parked outside the theatre. Hanfstaengl was glad to park the car and get out for fresh air. H had been at his most charmless on the long drive from Munich, talking on and on about his political scheme to defeat Social Democracy, restore the former glories of 1914 and conquer new lands. All the time he'd talked, neither wanting nor noticing answers, and as he talked he had farted for the Fatherland, filling the little car with a scarcely endurable sulphurous atmosphere.

The two men, Hanfstaengl towering over his companion, had slammed the car shut and approached the doors under the front loggia and found them locked. A side door was open, however, and they had managed to get inside. It was a mid-morning in spring. An eerie greyish-green light came from windows far to the back of the stage, while, front of house, the amphitheatre was in pitch darkness. By trial and error, through various doors, they found one marked STAGE. NO ENTRY – and entered.

They found themselves on a vast stage seemingly festooned with dust and cobwebs. To their left, carefully constructed in wood, was the house front of Daland, the Norwegian sailor. Behind, looming against the flat of the northern ocean, brooded the huge spectre-ship.

Putzi, whose American money put him in a different league from most of the Nazis, had a theatrical and musical background in his German family past. His great-grandfather Ferdinand Heine had designed the costumes for the première of *The Flying Dutchman* and for *Rienzi*. The overbearing, flatulent bully who had accompanied Hanfstaengl in the car became a different person, quietly and humbly fascinated by everything Putzi had to tell him.

Never forget this when you think of Winnie and Wolf. Those who suppose her a wicked person do not understand that the 'Wolf' she saw was the gentle opera lover who revealed himself to Hanfstaengl that cool spring day. We all present different selves to others. Sometimes we do it consciously, sometimes not. Winnie brought out the best in the man she idolized as Wolf. Maybe that was the worst thing anyone could have done. By allowing H to put aside the bullyism and the capacity to murder, and to become the polite, charming, opera 'geek' who remembered the names of contraltos in long-gone provincial productions, maybe she did herself, and the world, an injustice? H's niece who committed suicide must have seen things about her uncle which made death alone the salve to her pain. The woman unlucky enough to be made his wife on the last day of his life saw very little in those last so fully documented days except a raving fanatic whose megalomania had been responsible for tens of millions of deaths and the total destruction of our country. He almost never showed this side of his nature to Winnie.

My shame is that in the moods when I hated him I did so for all the wrong reasons. I did not hate him because of his poisonous opinion of the Jews, or his more generalized contempt for humanity: I did not hate him for his vaunting pride, which enabled him, a no more than average architectural draughtsman, to compare his artistic achievements to Michelangelo. As a matter of fact his ludicrously high opinion of himself, believing that he was a Frederick the Great redivivus, for instance, could be seen, in a poverty-stricken Austrian corporal, to have something touching about it. I only loathed him because Winnie loved him. Because Winnie loved him, I would not admit there was anything wrong with loving him, a contorted state of mind that led me to the ludicrous and disgraceful position of defending H when he was attacked by my scrupulous and morally intelligent family.

Love's obsessiveness forces us into the most painful imaginative experiments. A friend is absent and we think of him with fondness or not at all. A love object is absent and it is a gnawing ache. We envy all who are with her – her children, her friends, her dogs. Anything she touches, we envy. How much, that afternoon when Wolf enacted the fisherman and his wife, did I envy baby Verena on Winnie's lap, her hands enclasped in Winnie's hands, her bottom slithering between Winnie's thighs, her back pressed to Winnie's breasts.

In the time I was in love with her – is that time over? I will rephrase that. In the time when love was at its most persistently, gnawingly obsessive, I imagined her actually doing it, promiscuously, as Fidi did. If, cig between her fingers, she touched another man's arm in casual social conversation or if a male member of the opera company called her 'dear' or 'dearest' – many did, for she was an affectionate, bubbling, laughing girl – I winced with pain. Sometimes I actually imagined that these innocent exchanges, touches, glances were clues of a carnal relationship she could scarcely bother to keep secret. Later, of course, when her entire existence was dominated by just such a liaison, I could see the world of difference that exists between a woman under another man's thrall and one who merely enjoys male company.

At this first and early stage of loving Winnie, however, I was tormented by jealousy of all: but her passion for Wolf, as she always called him while he was alive, caused me particular complications of pain. Contrary to my own sensible family, I could entirely see why Winnie idolized him – and this even before he had performed the political and economic miracles, as they seemed at the time, of his early years in office. To tell the truth, although old Mr Chamberlain spoke of H as a national saviour in the early 1920s, I do not believe any of them really thought then he was going to get anywhere. At the time we are talking about his 'party' consisted of at most a few hundred activists – a mixture of thugs and harmless cranks. No – it was not the Party – it was *he* who captivated.

Yet the fact that he captivated *her*, as it seemed to me in a particular way, made me have the most complicated feelings towards him. As a member of the Wagner family circle now, albeit as amanuensis to Siegfried a very minor one, I naturally felt ashamed to differ from them in their views. They all adored 'Wolf', especially the children, and his visits had become high spots. Contrary to my own family, I moreover believed, roughly speaking, in the *völkisch* solutions to our poor nation's problems: a restoration of our borders, an end to 'reparations', anything to stop the economic chaos and the ever-present threat that we should become a Communist, anarchist state, embroiled in civil war as Russia had been, with millions killed. Pride in our nation, language, traditions – belief in our future – where was the harm in that?

So yes, I saw the nationalist programmes as the only ones – most Germans did except for Communists and perverse and fastidious people like my family. This did not remove the knot of pain that came into my chest when I thought of Winnie in Wolf's arms. Whole love scenes between them played in my head.

I tortured myself by envisaging, during one of those winter nights when he arrived alone at Wahnfried, that they had consummated their union. So fixedly had this fantasy lodged itself in my skull that I could follow every stage of the evening as if watching it on film. An abrupt telephone call 'Hello'. This Winnie.

'It's Thou' – from their first meeting they had dispensed with the formality addressing one another in the third person.

'Where?'

He would be saying that he had put up at an hotel a few miles out of town where they were sympathetic to him and where he could feel secure from the Secret Police who did indeed watch him carefully after his release from prison. I imagined her cranking her car, which she nicknamed Presto, into action – she was the first woman in Bayreuth to get a driver's licence – and when the engine

47

was running, taking her seat behind the wheel, driving at full throttle to the hotel a few miles out of town, which was Wolf's favoured hiding place at this date. The fact that this fantasy caused so much pain did not prevent me from revisiting it repeatedly. I saw, or felt, or imagined, the excited embrace between the two of them in the darkened hotel courtyard. I saw her being led into the hotel, hurrying furtively hand in hand with her lover down the corridor – and then, as the lederhosen or blue serge trousers of our future Leader fell to the ground, I forced myself to imagine her moans of pleasure. The only relief to my agony as these painful images filled my mind would come at the conclusion of the business. Winnie and Wolf would by then be completely undressed and on the bed. My tortured brain could even hear the squeaking bedsprings and see her ringed fingers clutching his mole-dotted naked back. But then at his moment of release there would come one of his explosive farts and I could hear Winnie laughing. Winnie had an earthy sense of humour and any bodily malfunction – for example, Eva Chamberlain's tendency to burp – always made her chuckle uncontrollably. Wolf's flatulence was out of control. I imagine that for most of his early visits to the Villa Wahnfried he was just about able to hold it all in with one of those preternatural displays of will-power that enabled him in different contexts to face down opponents, to conquer nations. But there are some occasions when all the muscles in the body relax and when wind, however fiercely held in, would be bound to burst forth. The moment of sexual ecstasy must be such a moment.

Upon sober reflection over many years I still believe in my flatulence theory as a general explanation of why he appears to have slept with few women. Such a man would never have been able to endure laughter at that point and there can be no doubt that his own explosion would have been met by a trumpet of mirth from his partner no less uncompromising than the outburst that provoked it.

But Winnie was different – there was the non-noticing side; there was also her hero-worship of Wolf; and there was her great warmth of heart.

This is a leap ahead too fast in a story that is principally meant for *you*.

Whatever the truth of his relationship with Winnie I offer my flatulence theory to the biographers and historians as an essential factor in determining his relations with other women. Those who dismissed him as a neuter with no interest in the physical aspects of love perhaps overlook how very carefully he would have to look about for a woman who could be relied upon to be neither disgusted nor amused when the explosion took place. In the time I knew him, over about a decade, the flatulence problem grew ever more pronounced and it is impossible to detach it from whatever thoughts he might have had about sex.

Perhaps Fidi, in his very Fidi-ish way, hit the nail on the head when he stood in one of his most characteristic postures one day in the salon. His right hand was balanced on the waist of his yellow shooting jacket. The left, between whose fingers dangled the ever-present Sanoussi cigarette, was laid with the back of the hand against his brow. Winnie, or the children's governess Lieselotte Schmidt, must have been indulging in one of their periodic encomiums in praise of their hero and Siegfried listened with that amused expression on his face. After a while, when Wolf's eloquence, courage, wisdom etc. etc. had been eulogized, Fidi chirruped – in his fluty tones – 'Of course, my dears. I agree with every word you say. But – great as he is – it's very hard to imagine anyone *fancying* Wolf.' His face, unhealthily florid and glistening with sweat, was wreathed with merriment as he said it, his lips pursed against any contradiction.

Winnie flashed a glance at her husband which was angry, defiant; but he was much too experienced a marital fencer to allow her to dissent from his words. 'Winnie, have you been on to Urchs?'

'I spoke to him yesterday—'

'But still no *bloody* cheque . . .'

Ernest Urchs was an American who had helped raise the funds for the Festival when Winnie and Siegfried made their tour of the States in the previous year.

'We're all going to bloody starve ... We need money, Winnie, money.'

'I rang Zurich yesterday,' said Winnie patiently.

'What good is bloody Zurich ...'

'Zurich is where the money is deposited.'

When Fidi began one of his tirades, Winnie sometimes fought back, but more often she used the ploy of sweet reasonableness calming a tantrum.

Although Fidi liked expressing the idea that without him the Festival would collapse, it was in fact Winnie who patiently ensured that all the details dovetailed.

'If we converted the money into Reichsmarks it would be valueless by the end of the week – then we'd find ourselves without any money to pay the orchestra and Wotan would understandably be staying in Munich.'

'Is Friedrich's' – he spoke of Friedrich Schorr – 'room booked at the Anchor?'

'Of course. He's coming to dinner tonight here. Tomorrow you have piano rehearsals with him in the morning. In the afternoon an orchestra rehearsal with him and Olga.'*

It was the first year that Friedrich Schorr was to sing Wotan at Bayreuth and I was keenly looking forward to the privilege of sitting in on the rehearsals. I had heard him sing Sachs at a *Meiseringer* performed in Munich, and I had also heard him sing Lieder in a concert in Berlin which – it being chiefly songs by Schubert and Schumann – my parents had consented to attend. His voice survives, so you can decide for yourselves by playing the discs if, unlike me, you possess a turntable. There's no music in this flat outside my head. In my opinion, there has never been a more warm-hearted depiction of Sachs, nor a more touching Wotan in that scene, the greatest in the whole Wagner canon, of Wotan's Farewell in *Die Walküre*. The bass-baritone was played like an instrument over which he had pure control. The voice, velvety and rich, has great steadiness, total purity of legato.

* Olga Blomé.

And this I was able to hear, not just in the dress rehearsals and grand performances that summer, but also in the many smaller rehearsals upon which Siegfried allowed me to sit in.

Schorr was a good man. This was one of his palpable qualities: perhaps it is why some purists think he is at his best in the genial role of Sachs and lacks the treachery, duplicity or sheer cruelty necessary to play Wotan. I don't agree; I had heard, by then, Fidi conduct many rehearsals. He was a brilliant conductor and director: I never saw any of the great singers whom it was my privilege to hear with a more total grasp of a *part* than Schorr – and he built up his effects, patiently accepting every bit of direction and advice Fidi could offer him. It was during these rehearsals, too, that one was able to learn so much about the genius of Wagner himself, the way he had translated into incomparable musical innovation such a multiplicity of complicated thoughts and ideas and emotions with a kind of instinctual cleverness. Yes – *there*. Yes – *that's* right. As Fidi and Schorr took the score to pieces and reconstructed it again one was witness to the dissection of pure genius, interpreted with astounding penetration.

In fact, the arrival of Schorr for rehearsals, with his high straight brow, hooded eyes, barrel chest and genial smile, made everyone feel confident about that year's Festival. The daily, often hourly, crises – two female harpists eloped, by bicycle, to Austria and another suffered from appendicitis; a major quarrel broke out among scene builders; one of the prettier boys in the chorus (Norwegian sailor and Grail Knight) claimed Fidi had given him the clap, provoking one of his better put-downs: 'Now, dear, you're just showing off', and the endless money worries – all calmed down since we knew, we at Wahnfried, that with Schorr singing in *The Ring* the Festival, which had been revived the previous year for the first time since the war and which had got off to a rocky start, was now destined to be a triumph.

The levels of stress and tension before the Festival would be difficult to exaggerate and we were all extremely busy, so that although I continued to love Winnie in the same tormented way, the emotional torture was numbed for much of the time by the narcotic of work. She, Fidi and I worked the hardest – in the household – though the Festival Theatre itself, its warren of offices, sewing rooms and rehearsal rooms, was a positive anthill of activity.

One feature of Winnie's character which I should perhaps have sketched in earlier was a capacity for besotted crushes. The Wolfmania was something a little different, or so I have concluded, though obviously it was of a piece with the ease with which she fell in love with people – with anyone but me. Her current crush was a young visitor from England, Hugh Walpole, destined to be celebrated in his day as a novelist. I never read him and I found his epicene and self-satisfied manner annoying. To make matters worse, I could not really understand what he said since he spoke English at all times: it is a language which I read with difficulty and which I have never had much occasion to speak.

In all the agitation, the daily small crises leading up to the Festival, I was painfully aware that Winnie was emotionally fixated on Hugh. Whenever I came upon them they were talking in the man's language and often laughing. It was at the height of the Norwegian-Sailor-Grail-Knight-clap business. Winnie as usual took no notice and one could not tell whether she did not know her husband had been messing about with a man in the chorus – whether, moreover, she genuinely did not know that the entire orchestra and chorus spoke of little else for about ten days – or whether she simply chose to rise above it. That is what I meant earlier when I spoke of her Welsh reserve. Perhaps she was trying to make her husband jealous by the hours of English conversation with Hugh Walpole? If so she did not noticeably succeed since Fidi appeared quite at ease with Hugh, perhaps too much so, and spoke perfect English.

Anyhow that Festival is defined for me by two robust exchanges in which I saw Winnie at her most magnificent. You may wonder, as I did then, how she found time or energy for such spats on top of her busy preparations for the Festival, but perhaps it was precisely the anxiety caused by the Festival that gave force to her outbursts?

The first was a row whose gist I did not really catch since it was conducted in English. It happened about a week before the Festival began. I had left Fidi in the orchestra pit doing a choral rehearsal and had pedalled the mile or so from the Festival Theatre into town and down to Wahnfried where, over a cup of lemon tea, I had intended to address some of the correspondence that mountained on his desk. Tea, with a selection of cakes and biscuits, was put out in the salon at about half past four and it was to that room that I made my way first, hoping to take my tea into Fidi's study. As I entered the room Hugh Walpole and Winnie were not merely having a heated exchange. They were having a row.

I dare say that the real reason she was angry with him was emotional disappointment. She must have hoped for an intense and unrealistic period that Hugh might have become her lover. The fact, obvious to the rest of us, that if he had chosen to have an affair with either of the Wagners it would unquestionably have been with the husband might at last have dawned on her mysterious Welsh soul. Whatever the truth of that, she had chosen to quarrel with him about Wolf. I couldn't make out what they were saying, but the phrases Landberg – where Wolf had been imprisoned – and *Mein Kampf* were discernible. Later – years later – when Hugh Walpole was just a memory, Winnie would tell me how angered she had been by his snobbery about Wolf, wondering how anyone could seriously imagine a man 'like that' becoming a great political leader. ('Like that' meaning a poor man, of no family.) Walpole stayed on in the house for about ten days afterwards and attended Schorr's performances in *The Ring*, but it was clear, and a source of satisfaction to me, that he had gone too far. She did not forgive his slighting references to Wolf.

As for the hero himself, however, even he was subjected to one of Winnie's rebukes. Just as I felt her anger with Hugh Walpole was inspired by emotional disappointment, so I wondered how much this unwonted snappishness with Wolf was not in part inspired by resentment that when he came to the Festival that summer, rather than staying at the Villa Wahnfried, Wolf was put up in a house very nearby which had been taken by Helene Bechstein.

Frau Bechstein, thirteen years older than Wolf, had seen both him and Winnie in their as it were unformed or unfinished state. As wife to the most distinguished piano manufacturer in Berlin she was bound to know pianist Klindworth and had seen the spindly-legged East Grinstead orphan soon after her arrival in the homeland. Little 'Senta' had been astounded, after the exigencies of the orphanage, to step into the villa which stood in the park of that piano factory and to see its wide marble staircase, its thirty-six rooms, its panelled walls hung with tapestries and paintings by Velásquez. In summer the Klindworths had been invited to the Bechsteins' country estate. It was there that Senta had flown her first kite, a gift from Frau Bechstein, and learnt to row a little skiff on the boating lake.

The Bechsteins were fervent conservative nationalists and, after the war, Helene had welcomed the young H to her salon when he had been brought along by the novelist Dietrich Eckart. Enchanted by the orator, Frau Bechstein conceived it her duty to make this Man of the People acceptable in society. She taught H how to bow and kiss a lady's hand. She explained to him how to sit at a table, how to take the napkin and unfold it on his knee, how to hold a knife and fork. There were occasional lapses. His tutor had difficulty explaining that a knife is not held in the same way as a pen; but on the whole Helene Bechstein was proud of her Pygmalion role in transforming him.

There was more than a little rivalry between the two ladies, Frauen Wagner and Bechstein, when it came to offering Wolf accommodation, though Winnie could see that while she was so busy with the Festival it made sense for Wolf to stay with the Bechsteins and come round to Wahnfried for visits. These visits themselves, sometimes made when Winnie was at the theatre, gave unfailing delight to the children, but were greeted with stiffness or even downright hostility by the old ladies. 'Winnie, my dear,' Eva remarked acidly over luncheon one day, '*shorts!*'

'What is that?' Winnie's response to the sisters-in-law whom she detested was to assume her impenetrable grin and to 'humour' them as a form of humiliation.

'We thought . . .'

'We, in this context, being?'

'Only, in the *house*.' She simpered and attempted to subdue one of those irrepressible burps, which never failed to entertain Winnie and which always came upon her after food. 'I mean he was even . . . the Divine Mother' – burps – 'suggesting he visit the Divine Mother wearing . . . lederhosen.'

It is true that in the intense heat of our Franconian August, Wolf had abandoned the navy-blue serge suit of a previous visit in favour of traditional Bavarian costume – stockings to the noticeably hairless white knees, leather shorts, embroidered braces and a white shirt. Winnie once told me that when he was doing one of his public performances he could drink as many as twelve bottles of mineral water, sweating it all out as he roared his message of salvation to the crowds. She spoke as if all he did – even sweating – was an achievement worthy of congratulation. True it was hot and we were all sticky in those weeks, but even without the mineral water and the public oratory, Wolf's face was always glistening, the armpits of his shirt two splodgy maps of the Greater Germany. There was a pungency about his presence which was almost of the farmyard. It was not to this that Eva, on behalf of the Divine Mother, objected, however. It was the bare flesh. No one older than a child had ever worn Bavarian National Costume in the house before.

Whether he really penetrated to the Divine Mother's quarters remained for the duration of the Festival, by the way, quite a mystery. Old Cosima was not demented, but even more than most members of the household at that stage, she lived in a world of dream. Her German, when spoken at all, was more and more accented and idiosyncratic, and much of the time she drifted into French. On a number of occasions during the Festival it was I who was designated to take her for one of her little walks in the Hofgarten. Sometimes she managed the 500 metres or so to the New Palace but more often we just walked past the graves of her husband, of her parrots, and his faithful Newfoundland Russ and pottered to the ornamental bridge beneath the chestnuts. She might be silent or speaking quietly in the

French which was my second language but of which my mastery was far from perfect. '*Et quand nous sommes arrivés à cet endroit-ceci*' – she teetered by the stone grave slab – '*il m'a dit – le Maître – nous appellerons la maison la Bonheur Finale – zum letzten Glück . . . Le professeur a-t-il nous visité aujourd'hui? . . . oui, oui, pauvre petit Professeur Nietzsche . . . si triste . . . pauvre professeur . . . ah, mes jardins . . . si parfaits, si parfaits avec . . . les Luxembourgs . . . Le Père, il est ici? Le Père? Depuis quelques heures je n'ai pas vu Le Père . . .*'

The characters who swam in and out of her consciousness, and to whose presence her semi-audible commentaries attested, had most of them been dead for years. Nietzsche came, as did Wagner and Liszt – and sometimes her first husband Hans von Bülow put in an appearance to convey forgiveness or blame, depending on her mood.

But there was another presence today in her mind and one could tell that he agitated her by refusing to leave her head. '*Un jeune homme si – si –*' It was, however, as if no French word quite suited this particular visitant and she eventually settled for our German 'weird' or 'strange': *seltsam*. '*Der Himmel hing voller Geigen. Il me l'a dit! . . . Mais il me semble qu'il se croit une espèce de génie – il m'a raconté l'histoire d'un opéra qu'il a composé lui-même . . .*' During the walk itself the identity of a young man who thought himself a genius and who had composed an opera was completely mysterious to me. It was only a few weeks later that Kiki, the Divine Mother's parrot, remarked in Wolf's most oleaginous drawing-room manner, 'Gracious Lady!' followed by the inevitable raspberry noise.

But I was in the middle of explaining the extraordinary little squall which blew upon between Winnie and Wolf. It happened at the Festival Theatre about half an hour before the first day of the *Ring* cycle. We were all very excited. I had heard Schorr now many times in rehearsal and with each performance his Wotan grew in terrible authority. It was cast iron clad in rich velvet.

But here, on the balcony, which led into one of the very few boxes in the theatre – the Wagner family seats – stood Frau Bechstein and her entourage. She had kitted Wolf out in evening dress, which must have been made for him. Unlike his lounge suit the swallow-tail coat, white waistcoat and black trousers actually fitted him, though the white bow tie was a little wonky. It was clear that he was in a state of great agitation.

Winnie had that expression on her face which betokened real anxiety. She nearly always wore it before curtain up. She joined us more than usually flustered, though, and I suspect she had had one of her innumerable tiffs with Fidi before he went to the orchestra pit to see Michael Balling, who was conducting the performance and had been unwell.

'I feel it is a betrayal of our *race* and this I must declare!' Wolf shot out. He was staring bulbous-eyed. 'It is a racial sacrilege to have the god of our German pantheon, Wotan' – he threw back his head – 'played by ...' There was no doubting the sincerity of his passion, yet, although these rhetorical pauses and eye-rollings had so mesmeric an effect on large crowds, in a small group gathered on the balcony it was different: acutely awkward, embarrassing, perpetually frightening. '... played by a *Jew*!' he bellowed.

'None of us wanted a Jew,' muttered Frau Bechstein, 'but perhaps they couldn't ...'

'Why not get Rode over from Munich to sing the role? What is wrong with ...' the opera geek Wolf began to reel off names of bass-baritones.

You will already have gathered my feelings about Winnie and I did not believe it was possible to love her more than I did. This evening she brought about that miracle. She appeared at first not to have heard. She was looking out over the balcony at the Wagnerians making their way up the hill and on to the terraces. 'Wolf,' she said. She was smiling as she said it. The many distractions of the evening had clearly, for once, put his feelings and concerns rather low down on her list of priorities. 'I and my family have supported you through *thick and thin*. When you first began your career in public speaking, I came to hear you – I came back here and told my family, *this is the man*. I know you can save Germany. We watched the failed putsch in Munich from our hotel window. We helped get your friends over the border to Austria. Fidi paid for Göring to go to hospital in Vienna when he was shot. When you needed paper and pens in prison to write *Mein Kampf*, we sent them to you. We stood by you when you were a state outlaw. And you are probably right that the bloody Jews want to take over the world. For all I know you are right about the depravity of being a queer. But just look out there –' she waved her smouldering cigarette in the direction of the opera goers. 'When you were fighting for your country, this place *closed down*. You want to hear the music dramas of Richard Wagner, right? Would you like to tell me which are the two categories of human being who enjoy him the most? Eh?'

She lit another cigarette from the butt of the old one and squidged the dead butt under a golden evening shoe. 'Do you know who paid for the revival of Bayreuth? The Jews and the queers. They are the people who *like* Richard Wagner. Half the chorus are pansies and one quarter of the orchestra is Jewish. If you love Wagner that is what you get. If you want something different, go in to Munich and hear *The Merry Widow* – or finance the bloody Festival yourself.'

I often wondered, when reading about H as a warlord who roared and ranted at his generals and air marshals, often directing them into catastrophic strategies and prodigious loss of life, what would have happened if they had delivered a comparable speech to him. Probably they would have been shot. I read somewhere that he claimed to have absented himself from that year's *Ring* on the grounds of Schorr's race, but like many of his claims this was a lie. I was quite close to him in the box that evening, and as the familiar and catastrophic chords began, and the strife among the divinely irresponsible inhabitants of Valhalla started its clash of voice, wind, harp, I could clearly see that it was not merely sweat but tears that cascaded down his plump, still youthful, face.

I was in the habit of returning each evening to my parents' house in the —— district of the town. On that evening I either was not bidden for a late supper at the theatre restaurant or at the Eule or the Anchor, or one of the other restaurants we liked in the town. Perhaps tiredness took me home, where the familiar front door of my father's parsonage was opened by Elsa, who prepared me what she called coffee but which was surely a mixture of ground acorns and chicory. Like everyone who did not have a Swiss or American bank account my family has been reduced to extremes of austerity, but unlike most of my acquaintances, my parents never made any comment upon the fact, slowly eating meals composed solely of root vegetables with the same decorum as, before the war, they had consumed roast meat. From the parlour I could hear the trio playing what my parents, and especially my father who played the violin, would call proper music. It was a piece by Haydn for violin (my father), cello (my brother) and piano (my mother). Sometimes, of course, I formed a quartet. More normally we played Haydn and Mozart, sometimes Brahms.

You of a younger generation often express astonishment that we could have *fallen for* the doctrines of National Socialism. And you simply can't believe it when we reply that most of us did not *fall for* anything or subscribe to any particular idea. We followed what we thought we wanted: full employment, national pride. It is not to our credit that we failed to notice the evil things that were there from the beginning, but the truth is that most Europeans say (and think) unpleasant things about the Jews. Although H, like Mr Chamberlain, took this to truly manic extremes both in what he said and in what he wrote, it wasn't the anti-Semitism that made him distinctive. Most public figures had that. What made him special was his mesmeric qualities of hope, his hypnotic faith in the future.

Winnie, more than most of us, loved these. But the orphanage girl had within her an anarchic desire to throw over the traces. It occurred to me that evening – if you had to find a reason why a nice and far from fanatical girl like Winnie should have been a National Socialist, you need look no further than the scene that presented itself in my parents' parlour as the Haydn trio ended.

My mother, her white hair in a bun, sat at the piano. She had a faintly flushed expression when she played music. Her pale-blue eyes blinked back into focusing on the room and her sons, after their acute concentration on the score. She wore a simple, immaculately clean, sky-blue blouse fastened at the neck by a 'good' old jewel – something, I believe, from Father's side of the family. My bespectacled brother Heinrich, with sandy hair parted in the middle, with a dark coat and trousers and a loose silk tie of sober colour, looked exactly like what he was: a teacher at the local Gymnasium who was considering following my father into the Lutheran ministry but who was held back by doubts about the miraculous elements in the New Testament.

My father – ah, my father – how can I write about you in the light of everything which was to befall you and my brother? How dare I write about you, you whose lives so put mine to shame? From the very beginning you saw through the madness which would one day possess our country. You never drank from the chalice that blinded the eyes, bewitched the gaze and numbed the senses of the rest of us.

At the time, my father's moderation, his measured, rational approach to life, his exactitude and probity and caution, were all qualities I found enraging. I foolishly mistook my family's quietness and *politesse* for being hidebound by convention. I even suspected them – here perhaps I had some justification for my suspicions – of snobbery. I'm sure it was from my mother I heard the objection to our local National Socialist candidate that one could not consider voting for someone 'like that' – Hugh Walpole's objection precisely – by which she clearly meant 'common'. My father's realism made him believe, as one government tumbled and another was patched together from its ruins, that Germany should struggle on. There were signs of economic recovery. The President and whoever happened to be Chancellor would one day persuade the Americans to force the French to lift the punitive sanctions on our country. One day French troops would move out of the Rhineland. It was certainly madness to speak of restarting the war. Everything my father thought and said was moderate, considered. That is what I mean by saying he was the absolute embodiment of everything that made impulsive Welsh Winnie into a Nazi.

She said she loved all things German but she didn't. The majority of Germans are like my father: quiet, patient, moderate and gentle. Wagner is not a typical German, any more than was his French-Hungarian widow, his Welsh daughter-in-law or his fanatical English son-in-law Chamberlain. You might add Wolf to the list of atypical unGerman outsiders. What made my father most intensely German to me was not so much his quiet methodical way of life, nor his musicality, nor his domestic authoritarianism (for he was firmly master in his own house) as his belief in reason. You might ask – as I did, and loudly – how a belief in reason squared with what he did for a living. He was a Lutheran pastor at one of the finer old baroque churches in our town.

This is a book about Winnie and Wolf, and if anything would die in this Communist republic of ours it presumably would be the faith of Martin Luther? So I'd have guessed until you revealed yourself to be a Christian in your teens. But my father plays a part in this story, so I ought to make a short excursus on his career. I think of him sitting there that evening with his violin. I thought of him as an old man then – a tiresome old man. He was – what? – born in 1870, so he was just fifty-five years old.

At about the time Nietzsche (professor of philology at Basel, later demiurge of modern atheism) was engaging his ecstatic imagination first with Wagner's and then no less violently rejecting him, Adolf Harnack was approaching the story of Christianity from the position of a rational historian. At about the time Nietzsche wrote *Beyond Good and Evil*, Harnack was beginning to publish his monumental *History of Dogma*.

Harnack is one of the intellectual giants of our country's history, but I find he has been ironed out of the story – I have never met a student who had read him. (Maybe things are different in the West.) He was professor at Berlin in the early years of our century – in spite of the protests of the Church dogmatists who pointed out that he doubted the Virgin Birth, the Ascension, the Resurrection and so forth. It was the Emperor himself who rescued his career, giving him the chair at Berlin, and eventually he was made the Director

General of the Royal Library, the largest library in Germany. After the revolution of 1919 he was still held in such high esteem that he was asked by the government to be the German Ambassador in Washington, but he turned the honour down. He was primarily an academic and his monument, apart from his books, which will endure for ever, are his pupils. They included nearly all the noted theologians of subsequent generations such as Karl Barth and Dietrich Bonhoeffer, and they also included my father.

Unlike Barth, who broke away from the disciplines set by Harnack and adopted a form of Fideism or Irrationalism which enjoyed a vogue in the German Church and the greater world, my father was a straight Harnack devotee. Harnack must have been an extraordinary teacher. My father once asked him how long it would take him to memorize one page of Greek he had never seen before. Harnack replied, 'If I read the page slowly, I would know it by heart.' He taught his pupils to be rigorous in their sifting of evidence, in their believing that their only duty was to the truth. This ultimately was what would lead his son Ernst, my father, and so many others to resist the National Socialists and to suffer accordingly – but that is to race ahead.

I had intended, as my brother did, to follow my father into the Lutheran ministry, but in my first few semesters I became bitten by the Nietzsche bug and the milk and water version of Christianity (as I perceived it then – my God) of those who thought like my father was a poor substitute for a true emotional engagement with the claims of Christianity. We had just lived through a war in which millions of young lives had been destroyed, in which thrones and altars had rightly been torn down, in which we had all found ourselves stumbling around among the rubble and the dust and the blood, our old values shredded like our houses, our limbs, our bank accounts. In such a world Nietzsche's fury with God for not existing, his assertion of a supremely irrational humanism, his desire to worship a God who could dance, his belief that morals had no power to make us good – they all spoke to me, as they spoke to my mentor and supervisor Martin H———. Nietzsche's idea, sustained even when he had fallen out of love with Wagner, that music might save us, or at least speak out our fears and desires better than religion, was true for me. It was what made the music dramas of Richard Wagner so repeatedly revisitable a source.

And there sat my father, with his violin, and his soft complexion and gentle eyes, thinking that the world would be a better place if everyone could be persuaded to be gentler and more rational. 'How was it?' he asked, meaning *The Ring of the Nibelung* I had just attended. I wanted to repeat to him the whole extraordinary conversation between Winnie and Wolf about Schorr. Something checked me. Both my parents, but especially my father, gave off the ever-lasting air of sitting in judgement. If I told Father what Winnie had said my narrative would have been complicated by all kinds of defensive reactions, I would sense both my parents, and my brother, wincing at the mention of homosexuality. And then again I did not want to be in the position of holding up Winnie to my family and saying, 'You disapprove of her political views; but here – you see – she is a decent person really . . .' So I left the story untold.

I talked instead of well-known faces I had seen assembled before the performance – seen, not spoken to, for I 'knew no one' unless Siegfried or Winifred introduced me to their guests. I had no entry into the greater world. I spoke of seeing Karl Muck, Thomas Mann and, to please my mother who would have been happy had Bavaria regained autonomy from the rest of Germany and brought back dear old King Ludwig III, I described various members of the European royal families who had come including Tsar Ferdinand of Bulgaria. I conjured up Winnie and Fidi bowing and curtsying to those pre-revolutionary ancients. The glint of large old jewels in the evening light, the brightness of white ties and stiff shirts, the tiaras and the, in the case of one visitant, sash with decorations had actually discon-certed me, recalling Nietzsche's disillusionment with Wagner, when he actually saw Bayreuth, and witnessed Cosima fawning upon the crowned and coronated heads. My mother would not have shared my or Nietzsche's views. I think it possible that she abominated the Dionysian raptures of Richard Wagner's music even more than

Father did, but she did think there should be a hierarchy in the management of society, and that kings and queens were conducive to an orderly and Christian life for the rest of us.

My mother made a few approving remarks about the Wittelsbach dynasty and commented – information gleaned of course from newspapers rather than personal knowledge – on the recent illness of Prince Rupprecht and the marriage of the Crown Princess Antonia. I do not suppose my parents ever discussed such matters as our (demoted and dethroned) royal family when they were alone together. Rather, these royalties provided a neutral conversational buffer which my family and I could erect between one another to disguise our lack of sympathy.

I tried to tell them about the English novelist, Hugh Walpole, but my father merely shook his head silently with a gentle smile, an habitual gesture which conveyed not merely that he had not heard of the persons under discussion but that he did not deem them worth knowing about. Then, rather suddenly, came the question which evidently all three of them had been wanting to ask me all evening. 'Was *he* there?' There could be no doubt, even at that very early date, that they meant H.

The directness of the question wrong-footed me, creating an unjustifiable defensiveness. My reaction would only have been appropriate had I been Wolf's political agent or if I had asked him to Bayreuth myself. 'I believe he was there,' I said, stammering out the name of the Bechsteins, as though it made things better or worse where he spent the night. There was a silence.

Then my brother, who had been largely silent ever since I got home, remarked with vehemence, 'It was a scandal that he was ever let out of prison.'

In spite of his subsequent rewriting of history and his claim not to have heard Schorr's Wotan, H returned to the second opera of the cycle, *Die Walküre*, the next day to hear Schorr's rendition of Wotan's farewell to Brünnhilde – *Leb wohl, du kühnes, herrliches Kind!* – which must be one of the most beautiful pieces of music ever composed. I do not believe anyone could improve upon Schorr's interpretation, so steady, so implacable, so heartbroken, as the divine father takes leave of his daughter and the nineteenth century knows that it is taking leave of its God.

H, as a Wagner devotee, must have known that he was hearing one of the great interpretations of *The Ring*. Presumably it was this which provoked his stream of letters over the next few years protesting against the use of Jewish artists at Bayreuth. I blush to record that Winnie tried to lure him back with the promise that she would find an Aryan understudy for Schorr on any night Wolf deigned to attend future Festivals, though she could hardly hope to replace all those in orchestra and chorus who either were, or were married to, Jews. My own belief is that H boycotted the next few Festivals not because of this painful subject but because of that powerful strain of superstition in his nature which believed he was being led by Fate from one phase to the next, but who also, having narrowly escaped death in the war, was never sure when nemesis might appear.

The final drama in the *Ring* cycle, *The Twilight of the Gods*, has no role for Wotan, so the anti-Semites among us could sit back untroubled. On this evening, however, all was not well, and the incident which took place on the stage of the Festival Theatre would have been disconcerting even for one who was not, like H, so acutely and superstitiously aware of portents and signs. The familiar story began with the three Norns weaving their rope of destiny and rehearsing the doom-laden mythology of the north – how Wotan came to drink of the well of wisdom and paid for his knowledge with an eye; how he carried secret runes on his spear taken from the World's Ash Tree, a token of his divine power; how he punished his daughter Brünnhilde by surrounding her with fire, which could only be broken through by a hero who knew no fear; how the dwarf Alberich stole the Rhinegold to win the arid triumphs of power without love; how the rope was tautening and snapping, and mere anarchy was loosed upon the world. Believe me, in 1925 such a story made a lot of sense.

Then the stage brightens and we are with Siegfried and Brünnhilde in their married bliss. The mortal hero whose sword has shattered the spear of Wotan is the embodiment of nineteenth-century man come of age – living without God. Siegfried gives the Ring of Power into Brünnhilde's possession and she in return gives him her flying horse Grane to carry him on his adventures. There were several stage horses used at Bayreuth in those days. Nowadays I believe Wieland's productions dispense with such stage business altogether and the Valkyries' flying steeds are imagined by the audience. But in 1925 Cosima (though it was years since she had actually attended an opera) was still alive and her daughters Eva and Daniela made it their business to protest if there was the slightest variation to the staging of the operas from the days of the Master. The same moth-eaten old furs, the same cardboard swords, the same creaking chariots and the same unconvincing Rhine waves were in operation that had seemed ridiculous as long ago as 1876. Had he produced *The Ring* several years running, Wagner would surely himself have seen the difficulties of working with real horses and would have got round the problem somehow or other since, unlike his wife and daughters, he had the stage in his blood and he was also always wanting to change, to adapt, to innovate.

That night, every member of the audience for *The Twilight of the Gods* must have been aware that the horse playing Grane was in no mood for four or five hours of a loud musical meditation on the nineteenth-century metaphysical crisis. At its first appearance to the ecstatic Brünnhilde and Siegfried in Act One it was tetchy and whin-nying, and as Siegfried led it down the ravine, it kicked one of the painted hardboard rocks with its back foot, then lifted its tail and defecated.

Winnie had expressed anxiety about the horse's demeanour more than once when we met during the intervals. The animal waited, however, until the last scene, before it upstaged the singers. Wolf cannot have been alone in that packed theatre in feeling that the incident, as well as being alarming in itself, was full of portent. For several weeks afterwards, even after our star tenor was on the mend and the injured stagehand had come out of hospital, we were all upset. The incident increased that feeling, always so strong in Fidi and which optimistic, healthy-minded Winnie resisted, that we had set our feet on a path to peril, to destruction.

Two puppet ravens flew into the air towards Valhalla over Siegfried's funeral pyre as Brünnhilde sang of her renunciation of the gold and of power. She sang of the end of the gods as lucre and struggle are overcome by the quiet music of nature. Olga Blomé's piercing soprano, as she seized Grane's bridle and asked, '*Weisst du auch, mein Freund, wohin ich dich führe?*' was too much for the beast. Do you know, my friend, where I'm leading you now? The horse leaped on the corpse of Siegfried, crunching several of Rudolf Ritter's ribs. It cantered towards the orchestra pit. Pio Jahn, an amiable stagehand, ran out to seize the horse, but it reared up, whinnying furiously and lashed at him with its hooves. He was lucky to escape with nothing worse than a broken ankle. At least he had turned the animal's head and diverted its intention, which would truly have been disastrous, of charging into the sunken orchestra pit. But the horse's behaviour had stopped the orchestra in their playing. Brünnhilde remained for ever poised on the edge of her husband's pyre never to make her sacrifice. The opera is meant to end with the human race at last come of age. That night in the sixth year of the Weimar Republic we felt dread in our stomachs. We had witnessed destruction without resolution; loss of power because it had been wrenched from us rather than because we had had the wisdom to renounce it; noise rather than music; chaos come again.

Lohengrin

I have woken up, alone. My eyes focus on the battered old puppet of Mr Punch who sits sadly on the shelf at the end of my bed. He has been on many journeys with me. His nose, on which traces of papier-mâché add to its grotesqueness, is housed over the Voltaire grin of the lips, which seems to be full of contempt for me, for my and for my country's history.

I have just dreamed of *Lohengrin*. When I say I was *in* it, I do not mean I dreamed that I was a famous tenor such as Max Lorenz, reedy, ethereal yet powerful singing that most beautiful of love duets –

Fühl ich ʒu dir so süss mein Herʒ entbrennen

– with Maria Müller. Rather my dream let me swim about in the music, a happy carp among flowing green plants and dark water, luxuriating in its lush sadness.

'From the very first *Lohengrin* to me was a call to arms – it is a direct political –' Wolf was not talking in my dream. The dream was pure delight, but as I come back to the waking world, memory superimposes itself upon dream and I hear again that rasping voice: '. . . in Linz at the age of twelve. It was my first experience of the work of Richard Wagner. Really – the whole story is there: the need for German reunification, for the strength of a Greater Germany.'

'Shall I tell you something, Wolf?' Winnie replied.

'King Henry comes to tell the fractious little people of Brabant that a German sword alone will unite them . . .'

'. . . I don't *think*' – she chuckled and lit a cigarette. 'When I finally sit down and hear *Lohengrin* or any of the other operas, I don't think. The drama is something that happens.'

'So long ago. *He* saw it, the Master . . .'

'There was no Germany ninety years ago,' Fidi interrupted. 'All those choruses in *Lohengrin* . . . it's like Verdi's choruses hoping for an Italian nation. There's the world of difference between aspiring for national unity you don't have and throwing your weight about when you do have it.'

'But your great father . . .' said Wolf.

'Daddy *hated*' – Fidi's voice rose to a squeak – 'Bismarck's Reich – in some ways as much as the old . . .'

'But in 1870, he and his ever-esteemed . . . your ever-gracious . . .' – there was something so oily about Wolf's manner with them – 'mother . . .'

'Everyone rejoices in a victory,' said Fidi, 'of course my parents were pleased that France was defeated in 1870 – all the more remarkably since she is French!' He squeaked with amusement.

One could never tell whether he noticed that his little interjections into Wolf's monologues sometimes had a deflating effect. The reminder, for example, that his father – our reason for all being in Bayreuth – had entertained many political views, some of them self-contradictory, in the course of a seventy-year-old life, but that by the time he came to Bayreuth for the sole purpose of staging music and drama he had developed quasi-mystic views, a sort of Schopenhauerish blend of Buddhism and Christianity, if that doesn't sound too much like nonsense. He practised vegetarianism, believed in peace through the relinquishment of power, hated political parties. He even repented of his strident former anti-Semitism and conducted, with admiration, the Italian Symphony of Mendelssohn. None of this deflected Wolf in his view that the legend of Lohengrin, a mysterious figure arriving by water and drawn by a swan, to rescue Elsa of Brabant from a charge of fratricide, contained messages about rearming post-war Germany.

'Was it not' – again Wolf adopted his oleaginous butler manner – 'your brother-in-law' – as he spoke his eyes brightened and looked first to Winnie, then to Fidi as if the very words 'brother-in-law' were a cue for the orchestra to strike up – 'who said that the whole future of Europe – the civilization of the world itself – rests in the hands of *Germany* and Germany alone?'

'Houston said that?' Fidi pursed his lips. Whereas Wolf's eye movements and the flicker of podgy fingers suggested an impatient desire for universal recognition, Fidi's lips and florid cheeks, and somehow his whole quivering *pose*, suggested dissension, at least in the matter of seeing his English brother-in-law as the fount of all wisdom. 'Do we have to exclude all the other nations? Eh? Italy has taught us a thing or two? About opera? Cooking? French cooking: not so bad. Come to that where would we Germans be without you, my dear Austrian Wolf, and Houston and Winnie who are pure English, coming and telling us how wonderful we are?' His laughter at this outburst was not appreciated.

'Now work, my boy, work!' He patted my bottom. We put down our coffee cups (no acorn-muck for the Wagners) and retreated to his study for an afternoon composing letters to some Americans, mostly Jews, begging for more cash and assuring them of the essentially international flavour of the Bayreuth proceedings.

As we left the room, Winnie had advanced upon Wolf and placed her hand on his. 'Don't mind Fidi's teases – he's on our side. Truly.'

It was true that Siegfried Wagner was an unsatisfactory mouthpiece for what might be called Wagnerian propaganda since (like Winnie, really) he was primarily interested in the operas as things to be performed rather than as encoded political programmes. Even Houston Stewart Chamberlain, Siegfried's brother-in-law, in his book about Wagner, admits that the composer's 'views' and 'philosophy' were a muddle. 'Art' – a product of genius which reflects general and absolute beauty and truth – can never act as a vehicle for a particular and specific teaching – that was what he thought once, anyway, though by the time he had become a Nazi prophet Chamberlain's views had probably modified somewhat.

Chamberlain's own views on Germany, on racial questions and on the Jews were not merely similar to Wolf's. They could be said to have fashioned them. If any one individual can be credited with the invention of National Socialism it must be this extraordinary Englishman.

Winnie, who took Chamberlain's pretensions with a pinch of salt and who openly disliked his wife, the burping Eva, used to say that he had the air of a sanctimonious clergyman. Once, when in a confiding mood – for she sometimes did and sometimes did not speak openly of her life in the orphanage – she would name one of these 'black crows': Father Carter-Bown, a prison-pallid man apparently who enjoyed the sycophantic attentions of some of the nuns. There was, as many visitors to Bayreuth noted, a quasi- or pseudo-religious atmosphere and in Chamberlain's smooth cheeks, extreme pallor, and fussy, slightly effeminate mannerisms you could have seen him as a man of the Church.

Not that I would suggest, by applying the epithet effeminate to Chamberlain, any hint of Fidi-like fondnesses for chorus boys. On the contrary, he had dropped Anna, the wife who was ten years his senior (he was twenty when they first met) and Lili Petri, his mistress of several years' standing, in order to leap at the possibility of marrying one of Richard Wagner's daughters – which he had done at Christmastime 1908 when she was forty-one. The marriage caused considerable scandal in conventional circles. Chamberlain's English family, from whom he had been long estranged, expressed horror at his easy abandonment of his legal wife and no Protestant pastor in Bayreuth could be found who would solemnize his union. Eva's mother, who had abandoned her husband in order to run off with Richard Wagner forty years before, was perhaps not in a position to take a strong moral line, but even she expressed reservations – especially when she heard of Lili Petri. But Lili was merely Venus: Houston assured his future mother-in-law she represented his imprisonment in the lustful lure of Venusberg, projecting himself as another Tannhäuser – not perhaps a very plausible role for a valetudinarian man of fifty-three whom I never saw out of carpet slippers and not very reassuring, for who would want Tannhäuser as a son-in-law? He assured Cosima that, whereas Lili had been Venus, in Eva he had 'found his holy Elisabeth'.

There was bad blood between Siegfried and his sister, and when Winnie married into the family she took her husband's side against the burping Eva. Such was her essential good nature, however, that Winnie was the soul of kindness to Eva in her widow's distress when Chamberlain died, cosseting her, taking her little meals on trays and doing everything short of verbal disloyalty to Fidi by way of listening to Eva's disgruntled complaints about family papers and about money.

Nowadays, of course, the only Chamberlain linked in history's ear with H is the British Prime Minister who declared war on our country in 1939. Thirty years before, however, Houston Stewart Chamberlain was one of the most revered thinkers in Germany, with disciples as famous as our exiled Emperor – who wrote long credulous letters in response to Chamberlain's idea that Jesus was not a Jew – or Albert Schweitzer who believed that 'what he had done for the advancement of knowledge will exist as a noble contribution for the good of the *Volk*'.

After his English boyhood (he was an admiral's son) Chamberlain had spent his life as a man of letters on the Continent, only interrupting his gentle existence (writing books and articles on poetry and philosophy) for a misguided spell of financial speculation on the Paris Stock Exchange during which he managed to lose his substantial personal fortune and become someone for whom money was always a worry. It was pure greed that made him a speculator but inevitably, perhaps, he blamed his folly on the evils of capitalism and on the Jews who supposedly control the mysterious movements of financial markets. Thereafter he saw the Jews as the enemies of culture, spirituality and all that is good. By one of those perverse contradictions which committed anti-Semites are often obliged to overlook, it was actually owing to two Jews that he was introduced to the music of Richard Wagner. The first was a Sephardic Jew whom he met at Interlaken, a music teacher named Löwenthal who played to him the Prelude to *Lohengrin* on the piano, following it up with some Klindworth arrangements of *Tannhäuser*. Once the sublime chords had seeped into Chamberlain's soul he was a converted Wagnerite, though it was not until he had met a second Jew, a Herr Blumenfeld from Vienna, that he heard about Bayreuth and the Wagner Circle. (Blumenfeld was a member of the Vienna Academic Wagner Society, which helped to finance the Bayreuth Festivals.)

The fact that Chamberlain owed his conversion to these two gentlemen in no way softened his hatred of Jews, and might even have increased it. (People have sometimes expressed surprise at H's ingratitude: they ask if he did not remember the Jewish owners in Vienna of small galleries who were the only ones prepared to buy his unremarkable architectural drawings, when he was an indigent doss-house dweller with holes in his boots. But would it not take prodigious levels of humility and gentleness, neither qualities obvious in H's character, to love those who had been such close witnesses of his life of abject humiliation?)

Chamberlain's *magnum opus* and the work which in his lifetime in Germany made him a household name was *The Foundations of the Nineteenth Century*, published in Munich in 1899. Here in these pages may be found all the racialist doctrines that underpinned the government's policies from 1933 to 1945. I can't claim to have read all this book. It is very long and it is written in a high hortatory style, which I find rebarbative. What struck me, when I attempted to finish it long ago, was that this foreigner's vision of my country in the last decade or so of the Emperor was not my vision. When I think of that Germany, the decade before I was born and when my parents were in love in Berlin, I think of travelling salesmen in curly bowler hats with curly waxed moustaches going from town to town on marvellous steam trains. I think of Adolf Harnack teaching my father and many students like him that Jesus was a gentle, ethically minded Hegelian. I think of stern schoolmasters teaching grammar and mathematics in every Gymnasium in the Reich. I think of neat small people in neat small towns having neat small thoughts. I think of clockmakers in low-eaved half-timbered buildings, of dreamers, philanthropists, scientists. I think of brilliant engineers and pioneer physicists. I think of superb bakers and proud glistening brewers. I think of miners and smelters and factory owners in the Ruhr. I think of families hiking on the banks of the Rhine or trying out new and superbly designed bicycles. I think perhaps above all of music, of little girls with blonde plaits thumping the heart out of Mozart sonatas as they sat at the piano, of choral societies roaring forth the sublime chorales of Bach, of families in chamber groups, of every small town with its symphony orchestra, and of course I think of the opera houses and the sea of sound that poured from them.

And yes, surely, when I think of Germany I think with pride of our united country ... There's nothing belligerent or sinister in that. I so vividly remember my brothers in their uniforms on the day that war broke out. I was twelve years old, Ernst was eighteen, Heinrich twenty. My parents and I joined the crowds to cheer on the departing troops. There was such ecstatic hope in those cheers of 1914. My mother's eyes were moist. My father, as always, looked steely and gave nothing away, but even he admitted later that evening that it had been 'very moving', a remark which in his scale of emotionalism was positively Dionysian. My brothers were risking their lives for good things. That was what they, and I, and my parents believed. They were fighting for the preservation of the Austrian Empire against terrorism and Slavs, for the preservation of the Ottoman Empire against the chaos that ensued once the war was over; and in our own Germany they were fighting for our Bavarian King, for our royal family. Heinrich, who has already appeared in this narrative as the shy schoolmaster playing music with our parents, survived the war, in spite of being gassed at Mons. Ernst died at the Battle of the Somme. As in most families to whom that has happened, my mother was never happy again. Germany itself when the First World War broke out was forty-four years old; exactly my father's age.

My dear old father never really wanted to live in the kingdom of Bavaria, still less in Franconia. He was through and through a Prussian, on his mother's side from a respectable family of yeoman farmers in East Prussia – all part of the Soviet Union now – and on his father's side, two or three generations of Berlin scholars. He had fallen in love with my mother when she was in Berlin, visiting relations. When his studies were complete, he had hoped to pursue his academic career in Berlin, but the illness of mother – I never really understood the details – led them south. My mother came from a small town in Franconia. After my father had been ordained in the Lutheran Church, he took the pastorate of the Peterkirche in Bayreuth as a stopgap. He was thirty, my mother had two small children and another on the way, they were both kindly to my impoverished and sick grandmother. Somehow or other they got stuck in the city adopted by and for ever associated with Richard Wagner. Still, decades after his 'mistake' (coming to live here in the first place) my father loved the Peterkirche. And that too was an embodiment of a Germany you would not find in the pages of Chamberlain – its high baroque ceiling dotted with heraldic devices of the local nobility who had endowed the church; its superb eighteenth-century organ case; and its choir, who in the course of every couple of years sang through the body of work which, to my father's way of looking at things, constituted the most sublime productions of the human brain or heart: the cantatas and chorales of J. S. Bach. But Chamberlain, who had lived in Switzerland and France and England for most of his life, saw a quite different Germany – a racialist empire of conquest whose most typical representative was not the clockmaker or the theologian but the soldier.

One of the few books I have in this little flat where I now live is *The Idiot* by Dostoevsky. Do you remember the passage where the Idiot says, 'He who has no roots beneath him has no god! That's not my saying. It was said by a merchant and Old Believer, whom I met when I was travelling. It's true he did not use those words. He said: "The man who has renounced his fatherland has renounced his god."' All the terrible qualities Chamberlain praised as quintessentially German were aspects, the worst aspects, of Britain. True, Germany had a few African colonies but its empire was absolutely tiny beside the vast tracts of Africa and Asia, not to mention Australia, New Zealand and Canada, which constituted the British Empire. We Germans never had an Indian empire and we never put down uprisings with the brutal severity used by the British in their Indian Mutiny in which they fired human beings out of cannons and even slow-roasted them over fires. It was the British who invented racism and, in South Africa, concentration camps.

Twisting all this round, Chamberlain invented or discovered a link between all the Aryan peoples, that is those who spoke the Indo-European languages from Sanskrit to Icelandic. These Aryans were the pure-bloods but they had weakened themselves by mingling with other races. The Jews had allowed themselves to maintain race identity while surreptitiously undermining the racial purity of the Aryans. This they had done by allowing their daughters to 'marry out' with influential Gentiles. Chamberlain saw the land of his birth, England, as having sold out to commerce. The aristocracy had married money to preserve its old privileges rather as the old gods in Wagner's *Ring* had stooped to alliances with dwarfs to get their hands on Nibelung gold. Disraeli the Jew had bamboozled England. The pure English aristocracy was corrupted by Jewish gold. America was likewise a mere 'dollar dynasty'. One nation, and one nation alone, that of the pure Teutons, could redeem mankind. 'The future progress of mankind depends upon a powerful Germany extending far across the earth.'

War would purify the Teutonic spirit. But it would also be necessary to purge the German Reich of its most pernicious enemy within: the Jews.

This was the strange set of doctrines propounded by the English admiral's son educated at Cheltenham College. (I have never managed to find out what Cheltenham is like but since it is, according to *The Gazetteer*, a Spa town, I imagine an English Baden-Baden.) Although his ideas were hugely popular in Germany, I honestly believe they would never have been propounded in the first instance by anyone other than an Englishman. The English sense of racial purity at that time in history, their obsessive desire to exclude Indians from clubs, tennis courts, European hotels, transport and so on, was of comparatively recent vintage, differing markedly from the eighteenth-century nabobs who took Indian brides and often adopted Indian religions.

Anti-Semitism, too, never rife in Germany where only a tiny proportion of the population were Jews, was an English obsession, especially when Disraeli's premiership was followed by a large influx of poor Russian Jews into London.

My father used to joke that it was because he was half English that our Emperor was so militaristic and there is more than an element of truth in this. Of course there was militarism on both sides and it destroyed both our countries. Anti-Semitism after the war seemed to explain a lot: the Russian revolution, the collapse of money markets, which made most of us poor and a few internationalist capitalists rich, and so forth.

Chamberlain's attitude, however, went beyond run-of-the-mill half-baked dislike of Jews. It was a mania. My father once told me that when his old professor, Harnack, met Chamberlain in Berlin, he praised parts of *The Foundations of the Nineteenth Century*. Indeed, like most educated Germans of those pre-war years, he kept returning to it, rather as we all read and discussed Spengler after the war. 'But', said Harnack, 'you really are possessed by an anti-Jewish demon, which dulls your vision and disfigures your excellent book with a stain.' What troubled Harnack's civilized liberal Protestant mind was that hatred, not merely of the Jew, but hatred generally, was deemed by Chamberlain to be necessary for personal and national regeneration.

Well – I've said enough about him to show why Chamberlain was a hero to Wolf and friends. Although Winnie, when she married Fidi, adopted his hatred of Eva, she always got along well with 'the old gentleman' as she called him – a rare instance of her using an English phrase. (As a mark of their German patriotism these two English persons living under the same roof spoke German to one another always. Chamberlain did not even get German – Bavarian – citizenship until halfway through the First World War. I heard, incidentally, that after the Second War Winnie reverted to British citizenship. I don't know if it is true.)[*]

[*] It is true. H.M.

Chamberlain, quite as much as Richard Wagner, was a 'draw' for National Socialists. And so it was, on that day in 1923, when I was still a student working on my philosophical doctorate and doing part-time work, when they were short-staffed, as a waiter at the dear old Golden Anchor Hotel. (In later days it was considered quite normal for students of our social class to make a little extra holiday money by working as waiters, porters and so forth. We had no money – quite literally *no* money – after the war, but it was certainly a torment to my parents to see me 'lowering' myself doing such work.)

If you had told me in 1923 during the 'German Day' in Bayreuth that the National Socialists would achieve absolute power within a decade or that H would become the Chancellor of Germany I should have dismissed you as a crank. The more *völkisch* among us enjoyed these 'German Days', which were occasions for demonstrations of national unity. Girls and boys in Bavarian national costume paraded: there was some folk dancing, in some towns there was a church service. In Bayreuth I remember the bells of the Spitalskirche at the far end of the market tolled out in memory of our war dead. For conservative-minded people such as my parents there must have been a great tug of loyalty there. The anniversary of the Armistice was as solemn a day for my father as was Reformation Day in our church calendar. My eldest brother, several cousins, and my mother's younger brother had all been killed in the war.

'Don't you *see*,' my father said, when I made some remark at the time, tolerant of the *völkisch* viewpoint, 'those people are hijacking the decent patriotic feelings and fears which we all feel.'

'If we all feel them, what's wrong with wanting to *do* something?'

My father shrugged. 'It was very wrong of P——' – he named the Pastor of the Spitalskirche – 'to let his church be used in that way.'

'They do say', said my mother, 'that if only Ludendorff became Chancellor we'd get the Rhinelands back.'

'Yes, yes, and solve unemployment at a stroke and reduce inflation and defeat Communism overnight. It's all so easy if you view the world in their baby terms,' said my father.

'They say this young H is quite a firebrand,' my mother had observed, 'just an ordinary common soldier, but with quite a gift of the gab.' She gave a nervous little laugh, adding that she wouldn't mind going along to the Riding Hall tonight to hear him.

The handsome old indoor riding school, built in the eighteenth century by the Margrave who also built our old opera house and the Eremitage and who laid out the Hofgarten, had been hired for the evening. My mother's sprightly claim that she'd've liked to hear the speaker was met by a glare from *Vati*. The idea had not been seriously entertained. She never went anywhere without him and little, apart from very occasional dinner invitations from friends or concerts of the classical repertoire, drew them away of an evening from their own hearth, their own music stands, their own books and comforting pots of ingeniously concocted beverages.

'He'll turn out to be a fly-by-night,' was my father's verdict on the speaker.

I did not go to the Riding Hall to hear H speak. To judge from the reports in the *Oberfränkische Zeitung* it was a piece of fairly standard patriotic stuff: the Reds who had dragged our country down for the last four years should go and live in Moscow with their comrades; France should be made to give back the land it stole from us after the iniquitous peace treaty. What Germany needs is not ten million academics or ten million diplomats but ten million soldiers.

It was after this speech that H walked the few hundred yards to the Anchor and a small reception was held. I handed round trays of refreshments and so it was that I witnessed the first meeting between Winnie and Wolf. The reception was hosted by the Bechsteins and I suppose there were forty or fifty people in the Anchor's small panelled dining room.

H – remember, I had not heard his speech – made very little impression upon me at all. He had on a navy-blue serge coat whose lapels were shiny with wear, and a plain dark-blue tie. It would not have been surprising to be told that rather than being the guest of honour he was Frau Bechstein's chauffeur. There is a little alcove in the dining room and he stood there nervously twiddling a glass of very good Moselle, the best in the hotel's cellar. I hovered nearby with a bottle and although he had barely consumed anything I asked him if he would like me to fill up his glass.

'No, no.' He was perspiring heavily.

I was reasonably handsome. Even if you would not agree with this verdict, I was still of an age when the bloom of youth was upon me and felt the eyes of others upon me, especially in crowded rooms such as this. I had already received the distinct impression that Frau Bechstein, with her swept-back blonde hair, her very moist skin, her expensive scent and her fur wrap, was a femme fatale who wanted to seduce a waiter. Now I felt those night-sky eyes of H's upon me. He was staring as if he wished to bend me to his will: at the same time there was something doglike, beseeching, about his expression. 'Could you ... I do not know if there is the possibility ...'

'What can I get you, sir?' I tried to keep any suggestion of flirtation from my voice by now taking in the body odour and, what I have always found a particular turn-off, the moist sweat on his upper lip, so that the small moustache and the skin on either side of it shone wetly. What was he going to ask me?

'Could you bring me, please –'

'Anything for sir.'

He whispered – spoke so quietly that he in effect mouthed the words 'sugar lump' and pointed a plump index finger towards his hock glass. It was the awkwardness of a child unable to digest any of the food or drink on offer at a party for grown-ups.

When I returned with the sugar bowl and the silver tongs, he did not use the instruments provided but plunged his hand into the bowl. By that time Frau Bechstein was approaching. Her expression of disapproval, the raising of her painted pinkish-orange eyebrows, first at the sugar tongs, then at myself, seemed to imply that he had only performed his act of clumsiness at my suggestion. 'May I introduce Frau Wagner?'

Winnie was twenty-seven and she bounded up with tremendous heartiness, a schoolgirl being presented with a trophy for basket-ball. Her clear complexion, as natural as Frau Bechstein's was oiled and creamed and pampered, flushed an excited scarlet as her hero clicked his heels together and bowed to touch the back of her hand with his moustache.

As if in slow motion, I saw it all happening: it was indeed as if I saw it slightly before it happened, the glass flying, the Moselle splashing, the bowl, the tongs. The sugar lumps raining like hail.

'Oh my goodness!' This from Frau Bechstein.

'I will fetch a cloth.' This from me.

By the time I had returned, very quickly since the glazed door into the kitchen was only a few feet away behind a screen, the three of them were in what I came to see as highly characteristic poses. Frau Bechstein was furious and had made matters worse by calling out to another of the waiters and trying to dab herself with a napkin, every step she took crunching sugar into the carpet.

Winnie was roaring with laughter, laughter which put the guest of honour at his ease.

First meetings are definitive. In the unimportant encounters of life this might not be so, since to mere acquaintances we give nothing away. The first few moments of an encounter with a person who will make a difference in our life is quite otherwise. A part of ourselves knows, not merely that we stand on the threshold of a love affair, an important friendship, a life-changing meeting of minds, but also the very terms on which all future encounters are to be conducted.

Wolf's abject awkwardness when I had first set eyes upon him in the panelled alcove no doubt owed something to that chemical depletion which overpowers great performers when they come off stage. I have seen Friedrich Schorr, Lauritz Melchior, Lotte Lehmann or Heinrich Tessmer similarly wilt when, having thrown their all into the previous two or three hours of music, they had, for a while, nothing inside them. They become like empty bags from which all content has been removed. By all accounts, H's speech that night in the Riding Hall was not one of his truly legendary displays of emotive oratory. Nevertheless, I do not believe that he ever spoke in public without some deep expenditure of emotional and psychological energy. Afterwards, though centre of attention and hero of the hour, and clucked over by the overbearing Frau Bechstein as her pet, her creation almost, he must have felt emptiness, even desolation. Also (the sugar lump) perhaps the body craved the lost energy which only a boost of sugar can provide. Having seen the gloomy, shy figure in the panelled alcove, and not witnessed the public spectacle of an hour previous, I had not taken in, as I would do in retrospect, the significance of these things.

Much as Winnie admired her Wolf from a public and political viewpoint and proud as she is to this day (as far as I know) to be the 'only Nazi in Germany', the nature of their strange relationship was not to be seen in terms of H's public life. During the sugar drama there was a look in his upturned sweaty face which was not that of one grown-up being introduced for the first time to another. He was in his early thirties, but what I saw, in the combination of expectancy and relief in his smile, was a child who had been anxiously waiting at the school gate for its mother to arrive. Finally, after a few minutes of agonizing delay in which the worst of fears had been making their nightmare march through his brain, he sees her – Mummy! That was what I saw. As well as seeing a boy of about eleven in the soldier's face, I also saw a countryman. I very seldom saw this in H when he became the best-known face in the world; in the domestic setting, however, one was conscious of it all the time. He was the young subaltern returning to his village on leave; even, a Brueghelesque figure who had come back to the house for an hour before resuming mowing or cutting in the fields. His complexion, no longer crimson with embarrassment, had resumed its bucolic appley pink.

'And, please,' said Winnie, who had 'taken charge' of the conversation as she often did, 'you [thou] must call me Winnie – please, please. And don't stand on ceremony.'

'Thou art too kind.'[*]

'And shall I call thee –?'

'Wolf!'

'I shall – Wolf it is. Wolf, thou must come back to Wahnfried' – this was said after the final brushings-down, the expressions of horror by Frau Bechstein when I was foolish enough to attempt to wipe away the sugar with a wet cloth.

'You fool! Do you want to cover us all in treacle . . .'

'Come back now for a late supper.'

'That is not possible,' said Frau Bechstein. 'We have important business here – and the crowds outside are not going to allow our most honoured speaker to retire without an encore.'

'Then breakfast tomorrow,' Winnie insisted.

Once again, what one saw in his delighted face was a child who suddenly discovered that he was wanted.

Shortly after this hastily concluded agreement, H was swept up by Frau Bechstein. The atmosphere of the dining room, which I dutifully circulated in my capacity as a waiter, was less that of a fanatical political rally than of a church social. One overheard phrases such as 'It all went really well . . .'

'Weren't the costumes wonderful? I thought the young girls dressed as . . .'

'I met young Thomas Koseleger on the corner of Ludwigstrasse and said that's a fine warrior you are, and he replied . . .'

'I thought the flowers in the Spitalskirche were . . .'

'I'm not just *any* warrior, Frau ——, I'm Wallenstein!'

'I see Frau Wagner put in an appearance . . .'

'The young Frau Wagner . . . She managed to speak to . . .'

'Did you see the way she simply rushed up to him?'

---

[*] I have here translated the words literally as they appear on N——'s page. What H is saying is that he wishes, from the first, to address her as an intimate and an equal. In all formal relationships between grown-ups it would be more usual, even today (how much more so in 1923) to use the third person (*Sie*). Such gradations of politeness do not exist in our language as they do in French or German. H.M.

'He's going out on to the front steps now to address the crowds . . .'

I have emphasized more than once that the Wolf we all came to know at Wahnfried was a private family person. Indeed, when I have meditated upon it I have sometimes wondered whether Winnie offered Wolf something he never had anywhere else: a family life where his sad past, his struggles, and his political world did not intrude. Complicated as Winnie's relationship with Fidi may have been, it was always able to be maintained with a level of normal good humour or normal bad temper as normal family life might be. Strange as it must have seemed to many and distressing as she found his forays in the direction of boys, the central fact of their lives together was that they were parents; in their fashion they were both extremely good and affectionate parents, and it was into this well of parental love that Uncle Wolf could dip his needy bucket.

But now we were all edging forward in a crowd into the hall of the hotel, past the reception desk and towards the glass front door. H was presumably ahead of us, since at a certain point we could hear a roar from the crowd.

It was then that one of Frau Bechstein's entourage, a cadaverous and instantly dislikeable young man with a heavy club-foot, approached me, with dear old Herr Graf, the proprietor of the Anchor. 'N——,' said my boss, 'this is Herr Gobelin from Berlin. He thinks that our speaker will not be audible from the front steps.'

'There is a big crowd out there,' said the thin man. 'Only the first few dozen will be able to see. We shall not have any difficulty in making our speaker heard, I assure you, Herr Graf.'

It was contrived that H should address the crowd below from the central bedroom on the upstairs landing, which had a window opening directly on to the Market Square. Herr Graf was uneasy with the immediate entourage, especially with the thin gentleman from Berlin, who resembled Nosferatu. In spite of his limp, perhaps because of it, he gave off an air of physical as well as of psychological power. He limped with purpose, even aggression, and one felt that all his energies were devoted, like some arcane practitioner of the dark arts, towards the summoning up of power for its own sake.

A small group of us, when the arrangement had been made, conducted H, his friend from Berlin, Frau Bechstein and a number of strange, thuggish individuals who I did not believe came from our town.

'Quick, quick!' said the thin limping young gentleman from Berlin as I fumbled with keys.

'I am doing my best, Herr Gobelin.'

'It is Goebbels,' he said, in a harsh, precise voice. 'My name is Goebbels.' He had moved forward and seized H fiercely by the elbow.

I went to the window to open it wide and H was on the verge of rushing forward to satisfy his public.

'No, no,' said Goebbels. 'You must wait. Create a sense of expectancy.' It was as if, from the background of the large white bedroom, the little limping dwarf knew how to control the crowd below, rather as our choirmaster could, while sitting in the director's chairs in the body of the Festival Theatre, control the volume of the swelling choruses.

The waiting did indeed create an effect. The first few rows of people in the cold square below had seen their hero. Then he had been withdrawn from them. There were murmurings. Then they began to call out their hero's name. Inside the bedroom, like a greyhound anxious to leave its traps and begin to race, he was transformed from the person I had served with wine and sugar into something different, a performer who needed his audience.

Only when the crowds actually began to shout did the Nosferatu figure himself lean out of the window and call with a cold sneer, 'Who do you want to hear?'

They shouted back their hero's name.

'Who was that?'

Again and again they called.

'Now!' said Goebbels. 'We've got them eager. Now you can go to them.'

Standing behind H in the bedroom, we could only see his back, his bottom and the lower half of his blue-serge legs as he leaned right out of the window and addressed the townspeople. 'A triumphant day . . .' the harsh bass-baritone resonated. He was not making a speech, as such, merely acknowledging the emotion of the people before him.

'A German Day for the German people!' Roars from below. 'A proud people . . . A people who have had enough of being lied to . . .' Roar. 'Had enough of being deceived . . .' Roar. 'Had enough of being bled to death by international finance.'

With each phrase proceeding from the orator's mouth, a phrase which moved the crowd below to an ever-greater sense of patriotism, his body gave a jerk, and the buttocks let out the quickfire whumps and cracks that accompanied the volleys firing from the mouth, and the room gradually filled with a gaseous sulphur odour. The acoustics of the situation was such that one heard only one word in twenty, whereas each rectal contraction and thunderclap, from where we stood behind him in the room, was shamelessly audible. Thus came about the surreal impression given by the buttocks, and the invisible torso, over which white lace curtains were draped, that the crowd were expressing their congratulatory applause for the shot and shell erupting into the bedroom at a truly heroic level of volume and smell rather than for the uplift of his spoken words.

'November crimin – pfff –'

Cheers.

'Pff – pff – raspberry roar – pff –'

Yet greater cheers.

'And I say this with my – pfft – pff – *TRUMPET BLAST* . . .'

'Germany will – *pfff* – and we will – *PFFf* –'

At this last Vesuvius of an outburst the crowd had begun to sing 'Deutschland, Deutschland über Alles'.

The visit to Wahnfried next day has passed into legend, but since I was not present it does not seem right to comment on the plausibility or otherwise of the stories. Some say that, upon meeting the pasty old Englishman with his prison pallor, H fell to his knees.

Others deny this, while admitting that Chamberlain was chair- or bed-bound, and that some degree of stooping was unavoidable on the part of any visitor to the writer at this date.

What is on record is the letter Chamberlain wrote after the younger man's departure:

It has been occupying my thoughts why it should have been you in particular – you who have such an unusual capacity for awakening people from Sleep and from the mundane – should have given me a longer and more refreshing sleep than any I have experienced since that fateful day in August 1914 when I was struck down by this insidious illness. Now I believe I can understand that it is precisely this which characterizes you and defines your very being: the true Awakener is at the same time the bestower of Peace.

You had been described to me as a fanatic but you are not one at all, in fact, you are the complete opposite of a fanatic. Indeed, I would describe you as the polar opposite of a politician, for with you all parties disappear consumed in the heat of your love for the Fatherland.

It was, I think, bad luck that our great Bismarck became so involved in a political life – may you remain spared this fate.

You have immense achievements ahead of you, but for all your strength of will-power I do not regard you as a violent man. The fact that you brought me such peace is very largely owing to your eyes and your hand-gestures. Your eye actually works like a hand – it grips and holds a person. And you have the singular gift of being able to focus your words on one particular listener at any given moment. As for your hands, they are so expressive in their movements that they rival only your eyes. Such a man brings Peace to a poor tormented spirit.

My faith in Germanness has never wavered. But that Germany should, at the hour of its greatest need, have given birth to you is proof of its vitality. I was able to sleep without a cure. May God protect you!

That one of the most popular 'thinkers' of the day should have responded in such a manner was of immense importance to the campaign managers who saw H's oratorical skills as their greatest asset.

In the first years in which I came to work in the Wagner household, as I have indicated, the public aspects of Wolf's life were discussed in his absence, but he presented himself during his visits as a family friend, a music lover, a playful uncle. Thus, when I first went to work for Siegfried in 1924, 'Wolf', as they always referred to him, was in Landberg Prison for his pivotal role in the failed Munich putsch of the previous November. This was when General Ludendorff, Wolf and others had announced to a pre-warned crowd of supporters in the Hofbräuhaus in Munich that they had taken over the government and were to march on Berlin. Siegfried was in Munich, poised to conduct a celebratory concert when their friends seized power. Siegfried and Winnie had watched the counter-revolution from their window overlooking Maximilienstrasse in Munich – they had seen the swastika flags hung from windows, heard the outbreak of gunshot as the authorized government led by Gustav Ritter von Kahr defeated the putschists. When their friend was imprisoned in Landberg, Winnie had done her best to keep him supplied with nice food and had sent Hess, to whom H was dictating his memoirs, a ream of paper, or so she claimed.

I know how important all this was to Winnie because I first worked as her husband's assistant while they were away fund-raising in the United States. It was my task to prevent the unanswered correspondence becoming too mountainous either in his office at home or in the office at the Festival Theatre. But as well as receiving incoming letters it was also my task to send out boxes of chocolate (difficult enough to come by), sketch pads, pencils and paints to their friend in prison.

During this period, whenever the Wagners were present at their house in Bayreuth they would discuss the political situation in Germany at large. We all did, all the time, without being able to stop ourselves. It is one of the great differences between my life now and then. Today it is not worth discussing the situation in our country. Apart from the fact that it would be dangerous to do so, and that there is no one left in my life with whom I might have such a discussion, there is also the fact that for East Germans today there is nothing to discuss. I see no way out of our situation. We live in a Russian colony and will never get out. Communism will last for ever – what is there to destroy it?

In my early twenties every day was a state of flux – a new government, a new currency, a new anything was possible. It became impossible not to discuss every failure on behalf of our elected democratic representatives to form a lasting administration. Would the Communists take over and enslave us as the Russians had been enslaved? That was how we viewed things then. Or would we be saved by our Swan Knight from the Austro-Czech border, drive the French from the Rhineland and begin at last to be a proud, peaceful etc. etc. etc? You couldn't not speak about it. Obsessively. All the time.

But when Uncle Wolf was on a visit this was not the case. Then, the children were in a state of high excitement knowing that here was a grown-up who was prepared to focus upon them his undivided attention. Then, his concentration upon physical games, romps, Grimm's fairy tales, puppet shows, jokes and teases was absolute. I think I can say I never knew a man with a more natural empathy with children. When I think of my own childhood and that of my brothers, it was a very different story. How much at the time would we have valued an Uncle Wolf. My parents' idea of 'fun' was musical practice. I do not recollect either of them larking about. Anything such as the visit of other children or of relatives, who might display slightly more willingness than my parents to let their hair down would be deemed, especially by my mother, in danger of getting us, Ernst, Heinrich and me, 'overexcited'.

I am speaking of Wolf's visits alone to the Wagner household. There were several occasions, however, when he visited not the Villa Wahnfried but the Chamberlains' house – more or less next door in Franz Liszt Street. We did not always witness these visits, Eva by then getting on poorly with Fidi and Winnie, and Mr Chamberlain himself being immobile and all but incapable of speech. The strange old half-corpse was still capable of writing, and continued to pen essays and articles about the vultures of revolution, the Jews, inspiring the breakdown of government in Weimar.

'My dears, the creatures you see going in and out to visit Mister C,' Fidi would say, pursing his lips with malicious amusement. 'That horrid little Dinter person.'

The Wagners had one of Arthur Dinter's best-sellers lying around, and I had heard one or other of them praising it – *The Sin Against the Blood*, the story of a young scientist married first to the daughter of a Jewish financier and then, when he realizes his mistake, to a nice German girl. Then, horror of horrors, she gives birth to a baby with Jewish features. The explanation was not that she had double-crossed her German husband. Rather, in her youth she had been seduced by a Jewish army officer. This one case of 'crossing' the races had been enough to drive out the 'good' German blood. We had all been sophisticated enough to laugh at the sheer scientific nonsense of Dinter's novel but it *had* impressed Fidi. I once heard him speaking with admiration of Dinter – until, that is, this purveyor of nonsense began to call on the Chamberlains.

Sometimes a whole entourage would turn up to pay their respects and it was not long before the end that Julius Streicher, Josef Goebbels – and Wolf of course – came for one last visit. By then the mumbling, speechless philosopher could do no more than stretch forth mottled hands from the bed and clutch at Dr Nosferatu's hand. He had wept, he had dribbled.

'I suppose you could say it is *kind* of them to have come,' said Fidi when he heard about it. He was blind to the ingenuity with which these people could turn anything to their use.

After Chamberlain eventually died, in January 1927, it was natural that his mother-in-law should have been consulted about the funeral arrangements. 'It will be quiet,' she had murmured. He was to be buried in the frosty earth up in the largest town cemetery.

Eva was proud to receive notification that royalty, albeit exiled

Prussian royalty, would be attending – the exiled Emperor's son Prince August Wilhelm – and we all knew that local dignitaries would come. The coffin was laid in the hall of Wahnfried for a few days before the funeral. The undertakers arrived about an hour before the ceremony to load the casket on to the hearse, but they were interrupted in their work. Fidi was sitting with his sister Eva when the lugubrious Herr Fischer, the undertaker, tiptoed up, asking if they were ready. Eva, dabbing her eyes with a handkerchief, was too distraught to be wholly coherent but she appeared to be saying that the undertakers' men were unnecessary, and that . . . other arrangements had been put in hand.

'Other arrangements? But darling, I told you, Mr Fischer . . .'

'Yes, but . . . Dr Goebbels . . . so nice . . . so kind . . . so infinitely obliging.'

At this point the front doors of Wahnfried, which had been closed behind Mr Fischer to keep out the wintry cold, were roughly flung open and a group of men, perhaps a dozen, marched in. Four each linked up on either side of the coffin and two others stood guard by the door. They wore brown shirts and armbands of the familiar red, black and white with swastikas. They were young – in their teens – acned and at least a couple looked frightened of the coffin. Upon the barked orders of the man who had opened the door – who was perhaps in his mid twenties – they advanced upon the coffin.

'I say!' exclaimed Fidi. And he raised a black sleeve in a well-manicured protest. But the boys were carrying out the coffin and, short of creating a ridiculous scene, Fidi could do no more than pick up his tall silk hat, offer an arm to his heavily veiled widowed sister and troop after the cortège. The coffin was placed in a horse-drawn hearse and the Wagner family, accompanied by myself, followed in cars. There was a much bigger crowd than Cosima had expected. (She stayed at home. Public outings were now a thing of the past and in any event it would not have been deemed wise for her to venture out on so very cold a day.)

The pastor at the church managed to conduct the funeral as a purely religious ceremony, but as soon as the body was conveyed out of the church the Brownshirts, who had assembled in great number in the churchyard, burst into song – first 'Deutschland, Deutschland' and then various others of a military flavour quite unsuited to the burial of a bed-bound, pampered old man who had spent his life among books and women. At a certain point H raised his hand and the entire crowd became silent instantaneously as if they were voices on a wireless which he could turn on or off.

I cannot remember all the words. I remember the intense cold, the thick snow on the ground, the gaping brown earth of the grave almost a desecration of the snow. Into the clear winter air that rasping voice spoke of the sword of Siegfried which would one day smite the staff of Wotan. The great and honoured friend to whom we said farewell at this graveside was not privileged to live to see the day when that sword would one day be raised. But it was on his anvil that the sword had been forged – the flames of his words had heated the anvil. One steady hammer . . .

To tell the truth, the metaphors of the tribute were all somewhat muddled. Who was the Siegfried in this convoluted analogy? H himself presumably. But did this make Chamberlain into the despised dwarf Mime in whose hut the magic sword is forged? Most of the older mourners did not look too troubled by such niceties. The great question for them was how long the speech, or speeches, were going to be. And sure enough there was a speech from the mayor, and a speech by strangely eyebrowed Rudolf Hess. As the coffin was eventually allowed to be lowered into the frozen earth the uniformed attendants, heavily outnumbering the family and 'civilians', raised their right arms and called rhythmically, 'Hail! Victory hail! Victory hail!' I shivered, and not just with cold, when we returned to the cars.

Siegfried Wagner was born, interrupting the composition of the opera after which he was named, in Tribschen, Switzerland, on the shores of Lake Vierwaldstätt, near Lucerne. He was his mother's last child. Two – Daniela and Blandine – had been born to her husband, Hans von Bülow. One, as I have mentioned, Isolde, was of questionable parentage. Then Cosima had made open her relationship with Richard Wagner and they had run off together.

Cosima's *Diaries*, more dramatic than any novel, begin in 1869, when she has made the break with her husband and set up a new life with Wagner in Switzerland. She is by turns ecstatic with joy in her new love, melodramatically guilty about her husband and tormented by the necessary separations from her children when they remain with their father. It is a strange fact, but I was the first person, after Richard and Cosima Wagner, to read these diaries. Just as Richard Wagner had to wait for decades before anyone saw a performance of his *Ring* cycle, so no one has read Cosima's account of her marriage. I do not even know for certain what has happened to these magnificent diaries, but I feel sure, if they survive in Bayreuth, that one day they will be published and the world will see what an extraordinary bond between two kindred souls this marriage was. When I think of the grumpy silent evenings I have spent in this flat with my wife in the latter stages of our marriage, it is with envy that I recall those rapturous pages in which Cosima describes evening after evening, reading Shakespeare or Goethe or the Greek tragedians, and discussing philosophy, music, politics, religion and the characters of their friends.

No friend, perhaps, fascinated them more in those early days of their shared domestic life than a professor of philology from Basel named Friedrich Nietzsche. They first met in 1869, the year of Fidi's birth. It was because of my proposed thesis subject – Richard Wagner and nineteenth-century philosophy, with special reference to his reading of Schopenhauer's *Die Welt als Wille und Vorstellung* – that Fidi, with great boldness, simply went to his mother's quarters and removed the sacred volumes of the diaries for me to read, explaining, as he flicked ash over their pages, that there would be bound to be 'stuff in there to interest you, my dear'.

'Have you read them?'

'I couldn't possibly, couldn't possibly. Would *you* want to read your mother's diaries? All her sorrows about one's father's mistresses, all her sexual guilt, my dear, I couldn't bear it.' Oh, how different our mothers! The idea of my mother having any sexual feelings at all, or my father having mistresses, was so absolutely alien that I could not hear Fidi's words without a smile. Naturally, when Eva discovered that he had been showing the precious diaries to 'your young fancy man', as she flatteringly but wrongly described me to her brother, there was a tremendous hullabaloo.

My friendship at Freyburg with Martin H—— had actually persuaded me that Nietzsche was a much more interesting philosopher than his hero Schopenhauer; that he had (really from his first utterances in *The Birth of Tragedy* about the Dionysian impulse in humanity, from which the great dramas of Aeschylus and the great music dramas of Wagner came) anticipated, as no other writer had, our twentieth-century follies and horrors. By chance, Nietzsche was staying in the house at Tribschen on the very night that Fidi was born. One writes 'by chance', but since he made so many visits to the Wagners that year it was hardly very surprising that he should have been in the house that June when Cosima went into labour.

Cosima was thirty-two years old, her lover fifty-six, when their son Siegfried was born. Nietzsche was a mere twenty-four. Wagner felt too old to be the father of a baby boy and, in the letters that survived that stormy friendship, we read him exclaiming to Nietzsche that he felt more like a grandfather to the baby. 'We need someone to form a link between him and me, a link like that between son and grandson such as only you can provide.' A few years later, when trying to persuade Nietzsche to come and live with them and be Fidi's personal tutor, Wagner would exclaim, 'He needs you! The boy needs you!' By then the friendship was on the rocks. Nietzsche, who had written *The Birth of Tragedy* as an act of homage to the greatest genius of the age, had become completely disillusioned by Wagner and his cult, distrusting its bogus religiosity. Once the shrine at Bayreuth had been established, the scales began to fall from the young Nietzsche's eyes – '*Bayreuth – bereits bereut*' as he famously quipped.[*]

Adultery is a lonely business and however many of Wagner's musical admirers clustered around them in those early days in Switzerland, they somewhat lacked for intimates. Both of them formed that passion for a third party which is a periodic feature of married life, but which is especially a feature of the newly formed adulterous pair, who feel estranged from many of their former associates. Thus, while having many conversations with Nietzsche about Schopenhauer, Beethoven, Goethe and the Greeks, and while playing music with him to their mutual delight, both the Wagners delighted in adopting the young man as their own and setting him all manner of tasks, as if to bond with him the better.

They liked sending him on shopping errands, particularly for chocolates, sweetmeats and delicacies unobtainable in Lucerne. Sometimes the items on their shopping list were considerably more elaborate. Wagner had for long coveted a lamp designed by his old revolutionary comrade Gottfried Semper. It was still in Dresden, where Semper and Wagner had manned the barricades in 1848, and where some said that Wagner had set light to the opera house of which he was the young orchestral director. There was a difficulty about the lamp, apart from the obvious one that Wagner had no money to pay for it. It had been bought for the synagogue and consecrated for use. Since writing his controversial pamphlet 'Das Judentum in der Musik' – the most catastrophic mistake of his professional life – Wagner had made many enemies. Many Jews, in deference to his musical genius, were prepared to overlook the fact that, in common with so many figures of the nineteenth century, Wagner was infected with the poison of anti-Semitism.

Some of the greatest Wagnerian performers and conductors were Jews, but those of them who came close to him, most notably Hermann Levi, were compelled to tread the tightrope between the

[*] Reached Bayreuth and already regretting it.

moods in which the Master repented of his pamphlet and of his anti-Jewish views, and times, especially alcohol-induced, when he fell back into the vulgar clichés of Jew hatred. Nietzsche, too, was both people – someone who saw and deplored the essential vulgarity and folly of hating or blaming a whole category of people for the ills of this world, and the gut instincts of anti-Judaism. Indeed, the whole of his *Birth of Tragedy* was posited on the idea that truly creative art is Dionysian – Greek – and that its enemy is the Apollonian. Apollo he associates with Socrates, the cutter-down of romance to size, the logic chopper, the empirical materialist – the Jew. Socrates in Nietzsche is a code word for the Jew and *The Birth of Tragedy* is, while being an infinitely more interesting book than Wagner's earlier pamphlet, a sort of rerun of ideas that were to be found in *Das Judentum in der Musik*.

Worried by her husband's health, his breathlessness, his weak heart, his over-indulgence in alcohol and tobacco, she begged their young friend Nietzsche, 'a request as from a mother to a son. Do not stir up this hornet's nest. Do you understand what I mean? Do not refer to the Jews by name especially en passant.' As ragingly anti-Semitic as the rest of them, she nevertheless feared that once they got on to the subject Wagner might have a seizure.

Hence it was that Nietzsche was dispatched to Dresden to buy the lamp. Nietzsche made enquiries at the jewellers Meyer and Noske and with the 'Elders of Israel' at the synagogue and did, amazingly, return to Tribschen with a replica of the synagogue lamp. He told the jewellers that he was purchasing it on behalf of 'a lady of rank'. Had he told them he was buying it (with bouncing cheques) for one who considered them to be 'teeming maggots on the rotting corpse of German art', it is possible that they would have parted from it less willingly. Whether the 'lady of rank' was Cosima or Richard, Nietzsche did not vouchsafe. As is well known, after he grew disillusioned with Wagner, he posited the view that Wagner was in all essentials a woman. He hints naughtily at Wagner's taste not merely for silky soft furnishings, but also for cross-dressing in women's underwear. And he concluded that 'Wagner was unmistakably *femini generis* – the bisexual god in the labyrinth – the labyrinth of the modern soul'.

In the first year they knew him, however, Nietzsche loved both the Wagners unreservedly and happily did their errands. He went to Basel to have Wagner's books re-bound, the Roman authors in yellow ochre, the Greeks in sienna, with marbled paper and calf spines, the very same volumes that I myself handled daily in the library at Wahnfried. Closer to me still – for did I not begin this meditation with a puppet sitting forlornly with me in my foul little flat? – was Cosima's commission to get the young professor to buy the children wooden puppets and the whole paraphernalia of a puppet theatre. He purchased it in readiness for Fidi's first Christmas in the world, 1869, which they all spent together in the Villa Tribschen. Cosima's diary describes the idyllic Christmas scene, including the arrival of Knecht Ruprecht to the appropriate screams and shouts from the children. During my childhood we always had this cere-mony – with Saint Nicholas distributing presents to children who had been good and his villainous sidekick offering pieces of coal to children who had been bad, on the Feast of Saint Nicholas (6 December) but the Wagners, who followed their own star, used to do it, even in my days with them, on Christmas Eve.

It was strange to think of that puppet theatre, which I myself knew so well in the 1920s, and early 1930s, having been purchased half a century before by my favourite philosopher, and the same lady who had commissioned their purchase still being alive.

It must have been after the death of Mr Chamberlain – in fact, I am sure it was a good while after his death. (My chronology does get muddled. Though I would vouch for every fact in this narra-tive, I would not go to the firing squad to insist I have everything in the right order.) But I should say that the next incident I recol-lect was about two years after Chamberlain's death. I date these things from remembering the children, and Friedelind, when she accosted me that afternoon, had grown enormously in all directions from the plump girl who had told me about the performance of 'The Fisherman and His Wife'.

She must have been about eleven, but a substantial maiden, with none of her sister Verena's delicacy. She looked like a version of what Winnie might have been if her face had been fat. 'Don't eat so much, for heaven's sake, Winnie, stop stuffing yourself, my *God* you're greedy!' These were the constant mealtime expletives of Fidi in those latter days. Although my beloved Winnie grew to be a substantial goddess, it would have been wrong to describe her as fat. She burnt off her energy with hyperactivity and cigarette smoking. Friedelind was definitely obese. But she was also tall and, for her age, disturbingly womanly. There were the beginnings of breasts on her already wobbly chest. But more than that, her moist hands, her pouting lips, her particular and inviting way of standing with one foot in front of the other suggested even at this early age the keen sensual interests that would be so marked a feature of her adult life.

Strangely, when she told me about that particular day's puppet show, it was of her that I instinctively thought 'Aren't you a bit old for that sort of thing?' rather than applying the judgement to her two elder brothers, Wieland and Wolfgang, who were by then beginning to be teenagers. 'It's "The Jew in the Thornbush",' she said. 'Uncle Wolf is doing "The Jew in the Thornbush".'

'How exciting.'

'I thought perhaps "The Maiden Without Hands",' she said. 'We could have adapted one of the puppets for that.'

I laughed, because I was so evidently supposed to do so; also because Friedelind was always a sympathetic person and when she laughed the world laughed with her.

'"The Seven Ravens",' she said, 'but in the end, we've opted for "The Jew".'

'Great!'

'Wieland's got the old puppet – you know, the Punchinello from Grandmama's puppet theatre?'

'I think I remember it.'

'He's added a new nose – made it even bigger! It's a real honker now. Uncle Wolf says we're to give him a right beating.'

She announced the programme as if nothing could be greater fun and I cannot now, at a distance of over thirty-five years, recall what I felt. I mean, obviously I should like to record that I felt some revulsion; or that I had remonstrated with Friedelind as she took my hand and led me into the salon. Her hand, as always, was plump and moist. I felt the pressure of the fleshy fingers against my own and was disturbed by the powerful erotic effect this girl had upon me. You see, that is something I can remember. But I cannot remember how I reacted to her excitement about 'The Jew in the Thornbush'.

You remember the story, I am sure. A young apprentice works hard for his master for three years without being paid and at the end of that period all his master gives him is a measly three farthings. But he is a happy, easygoing German and he goes on his way cheerfully singing until he comes to the middle of a wood. There he meets a little man who persuades him that, since he is an able-bodied youth, he can easily earn another three farthings, whereas the manikin is weak: 'If you give me the three farthings I will grant you a wish for each of them.' So the youth hands over his money and he makes three wishes: the first is that he wants a fowling piece which will hit any target he aims for; the second is that if he plays his fiddle, anyone who hears it will dance to his tune; and the third is that if he makes any further requests, no one will be able to refuse them.

By and by he comes upon an old Jew. In the original medieval versions of the story the youth meets a swindling friar, but by the time the Brothers Grimm had heard oral versions of the tale, in Hesse and Paderborn, the villain of the story had been changed from a dishonest churchman into a Jew. Wilhelm Grimm, in his revisions of the story, makes the Jew into an even greater caricature than in the originals, adding his long goatee beard, and making him speak with the exaggerated lisps and distortions of the stereotypical Jew. What follows is sheer brutality. The Jew is standing, innocently enough, listening to a bird singing in the woods above a patch of thornbushes. He wants the bird alive, as a pet, because he likes its singing voice, but the youth shoots the bird down, then makes the Jew dance in the thorns until his clothes are ragged and he is covered in cuts. The youth steals the Jew's purse full of gold.

In an effort to establish his rights, the Jew takes the youth into the nearest town and drags him before the judge. 'Sir judge, this young man has waylaid me on the public highway and robbed me and ruined my clothes.' The judge condemns the youth to be hanged, but as he climbs the gallows he asks for one last request – to be allowed to play his fiddle. Because the youth is charmed and no one can refuse his requests, the judge lets him play the fiddle in the public square. Everyone dances to his tune: the judge, the towns-folk and the Jew. Fat, thin, old and young, they all dance madly at the young man's enchantment. At last the judge promises to grant him his life if he will only stop the dance.

Then the youth is led down from the gallows and he goes up to the Jew who is lying exhausted on the ground. 'You thief,' he says. 'That gold was not yours. You are the one who deserves to be hanged.' The Jew confesses that he was indeed a thief. The rope is put round his neck, rather than the youth's, and he is hanged.

By the time I entered the salon to watch the dress rehearsals, Uncle Wolf had the children all ready with their parts. Wolfgang, a finely chiselled ten-year-old, was speaking the part of the wicked employer at the beginning of the story. Wieland, two years older and with a far greater histrionic gift, was playing the Jew. Verena who was eight played the bird and the judge. Friedelind played the part of the charmed youth.

Uncle Wolf had on this occasion been staying in the house only a couple of days, but he had rehearsed them well, not only in the speaking of their lines, but also in their adaptation of the puppets. For example, they had used the policeman from the Punch and Judy puppet show, but placed an ingenious top hat on his head to cover his helmet so that he resembled a capitalist exploiter of the masses. The Jew, originally Mr Punch, had, as Friedelind had reported to me, been given an even bigger nose than the Punchinello puppet, and a long straggling grey beard made of wool. The youth, slightly smaller in proportion than the other puppets, had not come with the original set of Punch and Judy figures and looked, from his tunic, his green stockings and his hunting hat, as if he could have played Tannhäuser, or indeed any conventional rustic German hero out on the hunting field. The children played the dramatized version of the story with tremendous brio, and much spluttering mirth. When Friedelind/The Youth played the fiddle, Wolfgang, his part as the employer finished, took up his own violin and produced frenzied jigs for the puppets to dance to.

The rise and rise of H and his political friends had undergone a considerable check in the previous few years. There were certain signs that the ever-volatile economy was recovering. The disastrous levels of inflation were falling. Then, in 1929, the charmed Youth started to get his wishes coming true and everyone began to dance to his fiddle. The Nazis formed a bold alliance with the Conservatives in opposing the Young Plan – an American scheme to rationalize the repayment by Germany of reparations to the Allies. If it had succeeded, the liberal schemes of Chancellor Stresemann might have succeeded. On one level the plebiscite was a triumph for the liberals – Hugenberg and H combined needed twenty-one million votes to defeat the Young Plan, and they got a mere six million. 'What is Alfred Hugenberg *playing* at?' I remember my father asking despondently. It was as if he had heard a valued old colleague had been very mildly misbehaving – flirting with a secretary, for example.

The alliance with Hugenberg's bourgeois followers did H little good with the revolutionary rank and file of his own party, the storm-troopers and maniacs. But it brought him a lot of kudos with the sort of voters who had feared he was not respectable, was not on their side. The farmer, the miller, the small shopkeeper and the provincial pharmacist saw H lining up with solid Conservative politicians on a ticket of Stopping the Foreigners Interfering in Our Economy. As soon as the plebiscite was over, H disguised the humiliation of its failure by blaming everything on Hugenberg and breaking the alliance at once. But he had collected many potential supporters in the process, from the ranks of those who were no storm-troopers, but simply respectable people. He had also befriended big business, many of whose magnates were now prepared, if there was a downturn in the economy, to support the more radical proposals which the Nazis had to offer.

If Stresemann had lived . . . But he died before the plebiscite was counted. If the economy had somehow picked up . . . But the world-wide depression that year culminated in the Wall Street Crash and by the end of the year there were three million German men unemployed. The next year there was yet another general election. The Nazis had a mere handful of seats in the Reichstag. In the two years since the previous election they became the second largest party in the Reich. On 13 October 1930, 107 Nazi deputies took their seats in the Reichstag, each wearing a brown shirt and shouting out the surname of Uncle Wolf as they answered the roll-call.

My brother Heinrich, who in early middle age had gone back to university to prepare for life as a pastor after all, was in Berlin at the time and wrote to us,

At the very moment those uniformed criminals were taking their seats in the Reichstag, their comrades, disguised in civilian mufti, were rampaging in the streets of Berlin. I was having coffee in K'damm. They strode past the window laughing raucously. They peered at us through the window. One had the unpleasant sensation of being encaged in some surreal zoo, for the diversion of sadistic apes, as though the normal position of the zoo were reversed and it was humanity locked up for the amusement of lesser primates. Were they going to enter the premises? Everyone in the café visibly hoped not. But we were lucky. The oafs strode on. It was evident from what happened at the next street corner what they had been looking for. They had been checking the name over the door and making sure we were an 'Aryan' establishment. (My God, this lunacy!) The next café along was not so lucky. The tykes picked up one of the chairs arranged at a table on the pavement outside and casually used it to smash the large plate-glass window. No one stopped them. They laughed and moved on to a large tailoring store – Schneider's – a few doors down. That too had its windows smashed.'

Tannhäuser

'*Caro mio*, of course we want you to do fucking *Tannhäuser*! . . . Of course . . . of course.' Siegfried was chirruping abruptly into the telephone, an angry blackbird who had just watched a starling swoop upon a worm. He held the speaking tube to his mouth with one hand and in the other, which held the instrument itself, there also smouldered a cigarette. Histrionically, he raised his eyes to the ceiling and moved the listening device away from his ear, so that the anxious voice of Toscanini, crackling down the wire from Berlin, could be distinctly heard agonizing about the suggestion that he should conduct Wagner's early erotic psychodrama.

'Darling,' shouted Fidi back, '*le tout* Berlin, *everyone*, my dear, said your *Tannhäuser* was a sensation . . . Why else should we be begging on our knees before you.'

The very mention of being on his knees before a man made Siegfried smirk at me, as though I could not even hear the phrase without mentally chewing off flybuttons.

'Dear heart – between you and me – *fuck Muck*! I know . . . I know . . . *Caro*, he is doing *Götterdämmerung*, he does it brilliantly – well, up to a point!' More conspiratorial grins at me. 'But . . . no, honey, that would be tiresome of you. Truly. Not at this stage . . .'

More crackling down the line.

'If I wanted to get heavy, *caro*, I should say it was because you were already under contract to conduct *Tannhäuser*.'

There was a weighty pause. Then he said, 'No, dear. You signed. Your agent signed, you signed, what the fuck difference does that make? But it isn't just that, you know it isn't . . . It's because we love you . . . You can have any views you like about his *Götterdämmerung* and he can . . . Exactly, my dear. So the rehearsals start in June . . . wait a moment . . .' With sharp, imperious gestures he pointed at me, then at the surface of his desk. I knew him to mean that he wanted his large 1930 desk diary.

He flicked the pages towards the summer. His fingers turned rapidly, reaching September, October. He was turning into dates, little did he know, when he would no longer be alive, virgin soil, Fidi-dead days; post-Siegfried Bayreuth.

'We said 26 June? Still *perfetto*! *Caro mio, sono in cielo! Sì, sì, e siamo tutti cosi felice, sì, sì, caro. Mia madre anche, sì. Naturalmente . . . E Winnie anche, sì, sì* . . . At a what? A rally, my dear . . .' He shrieked with laugther. 'She does love them, bless her. A Parteitag sets her up a treat . . . *Sì, nostrano Duce, fatto in casa, sì, sì! . . . Non te la prendere, tutto è sistimarà. Ciao!*'

'So, Toscanini . . .' I asked.

'Yes, he'll do the *Tannhäuser*. He knew he would. I knew he would, but he has to go through this stupid bloody charade of thinking bloody Muck wants to conduct it. Well, bloody Muck can want.' He threw his cigarette stub on the floor, whence I retrieved it, and stared into the middle distance.

Karl Muck, rumoured by some to be Richard Wagner's natural son, had a deep antipathy towards Siegfried, which was heartily reciprocated. He was a good conductor, but 'more trouble than he was worth', making endless mischief behind Fidi's back. Bayreuth was a hive of gossip, as you will already have gathered, and there were those who believed that Siegfried could not possibly have sired any of the four, increasingly disorderly, children. Some believed that Muck was the father of at least some of them.

As a would-be philosopher, endlessly trying to debunk my brother's would-be gruel-and-water Protestant theology, I would ask myself how he could say he believed things which serious reflection must tell him were untrue. He would sometimes come up with some spurious stuff about behaving as if you believed (say, in the Risen Lord, and this 'making' it true). This covered the mysterious area of behaving as if you believed, and making it true, while not with your mind believing. In matters of the heart, it is also possible for the corollary or opposite to take place. That is to say there are things you believe while not believing. In the former case the brain is trying to force the gut and in the latter it is the other way round. If asked to vote on the matter of was Winnie promiscuously unfaithful to Fidi, I'd have voted no, but with my gut I believed that she was wild and, even if she did not actually break her marriage vows, she wanted to.

This made loving her all the more complicated and painful. I was naive, unimaginably so, it now seems to me. My very inexperience and the romantic haze in which I had chosen to paint my crush on Winnie – a haze which conveniently disguised from myself my own shyness and awkwardness about sex – made it impossible to make a pass at her. Retrospect tells me that she would have been up for it.

Sometimes when these thoughts occur to me I say to myself, 'Everything would have been different if I'd been to bed with her.' But what does 'everything' mean in this context? That she would have married me? Scarcely. That I would have been different and absorbed in its totality her fatal political blindness? Or that she would have come to know my parents and my brother, and to have her doubts about Wolf? Doubts were not in her nature.

As with all other aspects of their matrimonial arrangements, it was impossible to reach a certainty of view about Siegfried's attitude to the passionate friendship between his wife and the rising political star. I never felt it was pure canniness which, in the last five years or so of his life, caused Siegfried to give H a wide berth. Winnie would always say, 'Fidi can't be seen to admire Wolf too much – it would upset our sponsors.' Or, 'For Fidi the Festival must come first. You know how stuffy people are – he can't espouse the Cause as openly as I do, but of course, he loves Wolf as much as I do.'

This was manifestly not the case. And with the hindsight of a grown-up perspective I do not see how Winnie's obsession with Wolf could have failed to be annoying, quite apart from any political or public embarrassment it would cause him. I remember an occasion, not so long before Fidi died, of her driving them both down to Munich. She arranged to meet Wolf in a restaurant for luncheon, and Fidi – 'Wasn't it sweet of him? He said, "I know you two want to be together – I'll have lunch on my own".' H had apparently expressed admiration for Fidi's extreme unselfishness about this, but the husband must have felt a bit snubbed?

Certainly, Fidi's way of discussing the Leader was less reverential than his wife's: 'Poor Win thinks he'll be our Mussolini. She forgets what a tremendously respectable country we are. As I know to my cost. Il Duce can take his trousers down on a daily basis and screw every secretary, film star and tarty little chorus girl in Rome, my dear. Insofar as the rumours of it all seep out, it just increases his popularity with the Eyeties. But here! You only have to see them sitting in their rows in church, the men in their stiff collars, the sole stiff thing about them, if you ask me; their plain, warty, well-scrubbed wives – I'm not talking about your father's church, my dear.'

'Of course not.'

'But you know what I mean – too respectable to have sexual feelings. God, what must they feel when they come to *Tannhäuser*?'

'They don't.'

'Don't say that. I've just spent a bloody fortune getting Toscanini to come and conduct it. Some Germans love *Tannhäuser* – presumably they heave a sigh of relief when he escapes Venusberg and then . . .'

'The strange thing about the opera is that you could read it as a story precisely as simply as that. He escapes the goddess and he goes in pursuit of the pure Elisabeth . . .'

'Nothing is simple about my father's work, dear, surely you have realized that by now. You know he wanted to call the opera "Venusberg" – the Mons Veneris! He might as well have just called it "Cunt" and had done with it. That's what it's about. Men's obsession with cunt, their inability to get away from it, the fact that they will do anything for it, even if it risks damnation – especially if it does. Makes it more exciting for them. Anyway, that's not a part of the body that Miss Wolfie interests herself in very much.' He allowed this morsel to drop into the air and watched it swirl like the smoke of his cigarette into silence.

Like many men who prefer their own sex, Fidi spoke habitually as if any male named in the conversation must, upon further thought or investigation into his character, turn out to be 'in the regiment', as he sometimes put it. At this date my own agonies about whether I qualified for a commission, or whether I could find happiness with a woman, my general muddle about sex and my feeling, on occasion, overwhelmed by directionless desire, were all so great that I had very confused ideas about grown-ups. Uncle Wolf was surely not in the regiment? I think I believed in the Proustian idea that regimental status could only be achieved by the effeminate, and that Wolf's soldierly bearing, robust language and rasping baritone surely suggested another area of preference altogether.

But this was not, evidently, Fidi's line of suggestion, since he airily continued, 'Of course, half the people in his movement are fucking pansies, my dear, that's as clear as daylight. They love marching around in their uniforms, with the prospect of a good bit of sadomasochism thrown in. Did you ever meet that Captain Röhm creature? My darling! Half its nose shot off, and about four feet tall and positively oozing queer love, oozing it, for the Leader. Winnie introduced us at Munich once. She said he was a "fine fellow". Bless Winnie. Do you think she notices *anything*, anything at all? Is that what she has in common with Wolf, not noticing? I'm sure Wolf hasn't spotted that the little Captain has the hots for him. Probably just thinks of him as a trusty little patriot who can be relied upon to stir up street fights, beat up a few yids . . . you know, my dear . . . But no! That isn't where Wolf's area of interest lies. *If*, my dear, the rumours . . . Of course, I know how terribly cruel rumours are, because they nearly always turn out to be true.'

He paused. He wanted, perhaps needed, the satisfaction of my actually asking, rather than simply allowing him to recite all the goodies uninvited. 'What are the rumours . . . the rumours about . . . Wolf?'

'Well, my dear' — in the tone of 'I thought you would never ask' — 'you know that they are in the money now — the Party? Rolling. Wish some of it would come our fucking way. Helene [Bechstein] has put them in the way of meeting some real money. You know, until very lately, he [Wolf, that is] was living in a little bedsit — no more than he was used to when he dossed down with the tramps in Vienna after the war. But it's all very different now. Not only has he bought the Barlow Palace for his Party headquarters, but he has also set himself up *very nicely* in a flat in Prinzregentenplatz. Huge place, nine vast rooms. Servants. Everything. Meanwhile his sister Angela — did you ever meet her? My dear, the complete peasant, you never met anything like it in your life — is down in the Berghof, his little mountain retreat at Berchtesgaden keeping house there. So who do you think is living with him in the flat? Angela's daughter, Geli. A medical student. The doctor can see you now.'

'Isn't it perfectly normal for a niece to live with her uncle?'

'I don't think normal is quite the word we'd use . . . I don't think the Faithful at all those rallies Winnie loves to attend would quite think it was normal, what young Geli gives Uncle for breakfast — to drink and to eat, my dear.'

I had never in my life heard of the practice to which Fidi referred, and it was necessary for him to spell out in more graphic detail than I need do on the page what was rumoured to go on between uncle and niece. 'You've surely heard of Golden Showers?' he asked me sharply. I suddenly felt that, as well as an encyclopaedic knowledge of Wagner's operas, part of my job requirement should have been a knowledge of the perversions of the human heart. 'Greek, isn't it? Philia, something you love, kopros, poo-poo. You know how fussy he is about what he eats and drinks. Yes, before she goes off to the hospital in the morning to cut up cadavers, young Geli has to give Uncle his little yellow face bath and feed him up with Number Twos. Or . . . *so they say.*'

I reeled. I literally felt the room swaying. Never in my life had I heard anything so disgusting. In fact, it was impossible for me to believe that I had actually heard these words spoken. Outside the window, in the bare twiggy branches of the trees, sparrows and blackbirds pursued their innocent lives. I could see the profile of the bust of King Ludwig, from whose nose drips of rainwater still clung from a short downpour that had fallen on the town some hours before.

Of course, when men are famous, rumours circulate about their erotic preferences and capacities which have no necessary relationship with the truth. Even at my immature stage of development I knew that. I knew in that moment that Siegfried Wagner had actually come to hate Wolf, and his association with his wife; and this hatred fed his desire to believe the rumours about the seedy private life. But it was surely revelatory that the rumours circulating Wolf and his innermost circle were so very unwholesome? His own mysterious attitude to sex, which bursts out on occasion from the pages of *Mein Kampf*, revealing an obsessive fear of syphilis, lends some plausibility to the idea that he preferred something a little different.

'Anyway,' I said, breathing deeply and looking at the garden, 'it is very good news that Toscanini is to conduct *Tannhäuser* this summer.'

'I must tell Mummy,' said Fidi. 'She'll be thrilled.'

The pale old head of Mummy was not, perhaps, beyond pleasing, but it was hard to know what it contained. So short were they of ready cash in that year that they allowed an American woman, a journalist, to sit up in Cosima's room for day upon day in exchange for 1,000 US dollars. Cash. Fidi and Eva fell upon the notes like carrion crows devouring the stomach of a dead weasel in the forest. Ten dollars in those inflationary days could keep you going for three weeks in Germany. On the streets of Bayreuth veteran soldiers, some with their medals pinned to their tattered chests, were begging for food.

Above, lit only by the winter daylight which cast its elfish silver glow from the back garden, Cosima reclined on her sofa. Her large nose already had the sharpness of death upon it. Her white hair, soft and beautiful, reposed against a white lace pillow. Her life music was playing inside her skull, sometimes in snatches, sometimes in extended passages, for the last time. The large warty face of her father sometimes leaned over her and the incomparable skill of his fingers on the piano made all other playing of that instrument seem not merely less good but a different order of things.

When Liszt played, the music came forth as if by nature, like the purling of a waterfall. You never *heard* him striving for effects. He had bestridden the two worlds – bodily lust and spiritual hunger. Cosima's childhood had been defined by her father's absences, the public's demand to hear him play and his desire to inhabit the magical kingdom of Venusberg. He had married none of them, his clerical status giving him the excuse to behave as perhaps all men wished to behave, pollinating one follower and then the next.

Cosima, a love child and the child of music, was left in Paris with her mother and her grandmother, while Liszt went off to another mistress and another musical assignment in Weimar.

Her century, the nineteenth century, had been posited on the notion that these feelings, the feelings which dictated her father's entire life, were unmentionable, shameful, perhaps non-existent. That was one of the myths by which the middle class was sustained. Home and hearth, a *bürgerliche* Madonna with her well-brushed children in their velvet frocks and lace collars. Yet music had given away the secret, hadn't it? Her father's haunting Hungarian strains told of the passion, but only in hints. It was Richard Wagner who let the cat out of the bag altogether: was that why bourgeois audiences always loved *Tannhäuser*? And why he wished so earnestly that he could have revised it and made it into a fully fledged music drama like his later work, rather than leaving it to retain, as it did, the elements of the old-fashioned opera with 'numbers'.

For what was it other than the simple difference between the world seen through the eyes of one in the thrall of sexual passion, and the world seen through the eyes of one liberated, if to lose desire is indeed a liberation? We think we are happy in the world of the bourgeois song contest and of the domestic, religious, sexless Elisabeth, who offers us security and warmth and pure love; yet a madder music draws us.

When she was seventeen, Cosima and her elder sister were sent by her father to live with a protégé of the Abbé Liszt's, Hans von Bülow, and his mother. Hans taught the girls music and helped to improve their bad German. Why did it make her shudder when his horrible moist hands touched hers on the keyboard? She did not fear sex. From an early age she had known her need of it, and from the instant she met Hans she had known his inability to provide what her soul and her loins hungered after.

Poor Hans! He was destined to become one of the most successful conductors of his generation, but when she was a lodger in his mother's house she saw only an impoverished and painfully nervous young man, in awe of her father certainly, but in love, not with her but with the music of Richard Wagner. She loved him for the dangers he had passed. It made her laugh to apply the Desdemona line to her feelings for Hans, since he had none of the heroism of the Moor. Once, when he was perhaps only twenty-five, he had conducted the Overture to *Tannhäuser* at the Stern Conservatory where he was a teacher. The public had hissed, so disturbing did they find it.

Waiting at home for his return, his mother had said that she would go to bed at the usual time. The servants had also turned in. Poor Hans had been so overwhelmed by the hostile response of the audience to what they conceived of as dangerous modern innovations that he had passed out. He had lain unconscious in his dressing room for a long time, and when he returned to his mother's house he had found but one lamp burning in the drawing room and the pale, intense, beaky figure of Cosima sitting up to wait for him.

Yet the love letters he wrote were not to her but to her father. 'For me Cosima Liszt transcends all other women not only because she bears your name but because she is in so many ways the exact mirror of your personality.' Poor Hans spoke true. Hans the Apollonian had fallen in love with a Dionysian. Had he not seen his hero, the Abbé Liszt, selfishly pursue music, women, women, falling back from time to time on the no less delicious raptures of penitence and religious ecstasy? This was what he fell in love with in Cosima and this he married.

She was glad to be loved. After the chaos of childhood and the many years when she felt no certainty of either parent's affection, Hans's spaniel devotion was very reassuring. Getting married had been his idea; all his idea? She could never remember. The only misgiving she could ever recollect was that she knew all passion was absent from those areas which she knew mattered most. Even before her first ecstasy, which occurred a few months after she married him and was self-stimulated, she had known that he would never send her into the dizzying realms of Venusberg, either by what they did in the bedroom or anywhere else. Some audience would always be hissing while in vain he conducted an opera to whose inner meaning and *raison d'être* he was totally deaf.

She'd met Richard Wagner when she was a child and he had evoked, as did so many grown-ups, feelings of angry jealousy, since it was obvious that Liszt cared more for the German composer than he did for his own children. When she married Hans the Wagner idolatry also got in the way. Hans did seem, quite literally, to worship Wagner. The spaniel eyes he had cast at her when she first came as a lodger to his mother's house were as nothing to the adulation he bestowed upon his hero. Taught by Liszt, Hans saw Wagner as a new comet in the sky, a new chapter in the history of music. Cosima was to see this, but only by tortuous paths did she come to the Heavenly City, winding up the purgatorial slopes and twisted paths of envy and jealousy and rage – envy not least of her sister Blandine, who seemed to be the one on whom Wagner had the crush.

Did any of it, this early emotionally confused pain of her marriage to Hans, flicker in and out of the old skull on the sofa in Bayreuth as she muttered to that polite American journalist? I went in several times during that fortnight. By morning light the head was silhouetted against the garden windows; one saw the nose, the wisps of hair, and beyond it trees and sky; in the afternoon light her face was radiated with the golden rays of the sun, setting behind the Hofgarten.

Tannhäuser is the dream of separation between two visions – the world seen when we are in lust and the world otherwise. It is not a celebration of sex, as such, it is an acknowledgement of its importance and of the genius human beings have for placing it in compartments. Hence the pivotal importance for nineteenth-century respectability of the brothel. Hence, perhaps, H's obsession with the Viennese prostitutes of his youth and the many raving references to syphilis in *Mein Kampf*, where venereal disease and racial impurity are sometimes intermingled as metaphors of social harm. With the advance of syphilis, so the book maintains, came the decline of German culture and the rise of cubism.

Liszt and Wagner chose to carry the chaos of their emotional and sexual burdens upon the carriage top and in the light of open day. True, the actual secrets of what each man *did*, or *liked doing*, might have remained a secret, though even in Wagner's lifetime his fondness for dressing up in silken female underwear was hinted at by the gossips. Neither man really needed the *Tannhäuser* dichotomy of the virtuous domestic hearth held in Hegelian balance by the Venusberg brothel or the kept woman behind lace curtains. They carried their chaos about, making everyone pay. When Liszt had abandoned the Comtesse Marie d'Agoult in Paris, he openly took up with the Princesse Carolyne von Sayn-Wittgenstein in Weimar. Wagner, cut to the quick by Minna's infidelities in their early married life, lost no time in making his own arrangements, and his life was punctuated by love affairs and a few *grandes passions*. Of these undoubtedly the most extreme, and the most artistically fruitful, was his unconsummated adoration of his neighbour in Zurich, Mathilde von Wesendonck.

The young bride Cosima used to weep at the mention of his name, Wagner's. By then she had stopped pretending, even in her head, that she found Hans's approaches anything but repellent, but if she were to hear him speak with adoration, it was of *her* she wished him to be the worshipper, not of this short, rather common, exuberant German genius.

But then, in those days she was always bursting into tears. Nothing now, as she lay half a corpse, remained of the passions, either of the anger she felt with poor Hans or the hopeless passions conjured by her imagination to escape the prison house of marriage. Whatever had happened to Karl Ritter, one of Hans's friends? Yet for one summer she and Karl had been so in love that they had rowed out into the lake at Geneva and earnestly committed themselves to a suicide pact.

At the time of these tempests Wagner was having troubles of his own. His wife Minna, who had lived through so many of his adventures, found the obsession with Mathilde intolerable and they were now living apart. She had come to be more and more conservative since the failed revolutions and she hated her husband's 'progressive' views on everything, and his desire to write 'modern' music that audiences hissed. Why not a few pleasant tunes that audiences enjoyed? The Mathilde obsession was being turned by Wagner into the first great piece of modernist music, *Tristan und Isolde*. He came and went between Switzerland and a very cold palazzo in Venice where, much of the time alone, he worked on that noble masterpiece.

Out of so much chaos ... Wesendonck eventually found the situation between himself and his wife so unbearable that, while continuing to pay Wagner's bills, he in effect sent him away from Switzerland. Minna, who had periodic attempts to meet Wagner and repair their marriage – episodes he regarded as unmitigated hell ... Cosima, trapped in the misery of her marriage to Hans and Wagner needing Hans as the musical interpreter of *Tristan*. Here were emotional circles of which Goethe himself could have spun another *Elective Affinities*.

It was to Hans that Wagner entrusted the task of making a piano score of *Tristan*, even as he composed it; and it was Hans who first played it through to Cosima.

And now she was fading. Her soul was possessed by music. So was her body. The intake of difficult breath and its exhalation heaved to the music of *Tristan*, to the ultimate yearning expression that love could find its fulfilment only in ... Hans playing the 'Liebestod' ... Hans conducting the first rehearsals of *Tristan* ... love ... death ... So many deaths around that fateful time when her soul and body became the possession of Richard Wagner. Her sister Blandine . . . her brother Daniel, aged twenty. Lying in the falling shadows of Wahnfried, the ninety-year-old shell, so soon approaching its shuddering separation from the soul, smiled across something which felt like a river of mist at her brother's kind young face. Her face, apple-pink but wrinkled: it was soon to become young again. She would feast on the apples of Freia and know eternal youth. Time was already in confusion.

Someone (it was the author of these words) and another (it was Winnie) was lifting the old lady under the armpits. Ever practical in her kindness, Winnie said, 'They become so uncomfortable if you do not move them.'

Was there a sob in the background? Is it Fidi sobbing? Is it a baby sobbing for its mother, or is it the universal cry of pain which the universe hurls back at the unjust gods?

She is being lifted, lifted.

The hands under her armpits feel her body. She feels the hands of Richard. Why is it so unlike the sensation when Hans touches her? Why is there such deep, deep excitement as the Master takes her in his arms? He was whispering to her. He was telling her his dreams. How many hundreds of his dreams was he to tell her and would she transcribe in her diaries? They were at the opera together . . . *Tannhäuser* . . . Paris . . . '*Comment a-tu osé avoir le courage et le mérite de venir ici seule?*'

They are in a box. She longs more than anything for him to possess her, there and then. She wants his hands, his tongue, his lips, his sex. She feels herself melting. Venusberg is now the centre of the universe, and all else has become a dream. Hans at the piano, her unhappy little affair with Karl Ritter, her baby . . . They are as 'in the background' as servants along a corridor, whose existence you acknowledge but who have absolutely no inner reality for you as you lie in bed drifting off into a deeper reality.

Long before the first wonderful union had occurred, and she had made love to the Master, Venusberg had come alive, its dry places had filled with hidden springs. That day he quite boldly, in front of everyone, in front of Hans, picked her up and put her in a wheel-barrow. They were staying at an hotel in Biebrich called the Beaver's Nest. His hands under her arms and then, as he carried her into the barrow, his hands beneath her buttocks, were so placed that one or two fingers, sticking up above the others, felt the ever-willing terri-tories of Venusberg.

Not long after that, came another moment – in a carriage, riding alone the pair of them through the streets of Berlin.

'I think she said something,' said Winnie.

'Oh, *Mutti*, *Mutti*, oh darling *Mutti* . . .' This was Eva leaning over her, but the girlish sobs in the background were Fidi's.

Cosima thought, 'The wheelbarrow had become for me a celes-tial wain, in which he bears me on and on towards our spiritual home.'

'Eva, let me near . . . oh my God, is she going – oh, *Mutti*, *Mutti*!'

'Fidi, darling.' It is Winnie, being comforting.

Now they are all kneeling beside the bed. They have managed to heave the body from the sofa to the bed. The old bones feel as brittle as biscuits. It is a wonder they can carry her without her cracking.

'She looks very comfortable.'

No one would know. No one could know what the union meant to them. There was no point in trying to find a word, which would either be some piece of smut, such as her father guiltily read, one of those novels from Paris that he concealed beneath his priestly soutane; or it would be an unsuccessful piece of 'poetry'. Music alone could convey . . . oh, must they shout and mutter and pray through the music?

'I think she's more comfortable.'

'*Mutti*, dear, we love you.'

'Hallowed be thy name, thy Kingdom come.'

I am coming, my Master. Our celestial wain is carrying me and once again I feel that heaving music, that ecstatic pleasure. With a great shudder, she shot from the room and out into the gloaming, the dusk took her. She swooped – the movement both was, and was not, of her own volition – towards Richard. The shudder was the greatest orgasm to which she had ever surrendered. She found his face, his smile. In the sardonic smile which sometimes on earth was cruel, she found only a benign indifference. He both welcomed and repelled her. She realized to her dismay, and panic, that she was not permitted to reach him: that, although she was coming to him, he was in some different condition from her own. She recollected quite distinctly at that moment their readings aloud together after dinner at Wahnfried – and the month they read the *Purgatorio* in which there was a long ascent and many encounters, before the pilgrim came fully into the presence of the Beloved.

'Twenty minutes' – Toscanini was convulsed with laughter. I record this fact not because I rate my talents as a comic anecdotalist but to show how different he was from any of the other great conductors whom I met at Bayreuth – all, that is, with the exception of Fidi, who had a highly developed sense of the absurd. Even Fidi, however, had not laughed at the twenty-minute *Parsifal* that had been shown at the local cinema, the Electric Palace. Cosima, in words her children helped her to frame and dictate, had written in the most grief-stricken tones to the city fathers. It would have been beneath her dignity to write to the manager of the cinema. One might have thought it was beneath her dignity to recognize the existence of motion pictures, let alone of a cinema in the divine Bayreuth. I remember the manager, a jolly cinematomane called Herr Tischler, reading out the Cosima epistle – 'The grief felt by all good people ... This sacred drama, uniquely and for ever associated with the town of Bayreuth ... desecration ... the truncation little short of blasphemy' – to the projectionist, Herr Bäcker, and the box office clerk, Fräulein Horn, with a mixture of incredulity and amusement. I of course had been the pianist aged about eighteen.

'I had prepared myself for the possibility that *some* truncation would have occurred,' I said, 'in adapting the drama for the screen. But only when Herr Tischler played it through did I ...' Once more

I laughed. Toscanini laughed – not because either of us had anything but the deepest reverence for the Master, and for *Parsifal* in particular, but because it was *funny* that the Edison Film Company – ages since, in the year I was born – had managed to make a film of this five-hour story and reduce it to twenty minutes.

'I wonder how short they'd manage to make the *Ring* cycle?' He spoke quite fluent German but with the strongest of Italian accents. Indeed, apart from making few grammatical errors and remembering his word order, something foreigners seldom do, he spoke the words themselves as if they *were* Italian, often adding vowel sounds at the end which did not exist in our language: *Parsifal-uh*. With his curly moustaches, dark, humorous eyes and swept-back black hair greying at the temples, he was the very embodiment of a dashing Lothario and I think Friedelind, twelve or thirteen when we were having this lunch together at the Golden Anchor, was already in love with him. But I do not think anything ever passed between them. Later she'd say he was her second father.

There were others round the spotless thick white tablecloth – Frida Leider was there, I remember, a great friend of Toscanini's. She was singing Kundry that year in *Parsifal* and she made Toscanini laugh with jokes about Furtwängler, his rival conductor.

It is hard to convey to you how grand the conductors were in those days. That season there were three – Muck, Furtwängler and Toscanini. In order to get these characters to come to Bayreuth, Fidi and Winnie had to write extravagant contracts. Furtwängler insisted not only upon his own private chauffeur and car to convey him from the bachelor house to the Festival Theatre but also a horse-drawn carriage with equipage as back-up for the days when the car was temperamental. He himself was temperamental always and the servants, not only in Wahnfried but also at the hotels and restaurants in the town and in the theatre restaurant, all regarded him with loathing.

Karl Muck was similarly capable of creating a fuss about trivia and only that morning, the morning we were having lunch at the Golden Anchor, Fidi had been driven half mad by a row invented by Muck because he believed Furtwängler and Toscanini were given better dressing rooms, more attentive valets – I forget the trifling nature of the complaint.

As well as having to contend with Furtwängler, there was also his formidable secretary, Berta Geissmar, who went through his contracts and negotiated on his behalf, an iron-grey-headed bespectacled person who terrified Fidi.

Toscanini was 'difficult' with the orchestra. (After their first rehearsal with him they christened him Toscanono.) But in person and as a domestic guest he was popular with the staff. He enjoyed his food, did not complain or send dishes back to the cook, as Geissmar so often did on Furtwängler's behalf. He was above all charming with the children. In the past year they had got so out of hand, and Winnie and Fidi had become so busy, that they had been dispatched to boarding schools in England. They'd only lately come home for the holidays as the Festival began. They brought with them all noise, chaos and life. We'd been working flat out in the weeks before the Festival but it was only when they all returned that I noticed (however short-tempered both parents could be with their offspring) how much happier Fidi and Winnie both were. Furtwängler would behave as if the children were an offensive smell it was heroic to ignore. Toscanini made friends with them, especially with Friedelind, and during any free time he would take them, or any member of the household who was willing, on picnics to the Eremitage, drives to the pretty Franconian villages round about, or to meals at the dear old Golden Anchor. 'Come on,' he'd said that day, 'Frau Wagner is being a good wife at the theatre, Herr Wagner is working like a Trojan – the house is full of people – come and join us for lunch at the hotel.'

After some joke about the Geissmar, I remember Frida Leider leaning forward and saying – directly to Toscanini and across the heads, as it were, of us Germans – 'What will we *do* if these people have any more success?' A little silence fell on the table. It was clear enough what her question meant. The formidable Geissmar was Jewish. Frida wasn't Jewish, but her husband, Rudolf Deman (leader of the orchestra at the Berlin State Opera), was. 'You know what Frau Wagner said when Siegfried got me to do Kundry? "*The synagogue is filling up*." That's the way people speak now –'

Toscanini created an atmosphere around himself of benignity and good humour, but also – a crucial fact – he was not German. Those who were and suffered under the burden of the times latched on, from now onwards, to foreigners. Far from thinking this natural, then I considered it unpatriotic. I thought, 'Is it any wonder you are hated if you shout out such thoughts to a foreigner?'

And yet only a minute before I was laughing with Toscanini about an American film of *Parsifal*. I admired Frida Leider's Kundry and I liked her personally. Yet at this sudden dismissal of, as it seemed, German patriots, something much stronger than the genial, grown-up top half of my brain was operating.

When she asked what she could do if 'these people' had success, Frida was alluding to the enormous surge in popular votes for the Nazis. In the Reichstag election of 1928 the Nazis had twelve seats. In the election of 1930 they won 107. In Bayreuth the SPD votes stayed steady at about 8,000. The Nazi votes leaped to about the same number, having been less than half. One of the inhabitants of Bayreuth who had voted for them – his first vote for them – was myself. Of course, at home my parents spoke of little else. It especially grieved my mother that there now seemed no prospect at all of the Bavarian royal family returning to power and that local politics had descended to fisticuffs. When Schemm, the Nazi leader in Bayreuth, spoke in the chamber of the City Council they could count on fights breaking out, chairs and glass being broken, ashtrays and blotters and even steel pens being used as weapons as though the violence lurking beneath the polite surface of things was now like some uncontrollable volcanic lava threatening the conventions and structures of even such dull assemblies as our own.

'Rudolf' – her husband, Frida was still talking – 'says Germans are too sensible. They have voted these people in to give the Conservatives a shake-up. Next election he says we'll be back to dull politicians with watch-chains and frock-coats and Points of Order.'

'Our beloved Duce,' said Toscanini, 'as well as making us *ridiculous* in the eyes of the world, is so *inefficient*. He declared the price of eggs was too high. Any farmer who charged an economic price for his eggs would *be shot*. It meant that for three weeks the shops were full of cheap eggs. Now there are none. If you want an egg at any price you have to buy it on the black market.'

'Uncle Wolf imitates Il Duce brilliantly,' blurted out Friedelind.

It was she and not I who had been brave enough to declare an allegiance and to bring this line of talk to an end. Of course, the conversation was overshadowed by what happened immediately after it; but Friedelind and I were both, I am sure, to revert to it in our minds in later years. Only the previous day I had cravenly assented to Winnie's expressions of rapture at the Nazi electoral successes. When Frida showed herself to belong to a radically opposite viewpoint, the demonic side of my soul felt with complete certainty that Uncle Wolf was right about the Jews. His followers might not have been right to be violent towards them, but their loyalties were elsewhere. Look, I said to myself, look at this Jew (I knew she wasn't one) leaning across the table to talk to this Eyetie – I admired and liked Toscanini with a large part of my being – to deplore the patriotism of the German people. Such double-think went on *all the time* in my brain. For example, I thought it was heroic of Winnie to drive to Zurich so often, sometimes as often as once a week, to get Swiss francs and US dollars out of the bank to pay singers, players, conductors and even on occasion the butcher and the baker. The successive governments of Weimar, soppy liberals or downright Reds, had driven all enterprizing Germans to such expedients.

Yet when I went to get my teeth fixed a different set of standards suddenly applied. The guileless, boring figure of Erik Hügel, leaning over me with miniature circular mirror and one of those chrome-plated hooks for fishing about in the gunge between teeth, would give his views on the economy. 'My wife and I both agree that to keep your money in German marks is the equivalent of putting it – you'll excuse the expression – putting it down the drain. A little wider please. Thank you. We all got stung after the war, like everyone else, but – a little wider, thank you – the war, but my wife said to me – if you'll excuse the expression – enough is enough.'

Whereas for the Wagners to have a Swiss bank was enterprise and sensible, for the Hügels to have one – a much more modest one, I'll be bound – was evidence that they did not really have this country's interests at heart and were somehow immune from the financial insecurity that plagued the rest of us. The Hügels' banking arrangements, about which he was speaking so openly and artlessly, translated themselves at once in my brain into something *underhand*, sneaky, conspiratorial, typical of *them*.

'Anyway, young lady, tell us about English school,' said Toscanini, who had evidently discerned from my face that, politically at least, neither he nor Frida was among friends.

Friedelind was in one of her high, histrionic moods, imitating an Irish teacher of Winnie's – she'd taught at a school near Berlin that Winnie had attended as a girl – named Miss Scott. This good woman now ran an establishment in the north of England. Friedelind's grasp of languages was excellent. I suppose I felt reproved by the company. When I had Toscanini's full attention and was talking about something I reckoned to know about – Richard Wagner's opera on film – I felt liberated, stimulated, by his company. But as the talk grew more political I had felt excluded by their cosmopolitan liberalism. It was all right for them (in this sentence 'them' was not a euphemism for the Jews, just for my immediate company), for them there was always abroad. But what about *us*, the Germans stuck in this country, which was determined to lurch from one bankruptcy to the next lunacy to the next? *What about us?*

So I was sulking – involuntarily – as Friedelind imitated her English teachers and bandied about English phrases, which made Frida and Toscanini and the others laugh but which I simply did not understand.

Perhaps it was because I did not understand the English jokes and because I was sulking that I was the first to see Wieland Wagner coming into the dining room at the Golden Anchor. All the tables had been taken, so that you could see the waiters looking at the boy and wondering where he intended to place himself. Indeed, in my mind there floated for a few seconds the possibility that he had decided he'd get a better lunch if he left Wahnfried and scooted off to the town's best hotel. The fact that he was not 'properly dressed' – he had an open-necked shirt and no coat on that hot summer day – might have been attributable to his family's incurable bohemianism, but even the Wagners minded their ps and qs in the sedate old Anchor. Besides, it was his expression and not his clothes that told Wieland's story and it took only a few seconds to read his stricken face. 'Mausi,' he said, coming up to his sister. 'Mausi – it's Daddy.'

Rehearsing *Götterdämmerung* on the stage of the Festspielhaus he had shuddered into unconsciousness and when some hours later in hospital an embolism finally brought his heart to a sudden halt, Brünnhilde continued to call out to the dead body of *her* Siegfried; the ravens – not the puppets used in the theatre but huge black-winged creatures – fluttered around him, poised for flight back to Valhalla. They played the music of Siegfried's funeral in the Festival Theatre on the day they buried the body of *our* Fidi in the town cemetery as Brünnhilde mounted her steed and rode bravely into the flames, and as the music of the Rhine reasserted the enduring world of nature at peace when the vain human striving for power had been cast aside.

Wolf did not come to the funeral. Winnie told us all that he had telephoned her to say it was better he stay away. He did not wish to cause her any embarrassment by making Fidi's obsequies 'political'. I had no doubt at all that these feelings were perfectly sincere. Though Siegfried had entertained very mixed, decidedly satirical views of Wolf and his antics, the satire was not reciprocated. H was slavish in his devotion to the Wagner name.

Winnie was never more magnificent in my eyes than in those days and weeks after her husband died. She was a thirty-five-year-old widow with four children to care for – but she made sure that the Festival went on and that she should be in charge of it.

On the very day after Siegfried died I rose early and cycled down to the theatre. Some instinct told me that she too would be up early and, sure enough, when I reached her husband's office, there I found her in a black dress seated at his desk. If I were not already in love with her I should have fallen in love that morning. Her abundant hair was neatly brushed and arranged in a bun at the back of her exquisite nape. Her hooded triangular eyes were sad, but not red, not yet. They had a look of sleeplessness but at this stage of the day lack of repose, rather than making her torpid, was acting as a stimulant. 'I thought you'd come,' she said to me. 'Thanks.'

She was seven years older than I was but suddenly we seemed of the same generation.

'I'm expecting visitors.' She smirked and for all her air of sorrow I recognized that love of a fight which was so much part of her Celtic nature.

'Oh?'

'Fidi's will,' she said and lit up. The next few words were borne on the diagonal lines of smoke coming from mouth and nostrils. 'He drew it up a couple of years ago. He named me as his outright successor as Director of the Festival. That means all this' – the hands and the cigarette were waved over the desk, then in the air to indicate the entire Festival Theatre – 'is my responsibility, raising the money, paying the chorus, paying the orchestra, hiring the principals, negotiating with the conductors . . .'

After a silence I said, 'I'll help you.'

Her laughter was not unkind, but she laughed. 'I gather we'll receive a little delegation from the mayor at nine a.m.,' she said firmly. 'His worship the mayor and his corporation think they know better than my husband how to run an opera festival . . .'

She asked me to stay for the mayoral visit. The mayor came in person, a sweating, porcine man whose pink neck tried to burst from his winged collar and whose pince-nez made red marks on each side of his greasy nose. There was a great deal of 'gracious lady . . . honoured lady . . .' but their meaning was clear. 'We have found you an . . . ahem . . . Mr Town Clerk, you have the particulars, I believe.'

'Certainly, Mr Mayor.' The town clerk, also in winged collar and frock-coat, was as dry and yellow and lean as the mayor was moist and round. '. . . in a *very* salubrious – as you might say – neighbourhood.'

'*Neighbourhood*!' exclaimed the mayor. The word might just have been coined, so novel did it seem to him. 'I think, Mr Town Clerk, we'll ask *you* to speak to this one . . .'

'Thank you, Mr Mayor. Gracious lady. We – that is to say I. That is to say the Corporation on behalf of all the people of Bayreuth – offer our most *heartfelt* . . . but felt it would be wrong to let this day go by . . . too big a matter for . . . Richard Wagner not just the possession of his immediate family, but of the world . . . The town would like to offer you for your lifetime occupancy of . . . A very handsome accommodation . . . The Villa Wahnfried could become a Richard Wagner museum . . . The papers, musical scores, diaries and memorabilia would be . . . *ahem, in the public domain.*'

Writing down these words of the town clerk thirty years after he spoke them, writing them moreover in a Communist country, they do not seem so very unreasonable. I gather that Wieland is doing wonderful productions at Bayreuth these days, but isn't there something absurd about that theatre having turned into a family fiefdom? But the mayor and town clerk chose to make their tactless proposals within hours of Fidi's death. That was why I felt so proud of her when she rose to her feet behind her desk – she was fully six inches taller than the mayor – and said, 'Gentlemen, I am grateful for your concern. My husband and I restored this Festival single-handedly after the war. We financed it from loans and donations raised in America and this year, largely thanks to the enormous popularity of Herr Toscanini, we shall be looking at a very healthy profit; all of which, I need hardly tell you, will be reinvested in next year's Festival. I do not believe in public sponsorship for the arts.'

The moist, plump mayor showed himself unexpectedly ready for this claim: 'There, dear lady, you differ from your distinguished father-in-law who not only enjoyed the royal patronage of King Ludwig II but who also openly advocated state funding – taxpayers' money! – being used to subsidize operas.' He tried his best. He pulled himself up in his chair, he stuck out his waistcoat and watch-chain, he said he was only anxious to preserve for all time what the Wagner family had so gallantly begun. He asked what would happen, perish the thought, if the gracious lady herself ... none of us immortal ... Surely it would be better if the responsibility for running the archive, the house, the Festival itself and the theatre should not devolve upon one pair of shoulders ... a mother's shoulders ... a young mother's ... a, dare he say it, *a woman's shoulders*.

When the mayor and the town clerk had gone, she seemed quite in control of herself, even prepared to joke about it. We made some inroads into correspondence and about mid-morning, when we had a pause and coffee was brought in, Friedelind turned up at the office. There was nothing so very unusual about this, since early infancy the children had treated this theatre as their playground, but today was different. It had not occurred to me until she appeared that there was anything strange, on the day after a father and husband died, about mother and children spending the morning separately.

Friedelind had grown since her absence in England. If not yet as tall as her mother, she was, even though only twelve years old, now a woman, not a child, and when she came into the office there was something about her that even since yesterday, when she heard the sad news in the Golden Anchor, now marked her as a mature being: it was a seriousness I had never seen before. In any other circumstance a meeting with the mayor and town clerk would have been an occasion for Winnie to do a comic turn, to amuse her daughter with imitations of their pomposity, but now she had risen from Fidi's chair and came towards her daughter as she entered the room. 'Oh, Mausi.'

'Oh, *Mutti*.' Friedelind threw open her arms. It was she who had come to comfort her mother. As her daughter enfolded her in her arms, Winnie burst into tears. You could tell that they were the first tears since Siegfried died, deep sobs coming from the depths of a broken heart. Her children had lost a father but they still had one another, and Winnie and their membership of a family. But in some senses Winnie was alone again. She had lost the man who had rescued

132

her from her outsider's life in 1915, and as she wept piteously she was, for those ten or fifteen minutes, once again the orphan Senta from the East Grinstead orphanage.

Hearing one's own name always alerts the ears, as when, in a crowd, you hear a nanny or a mother calling it out, only to realize that she is calling a child of the same name, an experience I always find alienating, disappointing: for a few split seconds one had believed oneself wanted, loved. But on this occasion there was no doubt at all that when Winnie, on the telephone, used my name she was speaking about me. 'I couldn't say anything about it in front of N——! . . . Yes, yes, naturally . . . It will be public knowledge eventually. Wolf, I don't quite know . . .'

The conversation upon which I had chanced was evidently an important one, for she had come into Fidi's inner sanctum at Wahnfried away from the rest of the family in order to conduct it. And she had not risked using one of the telephones at the Festival Theatre. 'I do not want to have to discuss it in public, but I wanted you to know . . .'

Just to the right of the door into Fidi's sanctum sanctorum was a walk-in closet where files, stationery, semi-obsolete works of reference and the like were kept. Its door was open and I slipped inside, confident that without switching on the light I could both avoid knocking into a filing cabinet and hear what was going on. '. . . because . . .' Her laugh was coquettish, positively flirtatious. And this was – what? – only a few days after the funeral.

'The terms are clear,' she was saying. 'Fidi has left me in sole control of the Festival. I am the sole owner (*Besitzerin*) of Wahnfried, of the furniture, fittings, all the Wagner material which the mayor wishes to be put into a museum . . . Yes, yes, I told you, he thought he would . . .'

There was a long pause in which Wolf was clearly saying what he would like to have done to the mayor and corporation.

'Not if,' she replied, 'when. But you will have more important things to . . . Ah! . . . No, no, the scores, the diaries, the letters, the entire archive is mine, as is the control of the Festival, the choice of directors . . . conductors . . . everything. So you see, dear Fidi has left me with a very deep responsibility and I do know how much this shows he trusts me . . . I shall rely on you, Wolf . . . I shall rely on you to advise me about everything . . . No, everything . . . Fidi always said we should involve Tietjen . . . Tietjen . . .'

The mention of the word seemed to have a strange effect on her telephone receiver. Even from the cupboard I could hear the rasping voice of Wolf expressing himself at great length on the suitability – much more likely the unsuitability – of her choice of artistic director of the future Festivals.

'You could make that very objection to *my* presence here, Wolf . . . Well, if you say that Tietjen isn't German . . . His father was German, it was his mother who was English . . . And I am completely . . .'

She laughed . . . 'Tietjen directed his first *Ring* when he was twenty-five years old. When Fidi and I went to the Berlin State Opera last year, Fidi was really impressed by the way he'd been working with Furtwängler and Preetorious . . . Yes . . . I feel I owe it to . . . Yes, Wolf, I know, but Fidi made it clear he trusted Tietjen . . .'

Another very long disquisition on Tietjen's qualities seemed to follow.

'Wolf, if it does not work out, we can send Tietjen back to Berlin and start all over again. I know how important it is to you that he isn't One of Us . . . But we are hiring an artistic director, not a local party gauleiter . . . Well, we have differed about that before, my dear, and all I would say is . . . You don't have to run an opera house . . . You couldn't do it, Wolf, my dear . . . If the only people you hired were National Socialists, you wouldn't necessarily have a very good cast of singers . . . of course not.'

After this spat, they seemed to nestle into a tenderer phase of the conversation's music. I still had not understood what it was she had not wished to discuss 'in front of me'.

Clearly the main point of her telephone conversation was not to talk with Wolf about the advantages or otherwise of hiring Heinz

Tietjen as next year's artistic director. It was Fidi's will she had rung up to tell Wolf about. 'Yes . . . I have the house, the running of the Festival, the archives, and so forth and so forth . . . on condition that I do not marry again . . . I wanted you to know that.'

He did not say much in response to this, because she quite soon continued, 'I wanted your advice . . . Do you think it would be worth my while to contest the will, or would it attract unwanted publicity?'

He spoke at some length in answer to this. Sometimes I could hear the rasp down the wires, sometimes he was obviously cooing at her, for she cooed back: 'When you are Chancellor, you can do anything you like . . . Naturally, in accordance with the "Will of the people".' There were inverted commas round these words, but there could be no doubt that she believed them, believed them both – that he could do as he liked and that he did constitute, as his own rhetoric so frequently proclaimed, an embodiment of the German people's will.

At this stage my parents were still dismissing the possibility of H's ultimate political success. My father had this persistent belief in the electorate's 'good sense', which used to inspire me to say, 'If they had any sense they would sack von Papen [or Brüning or Stresemann on whatever date we were having the conversation and whoever happened to be the Chancellor], and have a man who undid the Versailles Treaty, built up the army, did something about unemployment . . .' The usual shopping list.

Of course my parents always had an answer to this, but it was at base – or so it seemed to me at the time – a snobbish base: namely that we did not want the affairs of the country placed into the hands of 'people like that' – they meant the small shopkeeper class, the non-commissioned officers, the disgruntled local civil servants who provided the hard core of the Nazi vote. It was my brother, who had now overcome his doubts and was about to become a Lutheran pastor like Father, who, during the elections of 1930, saw that something had changed and that very many 'ordinary Germans' (like myself) believed that enough was enough, that desperate times called for, if not desperate measures, then something more than a repetition of the tired old Weimar non-solutions.

No doubt, reading this, you will find it incredible that I should have considered National Socialism an answer to any problems, rather than being itself the greatest 'problem' to arise in European history. But you see, what I cannot emphasize too strongly is that it was precisely knowing Wolf that made us, at Wahnfried, so confident that everything would be all right were his political comrades to be elected to power. Some of them seemed very odd indeed, some of them were downright sinister, and the local Bayreuth Nazis, especially Gauleiter Schemm, were little better than thugs whom we all deplored from the beginning. But Wolf had the qualities of a magician. He had mesmerized his followers, and perhaps himself, into believing that he was capable of anything. Domestically, especially with the children, he was just a very gentle, genial person. I acknowledge in retrospect the compulsive talking and the flatulence, but at the time these did not particularly detract from his charm. I had come not merely to believe, with my brother, that the Nazis now really had a chance to turn our country round; unlike my brother I viewed the prospect with eager excitement. Anyhow, wedged in the dark in the stationery cupboard, the nation's future was not my immediate concern – except insofar as it seemed, for the duration of a telephone conversation, as if it might be connected with the future of Winnie.

I should love to have intercepted that call and to have heard, word for word, what he had to say to her. Sometimes she replied, 'But Wolf . . . you couldn't . . . You could not . . . The entire burden of the Bayreuth Festival and the performance of Richard Wagner's music in the place rests on me. But . . . I know . . . and there is no one who could share it with me more appreciatively, or more helpfully than . . . I know . . . but you will have on your shoulders the future of the German race and that is something important . . . even more important, I find, than the future of our Festival.'

There was more, much more, silence on the line while he spoke to her.

I am not fantasizing. It was clear to me that he was, if not actually proposing marriage to Winnie, discussing the possibility of a partnership of some kind.

The retrospect of thirty years changes one's perspectives of everything. I am trying to recreate for you exactly what my impressions were in that stationery closet. I became aware over the next few years that Wolf had other women in his life apart from Winnie. As I have said before about public figures, especially those with innumerable political enemies, rumours circulate all the time. There were Fidi's obscene speculations concerning what exactly happened between Wolf and his niece; I heard this story told by others in the coming years, especially after Geli's death. There was the talk, which I heard from about this time onwards, of prostitutes arriving at the flat in Prinzregentstrasse – though I always discounted these stories as being essentially out of Wolf's character. A little later there was the arrival upon the scene of Eva Braun, who was eventually installed as his semi-official companion. With her customary impenetrable Welsh mysteriousness Winnie never let on how much of this impinged upon her.

In the stationery cupboard that day in the late summer of 1930, however, I had no doubt that I was overhearing Winnie and Wolf discussing more than a friendly association, or a shared interest in an opera festival. They were contemplating marriage.

Did it mean that my earlier speculation was right and that, seven years before, they had become lovers, however briefly? Or had they kept alive a flame of love for one another precisely because it – whatever 'it' was – had never been fulfilled? *Tristan und Isolde* appears to have been inspired by Wagner's unsatisfied yearning for Mathilde Wesendonck. *Tannhäuser* is about the shocking disparities between our erotic selves and the 'rest of life'. We come back from Venusberg and find the same old world of decisions, routines, preferences – not erotic preferences, but how we like our coffee, or what newspaper we should buy of a morning – dominating life. The madness of 'before' is replaced by the comparative sanity of 'after'. Or, if that is a wrong reading of the myth, the enchantments of Venus are simply so strong that they blot out the rest of life and can (as when Tannhäuser cannot stop himself from blurting out his Venus song in the anodyne little song competition) make the rest of life fade. Yet it is always this 'rest of life' which comes back; even in the life of an actual erotomaniac it will return – family, work concerns, money, the ordinariness of everyday. I do not know if they had, technically, been lovers, but I did know, as I overheard her from the stationery cupboard, that they had not been to Venusberg together. This was not the talk of two people who were caught up in shared madness. It was plans for the future. What was so electrifying is that she felt she had to tell Wolf (before anyone else?) about Fidi's will and its forbidding of her remarriage.

Within a few minutes of her having hung up I began the speculation which, on and off, has haunted my mind ever since – why Fidi made that provision in his will. My first stab at an answer, which had entered my mind even before she had finished her phone call with Wolf, was that he had known she would have this conversation. It was precisely this that he had found more unbearable than any likely affairs she might have. Of course, with his family background, Fidi could see the nightmare possibilities of family quarrels. The lawsuit with his sister Isolde, who might or might not have been the daughter of Hans von Bülow, or of Richard Wagner, had been ample demonstration of what difficulties result when there is more than one father in the picture. Winnie was a young, attractive woman, she liked men, she liked sex, she liked children. There would be every possibility of her marrying again and having children who would – unless Fidi guarded against it by his last will and testament – aspire to take a hand in the running of the Festival Theatre.

This was the common-sense reason why he stipulated she could only control the Festival for as long as she did not marry again. But . . . but . . . there was, beneath the prancing surface of Fidi's mannerisms, beneath the jokes, the queenery, the outbursts of bad temper and the high vein of fantasy on which he liked to live, there was something more than sensible about him. I always felt he was a person who understood other human beings. He was a kindly father – the desolation of the children in the months after he died was awful to witness. He believed in those four children and, really more than the 'unnoticing' Winnie, he made convincing imaginative journeys into their inner lives.

I think he knew his Winnie very well indeed. I think he realized that, almost by chance, his mother Cosima, by accepting Senta Klindworth as the mother of the future Wagners, had bought the most extraordinary bargain. All she could have hoped for was a good-looking woman of child-bearing age whose background was sufficiently odd and disadvantaged to guarantee that she would be submissive, grateful even, for having been adopted into Wahnfried. None of them – not Karl Klindworth himself, not Cosima, not Fidi – could have guessed that this seventeen-, eighteen-year-old girl would have been the world's most ideal director of an opera house. Fidi must have felt this. Yet her Welsh soul, so unlike the punctilious German mind trained by Immanuel Kant, had the capacity for hero-worship, the Celtic compulsion to leap into the irrational. Fidi had seen what she thought of Wolf, or he thought he had seen it. He feared that the two outsiders, the Welsh orphan and the Austrian corporal, would form a wrecking alliance if they were to marry. Maybe, even, Siegfried Wagner was sensible enough, and patriotic enough, to see how disastrous it would be to give licence to Winnie's temptations to make the Festival Theatre into a political platform, or to Wolf's temptation to turn German politics into a tragic opera? Maybe he had seen what I had only half intuited in 1925 when Wolf, carried away by the story from the Grimm Brothers of the fisherman and his wife, revealed his need to go beyond triumph to self-destruction. Perhaps his last will and testament was an attempt to prevent that? In the coming years I was to see another side to Winnie and her dealings with Wolf. Perhaps this too is very Welsh – namely that, together with her unshakeable loyalty and fervent zeal for Wolf, she was capable of exploiting him. Perhaps, even as they spoke together on the telephone that day, he was sensing that?

Papa Toscanini conducted *Tannhäuser* two or three more times that summer after Fidi's death. The familiar hysterical themes, more distasteful, I think, to my parents than any of Wagner's music, transported three happy audiences into the troublingly familiar chaos of sex. After the incident in the stationery closet, I felt a whole mingling of confused and painful emotions. There was a surge of relief when I realized that, for the time being at least, Winnie could not belong to Another. Unrequited love makes that cruellest emotion, hope, create all manner of impossible future scenarios. I had begun to construct a future in which Winnie would rely on me, more than on anyone, for emotional comfort and support, that I would be her special little friend, now that she could not have a lover. Of course, Fidi's will had not made any specifications about whom she took to her bed and I had no sense at that stage of how important sex was to this healthy young woman seven years my senior. It was not especially important to me – not sex, in the sense of doing anything about it. Like all of us who became grown-ups in the 1920s I believed that sex somehow 'explained everything' in the way that God was once supposed to have done, but although erotic confusion and desire surged through my being, I had no particular wish to 'experiment'. Indeed, I was completely inexperienced, with both males and females, and could not imagine how one began the process of initiating a sexual relationship. Hence the comfortingness of thinking that Winnie and I could be special friends.

Her grief for Fidi was calm but real. She had lost her best friend and the life companion with whom she shared her children. How important that bond is. And how little I understood such things at the time.

Now, of course, it is obvious to me that the chief, perhaps the only, important thing lacking in her marriage to Fidi was something she would very quickly come to find with another man. And that man was not to be an inexperienced character such as myself. I don't think she even considered me as an aspirant lover.

When the Festival was over she arranged to be away, and on her own, for two extended visits. The first was to Munich, where I know she visited Wolf several times. What they talked about I do not know, but she came home very worried about his niece and the talk that was circulating about their intimacy. She said it would do him terrible damage at the polls if any of the malicious scandal got out and that she could not understand the malice of Wolf's enemies who were prepared to suggest things which were quite manifestly – manifestly to Winnie's adoring eyes anyway – absurd. 'They are uncle and niece. He is helping her in every way he can to become a student. That is the end of the matter.' She said it in her highly emphatic way. These emphases were often, in my experience, to have the reverse effect upon hearers of the one intended.

The other visit, a rather longer visit, was to Berlin, which she went to in, I should say, October 1930. When she came back she was highly excited. She had, she said, spent a lot of time with Heinz Tietjen. 'He is our man! He is our man!' she kept saying. At quite what point this became literally the case I could not say, but something in the churlish reaction of the children whenever Tietjen's name was mentioned – and this even before he came upon the scene – told me that they had nosed out, by the instinct which self-protective families always can, that their mother's interest in the new artistic director at Bayreuth was to be more than merely professional.

The year 1931 was one in which so much outwardly happened, both in the history of the Bayreuth Festival and of our country. Both Winnie and Wolf were living through the great crises of their respective careers. She was being tested in her first full year as the Director of the Festival, and he stood poised between absolute ruin and absolute power. Perhaps it was this very fact which led them both to inhabit their separate Venusbergs that year. For I have no doubt that against all the background of their public lives, which you can read about in the books, their imaginative inner lives were dominated by Eros, perhaps in both cases for the first time. My own belief is that the telephone conversation I overheard between them intensified this. After the death of Fidi there had been something 'obvious' about the idea of Winnie, if not proposing marriage, then floating the idea of it past Wolf. The very fact that it was crazy must have been what appealed to both of them and I have sometimes wondered whether it would not have been the ideal solution, both to their own and to the country's problems. He could have taken over the running of the Festival Opera and although, as she had told him, this would have meant a drastic reduction in the numbers of competent musicians in his employ, it would have kept his mind occupied. That isn't how I saw things at the time, of course. But I 'saw' nothing at the time, not even the rather obvious fact that there was another person, apart from Wolf and myself, who was in love with Winnie: the maestro Toscanini himself.

Perhaps allowing ourselves to be caught up in the enchantments of Venusberg is the best possible distraction from the crises of 'real life'? There was another thought of which, at the time, I would have been incapable. It certainly is not present in *Tannhäuser*, which is in many respects a simple-minded work. No wonder, as Cosima's diaries told me, Richard Wagner was dissatisfied with it to the end of his days and spoke repeatedly of revising it. Tietjen was an unlikely lover for her. Small, gnome-like, with thick spectacles and a cold, totally unwinning manner, he had none of Siegfried Wagner's charm. Perhaps this fascinated her. What he did know about was directing operas, conducting orchestras and making them work.

I soon learnt enough about his political affiliations to be able to guess what sort of things Wolf must have said about him on the telephone when he first heard of his appointment. He was said to be a card-carrying Social Democrat – the party supported by my gentle brother Heinrich. Certainly, Tietjen leaned to the left of the rest of us politically, but to imagine him as a softy would be a big mistake. I never met anyone – and this is saying something, coming from the pen of one who knew H – who gave off a bigger sense of absolute power when you were in his presence. No doubt if I'd seen H in action in his War Cabinets I should be telling a different story, but apart from his manic tirade against Friedrich Schorr, I never heard him misbehave himself at Bayreuth, whereas Tietjen would do anything to get his own way and he exercised a power over Winnie quite frightening to behold.

He was a strikingly clever man and he let you know it. Any remark addressed to him was received as if it were ridiculous and he would usually answer 'quite' (*genau*). He could inject such scorn into the two syllables of the German word. If it was a remark with which he agreed, the syllables implied, 'Any bloody fool knows that.' If it was something with which he disagreed, the word would be loaded with sarcasm and often followed by a whinnying laugh, which had much in it of the witheringly sarcastic teacher humiliating an unsatisfactory pupil.

He was very well read, in several languages, and his table talk, when not about the minute details of opera management and business arrangements, ranged over the books he could remember better than anyone else. Hearing I was a failed philosopher, for example, he quizzed me about my friend Martin H——'s *Sein und Zeit*, showing that he had read it. By the time I'd finished my blundering attempts to say what I thought of it, though to tell the truth – a truth no doubt obvious to Tietjen – I hadn't managed more than about half the book, he stopped me with 'quite'. And the laugh. And went on to speak about the clarity of Anglo-Saxon philosophy and, in particular, his fondness for the works of Bertrand Russell. He seemed in this respect much more English than Winnie, even though he was only half as English as she – like our Emperor.

We all – and by we all I mean the household, the servants, the children – watched with incredulity and horror as Winnie allowed herself to become more and more Tietjen's creature during that year. She was a different character from the rebellious, laughing wife of Siegfried. With Tietjen she was timorous. He often reduced her to tears by the sharpness of his tongue. And his absences in Berlin, welcomed by the rest of us, by none more than the children, caused her anguishes of jealousy, for he had no intention of dropping his mistress there.

Yet if Tietjen was a monster, he was a monster with a purpose, a monster with a passion for Richard Wagner's music and a desire to rescue Bayreuth from either the disastrous legacies of Cosima (turning the place into a shrine) or the disastrous possibilities of Wolf (turning the place into a platform for National Socialism). All he really cared about, apart from himself and his own advancement, was putting on good opera and in this he helped Winnie to succeed triumphantly. At times when their affair was going painfully, she was crushed by him. But there were other moments when even I, sexually innocent and jealously appalled by this development, could see that Tietjen had supplied more than just sex in her life. The sex had given her self-confidence; and with the self-confidence, she was enabled – forced and cajoled by Tietjen it is true – to establish a new regime at Bayreuth.

First, he made it clear that it was necessary to get Furtwängler and Toscanini to return to the Festival that summer, even though both these prima donnas had said it was impossible to work if the other were present. Like many power-brokers, Tietjen realized that the hatred between the two rivals was a positive asset to the Festival since, after all their huffing and puffing, both Toscanini and 'Fu', once persuaded to come, would be determined to outshine the other in the ears of the audiences. Friedelind, who confided in me more and more about her hatred of Tietjen, was confused and upset by the perpetual rowing of the two conductors; confused, too, by the fact that her beloved 'Papa' Toscanini should have such deplorable political taste. In May that year, shortly before leaving Italy to come and start rehearsals at Bayreuth, Toscanini had been conducting a concert at Bologna, which he refused to begin with the rousing fascist anthem 'Giovinezza' – a much jollier thing, by the way, than our own 'Horst Wessel Song', which must have been coming into vogue at about that time. A furious mob stormed the podium and tried to beat him up. He was badly punched in the face. Given his hostility to fascism and the fact that he could have found work anywhere in the world, it was on the face of it surprising that he should have chosen that summer to come back to Bayreuth, and to spend almost every day in the company of Wolf's most enthusiastic supporter.

The obvious, to those of us who are tormented by the pangs of love, is often the last thing we see. At first I imagined, as Friedelind, Tietjen and others all boasted, that the very simple explanation was Toscanini's desire to outshine Furtwängler. It was only the tone in which the great Italian said the syllables 'Winnie, ah, Winnie!' – we were having a drink together in the bar at the Festival Theatre – that made the full truth dawn. Until then, I may say, I had been hoping against hope that my suspicions about Winnie and Tietjen were unfounded and that they had simply entered into a very close business relationship.

Papa Toscanini was a little drunk. He had arrived at the Festival Theatre in time for a scheduled orchestra rehearsal and had been told by Winnie, halfway through, that he must cut it short. There had been a muddle over the schedules. Furtwängler had also been promised the afternoon for rehearsing.

Clearly, Winnie knew that it was going to be difficult to break this news to the volatile Maestro since she had employed the cowardly expedient of asking me if I'd like to come into the Festival Theatre to hear the last of Toscanini's rehearsal. It very nearly was the last, too. She sidled through the darkened semicircle of the auditorium into the director's bench, where sat Tietjen and two others. From this vantage point she called down to the Maestro, during a short pause, that he in fact had only ten more minutes rather than the allotted two hours.

Toscanini turned and peered up towards the director's bench with astonishment. 'But we have only just begun.'

'Arturo, I am extremely sorry, the rehearsal scheds have gone awry and Herr Furtwängler . . .'

'You have promised the theatre to Herr Furtwängler when . . .'

'I haven't promised anything, but he is arriving in ten minutes and the orchestra . . .'

It was enough. Toscanini displayed not merely anger, but a tempest. He raised his hand in the air and brought the baton down against his lectern with such force that it snapped in half. Reaching into the depths beneath the podium – for what? – he picked up the bewildered figure of Rigoletto, his little fluffy terrier. As he stormed out of the orchestra pit, several members of the orchestra also put down their instruments and began to walk too. A general chaos ensued.

Furtwängler got his rehearsal time, but it was a close-run thing whether Toscanini would ever be tempted back on to the Bayreuth podium again. Or so I thought, until coming across him at the bar. I suppose Winnie must have sent me along to see what I could do to calm down the great man. He was stroking his dog. 'This is all so much worse than last year,' said Toscanini to me. 'Ah, Winnie.'

And then I could see it all – not merely that Winnie was Tietjen's lover but, another equally obvious fact that had entirely escaped me through all the previous twelve or fifteen months: Toscanini was in love with her also. Presumably he had agreed to come back to Bayreuth in the hope of wooing her, but when he got there he had found Tietjen already installed in her bed and the National Socialists, whom he abominated, installed as a political fixture in her heart.

Later that afternoon, when his chauffeur had driven him, me and the dog back to the Golden Anchor where we continued to drink (a rather good grappa of deadly potency) in the dining room, he said, 'You know, my young friend, I would forgive her anything. I do not even mind all this . . . political nonsense . . . anything . . . It would have been good – a good combination, don't you think? Her and me?'

Winnie was presumably not tempted by film-star good looks or film-star qualities. She moved from the oddity of marriage to Fidi to the unprepossessing Tietjen, pausing on the way to sound out Wolf who, for all his mesmeric appeal on some spiritual plane, could never be called a model of masculine good looks. Perhaps she was simply too caught up in the crisis of Fidi's death to notice that Toscanini was in love with her; or maybe she noticed and merely thought it was a bit of a laugh. It must have added bitterness, either way, when he went to America and began denouncing the political slant of the Festival since Siegfried Wagner had died.

For most of that summer Wolf was touring and speechifying, and we saw little of him. He was maintaining his boycott of the Festival, which began the summer that Friedrich Schorr took the role of

Wotan, and his visits to Bayreuth were therefore in any event more sporadic than they had been and tended to take place in the winter. Winnie, too, was deeply preoccupied – by Tietjen and by the Festival. The victims in all this were, in Bayreuth, the children; in Munich, Wolf's niece Geli.

Whatever the nature of his relationship with Geli from a sexual viewpoint, he stood *in loco parentis* to her. Clearly, he vacillated between moods of great tenderness, when he took her around on his arm to social functions, never, I think to political rallies or speeches. There were long, notorious shopping expeditions in which he sat patiently in Munich department stores while she accumulated the bags and dresses and shoes. But at some stage during this summer he had also formed his liaison with the young woman who would eventually become his wife – Eva Braun.

I never met Eva Braun and have no idea what she was like, though of course I've seen her photograph. She was never mentioned, in my recollection, by Winnie, though by some stage Winnie must have known about her. Geli I did meet once or twice. Wolf brought her over to Wahnfried for lunch. He had by now reached the grand stage of having his own chauffeur, Julius Schreck, who spent a lot of time needlessly burnishing the already gleaming Merc while Wolf ran into the house, to the usual whoops of excitement from the girls and the boys.

Since Wolf was, as always, caught up with the children, Geli had me for company. At a loose end for conversation, I asked her how her course was going at the university. I was attempting, with an unsuccessful effort of the will, to banish from my mind all the things Fidi had said about Fräulein Raubl's relationship with her uncle. The only 'clean' thing I could remember was that she was a medical student. Like so many of the things one remembers, this was not in fact true. Insofar as she was a 'student' at all, Wolf was paying for her to have some singing lessons. But I persisted for some time in quizzing her – 'was she pre- or post-clinical, did she intend to specialize when she went into medicine, did general practice or hospital work more appeal to her?' – this line of questioning.

'Are you a doctor yourself?' was her response to this.

Geli, as she asked me to call her, was not conventionally beautiful, but she was very sensual. She seemed younger than her twenty-three years; she was almost as schoolgirlish as Friedelind, but whereas in Friedelind there was a latent sexuality, in the case of Geli, you were aware of something which was totally overt. She had thick, wavy brown hair, and the lips hung half open much of the time. She wore clothes on that late summer afternoon which seemed too old for her, too formal – a sleeveless, probably expensive, cream-coloured dress, cut vaguely square at the neck, and a large heavy necklace of amber and silver balls. Her pale skin was mottled with freckles.

'No,' was my response, 'I'm not even a doctor of philosophy.'

'Why "even"?'

We had wandered out of the house into the garden, and although it was not my intention to show her the graves – Cosima had now joined the Master, the Newfoundland dog Russ and the parrots at the bottom of the garden – that was the direction in which we were heading.

'I mean, I didn't finish my thesis. Don't know if I ever will now.'

'So – what do you do here?'

'I'm a dogsbody.'

'Who told you I was going to be a doctor?'

'I . . .'

She turned her face fully towards mine and looked up. She was smiling and it was the first time in my twenty-five years of life when I thought to myself, 'I might kiss this girl – she really wants me to do it! I could have a proper girlfriend.'

The moment did not last, naturally; and I did not kiss her, but it had created a feeling of conspiratorial intimacy between us. We were the two young ones in a world of grown-ups.

'I'm not, you know.' She laughed.

I laughed. 'You've given it up – medicine?'

'I was never going to be a doctor. I don't know where you could have picked up the story. I suppose everyone talks about us – me and Uncle?'

This statement was so direct that there seemed no point in denying it. 'I suppose they do.'

'It was Mum's idea, my moving into the flat. I liked it at first. The Leader! Great! Like, the Leader was my uncle – I was the Leader's little pet.' She did a twirl in her – as it now seemed – ridiculously middle-aged dress. 'What was your name again?'

I told her.

'Do you fuck a lot – fuck around?'

I turned away, completely unable to cope with the question.

'That wasn't meant to be rude,' she said.

'No, no, of course it wasn't. I . . . er . . . good heavens!'

'I do,' she said quietly. 'When I can. Bloody prison, that flat. It was Mum's idea – did I tell you that? Mum's idea that I move in with Uncle, but my God! I'm going to escape. You know Julius?'

'No.'

'The man in the drive.'

'The chauffeur.'

'Yup.'

'We're engaged.'

'You're engaged?'

'Uncle doesn't know yet.'

She got out a packet of cigarettes and offered me one. 'So this is the great Richard Wagner,' she said, lighting up over the composer's grave slab. When my cigarette was lit she said, 'You know my uncle . . .'

'A bit.'

But she wasn't asking me if I knew Wolf, she was beginning half a sentence. 'You wouldn't believe the things he expects me to do.'

The walk threw no light on this utterance, which was thrown out almost casually. I wondered if she was a little mad. I even wondered, rehearsing the conversation over and over again in my head, whether she was under the influence of alcohol or some other narcotic. Her directness of approach was certainly unlike anything I had ever come across. My mother would have attributed this to her 'commonness'. She certainly spoke with the broadest of accents, even broader than that of her uncle, but there was more to it than that. Her directness was that of desperation, knowing that she had only a few more minutes before her uncle re-emerged from the house and the Mercedes sped back to the luxurious flat in Munich. It was not long after that, no more than a few weeks I should say, that we heard the shocking news of Geli's suicide. She shot herself with a 6.34 calibre pistol belonging to her uncle.

You could go on speculating for ever about the causes of her death. For a few weeks afterwards the wildest of rumours circulated – that she had been pregnant, that she was pregnant by a Jewish musician, that her body showed signs of having been badly beaten, that she had not committed suicide but been murdered. Needless to say, for those who believed she was a murder victim, H was the prime suspect, even though he was addressing a multitude of admirers in Nuremberg at the time of her death and there were probably 5,000 people who could have provided him with an alibi.

It was not the suspicion of murder, nor even the suspicion of improper relations with his niece, which were damaging to H at this time. It was something much less specific and much deeper. It was a generalized association between H and death, H and disaster, calamity. A *Liebestod* indeed: love and death inextricably mingled.

'That luxury flat's more like a bloody prison' – this she had said to me on our short walk in the garden.

The gunshot was a wild signal to the outside world that all was not well, not merely within the flat but within her uncle. From the post-war historical perspective in which I write, this is so obvious. But it was not obvious to us at the time. You'll never understand our generation unless you realize that the optimists who supported the National Socialists were not all sinister, Jew-hating decadents in love with death. We thought this band of admittedly rough and ready types, forged into a great national movement, would bring about good things, not bad, life not death.

Baldur von Schirach wrote a poem at about the time that I went to work for the Wagners, some time in the early or mid 1920s.

Lieselotte made the children learn it by heart and it was applied unquestioningly to the man they loved as Uncle Wolf:

> You are many thousands behind me,
> And you are me, and I am you.
> I have had no thoughts
> Which do not vibrate in your heart.
>
> And if I speak, I know no word
> Which is not one with your will.
> For I am you and you are me
> And we all believe, Germany, in you.

He was, for those of us who believed in him, an incarnation of the good German future, and to this extent it is not absurd to speak of him as a sort of German Christ. I would later have this conversation with my brother. Heinrich did not think that Jesus had gone about believing himself to be the redeemer of the world. The peculiar historical circumstances in which he found himself, however, condemned by the Romans for political insurrection and the perceived leader of a dissident group within Judaism, made him the natural figurehead of the new devotion. Thus Heinrich's and my father's Hegelian Christ became himself the servant of the moment, a redeemer of precisely the kind required by the time.

Uncle Wolf was a different kind of redeemer, because we lived in different times. As long ago as 1922, in a speech in the Bürgerbräukeller in Munich, H said,

I say: my Christian feeling *points me to my Lord and Saviour as a fighter* [tumultuous and long applause]. It points me to the man who, once lonely and surrounded by only a few followers, recognized these Jews and called for battle against them, and who, as true God, was not only the greatest as a *sufferer* but also greatest as a *warrior*. In boundless love, as a Christian and as a human being, I read the passage which declares to us how the Lord finally rose up and seized the whip to drive out the usurers, the brood of serpents and vipers, from the Temple [tumultuous applause]! Today, however, two thousand years later, I am deeply moved to perceive that his tremendous struggle for this world against the Jewish poison was most profoundly marked by the fact that he had to bleed on the cross for it [stirrings in the hall]. Two thousand years ago a man was also denounced by the same race. The man was dragged before the court and it was also said of him, 'He stirred up the people.' So he too had been a rabble-rouser! And against whom? 'Against God!' they cried. Yes, indeed, he roused the rabble against the 'God' of the Jews, for this 'God' is only gold [tumultuous applause].

This sense of H as our national saviour was so strong among his followers that the questioning of it seemed like a blasphemy, and not merely among his more fanatical followers like Winnie or Lieselotte. The dark chords played by Geli's suicide were intensely shocking to those, such as myself, who placed a hope in the National Socialist movement as (I imagined) a short sharp shock of realism injected into our national life before we could get 'back to normal'. We saw him as wielding a whip, but as one which needed to be wielded before the temple was cleansed; and Geli's death, which was not merely tragic but sordid – as though for a moment in one of Bach's chorales the orchestra had suddenly played one of the more discordant and atonal psychological disturbances from Alban Berg. A corner of the veil had been lifted, but I for one did not wish to consider its implications.

It was about two years after her death that my parents and I went to the dull suburb of Berlin where my brother Heinrich was to serve as a curate in a middle-class parish. As before in this narrative, I cannot remember precise dates, but I know he was sailing near the wind. I cannot actually remember whether he was ordained before or after the National Socialists came to power, but this event must have seemed like an inevitability. Perhaps already the first of the anti-Judaic legislation had come into effect, or perhaps he was merely commenting upon this part of their programme as a coming inevitability. In either event, I so clearly remember that large, rather soulless church, so unlike the beautiful baroque building in which my father preached his weekly sermons. In his black robe and with his white neckbands, my brother looked much younger than his thirty-five years, like a child dressed up as a clergyman rather than an authoritative figure in the pulpit. For the first few sentences of his sermon, indeed, I wondered whether he would ever be able to raise his voice to an audible pitch. He was nervous, and his hands shook as he placed them on the pulpit and read the words he had prepared.

'My dear friends, I think today of Martin Luther, and his words, which are now so often quoted in political circles: "I was born for my beloved Germans: it is them I want to serve".' Unnecessarily (but how typical of Heinrich, as it would have been of my father also) he repeated the words in their original Latin, a tongue I could be quite sure was incomprehensible to the wives of businessmen, the doctors and dentists and accountants and shopkeepers who made up this prosperous congregation: '"*Germanis meis natus sum, quibus et serviam.*" And so it is for any minister of the Gospel, at this time or any time. And how can a minister of Christ's Gospel serve the German people at this time? Only by telling them the truth. Luther's words, Christ's words, any good words, have been appropriated in our day by the political propagandists and they have thereby deprived the everlasting challenge of the Gospel with a piece of empty flim-flam.'

Heinrich was no orator. His words might have been strong, but his voice was not. He always had a somewhat reedy voice, intellectual and gentle, and not at all suited to speaking to a large audience. This gave the words considerable power. 'Let me tell you, my friends, of a vision I had. I came into this church.' With a shaky hand the smooth-cheeked Heinrich gestured around at the white-plastered walls. It was a building of the mid nineteenth century, with box pews, a lumpy pulpit, in which he stood, but with very little adornment. The only conspicuous religious decoration, as I recall, was an oil painting of Christ on the Cross, which hung on one of the side walls. 'In my vision, dear friends, I was not standing here in the pulpit. I was standing at the back. The church in my vision is as full as it is today, of devout worshippers. There was another figure, not myself, in the pulpit, wearing a brown shirt. And he was declaiming, "Non-Aryans are requested to leave the church." Nothing happened, so the words were repeated, this time in a louder voice: "Non-Aryans are requested to leave the church immediately." Again, nothing happened. So the figure in the pulpit speaks yet more loudly: "I repeat: Non-Aryans are to leave the church." And at the third time of asking, my friends, Jesus Christ came down from that great golden frame' – here my brother pointed to the picture – 'and left us alone. He left us without him. I was born for my beloved Germans; it is them I want to serve. Those of us who have been given the responsibility of preaching the Gospel at this crisis in our national destiny can only tell the truth. My friends, National Socialism is not just another political doctrine, to be set against Communism or Social Democracy or Conservatism, beliefs which any rational person might argue about or entertain. It is a plague, a mental plague. It means lies, hatred, fratricide and unbounded misery. Its leader teaches the law of lies. And I must warn you, as your pastor, those of you who have fallen a victim to the deceptions of those lies – wake up!'

After Geli's suicide – shortly after, though I could not say how soon – the Mercedes pulled up at Wahnfried. Julius Schreck was not at the wheel. I do not know what happened to him. The figure who emerged from the back of the car was at first scarcely recognizable as 'Uncle Wolf'. He was dressed, as of old, in a dark-blue suit, with a white shirt and a dark tie – I think a black tie. Yes, I am sure he was in semi-mourning. He carried a trench-mackintosh over his arm, and he was wearing a trilby hat. His shoulders were now hunched and I was reminded of the depleted, shy being whom I had first encountered, eight years earlier, in the dining room of the Golden

Anchor Hotel, the man whose expression, when Winnie came bounding up to him, had reminded me of a child who had been awaiting its mother to fetch it from school. Before that meeting he had been crushed, entirely alone and strangely insignificant.

He almost dragged himself to the door of the house. His shoulders were slumped, his face was drained of colour and his eyes were red. They forwent the formalities of little bows and hand-kissing. Winnie was there at the porch, though his visit had not been announced, and she flung her arms round him, enfolding him in a great hug.

By the time the tea had been brought in, someone had been sent out to buy some of the confections he most enjoyed. There was a cherry-and-cream sponge concoction of peculiar ingenuity which our favourite baker in town, who curiously enough was called Fräulein Göring (though no relation, as far as I am aware) had made her *pièce de résistance*. Wolf normally brightened at the sight of these magnificent creations of Fräulein Göring's. The cream cupolas and multi-layers of different pinks and whites, interlaced with delicate eggy sponge, were in their way as ingenious as the rococo plasterwork in the churches and monasteries with which the Asam brothers, themselves originally pastry cooks, adorned Munich and its environs.

It was the first time any of us ever saw Wolf survey one of these cherry cakes of Fräulein Göring without at once setting to with his fork. He was slumped and utterly wretched. The unthinkable, about this all-but-teetotaller, crossed my mind: that he might be the worse for drink. Naturally, I soon dismissed such a thought and realized he was merely in the grip of a profound depression.

'Oh, Winnie, this is bad . . . bad.'

'Try to eat, Wolf.'

'That child . . .'

Winnie's own children burst in at that moment. Verena had a drawing she wanted to give to Uncle Wolf and the boys had some boring magazine with pictures of motor cars of which they were imagining themselves the owners. In normal circumstances Wolf would have cast aside any of his own conversational needs and given himself wholeheartedly to the children. True, he did take the drawing from Verena and say, 'Oh, I say. What have we here? Clouds!'

'They're sheep,' she said, her own crestfallen expression matching his misery.

The boys, however, hung back and Friedelind said, 'Uncle Wolf wants to be alone with Mum.' I thought this remark was addressed to me as well as to her brothers, but, if Lieselotte was sitting out Wolf's visit, I saw no reason why I should leave until I was actually dismissed from the room.

'Winnie – I think the game is up.'

'What do you mean?'

As it happened, Wolf's visit occurred at one of those many moments in Winnie's life when she was really too busy to be able to concentrate. There was a children crisis, there was an opera crisis and there was a Tietjen crisis. They were all, in a way, related. Tietjen's enemies, of whom there were many, were trying to persuade Winnie that she had made a mistake in hiring him as artistic director and that the unprecedented success of the 1931 Festival – a financial as well as a critical triumph – was all illusory. The local right-wing papers denounced her for harbouring a Socialist in her bosom and the left-wing papers denounced her for being a Nazi. The sisters-in-law were up in arms about Tietjen's proposed reforms of any future stagings of the music dramas.

Meanwhile the children were showing all the signs of emotionally intelligent beings undergoing the grieving process. Anyone could see that their persistent 'bad behaviour' was an attempt to draw attention to themselves. The English boarding school had said they refused to have them back and various attempts to engage tutors had come unstuck when the children had, as only they knew how, put these unfortunates through their paces.

Most disturbing of all was the violence, literal violence, which had developed in the relationship between Winnie and Friedelind. The child, who always had a tendency towards plumpness, had become obese in the year since her father died and this was an ingredient, one felt, in the real hatred her mother appeared to feel for her. Winnie and Tietjen spoke openly about Friedelind, in front of the girl, as a problem.

'Look at its wobbling thighs, I mean, Winnie, you've got to do something.'

'What do you suggest – starvation?' Winnie laughed.

Friedelind, desperately missing both her actual father and her father-substitute, Toscanini, developed a carapace of indifference, laughing off any of the gibes, insults, calls to order Tietjen tried to throw at her and being as openly insolent to him as he was horrible to her. It shocked me that Winnie allowed him to behave like this to her own children and that she was seemingly so indifferent to what they must be going through in the year after their father's death. But that was Winnie. I have never said she was a perfect being.

And here was Wolf, with his burdens, which he was attempting to lay at her feet. Another needy child.

Although I saw more of him, close up and face to face, than many human beings did, the psychology of Wolf, a subject which could be said to dominate the entire history of the twentieth century, was no more easily understood by me than by anyone else. Yet it is noticeable that before each of his strides towards a new stage of his violent life journey there was a sinking back, a near collapse. Geli's death was evidently a tremendous grief to him; it was also very nearly a political disaster. Yet in the peculiar rhythm of his life it was perhaps a necessary preliminary to the next stage of extraordinary fortune. He plummeted, then he rose. In hospital, blinded by mustard gas at the end of the war, H had made a decent recovery and his sight was restored; but then, the red flag had been hoisted over the Chancellery in Berlin, the Kaiser had gone into exile and the November Criminals had sold Germany to France, disbanded the army that had marched so triumphantly in 1870 and 1914, and undermined everything H had hoped for. He went blind again. Professor Edmund Forster of the Berlin Neurological Clinic diagnosed a case of hysteria. There was no physical cause for the blindness, and none for the peculiar and sudden recovery when his sight came back and he was able to feast on the extraordinary narcotic of public speaking that gave him strength. Then again, four years later, there was the extraordinary setback of the beerhall putsch in Munich, its abject failure and H's imprisonment. His political hopes plummeted to nothing and he sank into a deep depression. Once again, words, spoken words proceeding from his own mouth, lifted the cloud. Although Winnie was always proud to boast that he wrote *Mein Kampf* with pencils and pens supplied by herself on paper ditto, the book was in fact dictated to the faithful Hess who might, or might not, have used the paper from the Wahnfried stationery cupboard which, together with the Swiss chocolates and other luxury items, were regularly transmitted.

Now, after Geli's bloody death, another of these troughs had been descended. 'It's all over, Winnie. It's all over.'

The cream cakes remained untasted – by Wolf, that is. Friedelind made short work of them as soon as they had been cleared from the room.

When he said 'It's all over', he was shaking as he spoke, not shaking as he did when addressing a public meeting, when the veins on his face stood out, when his hands made their irresistible hieratic clawings in the air, when his whole body carried his hearers with its gyrations and choreographed gestures of hope or violence. He was shaking like the down-and-out in a doorway he had once been on the streets of Vienna.

It was during this visit, which lasted a few days, that I had one of the few personal conversations I ever had with him. As a shy, youthful backroom boy, I did not expect visitors to Wahnfried to take any notice of me and it certainly was never part of my ambition to be a member of H's entourage. So it was: I never knew for certain whether, from one occasion to the next, he even remembered having met me before. It was during this depressed, quiet, depleted visit that he found himself alone with me. He spoke as if we had often had conversations; also as if it would be perfectly obvious to me that he remembered my working as a waiter at the Anchor, and his strange moment of discomfiture having addressed a meeting at the Riding Hall in the summer of 1923. 'Those hotels! You know, you are a middle-class boy, eh?'

'I suppose you could say that.'

'Oh, come on! Your father is a pastor.'

I had never told him this. He had 'clocked' me. This was both highly flattering and slightly disconcerting.

'Your father is an old conservative Lutheran pastor who doesn't much like the cut of the National Socialist jib. Your brother in Berlin is a bit more of a firebrand, thinks we all come from the devil. And you – you'll do. You see the point. But even though you see the point, you are a middle-class boy. You got a job as a waiter as a bit of a lark – OK, we all need money, God knows everyone in Germany needs money. But you've never gone to bed hungry – with an empty belly that wasn't fed today and wasn't fed yesterday. You've always slept in sheets. You've always had a maidservant, someone to cook your meals, someone to serve you, huh?'

This was indeed the case.

'You know what I feel when I go into one of those posh hotels in Munich? Or here in Bayreuth, when I see the rich people coming out of the Golden Anchor – I see the Tsar of Bulgaria or Herr Furtwängler and his yid-assistant, and Thomas Mann and Sir Thomas Beecham and all of them, yes, even Frau Bechstein . . . I remember . . . I remember going up the steps of the Excelsior Hotel . . . They had given us brooms.' He was speaking as if he were in a trance. The very first time I ever met him, at the Golden Anchor that night, I had seen a little of this side to his personality. It was not Uncle Wolf, the confident, jolly family friend; still less was it the Leader appointed by providence to save our nation. It was an outsider of outsiders, awkward, fearful, even, with his highly polished shoes and blue suit, slightly deferential towards the society which had chucked him out '. . . to sweep away the snow . . .'

Who had given 'them' brooms? I did not ask, though subsequently I came to think this must have been some pathetic work scheme devised by those who ran one of the bums' hostels in Vienna where he had lived in the years of his greatest destitution.

'We were to sweep the steps of the hotel, sweep the snow, so that the guests would not get so much as a drop of moisture on their golden evening slippers and their patent-leather dancing shoes. And we could feel the cold damp coming through the holes in our boots. It was like being at the Western Front all over again ... And one night, as I swept there and stared up at the golden doors, there emerged from the hotel a boy with whom I had been at the Realschule in Linz. He was with his parents and one of his sisters. She was very grand, the sister. She was once painted by Klimt, a bloody decadent painter in my opinion. Klimt! All he was for was to paint yids, splashing on Jew-gold in the background and making their Jew-faces beautiful ... He was a Jew, my school friend. I say friend – he hardly ever spoke to any of us. Too lofty. Too sneering. Yet there was something about that kid, that Ludwig. You know, I liked him. I liked his seriousness. And for a few seconds I thought, all I have to do is to run up to the Wittgensteins and say, "Look, it's me! I was at school with Ludwig and then (like him) I fought in the war, and look where it has got me – help, please help!" I think they would have helped, actually. I am sure they would have done ... But I was ashamed. There was I with patched, ragged trousers and a pair of boots that leaked, and there was Ludwig Wittgenstein in a white tie and a swallow-tail coat. Coming out of the grandest hotel in Vienna. So I swept the snow from under their feet and his father tipped me – he gave me a few thalers. I looked at Ludwig's face but I could not tell whether he recognized me or not.'

I was on the verge of interrupting him and asking him whether he had ever read any of his friend's subsequent writings. After a pause, however, he provided a sort of answer to this question. 'Funny man, Ludwig Wittgenstein ... wanted to become an aeronautical engineer. Went to Manchester in England, like a lot of yids do. My sister knew England. Manchester is the yid capital. But!'

For the first time in this monologue he sat up straight. His shoulders had been sunk in self-pity as he recollected sweeping the snow from the Vienna hotel steps to allow the Wittgensteins to pass. Suddenly, however, it all became a new thing. His glistening countenance was lit up with a merry triumph. 'Do you know what happened to him? I heard about him from someone. Like so many of us after the war, he tried a little of this and a little of that; rudderless, directionless, purposeless man. Nothing, of course, came of his ambitions. He did not have the application to become an aeronautical engineer. I could have done it myself, actually. I have the strongest possible views on aircraft construction. But him! Do you know what he is reduced to doing? The rich man of Vienna's Jewson? He is a village schoolmaster somewhere in the Swiss Alps.' Wolf nodded when he had imparted this information and it slightly seemed as if it was no more than Wittgenstein deserved, having walked down some steps in the snow when H was standing there with a broom.

It was not, however, the telling of this story that lifted Wolf out of that terrible depression. Winnie's hands and Winnie's hands alone could lead him from that slough of despond. In the intervals when she was busy he would sit around moping. The children were not at this stage about – it was the last phase of Winnie's attempts to make them stay at boarding schools. Sometimes she sent Wolf out with his sketchbook and he would return with uninspired though reasonably accurate depictions of the buildings within a stone's throw of the house. One of them was a postcard-sized watercolour of the orphanage just opposite the New Palace. Another is of the back of Wahnfried from the Hofgarten. There is one of the twin towers of the Stadtkirche and so on.

For much of the time, and I was slow to notice this, Winnie and Wolf were alone together. They were discreet about it, but there could not be any doubt that this was the week, some time in the October of 1931, that the relationship changed. I had been exercising the dogs, not my favourite task, in the Hofgarten one afternoon when, before opening the garden gate near the graves, I saw the pair of them, standing beside one another. There was an angle to Winnie's gait, a freedom with which she stood close to him, which told me everything. I am not sure that they even noticed me, from afar, but I decided to take the pooches for an extra five-hundred-yards walk in the park before coming home. I had not needed to find them *in flagrante*. If lovers wish to keep secret the fact that they have crossed the border and actually begun to sleep together, they should avoid being seen together, especially in those first few days and weeks. Otherwise, they might as well go round with placards round their necks saying 'WE HAVE JUST BEEN TO BED TOGETHER'; for it is always obvious. I have to say that, after all my self-protective jokes – about the flatulence and so on – I was amazed. I had come to believe in my own propaganda. I had imagined he would be Uncle Wolf for ever and nothing more.

He stayed in the house for a few days longer and I decided to make myself scarce. Where possible, I worked in Siegfried's old office at the Festival Theatre and tried not to disturb the lovebirds. When he had gone back to Munich, I think it was said . . . I knew that everything had changed.

'Oh yes,' Winnie told Lieselotte with a confident smile. 'His enemies might have thought he was finished. But now Our Leader is like a giant refreshed. He will ride on now, to redeem our fatherland.'

Mastersingers

I am sure I shouldn't be writing this, but something compels my pen. And you shouldn't be reading this; these pages contain a story that should be left untold. The burden is too great for you to carry – and for your children and children's children. I should go silent to the grave. Although I am not old by modern standards, I know that in this pig of a town where the only consolation is to smoke, my emphysema and bronchitis will take me off soon. Whereas you . . . you will have to live with all this – if you read this book. Of course it was essential that your mother had no inkling whatsoever. Sometimes she taunted me for my sycophantic crush on Winnie. But what am I saying? I should be saying: sometimes my wife taunted me for my crush on your mother. Sometimes she said she hated the whole pack of the Wagners, but this wasn't true. However low her opinion of me sank, my wife, your mother, as we always called her, retained a huge admiration for the Wagner boys, and for Friedelind, as opera directors, and for Winnie. But my wife is dead now and we need not worry about what that unhappy woman thinks of me any more. The funny thing is she just accepted your arrival as one of Winnie's mad ideas. Winnie adopted another little girl for a few years, a child she had met in the hospital. Wieland was ill – an inflammation of the lungs – and at the small private hospital, Winnie also met this child, a three-year-old called Betty Steinlein, who was covered with the most unsightly skin disease. The family had a little smallholding just outside town. It was obvious they could not cope with the expense and distress of looking after this little toddler. Winnie simply had the girl to live with them – she was still living at Wahnfried, that child, when I went off to war. The place was alive with 'Winnie's lame ducks', as Fidi always

165

used to call them, sad students, children, friends of her own children. She was one of nature's mothers.

So when Helga, your 'mother', was told that we would be adopting a child from the orphanage as soon as we had been married, she accepted it – simply accepted it. So did I. Only I suspected the truth. It would have been impossible to 'confront' Winnie with my knowledge. You do not 'confront' the Welsh. But she knew I knew and I know she chose us. It was a great position of trust. And the reason she chose us, my darling, was not that we were respectable or anything like that (though we were); it was because she had seen my capacity to love. She knew that I would love you, as I have done. And now we approach our leave-taking . . . because I am going to smoke one cig too many one of these days and we hardly ever see one another anyway. I will die in this dump of a town, and you will have a successful career as a musician, who knows, in the West? And I want to do the cruellest thing in the world; I want to tell you the truth.

But ———, what can I call you? I dare not write down your name. If the Stasi were to find what I have written so far, it would be compromizing enough, I know – compromizing to me. But at least I have left you largely out of the narrative. But you are there, a small tadpole in Winnie's womb. I shall continue to say 'Winnie', rather than 'your mother'. The latter phrase, between us, will always denote the sad, cross person with whom we shared this flat until she applied for a divorce and successfully moved to Leipzig, and then died.

Which is where, of course, the scene now takes us. Oh, darling girl, I shall not bring you into this book by name, but since you are always in my thoughts, I cannot entirely keep you out of the pages of this story. For, in a way, you *are* the story. Yes, I know there is the damage done to our poor country by . . . by . . . by Wolf, by everything that happened. There is the sad story of my own family, and I shall wish to lay a wreath beside the noble memory of my father, mother and brother before I have finished writing these pages. But at the time of writing, you are twenty-eight years old. I entirely support your desire to leave for the West. I do not want to stymie that in any way. And yet – you do see this, don't you, my darling – although it would be better for you *not* to know, you do *need* to know?

I watched you growing as an infant and I thought to myself, this is going to be so blindingly obvious to everyone. The eyes. Even as a baby you had the eyes. The rest – your thick, wavy golden hair, your long face, your long hands – they all came from your mother. But how could anyone look into your night-sky, hypnotic, all-but-world-conquering eyes and not see what is looking back at them so clearly?

They looked at me the other day some months ago, through those earnest, Marxist-made steel-rimmed spectacles, and your lips, which are the lips of Winnie, said, in the voice that is very much your own, '*Vati*, I so very much want you to come to this *Meistersinger*.'

You know what has happened in my life. It isn't that I had made a self-conscious decision to give up attending the operas of Richard Wagner. You might as well say that the inhabitants of your local town gaol had decided to lay off the pâté de foie gras. I do not know what productions are on at what passes for a theatre in this 'town' – some dreary renditions of Bertolt Brecht whenever I see the posters flapping about in the fog. The only music worth hearing is at church, which I attend for that reason *and for that reason alone*. You believe – you seem to have believed since childhood – my church attendance loses me points with the comrades, but I know that I am already deep into minus points. My pupils at school complain about me for teaching the lyrics of Heine and Hölderlin rather than ploughing through the idiotic socialist-realist tales that are our set texts. My wife always attributed the absolute, the particular, lousiness of my job, my flat, everything, to the fact that I had hung out before the war with Nazis; and I attributed it to the fact that she hadn't been a good Communist, and for once in our marital strifes I think you could probably say that we were *both* right.

Anyway, it wasn't surprising that you became a musician like

167

Helga; and there you are, playing in the orchestra at the Leipzig Opera House, and telling me about this fantastic new production of *Die Meistersinger von Nürnberg*.

I have been bad at keeping records, bad at dating, and I find this gives me a confused impression of the past. Here perhaps I can make a late start and say that we are now in 1960 and the production in which you played was staged in June 1960, with Joachim Herz as the young director. (I reckon Herz is – what? – about six or seven years older than you? He's in his mid to late thirties.)

Before we set out for Leipzig we had an extraordinary conversation about Wagner and *Meistersinger*, and about the uses to which it had been put by 'my friends' in the 1930s. But not, of course, by the Wagner family. The extraordinarily paradoxical consequence of the friendship between Winnie and Wolf was that the Bayreuth Festival Theatre was almost the one area of artistic freedom left in Germany after H became Chancellor.

'What Herz was faced with,' you told me, 'was the perception of *Meistersinger* as a Nazi work. Nuremberg was the Nazi town, it was in Nuremberg that they held their rallies, it was in Nuremberg that they had their come-uppance in the trials. And here is this opera, set in the bloody place, with honest old Hans Sachs the German cobbler coming on at the end and saying, Forget the glories of the old Roman Empire, forget European art – stick to German art and German thought and German everything and you will be saved. It is practically Nazi, yet how was Herz to make out of this glorious music something that could be of relevance to us today in the East with our very different Germany and our . . .'

'But hang on. Stop! You don't think you've just given a fair summary of what *Meistersinger* is about? You know something? When all this nationalist nonsense was beginning, and Fidi and Winnie Wagner had just been round the USA raising money to revive the Festival, they opened again in 1925 and one of the operas they opened with was *Mestersinger*. After Hans Sachs's song, you know, "*zerging in Dunst / das Heil'ge Röm'sche Reich, / uns bliebe gleich / die heil'ge deutsche Kunst!*", the audience started singing

"Deutschland, Deutschland über Alles". So for all subsequent performances Fidi had leaflets put on every seat asking people *not* to sing, and he put up posters saying, "here we only support art".'

'That didn't stop people seeing the Mastersingers as Nazi-singers, did it?'

'It's so ridiculous, that. It's the supreme example of their genius, their absolute genius, the Nazis', for taking hold of something, adopting it as their own and making it say the precise opposite, the complete and precise opposite of what it actually says.'

'Well, that's what Herz thinks too. That's what he's going to do in this new *Meistersinger* in Leipzig, which is why, Dad, you've got to get on a train with me and come and see it.'

'I mean, here he is – Richard Wagner. It is the expression, really, of his whole credo; and OK, that credo kept changing, he was an intelligent man. The human mind doesn't stand still.'

'Try telling that to Ulbricht!'

'But there are shifts we make that are true reversals – we start believing in God, we end up as atheists; we start as Communists, we turn into high Catholic monarchists. Actually those sorts of conversions are rare, and even in those cases, when you examine them, you find that the minds in question are, as it were, in love with the same ideas, but seeing them from different angles. Wagner wasn't that sort of a mind anyway. He wasn't an analytical intelligence – he thought with his heart, as Tolstoy said of some other thinker. And all his life I think he was trying to work out why he was being led further and further into music itself. Not music as propaganda. Not music as an accompaniment for someone else's pretty words. Music. And it had begun during his theatrical boyhood when no one could have predicted what lay ahead for him – a life in the theatre, obviously, like his sisters, his mum, his stepfather. He was born with the smell of greasepaint. But you'd have expected something much blowzier, much more rough and tumble – until the conversion – when he heard Beethoven's Ninth Symphony as a boy, and transcribed it not once but six times, and became possessed by the knowledge that whatever it was he wanted to say, it was going to be in music. I think Richard Wagner's life is as simple as that in some ways, and all the talk I've heard in my lifetime about whether he was a radical, or a Marxist, or a Nazi, or a this or a that – it's so much balls. But when he wrote the sketch for *Meistersinger* in 1845, without the last speech of Hans Sachs, of course, it was just a latent idea. There had been the singing competition in *Tannhäuser*, and this was a sort of comic afterthought. He'd invent the . . .'

'Yes, Dad.'

You were smiling at me. It was one of those conversations we used to have when you were a little girl and you would interrupt me by saying, 'Daddy! *You're telling me things.*'

Remember the letter Cosima – Wagner's second wife, aged twenty-nine – wrote to King Ludwig II (aged twenty-one) about the ending of *Meistersinger*? Whereas the composer thought 'The drama is actually over with Walther's poem and that Sachs's great speech is irrelevant – it was the poet's address to the audience and he was thinking of omitting it – I argued the opposite. I pulled such a pitiful face that Wagner got no rest all night. He wrote the strophe out, deleted what I had indicated and sketched the music to it in pencil' (January 1867).

He did not do so because he feared the lines would be interpreted as ultranationalist. He just didn't think they were necessary in the opera. But insofar as they do correspond to anything he felt, either when he wrote them just after the failed revolution in 1848, or nearly twenty years later when he was orchestrating the completed *Meistersinger* poem, it is quite clear what Richard Wagner thought.

We Germans – what have we got to give the rest of the world? Napoleonic-style world domination? No – we are a collection of kingdoms and duchies and states, and our revolutionary idea of becoming one people of free-thinking republicans in 1848 is a dream, it's never going to happen. So let's forget our political ambitions and our military ambitions, and continue to be proud of what we are good at, always have been good at: music, art, philosophy. That is what Wagner thought. OK, like any man getting on in years, he became more 'reactionary'; OK, in 1870 he cheered when his own country won a war – who wouldn't? – and he was momentarily excited by the creation of a German state. But he never supported a political party and he was fundamentally anti-Bismarck. He was no more 'political' than any great man or woman has ever been – Goethe, Tolstoy, Dante. Dante learnt to hate the political party to whose membership he owed his life of heartbroken exile. Rough-hewn cobbler-poet Sachs sings that though the Holy Roman Empire – that is the military and political might of old Germany from Charlemagne down to the seventeenth century – fades into mist, German art will always be supreme. It may be a bit childish, this sentiment, and maybe that's why Wagner wasn't keen on putting it into the finalized version of *Meistersinger*. But the notion that it was a political manifesto . . . !

He was in mourning while he finished the composition of *Meistersinger*, in 1866. Two deaths. Pohl – a pointer – had died at the villa just outside Geneva, where Wagner was then living, Les Artichauts. He was absent when the poor creature died. Cosima, not yet his domestic companion, though she had become his lover, suggested he 'get away from it all' and go to . . . Lyon, of all god-forsaken places. 'These childish monstrous cities like a thousand-voice Italian opera unison! Not a sign of life!' It had been impossible to work there, and he had been preparing himself to leave his lodgings and return to Geneva when on the evening of 25 January 1866 he received a telegram from his friend and doctor in Dresden, Anton Pusinelli: 'Your wife died last night.'

Minna! Minna gone! Minna, with whom he had endured such humiliating struggles, and quarrels and journeys; such midnight flits from cheap hotels where they couldn't afford the rent; such terrible pointless rows in awful bare rented rooms; such bad sex, such resent-ment, such hate and yet . . . You can't be married to someone and not at some residual level love them more deeply than any friend or family or hero. You've been through so much. (That's certainly true of me and Helga, though you, who had the bad luck to see our quarrels, would find this hard to believe.)

When he heard the news he did not think of Minna alone, drunken and ill, so ill as now to be dead, in Dresden. He had not seen that Minna in . . . what? Four years nearly. Poor Minna. His consciousness filled with the years of implacable struggle in Paris.

That horrible little flat in the rue du Helder, and someone in the room next door, practising Liszt's Fantasy on *Lucia di Lammermoor* over and over and over again until they were both driven mad. It was the autumn of 1840. He was twenty-seven, she was thirty-one. They were days of great pain, but it was before the worst days, the days of their estrangement. Still recovering from her miscarriage, Minna was gauntly beautiful and in her chaotic way protective of him. He remembered huddling in smelly blankets, as they both drank from a bottle of spirits she had bought down the road, and the insults they shouted at the piano player next door until anger and despair turned to laughter.

He remembered, of course, Robber. Oh, how they'd both loved that dog, Robber. The gigantic Newfoundland which had come with them on their flight from Riga, shared the terrifying sea voyage which inspired *The Flying Dutchman* and come to London with them. Robber had endured such adventures. Wagner could remember himself and Minna arriving in a pathetically dingy lodging house in Soho – Dean Street. The luggage had been deposited by a surly cabbie, who had hovered, expecting a tip. Minna had turned to him with uplifted hands – 'What do you think I'm made of? Money?' People! The way they expected you to pay them for everything. She had always been very good at that, Minna – seeing off the brutes who expected payment. She'd got them into that three-wheeler – Richard, herself, the dog, the portmanteaux and cases. She'd shrilly insisted in three languages that they be taken to the centre, the centre. 'Whazzat? So-oh, yer min?' 'Ja, ja, Soho will do us well!' And so there they were, and after she had given him an earful instead of payment he had gone off, the menace, deciding as the weak usually did that you couldn't force payment if people hadn't got it. And she'd negotiated herself into the lodging house. And they'd stared at the English room – perhaps the nastiest yet in their whole downward spiral of humiliation – a room whose spirit memories would drown with sorrow if taped, for it was here, eight years later, that Karl and Jenny Marx would fetch up with their sick, only too mortal brood of children – and Richard and Minna Wagner had looked at the large blue-black patches of damp staining the wallpaper, the yellowing pillowcases where a hundred greasy heads had lain before them, the rags representing blankets on the beds, the hole-torn dusty rugs on the dusty floor-boards – and suddenly both had cried out, 'Where's Robber?'

In all the theatre of seeing off the cabbie, by a display of shouting and asking if he had any idea how poor they were and what they had suffered, Minna had forgotten the dog, and Richard was cowering, in the way he did when one of their minor frauds or confidence tricks was in danger of exposure. He too had forgotten Robber, the faithful friend. Oh Christ! As Minna had thrown herself on the fetid, cold, unpleasantly damp bed and sobbed, and begun asking him whether he had ever done *anything* right, anything at all – was it not she who had negotiated the taxi, the rooms, *everything* – he had sadly and quietly stepped out into the alien British street and searched for the dog. Clever Robber had gone all the way up to Oxford Street when the cab halted. Several people whom Wagner stopped in the street had seen him there.

'Dog as big as an 'ouse!'

But Wagner, tear-stained, had returned to the lodgings in Dean Street without him, only to find, when he flung open the door, Robber and Minna sitting there. The dog, who had never visited these lodgings in his life, had, after circumnavigating Soho, found his way home.

When they lost him in Paris in a similar way they had dared to be optimistic. Surely Robber would find them, even if they had been too feckless to keep a watch-out for him. But that was one of the horrors of Paris for them both, Robber's absence. Wagner had worked hard in those Paris years. Meyerbeer, successful opera composer; Heinrich Heine, great lyric poet; all these German Jews, conveniently enjoying the liberties that Paris then afforded them and which, with its heavy censorship and its cultural narrowness, Germany did not afford. And yes, they'd helped Wagner – Heine had supplied the idea of *The Flying Dutchman*, Meyerbeer had helped get *Rienzi* looked at by some theatrical directors, but ultimately . . .

No need to go down that road, but it was the poverty of his circumstances, compared with theirs, which made him subsequently resent those Jewish friends in Paris. Meyerbeer, both he and Minna came to feel, had not been a friend. What crap the music was, in any case, the music of Meyerbeer, yet crowds of people queued in the cold to hear it at the Paris Opera. Unadulterated crap.

Sometimes he and Minna quarrelled, sometimes they made it up in the cold nakedness of rented rooms and – oh God, the remorse, he realized with twenty-year hindsight that she had been so frustrated by his jerky, clumsy lovemaking. She had tried to teach him and he was too eager, too busy to get finished himself to see what she was trying, often so playfully, to teach. He set the joys of sex to music while she got drunk and masturbated, that was their story. Oh, Minna, he knew that now. If there had been some way of explaining it to him, as a young man, what all that stuff in bed was *about, for* . . . why women care about it . . . ? And her lost baby, that came back into his consciousness as he sped in the train away from Lyon having heard the news of her death, twenty-five years and more after those Paris times.

Robber, that was what had bound them together, not the bad sex and the common poverty, but the love of Robber.

Wagner had been to see Meyerbeer – again. Ever since they'd conceived the idea of running away from their debts and problems in Riga, Minna and Richard had set unrealistic hopes on Meyerbeer's powers to save them. Wagner had sent the successful composer drafts of *Rienzi* and begged him to send letters of introduction, to give him an opening with the Paris opera house. Meyerbeer had supplied the letters, but when Wagner got to the opera he had had no luck. And the next time he saw Meyerbeer – God, how he hated being beholden to this talentless man – he had gently said that the letters had been of no effect. 'I'm not surprised!' Meyerbeer had laughed.

But he had, Meyerbeer, given him, Wagner, some help, rustling up singers who would perform a piece Wagner had written called *A Faust Prelude*. And on that particular evening Wagner had called on Meyerbeer to see if the singers really were available – and thank God, they were, and Heinrich Heine had been there too, sipping champagne. That was the evening he suggested to Wagner that he should make an opera of *The Flying Dutchman*.

Anyway, with his head full of these promising possibilities he had raced off to the cheap restaurant, where you could eat for one franc, and found Minna waiting at a table. It was a warm spring night and she was sitting out of doors on the pavement. As someone who was herself a woman of the theatre, and horribly aware of the ups and downs of the profession, Minna was still prepared, at this stage of their marriage, to follow every twist and turn and up and down of Wagner's (at that date non-existent) career. And here he was, on the verge at last of getting something performed, and she looked up and said, 'Oh my dear!' With sympathy, because the despair on his face seemed to speak of such utter bereavement and sorrow. 'Damn Meyerbeer!' she had added.

'No, no,' he said. 'Meyerbeer has got the singers, they are going to do a performance of *Eine Faust Ouvertüre*, but you see . . .'

'But darling, that's wonderful!'

But as she rose to kiss him he burst into tears. 'Minna – by the Quai du Pont Neuf – I've just met Robber.'

'How do you mean?'

'I met Robber.'

'But why isn't he with you? What happened? Has someone stolen him?'

'I was walking across the bridge, you know, and I was about to turn right into the Quai du Pont Neuf . . .'

'You mean, where he has his bath – or used to?'

'Precisely.'

When they had first come to Paris, Wagner and Minna had walked with Robber to a particular spot on the Quai du Pont Neuf each day and allowed him to wash himself and swim about in the river, which he loved to do. The spectacle of this enormous animal in the Seine drew such crowds that the police had cautioned them and said they were causing an obstruction.

'When I saw him there, just near where he used to bathe, I called out, "Robber! Robber, my old boy!"'

'Yes? And? What happened?'

'Oh, Minna! Oh, Minna! He turned and looked at me. It was a look of such strange reproach. We fed him, didn't we? When we had no money to feed ourselves, we somehow managed to get meat and bones for Robber? And when we had no love left in our hearts for one another we loved him.'

'Oh, God, Richard, what are you saying?' Minna was crying now.

'He looked at me. And as I went towards him, saying his name and reaching out my arms to embrace him, he . . .'

'He what?'

Wagner could not finish the sentence without sobbing it: 'He ran away.'

'But didn't you chase him?'

'Of course I ran after him, but he had gone, simply vanished, and I've been looking for him for an hour. He's gone, Minna, gone.'

That conversation of 1840 replayed itself in Wagner's head in 1867 while Minna's soul, released from its unsatisfiable bodily hungers, swooped joyously towards the empyrean.

Wagner wrote to Doctor Pusinelli in Dresden asking him to arrange the funeral. He would not go himself. An overwhelming tiredness had come upon him and he wanted, after the mistake of Lyon, to return to the routines of work which life at Les Artichauts allowed: days ordered by his housekeeper Vreneli with delicious meals, and soft bedclothes, and walks with dear old Pohl, the pointer.

They were both inspired pick-ups, Vreneli and Pohl. He had met Vreneli – she was called Verena Weidmann – when he had gone to an hotel in Lucerne to get some peace and finish orchestrating the third act of *Tristan und Isolde*. Vreneli was his kind of person; they had clicked immediately. There was a bit of flirtation, but it was nothing in the nature of a sexual relationship. She had seen in what ways he needed to be cosseted. He immediately liked her sensible-ness, humour, her not needing to be asked to do things because she had already thought of doing them. She was uneducated, had no particular interest in opera or music; she was a peasant. She was a chambermaid at the hotel and, when he checked out, he sensibly took her with him. And she remained with him, supervizing the move of Cosima (when she became part of the story) and the chil-dren into the new-built house at Bayreuth.

Pohl was another fistful from the lucky dip. He was a fairly old pointer. Wagner and he would only spend three years together. It was when he went to live for a while at Haus Pellet on the shores of Lake Tarnberg, fifteen miles south of Munich in 1864. Pohl, this slightly lame old dog, was somehow around and made friends with Wagner almost immediately. By the time he'd left Munich to go back to Switzerland, it was unthinkable that he should leave Pohl behind. And now, travelling back to Geneva from yet another little exile, the mistake of Lyon, he looked forward to being greeted by Pohl's large dark eyes on either side of that thin, mournful face and, putting his face down to the dog's, feeling himself licked. That would be his greeting as he came into the hall of the Villa Artichauts, and it would soothe all his worries, and all the gnawing sadness and remorse for the past years with Minna that were gone and never would return.

But, oh, as he came into the drive and Vreneli opened the front door, he knew there was something wrong.

'Oh, Master! Herr Wagner!'

For a split second he allowed himself to hope. The hope was a quite specific one: that Vreneli had heard of Minna's death and (in spite of all she knew about Cosima and his other amours) she was offering the conventional condolences on the death of his wife. But it was vain to hope this. How could Vreneli, who had never met his wife, possibly know that she had died, far away in Dresden? He had only just heard the news himself, from Dr Pusinelli. No, it was obvious enough that a real tragedy had occurred.

He went at once to the point: 'Is it Pohl? Has he hurt himself?'

'Oh, sir!'

As the stab wound entered his heart, another part of him, the part of the artist's soul which will exploit any experience and any situation, thought – that is so eloquent. All you need to show that a death has occurred is, not to use words, but for the woman to lift her apron, and stuff one corner into her mouth and pucker her eyes and mouth. That says so much and the music can say the rest.

It was not Vreneli's fault, it was the landlord's, the owner of the house, that the decision had been made, in Wagner's absence, to bury poor old Pohl in the vegetable garden of Les Artichauts. Wagner at once set to work, getting the gardeners to disinter the corpse, which he wrapped in the dog's favourite carpet and enclosed in a wooden coffin. On the lid was a marble tablet, which he got the local stonemason to inscribe 'To his Pohl, RW'. The animal was reinterred in a more dignified setting, beneath a tree near the house.

They were bleak days that followed, and he was not sure, as he struggled with *Meistersinger*, which simply had to be completed, whether the sorrow that weighed on his heart was for the old days with Minna or the much more recent ones with Pohl. He felt it was Pohl he missed. He had loved the animal's way of nuzzling. That long nose came at your trouser-legs, or at your face, warmly expressing love. Or, walking along, Pohl would press his lame old haunches against Richard's legs in a companionable equivalent of a hug before lolloping a few independent yards away from his friend. Dear old Pohl.

Vreneli, who noticed everything, tiptoed round Richard Wagner's grief. She supplied him with favourite dishes: a fricassee of turbot, with shallots and truffles and cream; vast amounts of sausage; poulet au riz; a spectacular stew she used to make, out of oxtails, which he liked eating with beer.

It somehow did not matter that the butchers, the greengrocers, the bakers, none of them had been paid. Sometimes they remonstrated with Vreneli and told her enough was enough. But somewhere inside her peasant heart-mind Vreneli was a Wagnerian and she knew that the phrase 'enough is enough' is a piece of nonsense. The road of excess leads to the palace of wisdom.

She did not mind, either, that it was weeks since she herself had been paid. She had a bit of money put by. Savings. She knew how to salve his wounds. She knew that until they were salved, the work he was doing would not get done, and that if it did not get done he would be nothing more than what people saw – and what his enemies for ever would caricature and revile – a small, rather ugly, passionate man of wolfish appetites, uncontrolled emotions, frequently silly opinions, a cheap sensualist, a con artist. Vreneli was aware of the mystery that out of this hyper-energetic little person there came forth something which was good for the world. He was that unusual man, the one who could speak to millions, both while he was alive and after he was dead, speak to their dreams, speak to their fears, make sense to them of their passions and of the convulsions that had and would rock their world. In the earlier bit of her Bible, much thumbed, which she kept in the kitchen – it was the old Luther version of course though she was a Zwinglian – there were two stories that came to mind. Samson's riddle about the lion – out of the strong came forth sweetness. And later, much later, the cleverer riddle of the Apostle: my strength is made perfect in weakness.

Richard Wagner was sitting in the Villa des Artichauts having drunk his morning chocolate and wondering where in the devil's name Vreneli had gone. Drat and curse and damn the woman, he needed her. He wanted a particular shirt ironed. He wanted to send her shopping. He needed something sent to the post . . . He sat with his head in his hands on a bench by the porch. He could not face going back into the house where he knew he should be at work on *Meistersinger* for the King. All the pleasure of being, for the first time in his life, in demand, in royal demand – of being in a position where his operas were going to be performed – all this pleasure had evaporated. The anxiety about his love affair with Cosima, previously an uplift to the spirits, was now a jangle in the nerves. The relief at hearing of Minna's death had turned to numbness, regret, not mourning, quite, but deep sadness; and there was a gnawing ache where Pohl, dear old Pohl, had been. That was it.

Women, and men: they had never given to him – though Vreneli tried – what it was that he so easily established with his canine friends. It was not just slavish devotion. It was the uncomplicatedness of the affection, the fact that, once established, it could not be taken away, which was so comforting. He and Pohl – dear old Pohl – they knew one another. There were no icebergs on the journey. No sudden swimmings into the cold, no moodishness. And there was Vreneli, coming round the corner of the house. Where in God's name and all heaven had she been? She was coming round the side of the house, from the coach house rather than walking up the small path at the front. So she had been into town without telling him? She and her husband Jakob had taken the brougham? Without being able to justify such anger, he felt it swelling up – as a compensatory variation on the gnawing sorrow within, which clogged the music inside his head.

'I hope you are going to be pleased,' she said. 'And there's no need to put on that angry expression.'

'There's a shirt I expressly promised myself to wear today. The cream silk one? But you weren't around . . .'

'Jakob' – the coachman – 'has someone he'd like you to meet.'

'I cannot meet anyone! How many times have I told you that I am trying to compose . . . that the King has . . .'

But there was Jakob, grinning like a zany, in his breeches and his green waistcoat and his open-necked uncollared shirt, leading forward, on a short rope . . . Robber? Robber had been gone for twenty-five years and more. He must be dead, but this was . . .

A Newfoundland puppy, thickly black-furred and already as large as a German Shepherd, was at Jakob's side. As happened with the best relationships, anyway the best dog relationships, eye contact was made absolutely immediately.

'Come – come . . . Let him off the rope, he'll come! Vreneli' – as if it were he who had brought the dog and she who had been neglecting her duties – 'have you got a steak for the animal?'

'I thought you'd like to give him his first meal here,' she said.

'Would you like that?' he asked his new friend. The huge wet eyes peered into his. From the jaws of Russ, as he would be known, fell a great skein of anticipatory spittle.

I did not know, as you of course did, that our journey to Leipzig was to be our last together and that we would never see one another again. Sometimes I have felt bitter about this; not angry with you, because I understand completely: you had to get away, from me, from this insane country, from the whole thing. You needed your own life. And, given the degree of surveillance by the Stasi, by the Passport Office, by absolutely bloody everyone, it was inevitable that you should have kept your decision completely under wraps. It is not that you would have feared that I would relay your decision to the police. It is that if you live in a police state, any passing on of information, any at all, is in danger of being intercepted. You needed to get out. The forthcoming tour of your orchestra in Stockholm gave you your chance to defect and you took it. I have no idea what happened to you after that, because not long after our visit to *Meistersinger* at the Leipzig Opera I was given a flat in a better part of town. It was no bigger, but the smell of the chemical works was four miles further away and the air was just a little clearer. You never knew that address, of course. I do not know if you tried to write. As you know, none of us living in these condominiums has ever had a telephone. There was no way you could have communicated with me, even if you had wanted to. At least I have been spared the knowledge of whether you did or did not want to be in touch. You went. It was the right decision.

The fact that we were going to the opera together, itself an unheard-of adventure, was perhaps enough to make me think of the railway journey as 'special'. Anyway, we spoke as we had never done, on that occasion. I do not know how it came about that you asked about my father. I had never told you about him and as the train rattled on I told you things that had never come up in conversation before.

I do not know why the three of us – you, me, Helga – living together for fifteen years, never spoke. After the war I never much spoke to my wife, nor she to me, nor she to you, nor you to me.

You could say that you had grown up, first in an orphanage in Nazi times, then with us in the war, then in a police state and that this did not encourage chatter. You could say that the silence which gelled around my wife and me like ice froze out openness. But maybe we just aren't an especially expressive family? I certainly had no idea what was going on inside my father, my mother, my brother throughout my teenage years, which was what made their behaviour, after the Nazi seizure of power, so completely extraordinary to me. I had thought (rightly) that they were quiet, even stuffy people, whose interests did not extend much beyond their books, their family, their music and a small circle of acquaintances. For years and years I had allowed all four of them – *Mutti*, *Vati* and my brothers, Heinrich and Ernst – to become caricatures inside my head. And because, arrogantly, I had followed some of the same paths intellectually, and then branched off in directions I considered more interesting, I assumed that they had merely reached the buffers. The idea that there was actually something going on behind the shutters of their quiet houses had not crossed my arrogant mind.

I derided my brother Heinrich's 'doubts' and I even more derided his overcoming them to become ordained as an evangelical (Lutheran) pastor. As for my father's Hegel-and-water position (as I conceived it), what could have been more ridiculous? I had once tried to explain to him why I had lost any faith in a personal God. And if there was no God, what was the point of pretending that there was any value in religion, or quasi-religious poses? Oh, yes, the fine eighteenth-century church where my father presided each Sunday, with its heraldic devices dotting the galleries, its painted ceilings, its pale-grey painted pews and its high windows, made a beautiful little concert hall for the endless rendition of Bach chorales.

But, but, but ... There was a man called Charles Darwin who demonstrated that we do not need to invent a 'Creator' to explain why there are natural forms on this earth. And without this unnecessary hypothesis, we need not tie up our minds in endless knots of absurdity, trying to puzzle out how the creator of a universe so full of pain, injustice, pointless suffering, could be a 'loving God'. It was all so much eyewash; why waste time on it? And the patient way in which my father had tried to say there was a 'universe of value' and certain 'principles' enshrined in the Christian tradition which 'either as individuals or as a society we threw away at our peril' – well, this was just flannel.

My poor mother! At the time I patronizingly assumed that she found even my father's (and brother's) views rather 'advanced'; that she was still stuck at the stage of believing Noah's Ark to be historical, which at least had a kind of coherence to it. I assumed she would be shocked by their 'position' – I could not dignify it by calling it a philosophy, in spite of, no, because of, the invocation of Hegel, which always threatened in discussions with my father – and that my outright admission of unbelief must be a sword through her heart.

'It isn't very difficult,' I remember my father saying. 'It is tested again and again in life. Do you in fact believe in a world of value outside yourself? Do you think you could reinvent morality? Would it be all right to . . . perform an act of gratuitous violence on a child, for example? Of course you don't. That's the starting point.'

We left it there – somewhere in the early 1920s. I could not be bothered with it. I abandoned, first theology, then philosophy (for which I never really had any aptitude), then I threw in my lot with the Wagners. It never occurred to me, as he led his really quite idle and gentle life – reading Harnack or the Greeks of a morning, visiting a few lonely or sick parishioners of an afternoon, practising music in the evening – that my father was a man of passion. He held to what I considered his wishy-washy views – that there was some kind of decency 'out there' which it would be an outrage to infringe – with as much fervour as Lieselotte or even Winnie would attend a Parteitag in Nuremberg.

That was the shock. I had not been to a service at my father's church for years, so when Gauleiter Schemm, the leader of the Party in Bayreuth, arrived in person to interview my father, some time in the early days of the regime, I was quite unaware that, week in and week out, he had been denouncing National Socialism from his pulpit. There was also, apparently, a notice pinned up at the back of the church, next to announcements of the following week's music and the rota of volunteers to clean the church or arrange flowers. It ready simply, in my father's neat calligraphy: JEWS ARE WELCOME IN THIS CHURCH. It was a parody, of course, of the signs by then going up in many restaurants, cafés and bars: JEWS NOT WELCOME, one stage milder than the JEWS PROHIBITED notices that appeared elsewhere in places such as swimming baths. (I remember going to our local baths shortly after such notices appeared there. I met a very nice pair, mid forties, he the head of the Maths Department at the school where my brother taught, she a housewife and mother. They had gone for a little swim together in the afternoon and as we passed the JEWS PROHIBITED notice she said, this perfectly nice and decent woman, with a little smile, half-guilty, half-conspiratorial, 'How nice it's just us, eh?')

Gauleiter Schemm was apparently closeted for about half an hour with my father in his study. My parents made very little comment upon the man's visit. The first I heard about it was when I noticed that my mother had prepared a rather tasteless macaroni cheese for supper, and I enquired after Elsa. It wasn't her evening off.

'Elsa has left us,' said my mother.

'What? Just like that? Without warning?'

'Your father dismissed her this afternoon.'

It turned out that Elsa had, all along, been an enthusiast for Wolf and his cause, and many of my father's tarter comments about National Socialism, over the weeks and months, had found their way back to Gauleiter Schemm's headquarters. Some members of my father's flock had deserted him and gone to churches in the town more sympathetic to the extreme nationalist viewpoint.

Since you had a completely secular upbringing, at home and at school, you are probably barely aware of the fact that after the National Socialists took power, the Lutheran Church was asked to swear allegiance to the new Leader. Up to that point in history the Protestant Church had been rather loosely organized in Germany, but now there was to be a Reich Bishop, Ludwig Müller, presiding over a Reich Church owing its allegiance to the Leader. Since in those days most

God-fearing German Protestants saw the deepest threat to their Church as coming from Communism, hundreds of thousands of Germans enthusiastically expressed their allegiance to this Church. But not Dad. There he was, in his old frock-coat on a Sunday morning, looking as if very little had changed in Germany since Hegel had penned the last confusing sentences of *The Phenomenology of the Mind*, or Schumann had played his last 'Träumerei'; and yet, when the choice was placed before him he allied himself with the 'rebels' in his Church, the so-called Confessing Christians, such as a young friend of my brother's in Berlin, Pastor Dietrich Bonhoeffer, another Harnack pupil, who took it as axiomatic that National Socialism was a toxic, wholly incompatible with Christianity.

There were some more visits – not from Gauleiter Schemm this time, but from some of his heavies. My father was eventually asked not to speak on political subjects from the pulpit. I am sure he disobeyed this. They had endless trouble with the authorities as the 1930s advanced and his congregation dwindled to very few. Interestingly, those who were brave enough to stay and hear him envisage what early Christian Platonists such as Clement of Alexandria would have thought of the Nuremberg Laws were largely old ladies. Still – I had my own preoccupations during all these years as you have noticed – I was not really registering what went on at home, and my father's activities, such as they were, struck me as no more embarrassing than anything else he had ever done.

Then came Crystal Night, 9 November 1938. Some kid had gone into the German Embassy in Warsaw and shot a diplomat of ours, supposedly in protest at his parents, Jewish, being deported back to Poland from Germany. It was used by Goebbels as the occasion to whip up a pogrom across the whole of Germany. Tens of thousands of Jews were arrested. Shops were smashed or set on fire. In almost every German town the brown-shirted thugs made their way through the streets with their cans of petrol, making for the nearest synagogue.

I knew nothing about what had been happening during the previous few days. I forget what crisis at the Festival Theatre had been occupying me, but it certainly had nothing to do with politics. It was more likely a crisis with the plumber, or Tietjen, the artistic director, with whom I by then got on extremely badly, was probably bullying me to write to some orchestral agency about the cut they were taking from the musicians' fees. Something like that. And I had my other life – my private life, with you – because I was married by then and you were with us. You were aged six.

I finished work about six and came home, which was now the flat I shared with you and Helga. We ate our meal – she was a good, simple cook, as you would agree – and for some reason I went out for a walk in the streets.

I remember wandering at will, smoking cigarettes. Probably Helga and I had just had one of our pointless rows and I was stomping off to get it out of my system. At the corner of Friedrichstrasse I encountered a coarse brown-shirted couple of boys who yelled at me, asking what I was doing. Since it was only about eight or nine in the evening, it did not seem unreasonable to be out walking in one's own home town, so I gave a non-committal reply and walked on.

"'Ere – you was asked a question!'

'I didn't feel much inclined to answer it.'

'It's better to stay in – unless you want to help give the yids a licking.'

'What do you mean?'

'This time we're really going to let them have it.'

There never were, historically, many Jews in Bayreuth until the famous anti-Semite Wagner, for whose music they showed such a penchant, came to live there. In 1759 old Margrave Friedrich had bought the old Redoutenhaus from a banker called Moses Seckel and built a synagogue, a fine little building, for the thirty-four families who might wish to worship there. By the time Wagner had established his Festival Theatre, several hundred more Jews came to the town, and it was those associated with the theatre who accounted for the huge majority of Jews in Bayreuth. Nearly all who were left in Bayreuth at the beginning of the war, by the way, were deported, either to Auschwitz or to Riga, where they were murdered. But that's to look ahead, to days which none of us fore-told or understood. Even my parents and brother, who protested against the maltreatment and persecution of Jews, had no conception of the scale of what lay ahead.

But this was November 1938, and the lout in the street was yelling that the yids had had it this time, they'd really had their come-uppance. I don't think he was suggesting that we all went out and committed murder together.

'Yeah,' said his companion, who had particularly bad breath, I remember, you could smell it halfway across the street, 'we're off on a little cleaning-up expedition.' This was one of those strange transformations in our language which began after the change of government in 1933 and which was actually, well, terribly unGerman I always thought.

It certainly was not my idea to take part in an evening of Jew-baiting. The further down the road I had been led, at first condoning and once even actually voting for the Nazis, I had always, like any decent person, felt this side of things was sick. We turned a blind eye, while we hoped the firm tactics on offer in foreign policy and economics would deliver our shopping list – ripping up the Versailles Treaty, giving us back the occupied territories on the Ruhr, allowing a standing army and getting the economy back on course. That was what we wanted – not broken windows and burnt synagogues and frightened old ladies.

Further down the street I saw that the yobs had some pals and on the next corner there was something approaching a crowd. I absented myself from them all and cut down a side street into the Market Square. There, life seemed to be going on much as normal. People were drinking in cafés and bars. Some people, perfectly inno-cently, were walking up and down looking at the shop windows. But this was only a superficial reality. As I watched, I saw that more Brownshirts were moving – from the restaurants and bars, to the streets themselves, advising people to move on. What in hell's name was going on?

I do not know what possessed me next. You probably think, from what Helga used to yell, that I was at the very least a fellow-traveller with the Nazis and that I might even approve of the Brownshirt roughnecks on our streets. But I most decidedly did not. I was sober, but I made hasty steps towards the police station, which led down the side of Bismarckstrasse into Humboldtstrasse.

The desk sergeant was friendly and polite. We knew one another by sight. Everyone did in Bayreuth in those days.

'They are planning some kind of affray,' I told him. 'They told me so themselves. You can't let them go around smashing the houses of innocent people.'

'We'll look into it, sir,' said the desk sergeant with maddening slowness.

'But they are out on the streets *now*! There was quite a gang of them and they seemed to be saying . . .'

'Yours is the only complaint we've had, sir.'

'But surely you'll come with me and see what I mean?'

'When there is an incident, sir, you can be sure that we will investigate it.'

'You mean you will sit there and *wait* for a crime to happen, rather than come out and prevent one happening?'

'That is the usual order of events, sir.'

So – I went out again into the night. And all at once I thought of the old synagogue, which I had never even entered myself. They surely would not be so brutal, so utterly without mercy, so ignorant of the history of our town that they would be prepared to attack this beautiful little eighteenth-century building? Then I remembered the two Brownshirts I'd met at close hand only minutes before – Spotty and Badbreath – and it occurred to me that eighteenth-century architecture was not necessarily something to which either had ever given much thought. Nor did either of them seem to be especially overflowing with the milk of human kindness.

So I broke into a run, the short journey to the little synagogue on the corner of Ludwigstrasse. And there an absolutely extraordinary sight greeted me. There were indeed quite a crowd of Brownshirts, shouting their usual anti-Semitic filth. But they were not alone. All around the front of the synagogue was a human chain, holding hands. I could see my dentist, poor old boring Erik Hügel, how bloody brave of him. But the majority of those who formed the human chain were not Jews. It was five years, then, since the National Socialists had become our government, abolished trade unions and all opposition parties, sent political activists and dissidents to prison or concentration camp. There were very few political activists at large in the whole country and Bayreuth was not the sort of town, at the best (or worst) of times, in which you would look for political activists anyway.

That was what made this demonstration so extraordinary. It was composed not of Trotskyites or latter-day Rosa Luxemburgs. It was the ordinary townspeople of Bayreuth. Not a lot of them, it is true, but about a hundred, who had formed a human chain round the synagogue. And at the centre of the chain, standing by the synagogue door with a vast placard, I saw, to my total astonishment, both my mother and my father. My father was wearing the black gown, white Geneva preaching bands and chimney-pot hat of the Lutheran pastor. My mother, as if dressed for a winter walk in the Hofgarten, was wearing hat, gloves and tweed suit trimmed at the collar with a modest fur. The poster behind them, with a text from St Paul, asked the question, ARE THEY HEBREWS? SO AM I!

The little group, in the quavery voices of the old, were singing church hymns. Some very much only for aficionados, which was why, presumably, they so often reverted to the old favourite, Luther's 'Ein' feste Burg':

Und wenn die Welt voll Teufel wäre . . .

'And though the world were full of devils and wanted to gobble us up, we should still not be fearful, we should not give up. The Prince of this World, however angry he may seem, can do nothing to us, because he is already judged . . .'

Some of the people in that chain were in their eighties. My father was, what? Sixty-eight. I stood there for a while watching, unable completely to believe what I was seeing. I knew that if I had total integrity I should have simply gone to join my parents and that, if I had done so, it would have melted the ice that had existed between us ever since my childhood. I told myself the reason I did not do so was that I did not want to make trouble for you or for Helga, who had already been to a concentration camp for her political views. In reality, I was still worried about what the Wagners would think. Of course, I now realize with retrospect that this sort of robust defence of other people's freedoms and decencies was precisely the sort of thing of which Winnie would have approved, that she was completely illogical, adoring Wolf but actually hating many, if not most, manifestations of Nazism when she encountered them, whether in its attempts to take over her Festival, or in its insistence that her children join the various appalling youth cults. But I did not know that then and I was a coward. I went home, and I did not even tell Helga what I had seen, for fear she would say that I had been taking risks, getting her into trouble.

My parents and their friends stayed there *all night*, praying and singing and not allowing the thugs near the synagogue.

In the morning Germany, and the world, woke up to what had happened in the night, though, like individuals of a destructive tendency, they did not wish to acknowledge what had occurred during the hours of darkness and preferred to put it all quickly behind them. Out of 9,000 Jewish shops in the whole of Germany, 7,500 were gutted. Millions of Reichsmarks' worth of goods were looted: jewellery, cameras, electrical goods, radios and so forth. In Berlin alone, fifteen synagogues had been burnt to the ground – 520 synagogues in all were destroyed across the whole of Germany in one night. The synagogue in Bayreuth was one of the very few to escape the torch.

So in 1960 we hurtled on by train to Leipzig, you and I, and other passengers could have seen us, a thin, skull-like man, with close-cropped grey hair and spectacles, and a young woman, also with slightly longer hair, dark brown, and intense eyes behind her spectacles, and both are weeping, as at the back of their heads the largely flat landscape of East Prussia is put behind them. When they got home, they found that they had been less lucky than the synagogue they were protecting. The Brownshirts had smashed their windows and their nice little cat Nina had been impaled on the front door. In my father's study they had not actually started a fire, but they had pulled a lot of the books out of the shelves and someone had smeared shit on his photograph of Adolf Harnack. The cello was in bits.

It was not long after that that my father was summoned for yet another interview with Gauleiter Schemm. It was actually before the war that they placed him under arrest. My mother and I made two visits together. She was even more than usually thin and frail, from then onwards. It was years, probably decades, since she had been out, or done anything independently of my father, so that having to make the decision to visit him was a strange one. He was in a small concentration camp erected just outside Bayreuth, charged with unpatriotic behaviour and using his pulpit as a political platform to undermine the Reich. It surprised me, on our first visit, that my brother wasn't there, but my mother told me that *Vati* had asked Heinrich to stay away. He said it would damage 'the Cause' if they both got arrested, and it was better that the older man should be the one locked up.

On the second visit my father looked terrible, much, much older than his nearly seventy years. His eyes were hollow and he seemed completely distant, not only from me (which he always was) but also, much more shatteringly, from my mother. I have told myself since that the reason for this was that he did not dare show the emotions he felt, for fear of breaking down completely and thereby causing her yet worse distress. We were not allowed to visit him again. Sometime in 1941 my mother received a curt letter informing her that her husband had died of an infection. We never knew whether to believe this or not. Clearly the regime in that place was terrible, my father was used to a gentle life. Maybe it was simply the life there that killed him. My mother must often have asked herself whether he was tortured. I ask myself that question and it is not bearable. He was one of millions. But he had made his stand.

When I came out of the first act of that Herz production I was in a state of ecstatic happiness, and I think one of the reasons for this was, quite simply, the beauty of the set. If you had spent well over ten years, as I had, in the industrial suburb of ———, living in a very small flat; if your place of work had been a school built out of brutalist hunks of concrete; if, in order to get to it, you had a tram ride through grey streets lined with more concrete – Karl Marx Strasse, Friedrich Engels Strasse and so on and so on ... What a tribute to these inventive thinkers this glorious architecture is. Sometimes, sitting on the tram, I would think of two late seventeenth-century gilded angels blowing trumpets round the organ case of the Stadtkirche in Bayreuth, supposedly, according to what the children in the Karl Marx Schule are meant to believe, from a time when the human mind was imprisoned by dogma and the human race was intolerably oppressed. I think of the sheer joyousness of those angels, and of the twin towers of the Stadtkirche, which are of about the same date, presiding over the beautifully laid-out cobbled streets in Bayreuth, our town. The handsome buildings, school, hospital, orphanage, piano factories, had all been designed with as much dignity and care as the opera house and the New Palace. The Hofgarten was always, as far as I am aware, open to the public to enjoy. Until the desolations of war fell on Bayreuth, and the British and American war planes came after us as a punishment for having housed Uncle Wolf, I do not believe there was a single ugly building in Bayreuth, a single alleyway or street or stable yard which, when glimpsed by a passer-by, did not give a lift to the spirits. Whereas I do not suppose that anyone living in the sub-town of ———, where I have spent the last decade, has felt anything but depression as a result of the architecture.

So my first impression of that *Meistersinger* was the set. It was an intricate, highly realistic depiction of an old sixteenth- or seventeenth-century theatre with galleries, such as Shakespeare or Molière might have known. And it was here that the comical burghers of Nuremberg held their singing competition, thrown into disarray, first by the intrusion of Walther, who isn't part of their narrow circle – he is an aristocrat, he finds it difficult to fashion his songs into the narrow confines of their rule books – and also by old Hans Sachs, the poet-cobbler. Sachs's overriding characteristic is generosity. He is the best poet in the play, but he uses his skill to train Walther to win. He is in love with beautiful young Eva himself, but he allows her to go off with Walther. It is true that he tricks the fussy, drunken and pedantic Beckmesser. But in the Herz production even Beckmesser is given his due. His claims for the place of rules and formality in art are not, as I think they sometimes are, made to seem totally ridiculous.

Because you were in the orchestra and I therefore sat alone amid strangers in the stalls, I was able to give up my total delighted concentration to the opera. And although I must have seen it over a dozen times, and sat through many of Tietjen's and Furtwängler's rehearsals of it during the 1930s, I had never before been so very moved by it, nor heard how rich its music is, nor been more impressed by how generous it is, generous as Sachs himself, in its central ideas. And yes, yet again, I was overpowered by how unNazi it is.

After the performance I hovered rather nervously, feeling very provincial, very old, very out of things as I waited for you to appear. It was a bit like waiting at a school gate when you were a little girl. I could see other members of the orchestra patting you on the shoulder, quipping with you, lighting up cigarettes. That was your world and I was out of it. In my worn-out, terrible, dark-blue suit, which I'd owned since the end of the war, and my frayed mackintosh and my cap, I was as alien from your world, now, as my parents had been from mine when I was in my twenties. But you kindly took me in to the reception they held afterwards. I was never very much good at large assemblies of people and this experience told me that I had lost what capacity I had for social chat.

'*Vati*, I'd like you to meet' – and you were leading me up to a pleasant-seeming young man. He was little more than a boy. This was Joachim Herz himself; and of course if I had been a poised, social kind of a being, I should have had so many paragraphs finished in my head about the originality and spectacular humanity of his *Meistersinger*; I'd have praised the performers, the intense colour and sensitivity of the orchestration, in short the complete brilliance of the production. I would have said, 'You, Comrade Herz – truly a comrade to all who love Richard Wagner – have rescued this beautiful work of art from the Nazis, who made its stirring overture, brashly played, into their theme song at rallies, who made ironical, warm Hans Sachs into a militaristic buffoon . . .' But of course I only half twigged who he was, and just mumbled some embarrassing nonsense about being your dad, and made some silly joke, which I could see you hating, about not being able to hear your cello playing above all the singing and the other instruments. I'd wanted to pay a compliment to you, but this was the moment to pay a compliment to him and, by making this ridiculous cello remark, I of course seemed to be expressing total indifference to the production we'd just seen.

Herz just gazed at me a bit quizzically. He was in any case surrounded by people and, as we were being nudged out by the next lot who came up to pay their respects, someone of evidently high importance, to judge from their bossy bearing and their shoulder movements through the crowds, was leading up . . . Wieland Wagner.

So Wieland, Winnie's son, was here. He'd crossed over from the West to see what the opposition was up to. Some such terribly unfunny quip was springing to my mind and at that moment I was seized with a desperate desire to talk to him. He had never been the Wagner child to whom I had been closest; that, undoubtedly, was his sister Friedelind. But we had seen one another daily during his teens and here he was, a man of over forty, very handsome, clever-looking – your brother, or rather half-brother. He had a very touching look of his father Fidi about him that night, but also, in the brow and the shape of the head, and the intense expression, of his grandfather Richard Wagner. I had last seen him when he was a young soldier in uniform at the beginning of the war.

I do not know, in retrospect, whether you knew that this man being led towards Joachim Herz was in fact Wieland Wagner. I remember only the look of intense embarrassment on your face as I wriggled back into Herz's circle to hold out my hand and say, 'Wieland! Wieland!'

Wieland and Herz were exchanging polite remarks about *Meistersingers*, and both looked up at me with that expression of disdain bordering on alarm when a stranger bursts into an intimate circle. Combined with annoyance that bad manners are being perpetrated by an outsider is the flickering fear that they might be about to confront a piece of serious bad behaviour, perhaps even downright lunacy. Wieland in particular, presumably because I was overexcitedly repeating his name, looked at me as if I might be about to produce a gun or lower my trousers.

I said my own name, but he showed not the smallest flicker of recognition.

'Come on, Dad.' You were tugging at my elbow.

I said my name – again.

It was then that Wieland smiled, but there was no warmth in the smile. 'Of course – of course – how is life treating you?'

'I mustn't complain.' (Untrue. Here in the East I believe it is a duty to complain.)

'But, but . . . how wonderful . . .'

'And your mother?' I asked. 'How is your mother?'

The smile was totally glacial and turned into a 'social' mirthless laugh. 'Indefatigable,' was his reply. 'But if you will excuse me.'

'This is my daughter . . .'

Of course I was not going to say 'This is your sister. This is the daughter of your mother and . . .' But I had wanted you both to shake hands at that moment.

It was not to be. Your patience was running out and anyway, by then, very many were milling around the two great men of the evening – the director of this particular *Meistersinger*, and the man who, in the West, had transformed post-war Bayreuth and introduced 'modern' productions there. I could very easily imagine what Winnie thought of those. Dear Winnie, she must have been over sixty then – an incredible thought.

But here we are, milling around at the party. There isn't much to drink. The grandees seemed to have been given something fizzy. I wonder what it was? Soviet champagne? The rest of us had some form of fruit cup laced with schnapps, quite nice but one small tumbler each was all that was allowed.

'I think I'm going to have to be getting back,' I said.

We had worked out that it was just possible, when the opera ended, to get a train home, though only by changing at Dessau.

It was one of those sad moments that occur so often between family members when both have run out of things to say to one another; both therefore want to part; yet both feel the sadness of the parting. You must have felt it more than I did because you knew that you were about to make your brave defection to freedom.

'I'll walk to the station with you.'

'No. No, darling, you stay here with your friends.'

'Really? You all right, Dad?'

'I'm fine.'

We hugged. I hugged you perfunctorily to stop myself making a scene and breaking down in tears, for, even though I did not know that this was actually our last farewell, there were always long gaps between our meetings and the goodbyes were always full of pathos for me.

''Bye, Dad.'

The quickest way to walk to the enormous railway station at Leipzig from the opera house is along Goethestrasse, a wide, modern road, lined with the big museums, and framed at one end by the gigantic modernist university buildings. But what the hell, I strode past the museum into the old town and walked about in what was left, after Communism and aerial bombardment, of the old Market Place, and found (locked, of course) the great medieval Gothic Thomaskirche where Richard Wagner (in 1813) and Johann Sebastian Bach (in 1685) had both been baptized. Leipzig! It was a living, scarred embodiment of the truth which the Mastersingers of Nuremberg had expressed in music. Its streets and churches and houses and people had been turned to rubble by American pilots, and crudely, insensitively knocked into shape again by our new masters; both of whom had made the fatal and ugly bargain to sacrifice love in exchange for power. But why do we remember Leipzig? Yes, yes, an important market town since the Middle Ages, a population of such-and-such, a Prince of Anhalt-Dessau who built such and such a church, such a Rathaus or Schloss? Maybe. But that is what the obsessives remember. It isn't what the world remembers. They maybe remember that Martin Luther preached here.

But outlasting any political philosophy or regime, and of infinitely more relevance to human life – and of infinitely more interest – is the music of Bach. The exiguous refreshment at the party, where I'd made such a fool of myself, was hardly enough to make me drunk, but I was quietly sniggering, like a drunken loon, when I entered the dingy lobby of a small hotel – Bach beat Ulbricht! Tee-hee.

'Papers?'

After the nervous fumbling which in my case follows any attempt to find a tram card, a train ticket, I found my ID.

A completely joyless woman, with the statutory Communist halitosis, stated mechanically, 'You've made no reservation.'

I explained about attending the opera, intending to get a train home, but having missed it.

'You can't stay without a reservation and without a permission form.'

I got this reaction in about three little hell-holes. For about an hour I walked around in Leipzig, then I sat on a cold bench on the Central Square. I was numbed – by saying goodbye to you, by seeing Wieland, by the whole experience. But something mysterious had armed me against feeling crushed. I suppose it was *Meistersinger* itself, the brilliant reminder that art outlasts politics, that the sordid and cruel things we human beings have been doing to one another in the last century in Europe are not the last word, that music outsoars it and is stronger than it: that Bach outlasts Frederick the Great and that Wagner, too, outlasts his more outlandish patrons and admirers.

Human beings do exist, even in our present-day Marxist paradise. On my next peregrination I entered a small hotel quite near the station. When I began the fumbling process all over again – for inevitably, money, ID, train ticket had all mysteriously jumped from my left to my right pocket – the hotel clerk here merely smiled.

He was a bearded man, thin, in his forties. The ashtray in front of him was full but he was smoking as if he had an ambition to build a small mountain of fag butts. His amused eyes were red and his cheeks through the nicotine habit prematurely lined. 'I think we can let you have a room.'

He looked a little like the English writer D. H. Lawrence, whose Nietzschean romances of working-class life I had read with deep admiration when at uni. As he showed me to the box-like cell, the tiny bed with its thin bedding folded upon it, he gave me a strange 'look'. 'No luggage.'

'I . . . missed the train . . . didn't think . . .'

Have you noticed in this country since the war – perhaps further back, since 1933 – we always react to quite innocent enquiries with over-elaborate self-justification, as if officialdom is trying to wrong-foot us?

'Just hope you'll be comfortable.'

'It's very good of you.'

D. H. Lawrence stared at me seriously. Then, lighting another cheap cigarette, lingered a moment too long. 'You are all right?'

'Perfectly.'

I do not flatter myself that my almost sixty-year-old body is an obvious object of desire, especially to homosexuals who surely prefer lissome youth. But what if he were the sort who liked 'older men'? What if his sole reason for being kind to me, and allowing me to stay in the hotel without authorization, had been a sexual one?

So, as I lay beneath the flimsy sheet and blanket, clad in socks, underpants, vest and shirt, my mind was a jangle of memories, impressions, fears, thoughts. The town band at Bayreuth playing a travesty of the overture to *Meistersinger* to herald some awful parade, inspected by Gauleiter Schemm – the swastikas in their banners falling from the large elegant windows of the old Margrave's palace, now Party and Administrative HQ. The performance I'd just heard, the true music of Wagner disinfecting the earlier memory. The nagging fear, which kept coming into my mind, that a priapic D. H. Lawrence would come into the room – how would one cope? The thought of *your* sad face as you said goodbye to me, of the jawline and handsome brow in your face, and the hypnotic charm of the deep-blue eyes . . .

Rat-a-tat!

Silence. The man in the hotel cowered.

Is anyone there?

Another silence. Who would it be this time? Secret police? Or merely debt collectors.

'Excuse me – Herr ――?' This was the false name under which he was travelling.

'Herr Wagner? Please?'

It did not *sound* like a policeman. The voice was that of a gentleman. The accent was that of Munich.

'Herr Wagner – please. I have a message for you from His Majesty King Ludwig of Bavaria.'

The day before, in a café in Stuttgart, a stranger had accosted him and offered him a card, inscribed with the same words.

If you are on the run, anything and everything seems like a threat. And at fifty, Richard Wagner was yet again on the run. He had been living in Vienna. Work had not been going well. He had not finished the orchestration, either of *Tristan* or of *The Ring of the Nibelung*. But what was the point? The more revolutionary and innovative his musical conceptions, the less likelihood there appeared of his ever being able to see them realized on the stage. It was twenty years since he had sketched out *Meistersinger* and although he had conducted concert performances of the overture, no one had seen the opera. No one had seen *Tristan*, though he had more or less finished writing it five years ago, in 1859. It was his fate not to see his work performed. Even with the popular early work, his life of political exile had made it hard for him to see his compositions on the stage. (*Lohengrin* had been completed in 1848, and first performed in Weimar in 1850, conducted by the Abbé Liszt; but Wagner himself did not see it until 1861, performed in Vienna.)

When his nerves were frayed, when his belief in himself was challenged, when it seemed as if life was stacking all the cards against him, he needed to cosset himself. Since his motherly elder sister had died, there had been no one to cosset him; not really to treat him, as he wished to be treated, like a tender little baby. That was why he indulged in what his enemies supposed to be an extravagant way of life. True, the walls of his apartment were lined with silk. The floor was covered with innumerable soft rugs. The enormous bed, and the little sofas, were all festooned with silks and satins. Above and around the bed were enormous looking-glasses. In his bedchamber, into which no one was admitted except himself and a few intimates, were closets stuffed with women's clothes, flounces, frilly silk drawers, Russian bootees, suspenders, satin petticoats.

In Vienna he had linked up once more with a friend of his Leipzig adolescence, Marie Loewe. He had developed an obsessive crush on Marie's daughter Lilli* – lovely Lilli, with her delicate little lips and her translucent skin. Marie had brought the daughter to see him one day in his apartments. He had been dressed in a yellow damask dressing gown, over which he had thrown a black cloak lined with pink satin. Unfortunately, he had kissed Lilli with too much ardour and she had not come again. But Marie came, Marie who *understood*. Before he returned of an evening to the overheated Vienna apartment, Marie would spray it, over and over, with the most expensive scent until it reeked like a seraglio. And she would lay out 'his' clothes for him on the silken bedspread. Drinking champagne together (only the best), Marie would soothe him by dressing him as he liked to be dressed. She wore soft cotton-velvet black gloves, buttoned to the elbow, as she helped him into his tailor-made silken drawers, lingering as she pulled them over his thighs, and slowly buttoned them at the front. Then, there would be the laced liberty bodices, the negligées,

<hr/>

*Lilli Loewe, by then Lilli Lehmann, sang one of the Rhinemaidens in the first production of *The Rhine-gold* at Bayreuth in 1876.

decorated with ruches, tassels and rosettes. Over all this he would throw one of the many brightly coloured silk dressing gowns which the Viennese tailors made for him at huge cost. And while he lay there, sometimes being stroked and fondled by Marie, sometimes alone, he drank bottle after bottle of champagne.

He had no income and no means of paying for all this. Without it, however, there was no hope of finishing his life's work. *How could you explain this to the cretins who had never composed a page of music in their lives?*

Eventually the predators, the money-grubbers, closed in. The extraordinary and trivial matter of his owing them some thousands egged on their malice to persecute him. So had they persecuted Beethoven before him. All right, all right, so Beethoven died in an austere room, and lived a life of abject discomfort and poverty, but was that a reason for Germany to persecute all the great musicians? As in Riga, when he was a very young man, so in Vienna, when tiredness and dissipation made his fifty years seem much older, there was only one solution: flight. Clad in the comfort of women's clothes, though with a heavy travelling cloak round him, and with one of his large velvet berets on his head, he had fled Vienna by dead of night, on 23 March, hoping to get over the Swiss border to Zurich before he was apprehended by the police.

He broke his journey in Stuttgart and it was there that he had the nasty shock of being recognized. He had imagined he was travelling incognito. But the messenger had approached him with the card: *I have a message for you from His Majesty King Ludwig of Bavaria.*

This could only be some cruel joke by the creditors, who were homing in upon him. He had retreated to his hotel, shivering, and so much in need, in need of comfort. Most of his clothes had had to be left behind in Vienna, but he had enough here to bring some measure of peace. He had lain on the bed, wearing magenta silk stockings, tied at the thigh with scarlet silk bows. His drawers, as slinky and soft as an adolescent girl's palms, clung to his loins. Over them were draped two layers of silk petticoat, and above was a tightly waisted liberty bodice, again, of pink silk.

The thunderous knock at his door was like the Commendatore at the end of *Don Giovanni*. It was a judgement, a visitation of doom.

He did not know that the Norns who had been weaving his Rope of Destiny had changed ill fortune to fair. This was the year when the miracles, all at once, began to appear. Though he did not know it as he lay there in his hotel bedroom in Stuttgart, his old enemy Meyerbeer had just died in Paris and Cosima, not long afterwards, was destined to conceive Isolde, his first child.

'Herr Wagner!'

He hastily put on one of his silk dressing gowns and added a velvet beret to conceal the fact that it was days since he had groomed his hair. Then, with a self-conscious glimpse at his small feet, still ribboned into the pink Russian bootees, he opened the door.

The flunkey who stood there was called Herr Pfistermeister and he was indeed Private Secretary to the newly crowned King Ludwig II of Bavaria.

The Immortals exact strange bargains from their puppets. When we contemplate the strange relationship between Richard Wagner and his royal patron it is difficult to know who was exploiting whom, which of them came off worse. Wagner (whatever ghastly views he might sometimes have expressed about Jews, revolution, Germany etc. etc.) was fundamentally a free creative spirit, a mind on the move. He accepted King Ludwig's patronage in 1864 and immediately had to set to work denying his revolutionary past, which he did in a huge, fascinatingly dishonest autobiography, *My Life*, which he dictated to Cosima, to give the King the impression that he had played almost no part in the 1848 uprisings. He also omitted to mention that he was a lifelong republican. Had Bavaria been a stable and completely independent kingdom, had Ludwig been a stable and completely independent political leader, Wagner's career, and particularly his career post-mortem in the twentieth century, might have been very different. But six years after Herr Pfistermeister knocked on Wagner's hotel bedroom door in Stuttgart, the twenty-six-year-old Bavarian monarch in effect wound up his kingdom, sent his troops to France to fight alongside the Prussians and capitulated to Prussian-dominated

German unification post-1870. Lurching from one psychological crisis to the next, the King was eventually proclaimed insane and took his own life (or was murdered by his doctors) three years after Richard Wagner's death. By then the sentiments expressed in Wagner's pamphlets and prose writings could be enlisted as propaganda for the new militaristic Prussian state of Germany. And gentle Hans Sachs's plea for Germany to drop its revolutionary-political aims in favour of art could be twisted into a belligerent militaristic claim that just as the newly created Germany had the fastest-growing economy, the largest army in mainland Europe, the fastest-growing navy and the biggest industrial plants, so it was also best at art. The Wagnerians who guarded the shrine of Bayreuth after the Master's demise did nothing to dispel the idea of Wagner as a tub-thumping Bismarckian nationalist (even though he had detested Bismarck). Cosima and her son-in-law Houston Stewart Chamberlain represented this capricious rebel against political systems as an arch-reactionary. His splenetic and poisonous outbursts of anti-Semitism became part of the programme, rather than aberrations from the purer side of his nature. And so the stage was set, after the calamities of 1919, for new nationalists and new breeds of Wagnerian, to take the thing yet further and create the image of Wagner the National Socialist.

All these things, in a way, were the inevitable consequence of his opening that hotel door in Stuttgart on April 1864. But at the time it seemed like the most wonderful stroke of good fortune, that after waiting for years without hope that he would ever find the financial support or the artistic enthusiasm, or the physical venue to make the staging of his later operas a possibility, he had found ... his Lohengrin, his magic prince.

My father was not really capable of malice, but there was undoubted pleasure in his eyes when he used to recall the fact that King Ludwig II was almost completely unmusical. His music tutor used to say that the boy could not tell the difference between a Strauss waltz and a Beethoven sonata. The only composer who interested him was Wagner. My father liked to state that this was highly usual among Wagnerians.

It was Ludwig's grandfather, the great builder and aesthete King Ludwig I, who had built the Swan Palace in the mountains, the Hohenschwangau, whose walls were decorated with murals of the Grail Legend and Tannhäuser. This was allegedly the site of Lohengrin's palace, and there were swans painted on cornices, ceiling roses, and vases. The lakes in the grounds were full of live swans. As a boy, Ludwig had feasted on these stories and, aged about thirteen, he had discovered the libretti of *Lohengrin* and *Tannhäuser*, which he learnt by heart. He was sixteen when he first saw *Lohengrin* in Munich and not long afterwards he heard *Tannhäuser*. Those sitting beside the youth in the royal box were afraid he was about to have an epileptic convulsion when Tannhäuser re-entered Venusberg.

His father died young, Ludwig inherited the throne when he was aged eighteen, and his first act was to dispatch Pfistermeister to find Wagner.

Thereafter began the partnership that ultimately enabled Wagner's operas to be staged. But nothing in the composer's life was easy. If he had been prepared to sit down and finish the orchestration of his operas, and get von Bülow to conduct them in Munich, probably all would have been well. But the young King was besotted with the older man. They in effect fell in love with one another (though of course Wagner, unlike Ludwig, was not homosexual) and the proud royal patron could not hold back from giving the greedy protégé everything he desired. Not only did he pay off Wagner's debts, but he gave him a huge stipend, paid for out of the public purse, a large house overlooking Lake Starnberg and another large house in the centre of Munich which, naturally, had to be decorated with silken wall hangings and all the softest and most expensive upholstery. The first performance of *Tristan*, the first great work of 'modern art', took place in Munich on 10 June 1865, and it did nothing to make Wagner popular. Indeed, hostility to Wagner, both in court circles and among the general public, grew to such a degree that the King was forced to ask him to leave.

This was not without its conveniences. Although the King was an ingénu (he asked one of his courtiers 'What is a natural child?'

and on another occasion appeared not to understand when someone tried to tell him what rape was), it would not have been possible for long to disguise from him the nature of the relationship between Wagner and Cosima von Bülow. They continued to assure him, even as Wagner's child grew in her womb, that they had no more than a comradely relationship and Frau von Bülow's presence in Wagner's houses was often concealed from the King. But this was more easily done when he had gone into exile once more and they were living together in the Villa Tribschen on the banks of Lake Lucerne.

Meanwhile, with the King's desperate pleading and Cosima's firm insistence that he finish his great works, Wagner had *Meistersinger* ready by October 1867 (it was performed in Munich under von Bülow on 21 June 1868 and, unlike *Tristan*, it was an instant success with the public.

The patron – a harbinger of Bayreuth in the 1930s – took obsessive interest in the staging of the opera. In this – again, foreshadowing Wolf's Bayreuth – the crazed monarch perhaps understood more of the audience's response to *Meistersinger* than did its composer. Wagner wanted his work to be a generalized, all but a mythological work of art about art. To use the title of one of his prose works, it was concerned with the artwork of the future. King Ludwig insisted that Angelo Quaglio and Heinrich Döll, who were constructing the sets, be sent to Nuremberg and recreate an exact replica of the elaborately Gothic St Catherine's Church for the opening scene. Though the opening night took place two years before the birth of Germany as a modern nation, this opera was to be the rallying cry of German patriots for ever afterwards. What had been conceived as a statement about the transcendent power of art, a power that crossed national boundaries, was doomed to become the ultimate expression of strident nationalism.

As in a scene change during one of the old bel canto operas, which Richard Wagner saw off, we have been in front of the curtains for most of this chapter. In 1932 there was no Bayreuth Festival. In consequence there were no raised eyebrows about the fact that Winnie spent so much of the spring and summer of 1932 'away on business'. For five or six months I hardly saw her, though she sent me letters that I treasured:

It's about time, tell Lieselotte, that the children's nursery is to have a complete *clear-out*. Get it done before they come back from boarding school . . .

When you are next at the office in the theatre, give some thought to whether we should get new filing cabinets before the coming season . . .

Tietjen tells me there's been a nasty outbreak of flu among the chorus. Thank heavens it did not happen in a Festival year. *Avoid getting it yourself.* There is no need to be an out-and-out vegetarian, but a diet largely restricted to fruit and vegetables is highly beneficial and anyone can tell you that . . .

Don't *let* Eva bully you. I have given you authority to tell the Wardrobe Mistress to *get rid* of all those tunics which had moths. In last year's *Lohengrin*, by the final performances, you could *see* the holes in the Brabantian soldiers!!

I am sorry you are tired. Much of this is attributable to *diet*. You should not stuff yourself with fruit and vegetables all the time. Protein is what you need – as much meat as you can afford.

Why throw away perfectly good costumes just because they have a few holes? I detect Eva's extravagant hand here! Ask around and see if you, or she, cannot get a team of good needlewomen to *mend* some of the more basic items of costume – those tunics, for example, which we used for the Brabantians in *L.*, and for the pilgrims in *Tannhäuser*, are *perfectly usable* for the Grail Knights in *P*.

And so on.

There were seldom specific addresses at the top of these letters – 'Zurich' or 'Berlin' or 'In transit' was all the clue they gave of her whereabouts.

When Helga and I rescued you from the orphanage in Bayreuth in 1935, I noticed that your birth, which occurred on 10 July 1932, was recorded as having taken place in Berlin. Your parents were described as Anna Schmidt and an unknown father. But your first name – Senta – gave a pretty heavy clue.

All my letters from Winnie were lost in the conflagrations and air raids of 1945. But I have a distinct memory of a letter from her in what must have been a few days after you were born. The reason I remember it so clearly is that, unlike the other letters, so vaguely dated from 'Zurich', 'Berlin' etc., this was from a clinic, with a number and a postal code.

> *No one* is to *worry* about me. I am perfectly well, just exhausted.
> The doctors say I shall be back on my feet in a week. I think
> I had been trying to do too much, but some of the burden
> which I was carrying has now been delivered from me . . .

I distinctly remember punning words to this effect, though of course I did not recognize them as such. And also I remember – 'Wolf, even at this busy time, has been to see me, and brought fruit and flowers. This is of *inexpressible* comfort to me.'

The year of your birth was one of near anarchy in our country. Even in sedate little Bayreuth the poverty was terrible to behold. Some weeks there was very little food in the shops. Those who were lucky enough to be able to buy food would find themselves being waylaid by beggars as they came out of the shop. I can remember my dear mother once coming home empty-handed, admitting that a woman had stopped her outside the butcher's and implored her to give away her shopping bag – a nasty cut of mutton, some pota-toes – to feed a hungry family.

In the bigger towns things were much worse. On my visits to Nuremberg, either on business or for shopping, it was common to see fights. At the station buffet when I was eating a bun and drinking a cup of chocolate, I saw a man draw a knife on the waiter and demand to be fed. The police were called, but before they came a small riot had broken out, with chairs being thrown and food grabbed from behind the counter.

The Communists were very strong, but their street fights with the Nazis were only the most conspicuous focus of our national divisions. The truth is division and chaos were everywhere, and many of us who were actually neither Communist nor Nazi felt ourselves torn apart. We wanted justice for the poor. We wanted to avoid the slavery Lenin had imposed on Russia.

You cannot imagine unless you lived through it the sheer level of chaos. I cannot remember how many elections there were that year – old General Hindenburg's statutory term of office came to an end, so there was a presidential election. (He stood again and remained in office.) There were state elections, Reichstag elections, elections every few months; riots every few months; murders every few months. Hundreds of murders. Reds and Nazis fought on the streets of our towns, openly firing at one another and killing dozens on each side. But quite apart from politics there was an atmosphere of murderous mayhem. Many deaths took place that had no obvious political connection at all. Even in our small town a youth was found, in the small alley which joins Friedrichstrasse and Dammallee, his shirt open, his guts spilling on to the pavement. He had a deep knife wound from diaphragm to groin. Such deeds would have been unthinkable in our gentle little town until these times. Now – I will not say we took them for granted, but they seemed in keeping with the desperate spirit of the times.

Many Germans, especially the unemployed and the hungry, felt that almost anything would be preferable to the murderous anarchy in which we were living. However much old Hindenburg tried to cobble things together with new chancellors and vice-chancellors, the problems got no better – unemployment remained terrifyingly high; the economy was in free fall. We all sensed we were about to have a civil war.

'We must see how von Papen shapes up,' my father gently remarked, folding his morning newspaper and laying it beside his breakfast roll.

'At least he is a gentleman,' said my mother.

'Though a Catholic,' added my father.

They seemed to be living in never-never land. The appointment of von Papen as Chancellor did nothing to stop the hunger, the confusion, the violence.

Old Oswald Spengler and his wife hung swastika banners from the windows of their flat in Munich. ('When one has a chance to annoy people, one should do so,' he said – even though he believed H was a 'fantasist' and a 'numbskull'.)

'I do not see how anyone can be so irresponsible, or so' – my father paused – 'so *stupid* as to think *those people* could bring order to our country, when they are street fighters, gangsters.'

'You didn't think much of this speech, then?' I indicated the newspaper, reporting a speech H had made in Munich in which he invoked the Revelations of St John the Divine. The Laodiceans had been lukewarm and Almighty God had spewed them out. This was not a time for being lukewarm. It was a time for action against the 'world pest', Bolshevism. It was a time for all good Germans to unite – for full employment, for economic stability and for our pride in ourselves as a nation.

As always when he was losing an argument, my father merely shook his head disapprovingly and said nothing.

After a silence, my mother said, 'I don't know why they don't bring back the Emperor from exile – or if the Prussians don't want that, at least let us have our own royal family in Bavaria. Things have never been right since they declared the republic.'

Uncle Wolf did not make much of an appearance in the Wagner family circle that year. The electioneering and the campaigning were more or less constant. He had conquered his fear of flying and was now escorted round the country in a small plane, surrounded by his particular entourage of associates – the bespectacled head of the SS, the very sight of whom gave one the creeps; there was the fat soldier whom Fidi had rescued after the beerhall putsch, whom I privately thought of as the Mad Gamekeeper; and the sinister Nosferatu with a club-foot.

At one point in the year – I forget all the order of events now – there was a great crisis in the Party. I do remember it, because it was one of the moments when Wolf spoke openly among us about his political chances – rather than being an uncle who spoke only of opera, or cowboy stories by Karl May. 'Strasser is trying to betray me,' he told Winnie in my hearing. 'If he takes a place in the government – Streicher is offering him the Vice-Chancellorship – then I am finished. And if I am finished, then the pistol will end the story.'

'Wolf, Wolf – you think the German people will want to be governed by Strasser?'

The crisis passed. Gregor Strasser had been one of Wolf's old comrades from the first days of the movement. A Socialist, who always wanted to insist on that element in the National Socialist programme, he had indeed been offered a place in one of the coalition governments that year – possibly under some kind of military dictatorship run by General Kurt von Schleicher (who was briefly the Chancellor at the end of that year). Had it worked . . . It is one of the big ifs of history: a brief period of calm, with martial law and a firm military government; the Nazi rank and file united behind Strasser, but prepared to work with the conservatives in government and other parties in the Reichstag; the routing of the worst thugs in the SA . . .

It was never going to happen. As we now know from the history books, H did one of his most successful pieces of emotional blackmail, accompanied by threats. He sobbed, he ranted, he shouted that Strasser had betrayed him, betrayed the Party. Strasser went out into political exile. Nosferatu persuaded H that he should demand the Chancellorship or nothing. After that the Presidency and absolute power. Absolute power or nothing.

All your memories of mature life, all your political memories at least, until you made the decision to get out, are of a Communist East Germany, which has been extraordinarily stable. As you know, I have no truck with the comrades, but it seems amazing now that 'we all' thought that Leninism would be the ultimate catastrophe. I look out of the windows of my little hell-hole of a flat as I write these words and, well, yes, it's ugly, yes it's not much fun and no, we have no freedom. But we all have somewhere to live, something to eat. Your schooling was rather good – better than mine, I should say. There is a social justice of a sort. The great monolith of Soviet Communism will never ever be broken, as far as I can see. I don't see what there is that can break it. The most that can happen is that such things as that wonderful Herz *Meistersinger* in Leipzig will lead to a different kind of Socialism here in Germany, more benign, less intolerant, less fearful.

But this is your Germany, albeit the one you left behind. It is one of appalling dullness and of almost non-existent economic growth, and of political repression. But all your life with me in this town of —— has been stable. Sometimes there were queues for sausage or for boots, but not riots, as there were in 1932, not open civil war in bars, cafés, town squares.

Well, there was no excuse, we made our choice, we Germans, and boy did we get it wrong. And I was at the very epicentre of the wrongness, no doubt about that, with Winnie having no scintilla of doubt that her Lohengrin would lead us all to the Promised Land.

The Wolf whom we glimpsed that year, flitting in and out for evening visits and always remembering to bring presents for the children, was still the old Wolf – a warm, jokey family visitor and friend. But we all read newspapers avidly. And it was obvious that he was no longer just Uncle Wolf, but also the person who might, just might, overcome the anarchy and become the National Saviour.

You will find it unsatisfactory that I have no memories whatsoever of your birth parents together during that year of your birth.

It was a very hot summer, the year of your birth, and it must have been a month or so after you were born and brought to the orphanage at Bayreuth that I saw Winnie, in a loose summer frock, and knew what had happened. Of course she did not tell me, but I knew. The sustained absence in Switzerland in the late spring and early summer had all been explained to us, and to her children, as being of a business character. But apart from her visit to America in 1924 with her husband, what business had ever kept her away from Bayreuth for such an extended period?

I do not know if she flew around with Wolf on his whistle-stop electioneering and speechifying tours, but there is no doubt in my mind, looking back, that she regarded herself as his mistress, partner, all but wife, during that year. And of course it was at that time that the situation must have been obvious to his young Munich girlfriend. About a year after his niece committed suicide, Eva Braun also made an unsuccessful attempt to shoot herself.

This minor event was but one of the blood spats on the pages of the 1932 calendar. Some of the more melodramatic plays of the young Shakespeare have gratuitous deaths and murders in almost every scene, so that one more or less fails to make an impact. That is what the year of your birth was like. I can't even remember the exact date at which Fräulein Braun did attempt suicide. Obviously,[*] she had found out about Winnie and Wolf – and perhaps about your arrival on the scene. She herself, it need hardly be added, never persuaded Wolf to give her a baby. You are unique.

It was, as I have said, several months before Eva Braun's attention-seeking display that my hunch about Winnie and Wolf hardened to certainty. It was during that very hot summer.

Winnie was looking magnificent in that loose, polka-dotted summer frock. Wolf was paying one of his flying visits and the

[*] Obviously to N——, but not necessarily to others. This is one of the many moments in his narrative when N—— strains our credulity. Eva Braun shot herself with her father's pistol on 1 November 1932, but it seems to have been more a 'cry for help' than a serious attempt to take her own life. She was able to telephone for an ambulance after she had done it, and the Leader visited her in a Munich hospital, bringing a bunch of flowers, the next day. The day after he addressed a huge rally at the Berlin Sportspalast. In all the many attempts to write about Fräulein Braun, no one has ever, before N——, suggested that she had heard of Winifred Wagner giving birth to H's child. H.M.

children were all around them on the grass in the garden just outside the french windows of the grand salon at Wahnfried. 'We think you'll do, don't we, Wolf?' said Winnie to me, looking up in that slightly teasing way she always had of speaking to me.

'Yes, yes,' said Wolf.

She was absolutely glowing: with health, with sexual energy, and with – yes – with triumph. The man she loved was at her side. I suppose there were many things he loved about her. One was her unswerving loyalty and her unwavering fondness for him. But another was that she did not kowtow to him, she treated him like a person and if necessary she stood up to him. Here they were together and, oh, were they together that afternoon.

'Winnie, don't *eat* so much!' – her husband Fidi's constant outburst at meals had been made half in jest, half out of genuine exasperation. Over the years there was no doubt that Winnie had filled out, though she was still, and surely always would be, *magnificent*. It suited her to be fleshy, it added to her charm. But I now saw that her shape, only vaguely discernible beneath the summer dress, had undoubtedly undergone a great change. The brightness in her eyes and the softness of her skin also told me what had happened.

For any other woman, perhaps, it would have seemed a tragedy. She was – still is, no doubt – deeply maternal. Motherly is one of the adjectives that would inevitably come to anyone's lips who was attempting to describe Winifred. It would not be just a reference to her bodily figure. Yet there was always this robustness of spirit, and this strange impenetrable curtain, which I have concluded to be a specifically Celtic capacity to guard its secret soul, which made it impossible to know what was going on behind her smiles – or behind her anger and grief when they were in evidence. She did not expose herself.

'We've been talking. You don't mind that I've discussed your situation with Wolf?'

'Of course not,' I said, not quite bowing to him, but certainly feeling a sort of deference; more than that, a very definite glow, that this man, who was now on the front page of every newspaper in the world, every day, had been discussing me.

'Naturally, your work for Fidi at the theatre, and here, has been invaluable, and I don't want to backtrack in any way. You came to us, not just as a dogsbody but as someone who wanted to write a book about the philosophy of Richard Wagner. And you must do that, you must.'

'Have you read Schopenhauer?' Wolf suddenly asked.

The question really did summon up Spengler's image of him as a dolt (*Hohlkopf*). How could anyone even consider writing about Wagner and philosophy without having read Wagner's favourite philosopher (or the one he said was the favourite – part of my book would be to explore the mystery of Wagner's silence about Hegel – and whose ideas quite obviously permeate all the music dramas but especially *Tristan* and the *Ring* cycle, that is, the primary works).

But of course Wolf's question had not been a question. It was a cue to himself to perform one of his party tricks, which was to recite whole pages by heart of Schopenhauer's *The World as Will and Representation*. It was remarkable that anyone should have such powers of recall, yet, as he spouted the words and Winnie looked on admiringly, it was noticeable that she also had no hesitation, when there was a slight pause in the performance, about butting in with her own talk.

'Wolf agrees with me that as a stopgap arrangement it was satisfactory; but it is not ultimately right' – she began speaking in that extraordinary overemphasis which was her hallmark – 'for the grandchildren of Richard Wagner to complete their education in an English boarding school.'

She pronounced the last three syllables (*In-ter-nat* in German) with equal emphasis on each syllable. 'And so – what is to be done? Some local schools must be found for the autumn. But they need someone who can be like a tutor to them, a little like a sort of father figure, if you will. I have had to be away this year' – she smiled, both mysteriously and almost mystically, as though her absences might conceivably have been on another planet. 'One must be realistic. We have to think who will be here for the children. Their father, alas, is no more. Wolf has done all he conceivably can. But his place . . .'

Wolf, all the time she spoke, was continuing to recite Schopenhauer.

'His place is elsewhere. He has been kind, kind beyond measure to those children. But his destiny is to save Germany, not to be Uncle Wolf, simply.'

She lit a cigarette and gave one of her throaty dismissive chuckles. Her tone somehow suggested that she was putting up a struggle against those who had been arguing for Wolf abandoning his political life in favour of childcare. 'So, my dear N——— – I wondered, Wolf wondered, we both agree with one another – would you be prepared to . . . adopt a tutelary role towards the children?'

It was a fairly tall order. Wieland was now fifteen, Friedelind fourteen, Wolfgang thirteen and Verena twelve. I said yes immediately, as I said yes whenever Winnie asked me to do something, and wondered inwardly what I was letting myself in for. Whatever Winnie wanted me to do with the children, it was not going to be easy. She was the reverse of a disciplinarian. Presumably in reaction against her own regimented childhood, first in an English orphanage, then as the adopted child of very old people, deeply set in their ways, she imposed almost no structure or order on her children. Fidi had been completely at one with her in this, allowing the children to tumble up more or less as they pleased and believing that so long as they were 'cultivated' people who could speak a variety of European languages to the many grown-ups who came to the house, nothing else much mattered; except music, of course. But now Fidi was gone, where did I fit in?

Later, when Wolf had left, she expanded more generally on what she had in mind. 'I could not say, not in front of Wolf, but I am spending more and more time in Berlin. With Tietjen. He is going to revolutionize Bayreuth. It will be terrific. But we have so much to plan and he can't always leave Berlin. He is finishing off his work there at the State Opera and besides, the new designer he hopes one day to bring to Bayreuth, Emil Preetorius, is also in Berlin. You'll all survive without me for a bit.'

I almost felt emboldened at this point to make a declaration of sorts; to say that I was not sure I ever could, from now onwards in my life, survive without her; but that if the best I could hope for was to be her childminder, this was at least one way of staying close to her.

I did not ask, nor did I need to ask, what she meant by saying she could not talk about Tietjen in front of Wolf. It had been obvious from the first that the men loathed one another.

And so began my new life, in which my duties were much less specific than they had been when I was Siegfried Wagner's personal assistant. Half the time Winnie really did intend me to have the freedom to pursue my researches and to write some work about Wagner's philosophy. The rest of the time I was to take responsibility for the children who were no longer quite children.

'Do you believe in astrology?' This was Friedelind's question when I was sitting around with all four of them and we were presumably meant to be having some kind of improving, if not directly educational, talk.

Normally, when questions of belief were raised, I hummed and hawed. Ask me if I accepted this or that political or religious proposition and I began to stammer. But luckily, Friedelind had, for once, asked me an easy one. Did I believe in astrology. 'Absolutely not.'

Wieland, already a handsome young man more than he was a child, asked if I did not then believe in the Norns, or Erda, in the *Ring* cycle being able to foresee the destiny of mortals and immortals.

This rather threw me. I'd assumed he was an intelligent lad, which he was. 'It's a story, Wieland, it isn't . . .'

Wolfgang, his younger brother, who always wanted to 'score' off his brother – the two of them scrapped and fought all the time, and not merely verbally – intercepted my remark with 'You see, Wieland? It's all rubbish.'

'It can't be,' said Friedelind intently. 'Else why would Uncle Wolf consult magicians?'

While I tried to say that it was news to me that Uncle Wolf believed in magic, the four children all started talking at once. It was some time during this conversation, however, that the truth about Wolf began to dawn on me. I mean, the whole ghastly truth about this man and what he was about to unleash upon our country. It was, at this stage, only a glimmering. Irritation with my (as I thought) self-righteous parents still prevented me from seeing the whole truth. So did the truly anarchic and terrifying condition of the country. So did the surface plausibility of Wolf who, for all his strange habits and tendency to monologue, was a very dear friend of my dear friends.

'Erik Jan Hanussen is the greatest magician alive, according to Uncle Wolf,' said Friedelind earnestly. 'He can see into the future. He is going to go to where Uncle Wolf was born and dig up a mandrake root. If he digs up the root by the light of the full moon, it will be a sign that Uncle Wolf will become the Chancellor next year.'

I must have laughed at this suggestion, because an uneasy silence descended on the little circle, as though they did not want to share with me any more of the secrets Uncle Wolf had imparted to them.

It was the first time, really, that I became aware that National Socialism was, quite literally, an occult rite, a branch of the black arts, more than it was a political party. To this extent it was not really to be set beside Social Democratic or Communist or Monarchist Conservative views. It was burrowing away deep into the strange world which rationalists such as the Brothers Grimm, with their fairy stories, or Goethe, with his lifelong evocation of the Faust legends, had explored: that Gothic depth of the irrational which the Enlightenment, far from driving away or expunging, had merely driven underground. Its manifestations in post-Enlightenment times were the decadent art of Baudelaire or Huysmans, the later operas of Richard Wagner; and such disturbing aspects of the *völkish* movement as virulent anti-Semitism, which had not a scintilla of reasonable justification. (The more you tried to 'explain' anti-Semitism, the more you ended up constructing an implausible 'justification' for it, such as that there had been a lot of Jews 'behind' the Russian revolution. The truth is that anti-Semitism did not feed upon such 'explanations'; it grew in the fertile, poisonous soil of mythology, with the Wandering Jew standing at the foot of the Cross and mocking the suffering Christ, or tramping through Christian towns with a sack of Christian babies over his shoulder, which he intended to devour.)

Another – yet another! – point of difference was beginning to emerge between Richard Wagner on the one hand, and the National Socialists who had appropriated his name and his music for their own political purposes on the other. He saw the power, the strength, the *point* of mythologies. He knew why they were essential to any group, or nation or family, they were a natural and organic way which human beings had of expressing their shared concerns in story. The Greek tragedy was born in the shared, if buried, dreads, superstitions, hopes of *Greeks* – not the collective noun People but people, actual men and women. They responded to the Dionysian in art, religion, story – mythology – not to the formal ideas of Apollo but to the frenzied impulses of Dionysus.

Wagner did for people of the nineteenth century – not for The People – but for *people* – what Æschylus did for the ancient Greeks. Their fears about the collapse of society, about sex, about the disappearance of their god he refashioned for them in music. But the point of his dramas in a way is that there is no right or wrong way of performing them, they are endlessly available because art, unlike ideology, is fluid. Let us Germans stop being proscriptive; we've seen where wars and politics got us, let us see where art takes us – thus Hans Sachs, changed immediately by German audiences ever since into 'Deutschland, Deutschland, über Alles'. And then again, with the great mythological dramas he is saying: come again into these darkened, damp, dwarfish caves, come among the mossy rocks of the Rhine and re-explore these old stories of heroes and gods. History and mythology intermingle, play against one another like moving light flickering through trees beyond the window and dappling a room; but in the end history must be fixed in fact and can never therefore take us further into truth. Whereas mythology, once recognized as mythology, can.

To believe in the truth contained in *The Ring* you would have to disbelieve in any literal surface truth. (This I take it was the sort of area my brother, whom I had the cheek to mock, was exploring in his reading of the Bible.) When I heard the children saying that they *believed* in their grandfather's mythology – the Norns, the Earth

Goddess Erda foreseeing the future and so forth – I had a jolt. I thought I was with one set of people and I found myself to be with another. It was understandable to me that simple Bible Christians should think that theologians like my brother were undermining belief by saying that Noah's Ark never sailed in history or that angels did not fly over Jesus's stable birthplace, which was almost certainly not in Bethlehem. Understandable – but wrong. They were failing to see that far from disputing the truth of the Bible the demythologizers, as they were known, were working hard to reach it, like miners on their hands and knees, hacking at generations of accumulated strata that concealed it. But beyond the objections of these 'simple' believers were the much more dangerous 'fundamentalists' who failed utterly to see the nature of mythological material.

Maybe Wolf and the other Nazi Wagnerians were 'fundamentalists' on this level, able to miss the multiplicity of truths contained in the mythologies because they sought in them not the disturbing and ever-changing power of sound and story, but rather the hard confirmation of their ideology. Therefore it had to mean this or that. Alberich grubbing for gold, purchased through power at the expense of love, ceases to be a life-transforming general principle and becomes a cheap mask for Jewry: Hans Sachs, deprived of his generosity and irony, becomes a German nationalist.

To say one has been bewitched is not to deny the power of whatever magic has worked its enslavement. One is not denying the power; rather the creepy truth claims of the occult.

I had been bewitched by love of Winifred Wagner. I had watched the same thing happen to others – to Toscanini, for example. But although I now believed – *knew* – that Winnie and Wolf were lovers, I saw *him* as an enchanter of an altogether different order. His admirers were, definitely, bewitched – enchanted, mesmerized – one could say almost hypnotized. It was closely akin to the kind of obedience called forth by other religions. The goals offered were so attractive that self was lost in an ecstatic common cause.

Apart from watching Wolf from behind, as he leaned from a hotel window at Bayreuth in the very early days to harangue the admirers,

I had never seen the performances before huge crowds, phenomena that were already legendary. It was the Wagner children who initiated me into this unforgettable experience.

It was at a youth rally in Potsdam in October 1932. It was not, primarily, the chance of seeing Wolf as H, wowing the masses, that made me say that I would take the children. It was, primarily, the chance of going to Berlin accompanied by their mother, who would stay with us all in a hotel. While I was in Berlin, I also wanted to catch up with my brother. First and chief of all the attractions, however, was to accompany Winnie. Although, in her absence, I sometimes told myself that my love for her was finished – that it was simply too painful to acknowledge that she had slept with Wolf, had a child by him, loved him; and that, relentless as were her appetites, she was almost certainly prepared to sleep with Tietjen too – it only required one minute of her actual presence for all my slavish adoration of her to return. Every single part of her was desirable to me. Her fleshiness, the softness of her lips, especially when she sucked on a cigarette, her cheeks, her calves beneath the hems of her often boring dresses and skirts, her hair, her eyes, all filled me . . . of course with lust, but with a yearning, sadness, longing which I never felt for another woman. Sexual frustration, and inexperience, you will say, pure and simple. But is anything pure and simple? I've often said to myself since, since she was obviously someone who enjoyed sex and was by no means naturally monogamous, would she not rather have enjoyed launching me on my erotic life? But no hint ever came from her that she would be willing to do this and I would never have had the courage to make a lunge. Our relationship was determined, on my side at least, by yearning.

There could not have been a greater contrast between the two worlds I saw during that visit to Berlin. On the one hand there was the awkward couple of hours I spent with my brother in the rather dreary suburb where he was working as a pastor. No doubt my visit was inconvenient to him and I caught him at a busy time, but his impatience sprang from my real reason for being in Berlin. Naturally, he had guessed why I was there. Every street, every bus stop, every metro station was red with posters advertising the Youth Rally at Potsdam. In some districts these posters had been defaced, half torn down or scrawled over with Red slogans. There was an extraordinary atmosphere of tension, of violence, wherever one went. Small riots and outbreaks of fisticuffs were regular occurrences in the streets of Berlin. You felt that any group of people standing near one another – say, at a bus stop – might at any moment erupt into violence. I'm sure it wasn't just in my head, the suspenseful consciousness that something awful was about to happen. For some of us this 'awful thing', if we'd been asked to define it, was a civil war, or a Communist revolution, or both. For others like my brother there was no doubt what was most to be dreaded.

At first we kept off the subject. He gave me a cup of coffee in his book-crammed room – he was living as the lodger of a clergy widow in the parish – and then, apologizing because he could not give me more time, he asked me to walk with him while he went on a sick visit.

Heinrich had always looked much younger than his years. Now, at less than forty, he had started to look much older. His baldness – not total but affecting the whole of the top of his head – happened fast. There was a greyness of pallor about his face and he had lost quite a lot of weight. As we walked along the suburban pavement we talked about our parents in that ironical way we always had of discussing them – humorous, even satirical, but quite affectionate.

It was a blustery October afternoon. Light seemed to fade from the sky with every word we spoke to one another and the shadows between us, the intellectual gulfs, grew as we spoke family generalities. I could sense that Heinrich was working his way up to making one of his 'statements'. If he had not been Heinrich, always the bossy older brother, always self-righteous, if he had instead been a friend of mine, or better, a casual acquaintance, I should have been able, I think, to make some kind of response to the objections which I could anticipate him making to my attendance at the Potsdam rally. But Heinrich it was, and all the old rivalries and difficulties between us, probably going back to rivalries for our mother's attention in early childhood, returned. So, I was not able to say, 'Look. I do not go along with the madder mythologies of National Socialism any more than you do. I hate the SA thugs who beat up Jews and I don't believe the majority of decent Germans like that side of their movement. But something's got to be done in this country – we can't go on having a new government every few months and nine million people unemployed. We are in a state of anarchy and all your so-called reasonable parties have failed us – I don't want a confiscatory system of state Communism. So what do you propose? Why not have a short spell of what will in effect be martial law to see if we can get ourselves back on our feet again?'

I might have tried some speech like that, and I might have gone on to say that, whatever Heinrich and my parents thought of the Wagners, they had become my friends, and the children and their mother were entitled to have views that differed from those of conservative wishy-washies like Mum and Dad.

But there was that intensity in Heinrich's eyes as he turned to me. And I realized then that he had been lying to me when he said that he had to go on a sick visit that afternoon. For he had led me to the door of his church hall, a large barn of a building on the corner of this tree-lined street. There were posters on the door. On these posters there were two pictures. One was a reproduction of that Dürer painting of Christ crucified against a night sky, which hangs in the Dresden gallery. The other was a photograph of H in SA uniform.

WHICH OF THESE TWO MEN IS THE BEST GUIDE FOR YOUR LIFE?

That was the legend beneath the pictures.

Heinrich turned to me and suddenly asked, 'We are having a meeting here tonight, to coincide with . . . with . . . with the one in Potsdam. I'm hoping to get some of the young people in the area to come along and . . . and at least to see what's happening.'

'Heinrich, I . . .'

222

'Please. Would you consider bringing the children, the young people in your care, the Wagners, to join in the discussion here, rather than taking them to . . . that *charade?*'

Oh, Heinrich, oh, my brother. When I think of all the things that happened to you after that and how you suffered for your bravery. It pains me to record that I simply laughed at you.

The idea that the four Wagner children, who had been imploring me for weeks to accompany them to this big Youth Rally in Potsdam, would agree for a single moment to come out to this dismal suburb for a discussion group about Christianity with my brother Heinrich and a few earnest church adolescents with acne! It was very laughable.

'They might at least see,' he persisted through my mockery.

'The light?' I countered mercilessly.

'They might see that life is a bit more complicated than the Nazis are making it. They might see that life is not to be found in selfishness, whether it is personal selfishness or organized selfishness.'

'You don't think Germany needs to be a bit selfish, a bit collectively selfish just now? Well, I'm sorry, Heinrich, but I do.'

I felt my voice trembling and I realized I was losing control. It would have been so much better to have stuck to the generalities and the ironical jokes about our parents. But I could not stop myself now. 'Force me to choose between either of those gentlemen', I said, pointing to the poster, 'and maybe in an ideal world I wouldn't choose either. But we've had enough of being crucified.'

Heinrich stared at me. In the fading afternoon light his face had taken on an expression of infinite sadness. He wasn't out of control.

Then he spoke very quietly. 'The crucifixion hasn't begun,' he said.

I mind very much, when I recall that conversation in all its painfulness, that I was so angry. I simply turned away from him and did not even say goodbye.

In my tattered old copy of *The Idiot*, I kept my brother Heinrich's last letter, written from prison towards the end of the war.

My dear ——,

Something tells me this will be the last letter. I have written to Mother and Father, but I want to write a separate word to you, my brother. We are very different characters, with different takes on life. Sometimes, I have failed to see what you were trying to say to me, and I'm sorry not to have made more effort to understand you. Clearly, in the last decade we have taken very different views politically and this has led to a failure of sympathy on my part. I know that you are a good person and I believe you when you say that, for example, Winifred Wagner is a good person also. I would like you to forgive me if, in my anger at what has happened to our country, I have appeared to sit in judgement on you or on anyone else.

Maybe our early differences over Richard Wagner highlight what I am trying to say. It seems strange to be devoting the last letter I shall ever write to the subject of myth and music theory, but here goes. Do you remember that squabble we once had about the old Northern mythology and Christianity? You said that you thought that there was a nobility in the old Teutonic religion because, in spite of all the endeavours of the gods to build up their Valhalla, and in spite of the courage of Thunder and the virtue of Baldr, in the end they only face chaos and defeat? In Ragnarok, the Wolf Fenris devours the great World's Ash Tree and everything descends into fire and chaos ... And you said this was a truer picture of things than Christianity, which promised a fake happy ending, with hallelujahs for the faithful and tears being wiped away from every eye.

Perhaps you do not even remember this conversation. I confess when we had it (you were a student, and I was still a teacher) I did not really know how to answer it. My own version of Christianity was what you would call Liberal Protestant or Hegel-and-sodawater. I did not believe Christianity to be 'literally true', but merely a set of myths by which we could improve our lives. And well – maybe if that is all it is, who was I to say one set of myths was worse than another set of myths?

———, my brother, from my prison cell, from a man who is about to die, please let me tell you how wrong we *both* were. I was worrying my head in those days about whether the Gospels recorded true stories, and whether Christ ever performed miracles. But when I went to Berlin and began my work as a pastor, and started to take part in the protest campaigns of the Confessing Church, I discovered a quite different Christ, one who is alive, who takes possession of the heart and soul. When this has happened to a human soul, questions about the historical Jesus become . . . not irrelevant, exactly, but dry as dust. For it is *now* that we watch the water turning into wine; it is in our own lives that we feel our blindness turned to sight, the paralysis of our limbs leaping into joy.

The Nazis made me a Christian. For that I shall always feel a sort of gratitude to them, even as they take me out to be hanged. Poor benighted men and women, they have things so wrong. They have tried to invert Good and Evil. They have demonstrated it cannot be done. Good will always go on being Good, and Evil will always be Evil. Christianity does not invent a fake happy ending of hallelujahs. It discovers a God who reveals himself not in power and triumph but in suffering and in apparent defeat. We used to hear so many sermons about the sorrows of Good Friday being followed by the glory of Easter. These harsh times in Germany have taught us again that the Glory *was* the Cross. God's glory never shone forth so brightly as on the Cross. Only a suffering God could save us – not a false idol, not a muscular Nordic demigod like Siegfried who knew no fear, but a vulnerable Christ who knew fear and doubt and horror, and who died doubting.

———, my dear brother, forgive a sermon as my last word to you, but I so love you, although we have not always appeared close. And in my last words of love I owe it to you to tell you what now seems to me the only truth worth knowing. You will survive this terrible war, as will Mother, pray God. And even if the institutional Churches do not survive, and all Europe is in ruins by the end of the nightmare, Christ will survive – the fundamental truth about dying-in-order-to-live, and life-through-death-of-self, that will survive, through Jesus Christ Our Lord.

By the time I got back to the hotel the young Wagners were all vastly overexcited. There had been talk of going out to Potsdam by the excellent railway, but Winnie decided to hire a car. Needless to say, very good seats in the stadium had been reserved for us all.

Potsdam is now wrecked. Even as you and I were making our way to Leipzig in the train for *Meistersinger*, the bulldozers were destroying what was left of the City Palace in the centre; what was left, that is to say, after the devastating air raids of April 1945. I do not know even now whether the Palace of Sanssouci survives, where Frederick the Great entertained Voltaire and played the flute to J. S. Bach's accompaniment. For all I know that too has been demolished for ideological reasons.[*] The last vestiges of the Hohenzollern dynasty have probably been wiped off the face of the earth. And why not?

Before the war, however, all these magnificent rococo palaces and landscapes survived, and our drive into Frederick the Great's residential city, with its domes and churches and parks and pavilions, was very beautiful, for the buildings had been lit up and although we could not see the extent of the parks, it was like driving into a vast illuminated doll's theatre.

All along the way, young people were still trooping to the rally, and when we got to the field on the edge of the town where the speech and the parade were to take place, it was evident that tens, possibly

[*] N—— was unduly pessimistic. The Palace and Gardens of Sanssouci all survive, magnificently restored. The Chinese Pavilion, the Ehrenhof (Court of Honour), the Belvedere on Klausberg Hill and many other pavilions and palaces have survived the tragedies of the twentieth century.

hundreds of thousands of human beings had assembled. Winnie had by now attended many Party Days in Munich and Nuremberg, but this was the first really large-scale event I had seen. And absolutely immediately one was swept up into the excitement of it all.

Of the four Wagner kids, Friedelind was undoubtedly the most excited, pointing out boys in their SA or Hitler Youth uniforms, or those who, without uniform, nonetheless wore swastika armbands of red, white and black. 'Look at them!' (A banner saying 'We have walked from Prague'. Another saying 'The youth of Vienna salutes A—— H——'.)

Somehow the driver left us by the main entrance to the field and we were shown to our seats in the grandstand which had been erected in the field. The field itself was lit with spotlights and arc lights. There was loud music. Then one of the speakers, not a very good speaker, told us that the moment for which we had all been waiting was about to arrive. Our Leader was going to come and address us.

As if spontaneously, the crowd broke into the Horst Wessel song. For over a year now, this strange but haunting song had been the anthem of the Movement. Horst Wessel was a young SA leader in Berlin. He moved into some dingy lodgings with a prostitute called Erna, but neither of them would pay the rent and the landlady got the local Communist street fighters to come and turf them out for her. It happened that the leader of this particular Communist gang was also a client of Erna's, so he said, when he raised a pistol and shot the twenty-one-year-old Horst Wessel dead, 'You know what that's for.'

It wasn't a very edifying incident, but the Party's Nosferatu, Dr Goebbels, soon got to work. Horst Wessel had left behind a poem, 'Raise high the flags', which he used to sing to an old Viennese cabaret tune. Nosferatu made Wessel into a working-class German Jesus: 'Leaving home and mother, he took to living among those who scorned and spat on him. Out there, in the proletarian section, in a tenement attic, he proceeded to live his youthful, modest life. A socialist Christ!'

This German Jesus had died in February 1930 and the Mary Magdalene, Erna, had survived. Now we sang Horst Wessel's song, with the cabaret tune rearranged to fit (just about) a march rhythm.

> Raise high the flags, the ranks in close formation
> Of SA men march calmly and march strong.
> Our comrades shot by Reds and by Reaction
> March now in spirit with us, all the ages long ...

Winnie was making herself hoarse as she belted out the words and it was evident that her children knew them by heart already. For those of us who were new to this sort of thing, there were programmes with the words of this, and many other stirring ditties, printed.

> The streets are free now for the Brown Battalions,
> Free streets where Sturm Abteilung march ahead!
> Where swastikas hang out, there hope springs for the
>   millions
> It brings the day of freedom and of bread!

And then the most rousing chorus of all.

> For one last roll-call sounds the gallant bugle,
> For one last fight stand ready friend and friend!
> Soon over every street those flags will triumph,
> The time of slav'ry hastens to its end.

The tune is only a cabaret song, but when it is sung by over a hundred thousand voices it is hypnotic. And then, almost before the words had been finished, the Leader, with brilliant timing and perfect choreography, came almost running up the steps just beneath us. The arc lights were trained upon him and, as if the crowd were now not a hundred thousand individuals but one great creature, trained to his absolute will, we roared, we cheered and we raised our right hands in the Roman salute.

> Victory, Hail! Victory, Hail! Victory, Hail!

If one were to write down on the page the exact words spoken in the next half-hour, they would look quite unimpressive. In any case I can't remember them exactly. I do remember that he had tempered his words perfectly for a young, idealistic audience. He spoke of them coming from Austria, from Czechoslovakia, yes, from all over Germany. For Germany was not a place whose borders were determined by its enemies. Germany was wherever the German soul was to be found and wherever the German language was spoken. He thanked Almighty God that he had been born near the borders of two great empires, the Austro-Hungarian Empire and the Prussian or German empire. And now, after a gallant war and the betrayal of the greater Germany by its enemies, we had all been through the hardest decade of our history. But that time was over. Germany had awoken. German youth had awoken. And in all German lands, from the borders of Switzerland to the furthest reaches of Poland, from the Baltic to Bavaria, from Czechoslovakia (so-called) to Austria, the German people would one day be free.

And then, I do remember – he quoted, or rather he most revealingly misquoted, Hans Sachs:

Even though the Roman Empire should vanish into the mist, yet should remain – German Culture, German Art, German Youth and German Strength!

It was an extraordinary performance by any standards. We were all transfixed by it. I do not believe that even brother Heinrich, had he been present, would have been able to resist the hypnotism of that speaker. On this occasion his words were all positive and uplifting. There were harsh words for the enemies of Germany, but he did not spell out who they were. There was no coarse anti-Jewish sentiment. It was a kind of patriotic aria, ranging from quiet reminiscences of his own youth and childhood, and his yearning to serve his country in peace and in war, to the terrible condition of things today and to our determination to raise ourselves out of it.

You could not but be carried away by his mental music. It was mass hypnosis, mass hysteria if you will, of the most electrifying kind, all the more so, I think, because the audience were so young. After he had spoken the Youth organizations from all over Germany marched past the podium, carrying torches and banners, while we cheered and sang and raised our arms. Looking back, it seemed inevitable that this man, with such an extraordinary power to win over crowds, should have achieved the impossible: he became the Chancellor of Germany a few months later, at the end of January 1933. It wasn't a decade since I had offered him a sugar lump to put in his wine in the dining room of the Golden Anchor Hotel in Bayreuth. Not long before that he had been in prison, this man who in his youth had failed to get into an art school and had lived as a bum in the dosshouses of Vienna. A Triumph of the Will indeed.

Naturally, I did not tell my parents about going to the rally, though they must have guessed. The newspapers were full of it and my rather feeble attempt to explain away the visit to Berlin as a cultural event, in which the children had been to art galleries and concert halls, was not plausible. By the time I got home, they were much more worried by what had happened that evening at my brother's parochial hall. Astoundingly, he had managed to persuade about twenty brave Christian teenagers, evenly divided into the sexes, to come to his meeting. Not much had been said because they had been joined by some SA men (in mufti) who tore down the posters and threatened even the girls with violence. Most of the young had fled, but a few had remained, hoping to protect my brother from a beating. They did not succeed. He was found beside some bushes just outside the church hall, bleeding from the mouth and from the skull. He had lost about six teeth and for several days he was concussed. He had two broken ribs. My mother told me, with a mixture of terror for his safety and pride at his courage, that in spite of a swollen jaw he had insisted upon preaching the next Sunday. He had chosen for his text 'I have fought with wild beasts'.

Parsifal

One very cold winter morning in the winter of 1933–4 I took the bus to the nearest stop at the bottom of the Green Hill. I wasn't averse from riding my bike in the snow, quite the opposite, but after a skid on the ice the rear wheel needed replacing and I'd left it with the menders the previous afternoon. I don't know what impulse made me take the bus. I hardly ever took buses – our town is too small, really, to make such journeys necessary, unless you live in the sprawling working-class suburbs beyond and want to get to the centre, or to one of the outlying villages. Anyway – it is simpler perhaps to believe that Fate made me change my habits and take the bus.

It was fairly crowded at that hour of the morning, and there was a good fug of steamed windows and cigarette smoke as everyone chattered happily. But at a certain stop along the line a young oik wearing the brown shirt and swastika armband of the SA got on board. Though he was alone he had that vacant stupid look on his face which addicts of violence, often exhibitionists, wear: 'Look at me, while I kick someone's face in.' An expression that carries with it defiance: 'Any objections? If I kick this human face? Objections? Anyone?'

Winnie had often complained to Wolf about the street bullyism of the local SA lads, while having a personal fondness – I'll talk about this a little later – for Erich Röhm, the actual leader of the SA, that private Nazi army which had been so important a part of their personal mythology in early days. Now that Wolf was Chancellor, right-hand man to old General von Hindenburg and in cahoots with the regular army, the semi-, or actually criminal activities of the street army were a liability to him. Many thought he should wind it up, but it would have lost him many loyal supporters in the Party and the more his personal power grew – it was already approaching Napoleonic heights – the stronger grew his persecution mania and the certainty that Party colleagues were plotting his downfall.

The SA oik in the bus, with his nerdish peaked cap and BO, was an unimpressive person. Cigarette in mouth, he moved down the crowded bus until he was standing quite near me and then asked me, 'You wanna seat?'

I didn't know what he meant and made some dithering remark to the effect that I was OK standing, but that should the crowd thin out I'd sit down.

''Ere – you!' I realized to my horror that he was addressing an old lady sitting just beneath us. With sausage fingers he pushed her hat askew and prodded her bony shoulders. 'Didn't you 'ear the gentleman?'

The old lady looked up, her face tautened with fear.

'An Aryan wants to sit down,' said the oik. 'So stand up – *yid*.'

I protested that I did not want the old lady's seat.

'What's the matter? You a yid too?'

I was reduced to a stupid incoherence by this question. There were now murmurings round the youth. Some people seemed revolted by his behaviour, but I do not think I deceive myself when I say I remember some people talking about 'them' taking up space on 'our' buses.

'Well, if this poofter won't take your seat, I will,' said the youth and he pulled the old lady to her feet. He looked around, blushing slightly, but with a conceited grin, his behaviour in his own eyes deserving applause.

Courage, like music, is a matter of timing. I had hesitated for only a split second, but it was enough to give the thug his advantage. I should instantly, for I was the one standing nearest him, have punched his suppurating face. The old lady was badly shaken, as much by the brutal rudeness as by having been manhandled. But in the split second I had hesitated someone else had risen from her seat. 'Here. Take my seat.'

'It's all right, dear, it's all right,' said the old woman with a trembly voice.

'No. You sit down.' The person who said this was someone who could easily have been taken for a boy. She wore her thin mousy hair short, in a crop. She had a cigarette alight between her fingers, whose orange tips, like Winnie's, revealed the habit of chain-smoking. Her nails were very short, pared right down. The very dark-brown eyes animated her thin face. The elfin beauty was not immediately obvious, since the character breathing through the features was so strong that you were aware of the personality before you took in the appearance, a very unusual sequence in my experi-ence. She exuded confidence; the world was to be understood and accepted on her terms or not at all.

'I insist that you sit down,' she said, laying a gentle hand on the old woman's shoulder.

'What you, then, a lesbian?' The oik looked around the carriage for approval of his joke. I'm glad to say, for the sake of my fellow townspeople, that he did not get it. The atmosphere of menace he had created was, as well as frightening, acutely embarrassing.

The girl – she was only in her very early twenties – continued to caress the shoulder of the old woman, as if she were her grand-mother. She did not look at her, merely kept the hand there to comfort and to protect. 'Just tell me when you want to get off the bus,' she said.

After a few minutes we reached the stop at the bottom of Burgerreutherstrasse, where I should have got off for the Festival Theatre. So, too, should the girl, because I recognized her. She was the one that Winnie, who liked nicknames and jokey appellations, referred to as the Communist Hornplayer (*die Kommunistische Englisch-Hornspielerin*). Winnie's whimsy obviously had to do with her automatic sensing of other women's attractions to Tietjen. The KEH, as she was sometimes abbreviated on Winnie's lips, had lately joined the orchestra. It was unusual, though not unknown, for women to play wind instruments in those pre-war days, but no one had any doubts about the Communist Hornplayer's abilities. I could even remember the day of her auditions and Tietjen remarking upon the skill with which she had played her 'party piece', as he called it – the amazing, long cor anglais melody of the 'shepherd's pipe' at the beginning of the third act of *Tristan*.

I could not work out if the KEH had 'clocked' me as someone who also worked at the Festival Theatre. At that moment her attention was entirely focused on our fellow bus traveller who, it transpired, was going to visit a sister who lived in St Johannis, a village about four miles from the centre of town. The SA oaf had got off the bus long before this.

The old lady was pathetically grateful to the KEH, almost slavishly so. It was horrible to sense the way she had come, within less than a year of the National Socialists taking power, to feel she was living in Germany on sufferance, she who had lived here all her life. We took her up to the door of a small, neat house, surrounded by shrubs in pots, conveyed her safely to her sister, then walked back together to the bus stop.

'So!' said the KEH, lighting up her umpteenth fag. 'I think we'll have a long wait till the next bus. Helga Gerlandt!' Her handshake was surprisingly hearty and firm. Knowing nothing, I immediately thought of the SA thug's taunt on the bus and, putting the handshake together with her short hair, assumed lesbianism.

Perhaps it was this that put me so much at my ease in the first instance? There we stood, by a cold bus stop, waiting for the next one to come along (it took over forty minutes). She had indeed recognized me as someone who worked for the Wagner family. Was this why she did not make any allusion, any at all, to the incident of the old lady on the bus? Was it because she assumed an absolute political division between us? You couldn't be too careful in Germany then, as her subsequent experience showed.

I made some fleeting reference to how well she had behaved. But she still wouldn't pursue it. 'I wish I'd hit him,' I said.

'He's a bastard. They all are.' She threw her butt and it hissed in the snow. 'You don't smoke?' This question was accusatory.

'I do, but not that much.'

'Not as much as me? Go on' – she offered me one of hers. My gloved finger fumbled, her ungloved finger took a cigarette and our hands touched.

'So – quite a lot of trouble about this year's *Parsifal*.' Everything she said was tinged with heavy irony. This continued to be the case for all the coming few years until crossness – mutual crossness with one another – drove out the jokes. But that was much later, after we had married.

We began to talk about the *Parsifal* row, which was the talk, not only of Bayreuth but of the whole opera world that winter. Tietjen had been determined, during Winnie's 'sabbatical' (the year you were born), to tackle the problem of the stage designs and costumes at the theatre. Many of the props, costumes and pieces of scenery dated back to the time of Richard Wagner himself and were absolutely ragged. As were the two aunts, Eva Chamberlain and Daniela Thode, but this did not prevent them having strong feelings. When they heard that there were plans afoot to have a redesigned *Parsifal* they drew up a petition, for which they got nearly a thousand signatures from devotedly conservative Wagnerians, that the original 1882 stage sets should never be altered.

Winnie, who was now open in her hatred of the aunts, did not care about their hurt feelings, but she was rattled by the prospect of these thousand names, who might withdraw their support. Was there any guarantee that there were a thousand modernists out there who would buy tickets to take the conservatives' places? 'It makes me so angry!' she had exclaimed during one of the rows with the aunts. 'You might as well claim that it was going against the sacred will of the Master not to light the stage with gas, because that was what he did. *My children, make it new* – that was his motto. My God, it's a theatre, not a shrine.' But this heretical idea only confirmed the aunts in their view that, as far as *Parsifal* at least was concerned, they were right to resist any change whatsoever.

'It's a load of crap, total shit, of course, *Parsifal*,' said the KEH. 'Nietzsche for once in his life got something right.'

'You're just thinking of *The Case of Wagner*,' I said.

'No, I'm not,' she returned instantly, aggressively, passionately. I saw for the first time the anger that was always part of our relationship – her brown eyes blazed at the implied patronage in my suggestion that she had not read *everything*. 'His judgement of the contents of the *Parsifal* poem are all true,' she asserted. 'More Liszt than Wagner. Counter-Reformation – decadent drivel.' She giggled. 'All too restricted by Christianity.' She suddenly looked sternly at me and asked, 'You're not a Christian, are you?'

'No – no, of course not.'

'What a relief.' She puffed out smoke into the wintry air. Why did this remark make me so happy? Because it suggested she wanted to include me in her future?

'But he also recognized, the Basel loon, that the music of *Parsifal* was bloody marvellous – best thing Wagner ever wrote, I think. You remember, Nietzsche asks somewhere, "Has Wagner ever written anything better?" So although he hated Wagner for falling sobbing at the foot of the Cross and all that *crap*, he knew that the music cuts you through like a knife. That Prelude is just an amazing piece of musical juggling. You start with A flat major, all those arpeggios building up; then he repeats the motif with arpeggio harmonies a whole octave higher with violins, trumpets, oboes; then back again at the end, with the trumpet, to A flat major, with that slow building of C minor – oh, yes, yes!' She punched the air.

I began trying to say why I thought the Christian elements in *Parsifal* worked very well. I talked about the nineteenth century having got rid of God too brutally – with the young Wagner reading Feuerbach and deciding that Christianity had to go – but that later, when he'd read Strauss's *Life of Jesus*, Wagner had realized how crude those reductionists' views of the New Testament were and ...

'My Christ, you *are* a Christian!'

'Schweitzer talks about Tragic Christians.'

'That old Nazi!'

I had never heard anyone disparage Albert Schweitzer before. He was universally, and not just in Germany, regarded as a saint.

'He's just gone to Africa to assert the superiority of white men over black men. What's so clever in that? His so-called Tragic Christianity is just a reinforcement of the colonial cultural traditions we should be encouraging the Africans to throw off. It's so dishonest, it makes me boil. Schweitzer admits that Christianity isn't true, but he wants to go on living as if it were true.'

'Isn't there some nobility in that?' I was thinking of my brother in Berlin; it had not occurred to me that my parents were in a similar situation and would be equally brave, equally 'tragic', when the time of testing arrived.

'There can't be any nobility in living a lie,' she said firmly.

'But they don't want to lie, the Tragic Christians. Their tragedy is that they want to tell the truth. And incidentally, I think Wagner was one really. I think that's what *Parsifal* is about. I think it's about recognizing that Christian myths, even if they are myths, can still sustain and feed us – not just our imaginations but our capacity to be good.'

'No one can be good in a criminal society. Only when society is reordered can there be any virtue. Virtue without social justice is simply an illusion.'

'And who will do the reordering?' I asked.

'We will,' she said simply.

Then the bus came.

Christ left the nineteenth century because there was no place for Him in it. He could find no refuge in its lust for profit, in its industrial inventiveness, in its exploitation of child workers, in its grinding down the faces of the poor, in its boorishly material answers – Marx-Engels – to its spiritual problems. How could it come to have made so many moral mistakes: factories/colonialism/capitalism? In fact, once caught up in the capitalistic nightmare, no one could really escape it, though Tolstoy, rich aristocrat that he was, could afford to become a simple peasant-anarchist and pretend that the machine age had not arrived.

So they all railed against Him and, like Kundry, laughed at the Crucifixion. Hegel had spiritualized Him out of existence, made

Him an ideal, rather than the perpetual disturber of the human conscience, the perpetual upsetter of the idea of morality with the concept of grace and redemption. So came the materialistic inter-pretations of the New Testament and its origins, a New Testament without miracle, a Gospel demythologized by Feuerbach, Wagner's youthful hero, and by Strauss of Tübingen. Nietzsche thought he was banishing Christ by his childish anger against a non-existent God, but he did not realize that it was he, with his loud ranting, who had already been banished. (After their quarrel, Wagner wanted to send Nietzsche, as a gentle jokey reproach, a bust of Voltaire which he and Cosima acquired.)

Cosima had her own relationship with the nineteenth century's mad spiritual journey. She was brought up a Catholic and could never entirely expunge the mental habits it had brought along with it. But while she was falling in love with Wagner and putting aside her husband in order to be with him, the Pope was assembling his Vatican Council in which he would declare himself to be an infal-lible being. Against the relentless reason of the nineteenth century, its churning machines, its steel battleships, its steam pistons and its business logic, the ancient Italian aristocrat Pio Nono asserted the supremity of unreason, a gesture as violently angry, and as mad, as Nietzsche's declaration that God was dead. In fact, the Pope declaring himself infallible was the same gesture, for to blaspheme against the Holy Spirit so violently as to claim a property of divine infallibility for oneself must be the ultimate denial of God.

Cosima became a Protestant and confronted the awful raw possi-bilities of being fallible – about God, about sin, about sex, about anything. She found a sort of freedom in it for a while, but pretty soon had to construct a new religion. Living without the old idol-atries of Rome, she had to replace them with the idolatries of Bayreuth, and *Parsifal*, which she urged Wagner to write, was her sacred text. Ceaselessly and unsuccessfully she tried to petition the Reichstag to make it a unique text in the whole of German drama and music: she tried to make them pass a law which stated that only on the hallowed stage of the Festival Theatre could this solemn ritual ever be enacted. She went to her grave bitter that she had failed.

And there arose another, more fervent if possible even than Cosima, in his devotion to this text: 'If I had power,' said Wolf . . . 'If I had the power, I would indeed put this law through the Reichstag, that in Bayreuth, and in Bayreuth alone, could the story of Parsifal and the Grail Knights be sung.'

And as so often, the spirit of Richard Wagner laughed at the absurdity of his devotees and their mad reversals of everything he had believed.

Wolf was at his large desk in the Reichs Chancellery. The social misfit to whom I had offered sugar in the dining room of the Golden Anchor only eight years before was now Napoleon. But he was also a Grail Knight, awaiting the demise of the old wounded hero; for General von Hindenburg still lived on as President and his other old comrade in arms, Ludendorff, who had supported Wolf in his early days and even played a part in the putsch of 1923, now intoned his operatic warning: 'I solemnly prophesy that this accursed man will cast our Reich into the abyss and bring our nation to inconceivable misery. Future generations', he intoned to the old General, 'will damn you in your grave for what you have done' – that is, offer Wolf the Chancellorship.

Mistaking my turn, rather than entering the library where we had been told to assemble before the meal, I blundered into the dining room itself. To call it spacious does not convey the size of the place. It felt as if tanks could easily have been driven into it and still not brushed against the tables. In the middle was a large refectory table of polished mahogany. It would have seated thirty people with ease. But then beyond that, in a bay near one of the large windows that looked down on Unter den Linden, was a round table set for eight, as I quickly saw.

It was a striking table display. It could have been the slightly fussy luncheon table set in one of the more chichi Munich cafés. It was too ornate to be domestic. A large silver epergne, representing a youthful warrior, stood to attention in the middle of the table, around which were arranged clusters of white flowers, lilies of the valley, white freesias, white carnations, in which had been set very narrow candles, almost too small for table candles, practically the sort you would put on cakes. The napkins, too, were not of the kind you would expect to see either in an official residence such as this nor in a domestic setting. They were folded into the shapes of fans and inserted into the glasses. I stooped to look at one more closely and noticed that in the corner of every single napkin had been embroidered the initials A.H.

Disconcertingly, the glass containing the napkin moved, first an inch one way, then back again. 'That,' rasped a familiar voice, 'is straight, I think. People never give enough attention to the laying of a table.'

Wolf was squatting on his haunches, with his eyes at the level of the table top. He was making sure that every place setting was exactly regular and symmetrical. Without getting up he added, 'I had some English guests staying; very, very great friends. I gathered they found it amusing that my initials were embroidered on the napkins. And on the towels in the bedrooms. Eduard – he is a very good footman, he comes and tells me things – said that they sat on the edge of the bed, these young Englishwomen and their mother, and laughed because there were initials on the towels.'

'Really?'

Was there some kind of trick? Should I have been sharing in the laughter or was it an example of the general oddity, which the rest of the world has noticed over the last few centuries, of the things that make English people laugh?

'That should do it.' He moved a silver knife a millimetre to the left, then stood up, rubbing his hands. He stared at the table with the satisfaction of an artist. 'Winnie would perhaps know about the initials,' he said, 'though it is a long time since she was in England, of course. And this morning' – he spoke almost in a tone that suggested

I had come into the room simply in order to discuss the matter with him – 'I spoke on the telephone to Reichsbischof Müller. We are nearly there. What does your father think of Reichsbischof Müller?'

This, like the initials on the towels, was esoteric stuff. With some conversationalists you might have expected a trick question here, but in my experience, anyway when he was in Winnie's entourage, Wolf did not go in for trick questions.

'I told Bishop Müller that I belong to no confession. I am neither a Protestant nor a Catholic, I believe only in Germany. It is obvious that just as I have entirely reorganized the Civil Service and the other institutions, we should put our national Church, the Church of Martin Luther, on a rational basis. I'm sure most decent Germans want that – the vast majority of God-fearing Germans. I have always made it clear that our Movement is fundamentally a Christian movement, but it is not for us to propagate religion. That is for Bishop Müller, and your father, and his churches.' He looked me full in the eye. He conveyed the sense that he would do anything to help you, that the reorganization of the Church was something for which the majority of God-fearing Germans had been yearning, Sunday by Sunday.

My father's opinion of Bishop Müller would not have been repeatable in this setting and if I had told the Leader what my brother was proposing to do, when these Church reforms were put into effect, he would probably have been sent to a concentration camp. Müller was a puppet of the regime. Only that week Agnes von Zahn-Harnack, the daughter of my father's old supervisor and mentor, had written from Berlin to say that she had published a petition to all the Churches to stay clear of state control and to avoid adopting the ideas of the 'Movement', especially in relation to anti-Semitism. Frau Zahn-Harnack had written, 'In every area of our national history and culture they appropriate it and make it their own. You were so right to stay away from the 450th anniversary celebrations of Luther's birth in Wittenberg in November. Müller's speech was pure Nazi and at the statue of Luther in the town square the bishops actually raised their hand in the Roman salute! Everyone from our history is enlisted. Frederick the Great – imagine the scorn he would in actual life have felt for the mustachioed one. Goethe will probably be next. We must hold out against it. When Luther said *Germanis meis natus sum, quibus et serviam*, he did *not* mean he was a Nazi. In fact, now the best way we can all serve our fellow Germans is to tell them to *wake up* and stop before it is too late.'

That was the voice of Harnack's daughter. I suspected that many of the more intelligent practising Lutherans would agree with her. I no longer greatly cared. The *Kommunistische Englisch-Hornspielerin* had taken up residence inside my head and any faint sentimental feeling I might have retained of being a fellow-traveller with Christianity had vanished. As for my feelings about Winnie and Wolf, and about the current political climate, these too were in a jangle of chaos since the overconfident elfin figure of the KEH sat beside all my thoughts and laughed, inside my skull, at my hedging and fudging, and at the general weakness of my outlook and expression.

'I was brought up, as you may know, as a Catholic.' For a moment he stared into the middle distance. Then he smiled and, coming closer to me, patted my upper arm and said, 'Good, good!'

I had the disconcerting sense that I was supposed to have agreed to something, even though I had hardly uttered a syllable. He led me from the room as if a very satisfactory conclusion had been reached to a hitherto insurmountable set of problems.

It was Herr Treibel, who owned the small apartment block in Linz where they lived, who had made the suggestion. No doubt the lad's mother had chattered, a mixture of pride and desperation, for what was he to do with himself, this moody youth who thought that normal professions were 'boring', who said he wanted to be an 'artist', who whistled tunes from operas, who inhabited quite another world from the one all his contemporaries appeared to accept, the world where you work, bring home your money, make love to your wife, get drunk, sleep, go to work ... Someone had suggested he try to join the Civil Service, become a Customs clerk maybe, like his dada had been. She'd (without telling the youth) investigated it. His qualifications weren't up to much, they had not really esteemed him highly at the Realschule, which was anyway full of snobs.

He knew, the youth, that some such pathetic thoughts had fluttered in his mother's hopeless, irritating, ever-beloved heart. He thought of the Marriage Feast of Cana, when the mother of the Saviour had tried to push Him forward – 'Ask Him, if you want a miracle performed. My boy will do you a miracle!' And the Lord had replied, 'Woman – my hour is not yet come.'

None of them could possibly understand – not the teachers at the Realschule, who completely failed to engage with what was going on inside his skull; not his brutal father, thank God five years dead, nor the father's children by the earlier marriage, Alois and Angela – they all understood as little as his baby sister Paula. God understood, only he had discovered at an early age that God, as such, did not exist. What existed, to take you out of *all this*, out of the banality, the poverty, the conversations about the price of coffee, the tedious nothingness of the family's conversation, and to take you too away from the dread and the violence and the smell of his father – which still, though he was five years dead, could frighten him, that great hulking brute! – what could take you out of it all was *ceremony*.

He had first been aware of it when he was only five or six years old. It was the year they lived in Passau – the hulking monster-brute undeserving of the name of father had worked in the Customs office there, and then been assigned to a job in Linz, leaving the rest of the family *behind*. Every second that his father was there, you felt the threat of his presence – the smell of alcohol and sweat and tobacco, the bad language, the shouting, the violence – towards them all, but especially, it seemed, towards him, the little lad. So when the father was gone, away in Linz, Passau had been a sort of paradise. The mother had let him wander, much of the time, and he had liked to walk about in the cathedral and lose himself in the vast, whitish-grey baroque space. The twinkling lights before the statues of the saints, the priests muttering their private masses at the side altars, the murmured voices from the confessionals, all added to the strangeness of the place, but most amazing of all was when the curtain went up, and they did a show – Benediction of the Blessed Sacrament on a Sunday afternoon, with the Host in a huge gilded clock-like case, carried and waved about the submissive crowds, and rank upon rank of well-choreographed acolytes with candles and priests in their stiff embroidered robes. *That* took you out of all *this*! That redeemed you from the humdrum. Retrospect, from any of the tormented staging posts of his life, did not, when looking back on that carefree year in Passau, recall any personal awareness of the Almighty. It was later that that came, not mysticism – that he detested – but a sense that he was riding the thunderclouds, that destiny, great impersonal fate, woven by the Norns and decreed by the Earth-Mother Erda, had singled out his destiny above his fellows'.

The Passau experiences, added to by experiences in Linz, gave merely the simple consolations of taking part in large colourful ceremonies in buildings ten thousand times the size of home. Other aspects of Church life displeased him. Even more than being made to go to confession himself, he hated the thought of his mother going through that humiliation – she who had never committed a sin in her life. How dare they, the black-robed maggots, sit in their polished confessionals and force that sacred being to tell them of her sorrows and sufferings, when it was they, with their pot bellies and their sexual perversions, who should be made to crawl along the ground and lick the very dust before her feet. That thought made him, even as a growing boy, feel as if the blood in his head was quite literally boiling, and he had to stop and jump up and down with rage. For this reason, of course, he had made a mockery of the confessional from the very beginning and, when being prepared for his First Communion the year after they left Passau, he had told the priest a pack of lies – mainly about the lavatory, but also about his siblings.

'You must not make up fairy stories, this is a sacred place,' the priest had said. But it had only inspired the boy to go on and on with the filth. There was nothing the priest could do to stop him. Even in adolescence, when he had of course given up religion except as the most formal outward observance, he had sometimes felt tempted, when passing one of the confessionals in the cathedral at Linz, to go in and spew out the filthiest and most violent lies he could think of. Nothing the black maggot could do, with his craven commitment to keep the secrets of that sordid box until the grave. (A likely story in the Jesuit churches, of course – it was well-known that the Jesuit churches in Munich, for example, regularly sold the confessional secrets of their most distinguished penitents to a big Jewish operator in New York.)

By the time they were living in Linz, and his father was dead, he had already made up his mind to be an artist, and he had found another outlet for that 'feeling', for that need for the consolations provided by large spaces, large noises, bright colours, ritualized experience: opera.

Sometimes alone, sometimes with his only real friend of those days, Gustl Kubizek, who was going to study music, he had gone to the opera. Gustl liked Verdi and thought it was worth saving up to go to the grand opera house, the Royal Opera. The processional march from *Aida* was all right, of course, but there was something about Verdi that Gustl's friend disliked; maybe it was his geniality. Once, when they were walking along a street, they passed an organ grinder with a monkey, playing 'La donna e mobile'! 'There's your Verdi,' he had said, 'imagine a monkey-organ grinding out tunes from *Lohengrin*!'

No, he preferred the much cheaper theatre, the Burgtheater, where he had seen his earliest productions of Wagner and fallen under the Master's spell. In *Rienzi* the young demagogue who came from nowhere took all the Roman crowds with him. In *Lohengrin* the mysterious stranger from afar came to rescue a chaotically and badly organized little German state. Had Lohengrin passed any exams? Did he belong to a high social class? Was he fifth grade, sixth grade? He came because he was sent by destiny to awaken the power of the German sword.

The music worked its hypnosis over his soul. It was better than anything you got at High Mass or Benediction – the same, but better, especially when the massed choruses came. (That was the only drawback of the great *Ring* cycle, which he only came to learn later – so few choruses.)

His career as a teenage artist foundered. The Viennese Academy of Architecture, which was one possibility, would not take you without a diploma from the building school, and they wouldn't give you a diploma unless you had reached a certain grade and passed for a diploma at the Realschule – and it was too late for all that sort of thing now. He would just have to stay at home with mother and prove them all wrong, with his architectural drawings (he already had plans, aged sixteen, for the total rebuilding of Linz) and with his stage designs. It was time for him to design the sets for *Lohengrin*. His mother could keep him until he found his feet.

Even when trouble struck, at the beginning of 1907, he had not really understood. His mother Klara had been to see the 'poor people's doctor', Dr Eduard Bloch, a gentle clever Jew. A grotesque relation, Aunt Johanna, a dwarfish hunchback, had come to keep house for him and his younger sister Paula while Klara went to hospital to have a breast removed. When she came out she was too weak to climb the stairs, so they crossed the Danube and found a flat in a pleasant suburb of Linz called Urfahr. He wouldn't allow himself to dwell on what was happening to his mother. The doctor, at her request, did not tell her son that she had cancer. He filled the summer days by pacing the streets of Linz, making detailed plans for the town's reconstruction, and by nursing a Platonic passion for a girl who hardly knew him. Stephanie her name was, a tall blonde. As the hot summer wore on, he was programmed by some accursed protective device fashioned by nature not to notice his mother's illness. He thought her tears were the tears of pure motherly affection when he told her that the time had come to leave her, to go to Vienna to seek his fortune. And he'd gone, and shared a flat with Kubizek, and tried to get into the Academy of Fine Arts.

'Test drawing unsatisfactory' – that was their verdict. *Test drawing unsatisfactory*. It was a humiliation from which no recovery was truly possible. He kept it a secret even from Kubizek who, with his second-rate talents, had easily passed into the Academy of Music. He pretended to attend the Academy of Fine Arts, while actually wandering the streets in a state of abject sorrow. But that sorrow was as nothing, absolutely nothing, compared with what was to come.

He came back to Linz after a few weeks. The postmaster's wife had written to him to say that Klara, his sacred mother, was ... It wasn't possible. Dr Bloch, sorrowful and sympathetic, said that the operation on Klara's breast had been performed too late. The cancer had spread. Already there were metastases on the pleura. The only possible cure was an expensive and very painful procedure in which large doses of iodoform were applied to the open wound.

Expense! No expense would be spared. Autumn turned into winter. All their money was spent on iodoform, a stinking balm that was applied to gauze and held against the wounds of the suffering patient. They moved her into the kitchen since, as the weather became colder, it was the only room in the flat they could afford to heat.

A terrible calmness descended. He, the postmaster's wife and the hunchbacked aunt, often without words, nursed Klara twenty-four hours a day, taking it in turns to tend her. Sometimes a very faint whimper would come from the patient who was in such agony and occasionally a terrible shriek would pierce the whole apartment. But on the whole she was silent and they were silent. Her great grey-blue eyes looked back at his with intense yearning and sorrow. This was the terrible secret of the universe, which Wagner confronted in his last works: the sheer pitilessness, the irredeemable burden of suffering under which all sentient beings moved.

Caught up in the drama of the illness itself, however, you only half confronted the truth, as it progressed from one dressing, one turning of sore limbs, one wake-tormented sleep, one sleep-heavy vigil to the next. On 21 December 1907 the inevitable happened. In the darkened early hours, by the lights of a Christmas tree he had put up in the corner of the kitchen to cheer her, she died.

Two days later, wearing a frock-coat and a tall black top hat, he followed her coffin to the grave, which had been dug beside her husband's. She was forty-seven years old.

The next day, Christmas Eve, he went to the doctor to settle up the cost of all those innumerable home visits, those seemingly endless applications of balsam to the dying one's wounds. His memories of the scene were all disconnected – his sister and his half-sister in their full mourning dresses, chatting to the doctor in an almost social manner about arrangements. His producing the money and wondering if some mistake had been made – for, though it had eaten into about a tenth of Klara's savings, the bill was far, far less than they had expected. He had looked up at the kindly old doctor and grasped his hands. 'Never, never will I forget this kindness, your . . . kindness . . .' He could not finish his words.

Thirty years afterwards orders were given, by Martin Bormann, to have Dr Bloch, who was still practising from the same consulting room, photographed in the same spot, with the chair, now empty, where the Leader had sat in this abject, mythologically giant moment.

The last time he had truculently agreed to go to church with his mother had been after her operation, perhaps a couple of months after. He had insisted that if they were to go to church they should do the thing properly and attend the cathedral at Linz. It was Good Friday, the day when the Church remembered the Crucified, and the choir had been singing the grief-stricken and imagined words of the Saviour. It was incomprehensible, of course – what abject bloody nonsense to be singing Latin to good German people, it was an affront in many ways. But the atmosphere of it came back to him in those days after Klara's death. He was now bearing a Crucifixion, he was now bearing an intolerable sorrow.

The miasma of the sorrow surrounded the whole of conscious-ness, it was not really possible to speak or to hear through it. You were in a sort of fog of sorrow and other people, or trivial events such as purchasing a tram ticket or buying a cup of coffee, happened a long way off, noises heard through water. That Herr Treibel, for example, the owner of the apartment where Klara had died. What tomfool or perfidious reason had *he* had for visiting?

But he was trying to be fatherly. 'With your talents . . . And your dear mother always said to me that you had a passion for the opera. I like a good opera myself – *The Merry Widow*, now there's a good one. But the funny thing is . . . and I don't know if it will be a help, but every little helps, they say, every little helps. This man Roller, now. Alfred Roller. Heard of him?'

The answer to this question, happening somewhere out there in the sunlit realm where no grief was felt, and where people could go on talking about today and tomorrow without howling, the answer was an astonishing no. He had not at that date heard of Alfred Roller. And this man in Linz who owned a bit of real estate and happened to be their landlord was a friend, or acquaintance, of Alfred Roller, the greatest designer of opera sets in Vienna.

That first, fantastic *Tristan*, which he had seen during his few weeks in Vienna when the bastards at the Academy of Arts had turned him down. Could anything have been more magical than that *Tristan*? Gustav Mahler was on the podium, conducting, and when the brooding, everlastingly unsettling opening prelude was completed, the curtain went up and there was Roller's ship, at a right angle to the stage, with wind flickering the sails and Tristan in the prow.

Never to be forgotten Roller! But, when asked through the fog of grief 'Heard of him?' he had only shaken his head sadly, unaware of what Herr Treibel was suggesting, namely the impossible: that there might exist a link, in real life and not in fantasy, between the desolate kitchen in a flat in Urfahr, where happiness itself died to the light of Christmas candles on a tree, and a man who invented the magical scenery of the Court Opera in Vienna.

Treibel had scribbled out a note of introduction and recommendation. 'Go to Roller. Go and say old Treibel recommended you. He's a good man, Roller, he'll help you – who knows, maybe get you doing set designs for the operas? Now Offenbach – there's one to get your feet tapping.'

So back to Vienna he had come. He had spent some money on clothes before he arrived, a dark hat, a gentleman's overcoat, none of your rubbish, a walking cane. The letter remained propped on the chimneypiece of the small room he shared with Kubizek. Every day Kubizek went out to the Academy of Music and studied – in reality. Every day, he in turn would walk the streets pretending to be at the Academy of Arts, and he would come back to the room and stare at the envelope addressed to Professor Roller. Eventually he developed enough courage to take the envelope down. He had by now filled a portfolio with drawings. There were some proposed sets for *Lohengrin* and *Tannhäuser*. There were all the architectural drawings for the complete rebuilding of Linz, of course. He was beginning to wonder whether it might not be advantageous to demolish Vienna and rebuild from scratch; but that would come later. And he had set out for the Court Opera House, with the portfolio and the letter of introduction.

But what would he say when he was stopped at the door? 'Excuse me, I have come to see Professor Roller?'

'I'm sure you have, Sunny Jim, and I'm just off to see the Emperor, good day to you.'

What if he met with mockery? His grief was still at the raw stage when any setback, however slight, was capable of provoking either the most abject misery, actual sobs, or a return of his old rages. In a café the other day he had ordered a particular type of cake with a pot of coffee. The waiter had brought the wrong cake. When he saw the waiter coming, with a nut-and-walnut concoction instead of the cherry-and-cream one upon which he had set his heart, he felt the universe collapsing. Looking at the callous waiter, who couldn't give a damn whether he brought a cherry gâteau or a plate of raw human flesh, he had made one very firm decision: he was not going to burst into tears just to satisfy this young sadist. Quite the opposite. But although the decision had been made to stand firm, he had not quite reckoned on what happened next, since the wave of pure vitriolic rage that shook his whole being at the very moment of the waiter's arrival had in fact taken him completely by surprise. The cake had been hurled, the plate had been smashed, but much more dangerous had been the coffee pot flying through the air, raining its contents on the shoulders of others in the café. Naturally, he had found himself being escorted from the premises and set down on the pavement, with pompous comments about his good fortune not to have been handed over to the police.

Fearing a revisitation of such an outburst, he had come to the door of the Opera House. In fact, the commissionaire, in his splendid uniform with frogging and epaulettes, had been friendly, asking 'Sunny Jim' whether he could help. When he had shyly, almost inaudibly, mumbled the name of Alfred Roller, he had been told to go to a particular office on the first floor. But then courage had failed him and he had muttered something about not needing the Professor today; another day. He merely wanted to know where the Professor's office was, should he ever need it.

His cowardice nagged at him, all through a concert that evening which Kubizek took him to – the everlastingly wonderful seventh symphony of Bruckner! This would not do, this fear. The next day he would go and confront Roller. But the next day, and the next, though he managed to make himself go to the Opera House, he could not bring himself to beard the great man in his den. And, coming away from the Opera House that third time, he had been visited by an outburst of despair that made him dance with anger, and he had taken Herr Treibel's letter and torn it into confetti, hurling it into the air about him in the street.

For weeks afterwards he thought of writing to Treibel to get another letter of introduction to Roller, but it was no use. He did not have the nerve. Worse than this, he could not summon up enough energy to do it. For days on end he did nothing, simply did not know how the time passed. At other times he could do some work and he felt the quality of his draughtsmanship, especially of his architectural draughtsmanship, improving. Months, years passed. At some point he had applied to the Academy again and once again the bastards had turned him down, even though he seriously believed that some of the drawings in his portfolio stood comparison with Michelangelo. The money began to run out. What money there was he spent on going to the opera, and he saw all the Mahler–Roller productions, some of them many times over. Legends in the history of Wagner production and he was there! One letter, one measly letter might have allowed him to cross the bridge and enter the legend, become part of that world. He too could, like Roller, have translated what he had drawn in a notebook into a world of enchantment, a setting for the greatest music ever composed, which would transport the collective consciousness of one audience after the next in that packed opera house into the world of their true selves – not their world of petty debt or tedious work or party politics, but the true world of the spirit and the imagination. But it was not to be. He struggled on, trying to sell his paintings while living in a large hostel for indigents, little better than a dosshouse, and finally, defeated by the system, he had decided to try his fortune elsewhere and crossed the border into Germany.

Oh, it was good to be back. The German of his childhood had been the accent of Lower Bavaria and he had never got his tongue round the so-called sophisticated Viennese lingo. Surely he'd get a place at the Munich Academy if Vienna had rejected him? That, too, was not to be his destiny. By then the sombre orchestral mutations that follow the war cry of the Valkyries had already been played, and Wotan the Warfather was waiting for his daughters to sweep over the battlefields of Europe and fill the Hall of the Slain with heroes.

Wolf led me into his library, another room of colossal proportions where a battleship would have seemed as small as a waste-paper basket.

'Ah, Winnie!'

She came towards him – two hands outstretched, both of which he took. They stared into one another's faces with pure pleasure. Then he took the hands and kissed each in turn.

'My Leader,' she said. And meant it.

The children were there too. Wieland was now a lanky seventeen-year-old in a pale double-breasted suit. Wolfgang, two years younger, was similarly clad like a grown-up. They called him 'Uncle' still. The overweight of Friedelind, just sixteen, gave her an ageless, womanly appearance. Only Verena in her plaits had, at fourteen, a touch of the child about her. The KEH was here too. This might surprise you, but of course the others couldn't see her; she was inside my head; I now felt myself observing the whole scene through her quizzical, hostile yet satirical eyes.

'Before we go any further, My Leader, I really must tell you about some of the excesses of the SA. And the HJ in Bayreuth. You can't know what is happening at the local level but . . .'

'Later, Winnie.'

'I want to tell you about Gauleiter Schemm, who has really made himself objectionable . . .'

Whenever Winnie met him in these days she had a shopping list of grievances, which she expected him to solve instantly; of Jews in the orchestra or the chorus whose life had been made difficult; of her own children's intense dislike of the Youth Movement, which all good children in Germany were now expected to join; of the over-exercise of petty bureaucracy by party officials. She seemed to believe, and nothing in subsequent history, so far as I know, has ever made her alter the belief, that the manifest ghastliness of National Socialism and its adherents had nothing, or next to nothing, to do with its Leader. 'If the Leader knew of this, he would put a stop to it at once,' she would often say. Usually, H listened to her when she produced these complaints and quite often he heeded her requests.

But today he had something else on his mind. 'I want you to see these,' he said. And he led us to a large library table on which were propped up a number of drawings. One was labelled – 'Grail Hall', another 'Klingsor's Garden' and another 'Monsalvat'. 'They are, I think you will agree, a considerable improvement on what you have at the moment at Bayreuth.'

Wolf had been following every stage of the row with the aunts about the new production of *Parsifal* heralded for the next Festival. He had been very supportive of Winnie. 'They are driving me to distraction,' she said. 'You know about this petition? I told you about it – nine hundred and something names saying that we can't alter a flipping thing in the designs of the sacred *Parsifal*.'

Wolf was the same person as H, but he kept H very well hidden from us. One of the reasons, I suspect, that Winnie was able to continue loving Wolf, and admiring him even when the extent of H's atrocities had become obvious to everyone else in Germany, was that Wolf so much needed a place in the world where he *could* be normal, gentle, playful. It was a side of his nature which in other phases of existence he had only ever shown to dogs. He needed, when with Winnie and the children, to be someone who was, quite genuinely, as amiable as he almost always was with her. It was not that he was putting on an act. His Wolf-in-Bayreuth self was one of the things which held in check H's capacity for truly monstrous behaviour. But when he had heard about the Eva Chamberlain petition one saw the corner of the curtain lifted. He pressed the table so hard that the various stage designs for *Parsifal* began to flutter, judder, fall over.

'This petition, this attempt to thwart the *will* of the Director of the Bayreuth Festival – and you, Winnie, were made the Director quite specifically by the son of Richard Wagner ...' There were veins sticking out of the side of his head and the deep-blue eyes which, in Winnie's gaze, were enchanting in a purely romantic sense now took on a shamanic fierceness. They were eyes which could turn you to snakes.

'It is not *tolerable* that your plans should be upset in this way. So let me tell you now ...' Realizing that the fit of anger was not suitable for a Wagner family lunch party, remembering that he was with his old friends, that he was Uncle Wolf with the children, he visibly controlled himself. One hand went to his throat and stayed there for a while almost as if he were preventing the demons from rising in his gorge, then he smoothed the back of his head as he spoke: 'The new production of *Parsifal* will go ahead and the money will be no problem, because even if all thousand who signed this monstrous petition were to stay away, I could fill their seats five times over. I guarantee we will underwrite every seat in the house. Have no fear of financial failure in the 1934 Festival.'

This was an extraordinary undertaking and, incidentally, it was one he fulfilled. The KEH inside my head furiously began to kick me when I allowed myself the thought that here was a man who already, within a year of taking office, had reduced unemployment by over half, who seemed to have turned the economy round, who had revivified German industry and was also preparing to bring to pass what Richard Wagner had proposed, but only dreamed of: state subsidy of the arts. Today, in the 1960s, on our side of the border we take it for granted – but that is because if something in the DDR isn't subsidized by the state it doesn't exist.

'I want you to look at these.' His eye strayed nervously to the large clock on the mantelpiece. It was half past twelve. 'They are drawings I have been doing over the last few weeks of possible set designs.'

'Your own?'

Winnie's question was pertinent. I had been wondering who had done the drawings. My first hunch, that he had drawn them himself, was dismissed, partly because they looked too professional and secondly because I could not see how, on top of saving the Fatherland, he would have had the time. And then, as he began to show her the drawings, I remembered that saying which, as Uncle Wolf in the family circle, he must have quoted to us about the time of his poverty in Vienna, when he and friend Kubizek passed the hurdy-gurdy man playing 'La donna e mobile'. Was Wolf the monkey or the organ grinder? Here he was, almost within grasp of total power. Only feeble old General von Hindenburg, lingering on as President, stood between him and – what was inevitable – his becoming the Head of State. Yet there was this world we hardly ever saw. Winnie saw much, much more of it than I ever did, all Wolf's creepy friends in the Party, little Ernst Röhm, with his scarred face; the heavily eyebrowed Hess; the fat gamekeeper Göring, with his high complexion and his extraordinary country clothes, alternating with Ruritanian uniforms; the hideous bespectacled figure of Himmler, whom I once saw in Bayreuth, but who tended to stay away (like the pack of them, he hated Wagner); and most sinister of them all, Nosferatu himself, the evil genius of the whole propaganda machine. What if all these men – and the legions beneath them in the Party hierarchy throughout the ranks of the SA, the SS and all the sinister organizations of police, murder squads, private armies, and all the local administrators and youth leaders – what if they all, who were now enjoying their day of triumph in Germany, what if they were the power in the Movement? What if H was necessary to them only as a voice, as a figurehead, as a monkey gyrating to the music of the hurdy-gurdy?

Of course, it was the possibility of asking this question that in part contributed to H's preternatural popularity with the masses, since they did think of him as a creature apart from the Movement, just as the Saviour was distinguished from the errant and even treacherous Apostles. 'If the Leader knew of this . . .' That familiar phrase . . . Winnie herself used it, but his adorers all over Germany did so too. In this sense Winnie was entirely typical. So his strength lay in part in his detachment from the thugs, creeps, killers and controllers who believed in Nazism; while of course he knew, better than any of them, better perhaps than anyone who has ever lived, how to manipulate and exercise power over people. He was in fact both organ grinder *and* monkey, but it was necessary for his maintenance of power to pose as monkey; a high-risk strategy which led him to an everlasting paranoia about those closest to him in the Party, fearful that they wished to do away with him once he had delivered to them the only thing they craved: power itself.

'Here, for example, is Act One – and you see, at the moment when the door opens in the rocky cliff and the knights walk in procession to the Chamber of the Most Sacred Grail, we have . . .' He produced another drawing proudly. 'This. Something very simple, something magisterial – and you see . . .' He pointed with his stubby finger. 'This is the grave-like chamber where Titurel has been lying, then the old man comes out of there and greets his wounded son, Amfortas.' He rolled his 'r' when he said 'Amfortas' and looked at the ceiling with a hieratic expression, which would not have been unfitting on the face of the Pope while saying a public mass, and he muttered, in words which were perhaps almost a prayer, the old king's words '*O! Heilige Wonne! Wie hell grüsst uns heute der Herr!'* (Holy rapture! How brightly the Lord greets us today!).

It was never possible for a work to move forward unless Richard Wagner was immersed in what he called a musical aroma. The *Parsifal* story, in the medieval poem of Wolfram von Eschenbach, had been a sketch for an opera ever since that pregnant decade the 1840s, but it did not belong to the time of revolutions. The completed opera was not performed until 1882, at Bayreuth. His grown-up lifetime of spiritual and emotional experience had to be poured into the music. The long rambling narrative of the medieval poet had to be compressed, compressed, compressed into myth. The only thing in the history of the performing arts to be compared with the Greek tragedies is Bach's passion music – but it was all composed at a time when myth had been changed into dogma. It must be Wagner's task, after the storm clouds of the nineteenth century had darkened the skies, to refashion all that *stuff* as myth. 'I do not believe in God, but I believe in Godliness, which reveals itself in the sinless Jesus,' he said.

Wolf was saying, and Winnie stared at him with some anxiety as he expatiated upon the theme, 'You want to know why the Roman Catholic Church has been so strong for so many centuries – where its hard inner core of strength resides? A celibate clergy. The Popes knew a thing or two, I'm telling you. By compelling them to be celibate, the Church has built up huge reserves of power, emotional, spiritual power. This, undoubtedly, is one of the themes of *Parsifal*, I find. Amfortas is wounded, kaput because he has yielded to seduction. Parsifal can raise the sacred spear because it has not been tainted by ...

But the aroma, he could sense it, Richard Wagner, but not catch it. There were too many themes to be compressed. One day he told Cosima it was a purely technical matter: 'Stupid fellow, not D minor, it must be C minor – and then when I'd seen that everything was all right.'

Yet for years the words and the music failed to come together. He could not instinctually feel where the music was leading. Only with the chorus of the Flower Maidens in the second act, the girls who dance about the doltish Parsifal and try to seduce him, did words and music come together. And after *that*, though with painful slowness, 'everything was all right'.

They came to him, the Flower Maidens, in London of all god- and music-forsaken places. The London Philharmonic Society, in 1855, asked him to conduct a season of concerts, a selection of his own works. It was an interruption to life – he was finally getting down to the orchestration of his central, finest work, *Die Walküre*. His emotional life was, as ever, in chaos, with love for Mathilde Wesendonck and guilt about Minna, and an irrepressible lust that led to all kinds of more furtive encounters all taking possession of him. And his mind was not so much on the march as in a whirl-wind, the old revolutionary certainties having been blown away by Schopenhauer; the somewhat clunking rejection of religion and its mythologies in the writings of Feuerbach giving place to a redis-covery of what all that religious stuff was – not God or dogmas but our relationship with Out There, our lonely and intolerable awareness of our place in an indifferent universe of unexhausted suffering, a place where our own consciousness scalded us with the awareness, not only of our own unhappiness but that of others, and not merely of human beings, but of sentient animals.

Walking on a terrace during a reception at Holland House, some grandees' mansion in London, he had heard a peacock shrieking and formed the curious sensation that it might be trying to speak to him in Sanskrit, the ancient Aryan tongue, the ur-language of religious experience and of the Upanishads, the language of the murmuring Rhine water.

God, that concert season in London was hell! The publication of his pamphlet 'Judaism in Music' had guaranteed him a sticky recep-tion in the London press, so that his concerts received terrible notices.

Wherever he went he met admirers of Mendelssohn and Meyerbeer. Prince Albert and Queen Victoria had attended one of his concerts and when he had been presented to them afterwards the Prince had said, speaking of course in their own language, 'I especially liked the Prelude to *Lohengrin*. It had quite something of Meyerbeer about it.' Though a musical amateur himself, the Prince had clearly acquired the English cloth ears since marrying his quite monstrously plain little cousin, the Queen of England.

Richard had spent as much time as possible with his own countrymen. He had met the young man who was destined to be a close friend, and interpreter of his work, Karl Klindworth. A young pupil of Liszt's, Klindworth had come to London under the mistaken impression that he could live as a pianist and a teacher of the piano. Liszt's concerts in England were always a sell-out, but the entire musical life of the country took place in cliques and you could not rely on any interest in music on behalf of the generality of people. It was indeed a Land Without Music. Klindworth was leaving as soon as possible and going back to Germany.

Naturally, Wagner avoided the Royal Opera House where Meyerbeer was god and where the quality of singing was appalling. Those evenings not spent conducting selections of his work, he contrived more and more to spend alone. He paced the streets of London, a shocking mixture of unparalleled opulence and squalor. He fell – as who could not, they were so thick on the ground you literally had to press your way through them to get into a café or chophouse – for the charms of the whores, some of whom were friendly but most of whom were ill-mannered, greedy, quick, incompetent. He took boat trips on the Thames and the vast brooding warehouses, the ships coming in from every corner of the Empire and the fetid squalid tenements in which the poor were crammed like unhappy zoo animals all seemed an embodiment of the Nibelung slavery. No wonder that boring materialist Karl Marx had taken up residence here and saw it all leading to an inevitable collapse.

But one aspect of London was to be commended. The middle and lower classes knew how to enjoy themselves, and the pubs, the music halls and the popular theatres were all delightful. It was the time of year when Christmas was approaching and many of the theatres had enactments from Grimm and other fairy tales. There was a superb *Little Red Riding Hood*, which he attended more than once, and a very good *Cinderella*. Here, at last, was what was so lacking in any of the 'musical' circles he had discovered in England, a genuine connection between audiences and performance, a real appreciation of what was going on in a story.

Best of all was *Mother Goose*. The figure of the Bird Herself, in her silky festoons of artificial feathers, was a man, who sang ribald songs. Much of the meaning was impossible for a foreign-language speaker to catch, but the atmosphere was clear enough. And there was then the most sublime dance of Flower Maidens on the stage. He went back to watch them again and again. They exuded good humour, easy sensuality and that feeling of *lift* which good art always gives you, of taking off into the air. Here was something sublimely well done.

The drama of the Three Wishes, and the Golden Egg that results, would itself make a good opera. But as he sat, rather drunk, in the stalls, waiting for the coming of the Flower Maidens afternoon by afternoon, and night after night, a whole jumble of thoughts spread before him. Their mouths half open, their wavy, thick hair, braided with paper flowers, suggestive of the triangles of warm, moist hair and the caves of delight they curtained, beneath their floral costumes; their breasts not visible but evident as they danced. And yet what they represented was both an escape into paradise and a journey towards further and further enslavement to the world of sense; and if one could only rise above those feelings and be detached from them; if the everlasting tug of lust could be removed and we could see life clearly, as Buddhist monks, high above the mountains in the cloud-capped monasteries of the Himalayas, ancient seat of the Aryan purity, saw life; if we could be detached from lust, but not detached from pity – might we not enter into life, the true eternal life, which was not the infantile fantasies of the Christian Church, an everlasting hallelujah, but a still, deep awareness of Being itself, of life, such as patient dogs know, and show to us in their watery eyes and gentle faces?

Those Flower Maidens in *Mother Goose* never left him and, when the time came twenty years later to orchestrate *Parsifal*, they returned full blast into his mind, carrying with them mysteriously both the allurement they had held then and the message of detachment which, at the time, had seemed to be at war with them.

Yet nearly thirty years of experience after those London evenings had altered all perspectives. Young Klindworth had become old Klindworth, a close and dear friend. The Abbé Liszt his master had become Wagner's most tiresome father-in-law, and Cosima had become his muse: religious and tormented Cosima. After they had brought the children back to Germany and settled in Bayreuth, and she had left (or hoped to leave) her Catholicism behind her, she took the children to the Lutheran church, the Stadtkirche. After a lifetime of staying away from church, Wagner took to going with them, able at last to find in Christianity the core-myth without being distracted by the false dogmas. And she had said to him, one Communion Sunday when the dean had given them both the sacred bread and the cup, that the experience had given her greater rapture than anything except their wedding itself.

He knew she was being tactful. He knew that for her, as for her father the never-quite-reformed Abbé-roué or roué-Abbé, the religious ecstasy quite rivalled and at times obscured the pleasures of the flesh; that, more than that, the pleasures of the flesh merely provided a vehicle for yet more ecstatic religious guilt.

The wound of Amfortas – old Wagner carried that, ever more subject to wheezing, to bowel complaints, to sleeplessness, to exhaustion which made composition all but impossible. The energy of the celibate Parsifal, akin to the powerful energy of Jesus or Joan of Arc. So, little by little, and at the ever more frantic demand of his royal patron, he laboured on to complete that strange, incoherent, but everlastingly haunting work.

'And then, you see, in the second act – the Garden of Klingsor!' Wolf had it all worked out. 'Do you remember, when he was in the final stages of composing *Parsifal*, Wagner was so ill that he had to recuperate in Italy and eventually he reached the Palazzo Rufolo in Ravello. He said, "Klingsor's magic garden is found!" I have asked to be taken there when I make a visit to Mussolini in Rome later this year. Naturally, my Cabinet think I am mad – Heinrich –' For a moment I was startled, thinking he meant my brother, because he added, 'You haven't met the faithful Heinrich, have you?'

Himmler was meant. '. . . wants the performance of *Parsifal* banned. He thinks that his own Grail Knights in the SS are stronger than the knights in this drama. We shall see about that.'

After this surprising little revelation he smirked. A lackey entered and murmured, 'Professor Roller, My Leader.'

'Ah yes.'

Wolf had been beside himself with excitement and glee all morning, ever since I'd found him putting the finishing touches to his table decorations. When he was showing Winnie his sketches for the new production, I had put his good spirits down to the fact that he had been able to come up with designs that pleased him so much. I had not realized, nor had any of us, that he planned a spectacular little 'coup' which would, as he put it on another occasion, 'thoroughly scotch the 900 petitioners'.

The lackey led into the room the bearded, elderly figure of Alfred Roller. In 1908, aged eighteen, Wolf had been too shy to approach this man's door, for here was the king of opera design, who had created the sets on which Mahler's interpretation of Wagner had been staged. Now, as his country's Chancellor, Wolf welcomed the old man.

'I think we would all agree', said Wolf, when we had taken our places at the table, 'that a meal to celebrate this occasion, a meal which anticipates the greatest triumph in the history of Bayreuth, should not be at variance with the wishes of the Master. By the time he wrote *Parsifal*, the Master had enjoined many of his friends to become vegetarian. He regarded the eating of animal flesh as mere cannibalism and the message of the Last Supper was clear enough – Thou shalt not eat meat!'

'Well, Herr H———,' began Roller, who might or might not have had some views on this subject.

But Wolf had views on the place of carnivores in evolution. He spoke of Darwin, next to Wagner the greatest man of the nineteenth century.

'I believe,' began Roller, 'that when *Parsifal* was first performed that . . .'

'Which is why in all his later writings he makes it so clear that any kind of race mingling is really little better than minglings between the different species. Indeed, it is not at all clear that the Negro *is* the same species as ourselves.'

'As for *Parsifal*,' tried Roller once more.

'It is of all Wagner's operas the most complex,' replied Wolf. He told Roller the number of times he had seen it. He complimented Roller handsomely on all those productions in Vienna that he had seen with his own eyes – *The Egyptian Helen*, *Tristan*, *Rosenkavalier*, *Valkyrie*, all superb. And your *Parsifal*.'

'Which I was going to suggest . . .'

There was no chance during that meal of anyone, least of all the guest of honour, interrupting the unstoppable monologue. He told us that the beginner loves *Tannhäuser* for its melodies and melodrama. Later, one might develop a love of the *Ring* cycle. But for the true Wagnerian, the more one experiences of the Master's genius, the more one realizes that *Parsifal* contains . . . the Message! But this gnomic (and to me, to this day, not entirely comprehensible) dictum did not come pithily forth, still less was it laid open for further discussion. It was sandwiched between a long flow of talk about the miraculous recovery of Germany (had not Wagner said a strong absolute monarch means a free people?), the race theories of Darwin, but chiefly productions. He had an apparently encyclopaedic recall of every single opera he had ever attended since boyhood and Roller nodded in appreciation as the names of tenors and sopranos and bass-baritones were recited, and their respective merits assessed.

For me, the chief memory of the meal, however, was when he made that remark about the celibacy of the Catholic clergy being the secret of the Church's inner power, and the look of unstoppable shock that spread over Winnie's features as she chomped her way through the slightly flavourless spaghetti dish and ratatouille set before us, washed down with mineral water. I am convinced that he had summoned us all to the Chancellery not for one reason but for two. Yes, he wanted to tell Winnie that the 1934 production of *Parsifal* was saved. But he also wanted to tell her that though they would always be friends, they could no longer be lovers. Several years later he said, 'I have sometimes been asked why I have never married. I reply, a man in my position is married to the German Reich. It is not for his country's leader to give himself to one woman when Germany is his bride.' Perhaps by banishing Winnie from his bed, he also banished his last chances of contact with a decent and normal human being, who, for all her many faults, never let pity or affection die in her.

I did not tell Helga about our lunch at the Chancellery. I realize now that I should have done so, that I should have come clean about this. Winnie's involvement with Wolf was a matter of common knowledge, not only among the orchestra and chorus at the theatre, and the townspeople of Bayreuth, but throughout Germany. Nevertheless, my new and deepened involvement with Helga should have made me see that I owed her complete frankness from the first. Many complications would have been avoided later on in our relationship if she had known that ... not that Wolf was a friend of mine; he wasn't; but that I belonged to that very small band of people who had seen Wolf – rather than H – had seen a genial opera lover; the apple-cheeked yeoman-soldier in a dark-blue serge suit of my first few meetings with him, a man who with Winnie and the children was all geniality and who, in spite of a discernible vein of overenthusiasm, and an occasional coarseness of expression, was, or appeared to be, an essentially benign figure. The extent to which he was playing a part when he was at the Villa Wahnfried has often occupied my mind, of course it has. But, you see, I do not think he was. I think there was a side of him which quite conceivably regarded the demonic side to his nature with dread and retreated from it into the family circle that Winnie provided with hearty relief. If circumstances had been different – if, say, the economy of Germany had taken a great upturn and the normal, mainstream political parties had won back all the votes taken by the Nazis – it would have been the end of some of his cronies and gauleiters; but I honestly believe that it might have been the beginning for him. I don't think he'd have been a murderer in private life, if he had not been the Leader. I think if – unthinkable if – he had been voted from office and Winnie had, as it were, tamed him, and allowed him to become a set designer for the Bayreuth theatre, he might have been transformed into an amiable old gentleman. But I know this view of mine is totally at variance with everything people now believe about the all-out monster H, who ruined our world; ruined it irreparably. And it is frivolous of me, perhaps, even to voice these thoughts when so much damage has been wrought, so many lives destroyed, so many nations enslaved.

As far as Helga was concerned, the suspicions she had about my involvement with dodgy right-wing politics were set at rest at a fairly early stage of our relationship. She knew I was not a Nazi at heart, nor any more anti-Semitic than the ordinary run of human being who allows his mind to fall into unthought prejudices, base and coarse thoughts from which it is easy to cure oneself with consideration. My thoughts about Wolf were of a different order, almost a metaphysical thing. Like most people in Germany, perhaps in the world, Helga had profoundly superstitious thoughts about H. She had been brought up in a Catholic family in Munich, but had never taken religion seriously, and when she began to think about such matters she had decided she was an atheist. Nevertheless, she believed in Evil, possibly even in the Evil One. She certainly always believed, as soon as he came into her consciousness as a political leader, later as a voice blaring from radios and microphones, that H was out of the ordinary run of political baddies; that he was really Satanic. For this reason, if for no other, I owed it to her to explain that I had supped with the devil. In any event, when one loves another person one should trust them; else one lie leads to another. By suppressing the lunch at the Chancellery, I had to tell a number of outright lies about how the children and I had spent our time in Berlin.

'You want to get away from those lunatics.' She blew a puff of smoke as she said this.

The snow was still on the ground. It had been (for Franconia) an uncommonly long winter. We had made a short expedition to the Eremitage. In the summer, this eighteenth-century pleasure garden built for the Margravine Wilhelmine always had a sprinkling of visitors, and at Festival time it was crowded in the afternoons. Today, however, it was completely deserted. The statues were all boxed in against the frost. The principal grottoes were closed, but it still made a pleasant place to walk about, with someone with whom you were wondering if you had fallen in love.

That description went for both of us. We were wondering quite what had happened. Certainly, in the years to come, we had plenty of time to do some more wondering. That I did fall in love with Helga at some stage, and she with me, can't be denied, but we were very different types of people and quite how, or why, or even when this conjunction of souls took place I couldn't say. From the beginning there lurked in my mind a doubt. Was she my excuse to get away from the Wagners? Why was I lying to her about Berlin? Obviously, her politics were about as far away from National Socialism as it would be possible to be. But my silence was prompted by something more personal than that. I did not want her to think that I was a Nazi. My mind was in a state of absolute political confusion, which had been building ever since my brother had established himself in Berlin. The horrible incident on the bus with the SA youth made clear, as if it had not been clear already, what the dark side of the Movement was. Yet certain things could not be denied – unemployment was down and there was an atmosphere, in those early years of the Third Reich, of extraordinary optimism about the future.

'We've been given back our pride.' That was a sentence you often heard.

I'd begun to see, however, that the systems of thought to which my brother Heinrich and my friend Helga, in their very different ways, adhered had winkled out something inherently *wrong* with Nazism. Yes, Germany might be saved by systems of public works, new roads, new factories, new industrial bases, new hope. But if these things were to be brought to us by *these people*, we had already paid too high a price. Christians, Communists, a few lofty old aristocrats and royalists could see this; they could see, what hindsight makes transparent, that we had made our bargain with the devil, and we would not come out of the contract until we had paid with our last drop of dignity and blood. But I am not gifted with certainty and I did not see things clearly.

The fact that I had begun to do so, and had begun to feel sheepish about my besotted devotion to Winnie, was attributable to my new feelings about Helga. Hence, when she said, 'You want to get away from those people', I turned to her. Her face was pink in that snowy air. She wore a woollen hat, which framed her pretty, boyish face, and she was looking at me with the kind of mocking seriousness that was her most characteristic expression.

I kissed her.

I had never kissed anyone before, except for kissing my mother goodnight. I had seen erotic kissing feigned in films often enough and had no idea how it was done.

'Here,' she said and threw away her stubb, which hissed in the snow.

Gently, slowly, she coaxed my lips and teeth with her tongue and taught me how to kiss her. One of the many things for which I was always grateful to her was that she never commented on my lack of experience. She guided me by gentle degrees, with 'here' being the usual preface to the next stage. After kissing for a while, in the snowy sunken garden by the larger of the grottoes, she took my woollen fingers in her woollen fingers and rubbed my hands affectionately. Then she looked at me with very great happiness. 'I wasn't sure whether you wanted to do that,' she said.

'Yes. Very much.'

We started to sleep together that afternoon, after a lunch in a small restaurant in her district of town, beyond the cemetery where Fidi and Houston Stewart Chamberlain lay beneath the snow; and apart from being wonderful in themselves, the wonderful couple of hours in her single bed provided my deliverance from the whole National Socialist madness. Surprisingly enough, there were no bungles. It was complete bliss from the first try. I did not ask whether I should have been taking precautions. The matter did not crop up in conversation and since she so clearly knew what she was doing I assumed that everything would be all right. Whatever all right was.

What I liked so much about her, apart from the intimate and magical things that took place between us in bed, was her manner towards me when we had our clothes on once again – having cups of coffee, chatting in the Festival Theatre, or simply going about together. There was a jokey friendliness in it all. 'So, old comrade!' was often her way of greeting me and of parting from me, sometimes defiantly raising her fist, sometimes affectionately punching me. When I think of the ruin of our relationship, years afterwards, when we began to grate upon one another and annoy one another in a very small flat with you, our adopted child, I think with tremendous sadness of those jokes and that friendliness. To tell the truth, although I know we were lovers, nearly all the details of our lovemaking have vanished. But every second of our early courtship, of the quality of our friendship and companionship, remains with me, a torture of memory to contrast with the mean-spirited marital crossness which came to replace it. But that is not really the subject of this story.

I have entitled this section 'Parsifal', and that was the opera which loomed over the summer months of 1934. Helga was rehearsing – for she was also, of course, as a member of the Festival orchestra, playing in the *Ring* cycle – but there was something especially exciting for her about rehearsing *Parsifal* with Richard Strauss, even though Strauss had been inveigled earlier in the year into signing the infamous petition. With old Roller designing the sets, it was clearly going to be a ground-breaking production about which little

Tietjen was understandably excited. The day-to-day details of keeping this show on the road, together with the *Ring* cycle, were Tietjen's and Winnie's, and it was a frantically busy time in which I had much to do. The children were still, for as long as possible, incarcerated in various hellish boarding schools, and between my love affair with Helga and my work at the Theatre there was little time for noticing what was going on in the world that summer.

Had I done so, I would have realized that the unpleasant incident on the bus, with the young 'storm-trooper' making a nuisance of himself, was symptomatic of a crisis building in Germany, but especially in Bavaria, over the hated Brownshirts.

Winnie's Nazi life, which went back to the very origins of the Party in the years after the First World War, was never something of which I had been especially aware, knowing her – as I have already indicated – in the domestic and theatrical setting. Although, when Wolf became the All-powerful Leader, we started to see more of the High Command – and the whole intricate palaver of bureaucracy controlling public performances in theatres, concert halls and the like was placed, for example, under the unlikely supervision of the Fat Gamekeeper – we never saw much of these extraordinary people. An exception, however, was the strange little man who became the leader of the SA, Ernst Röhm.

Privately I considered him as one of Winnie's lame ducks, a category I easily recognized, since I belonged to it myself. He came to stay at Wahnfried on several occasions (without Wolf) and although none of us could quite see what she saw in him, I am sure it was not the same thing as his underlings in the SA saw. I think she saw a sad little homosexual with a scarred face – part of his nose had been shot off in the war, so he was especially ugly. I remember him once, half-sozzled with schnapps, saying to us after dinner, 'I can't live the life of the respectable bourgeois citizen. I'm not a marrying man – I like rent boys and soldiers. The war was fine for me – it was my best time. I'm not a good man. I'm a pervert. I can only operate in a sphere of violence and mayhem. Wolf wants to bring order to Germany – or so he says. Well, we'll see.' He'd laughed when he said this. He was always very open about being queer, and I think this was something Wolf appreciated. It was amazing to me that Wolf, in many ways an extremely strait-laced and conventional person with regard to social *mores*, entirely accepted Röhm's sexual predilections, even though I believe there were others who felt sure they were a liability.

Anyway, Röhm's words about only being happy in an atmosphere of violent mayhem made a great deal of sense to me, uttered as they were at some stage of Weimar topsy-turvydom when a packet of fags cost two billion marks and when every value, moral and monetary, we'd ever taken for granted was up the spout. Here was a self-confessed moral nihilist, who lived for street violence and anarchy. He seemed like a symptom of the times, rather than someone directing their course.

After the so-called seizure of power by the Nazis, words much loved by Röhm and mates because they implied that Wolf had become Chancellor by some bit of fisticuffs rather than by voting and manoeuvring, Röhm's position and that of the entire SA seemed redundant. Göring enlisted as many SA members as possible into respectable roles, trying to make them abandon the brown shirt and join the police force, for example. Plenty of policemen and prison warders were needed for the newly established concentration camps, which had been set up almost at once to deal with political dissidents.

But there were fears, from the moment that Wolf got into a Cabinet with von Papen and the other 'stuffed shirts', that he would betray the grass roots of the Movement and forget the Socialist ingredient in the National Socialist mix.

In H's first year in power, Röhm, down in Munich, enormously increased the membership of the SA and discontent spread among its ranks. SA yobbos were running amok in many towns, especially in Munich. As the weather heated up, their drunken routs turned into threatened riots and Röhm, presumably – we hadn't seen him for years by then – was a happy little man, egging on his skinheaded ugly boys to bait Jews, vomit on street corners and smash windows.

And his fear was a self-fulfilling prophecy. General von Hindenburg and others did indeed tell H that enough was enough and that the SA must be brought under control, if not wound up altogether.

Whereas the respectable or semi-respectable politicians such as von Hindenburg and von Papen, and the army chiefs, saw the SA as primarily a threat to public order, H's perspective was very different. He was acutely aware of the way Röhm's queer mind worked. Between the two men grew up feelings of twisted disloyalty, paranoid fear. H had used the SA ruthlessly as a means to power, both within his own movement and at local political levels all over Germany. Membership of the SA swelled wherever there was discontented, unemployed moronic youth lurking at street corners. They were enlisted with ease by promises of barely controlled hooliganism and plenty to drink. But they were really an anarchist army and, now that he was in power, they could only be a personal threat to him.

When news reached him that Röhm was being openly disloyal and making speeches to the yobbos in which he criticized the leadership, H decided to act.

On 30 June Strauss had his first full orchestra rehearsal with the chorus and singers on stage. Tietjen and Winnie sat halfway down the amphitheatre at their director's bench. Helga and her fellow players were in the invisible orchestra pit and the first act began — the strange story of a band of celibate knights, fed by the Eucharist alone, who were tending a fatally wounded prince, Amfortas, whose sores and wounds had to be bathed each day; a band of knights into whose midst two strangers come, the utterly mysterious Kundry, wild woman, witch, bringing her healing Arabic balsam for the wound, but also her bewitching and sexual spells; and the Fool, the Wild Man of the Woods who barely knows his own name and whose act of casual, ill-considered violence has led to the death of a swan.

Three thousand SA troops had rampaged in the streets of Munich the previous night. H travelled through the night from Berlin,

flying in a three-motor Junker 52, and being driven at speed in a
Mercedes to the Hanselbauer Hotel in Bad Wiessee at six in the
morning.

'We'll take that from the top,' said Richard Strauss from the podium.
'Before the plundered sanctuary, in prayer impassioned knelt
Amfortas.'

The SA High Command had been doing some serious drinking the
night before and they were in no condition to resist the intrusion
of H himself, who was accompanied by armed detectives. The rival
SS had the building surrounded in case of trouble. The only person
who was not in bed with a boy was a cousin of Röhm's, Max Vogel.
They found him with a frightened, naked chambermaid. Otherwise,
in almost every room they entered they found a naked senior SA
officer in bed with some eighteen-year-old youth, male.

H entered his old friend's room, carrying a whip. He pulled back
the covers. The detective who followed H into the room dragged
the toyboy out without even giving him the time to dress, while H
produced a revolver from his pocket. 'Ernst,' he shouted, 'you (*Du*)
are under arrest.' Röhm was given the chance to get dressed in a
crumpled dark-blue suit.

By mid-morning a hasty court martial had been arranged at the
Brown House, the SA headquarters in Munich, and Röhm and the
other conspirators had been condemned to death. The difficulty was
in finding someone who would be prepared to shoot the old hero
of the Movement, who had been there from the beginning of this
socialist and nationalist adventure, taking part in the putsch of 1923
etc. etc.

'Try that again,' suggested Tietjen. 'Amfortas, you are holding back
the boys, but only with a gesture of the hand. You are wounded,

grievously wounded – "What is the wound and all its tortures wild"
– try that.'

'Spare Röhm,' said H suddenly in the middle of the morning. Rather, it was Wolf, awkwardly aware of what H was up to; like a fanatic who has been in a trance and wakes up to find his hands on a bloody knife, he does not quite know what he has done and tries to persuade himself that he is still dreaming. He was speaking to General von Epp, who had arrived at the Brown House and was determined that the SA menace be finally stamped out. H began raging – one of his real tantrums. The general walked out of the room muttering, 'This man's crazy.'

In Berlin, Himmler, Heydrich and Göring, cock-a-hoop at the prospect of a bloodletting of old enemies, had already begun a series of arrests and killings. General Kurt von Schleicher, one of von Hindenburg's oldest friends, who had prevented H becoming Chancellor two or three years before and taken the job himself, found two Gestapo agents in his study. When his wife, in a neighbouring room, ran in to follow the noise of gunfire, she too was shot.

H always gave it out that he flew straight away to Berlin, but by a strange compulsion his morbid sado-pity for Röhm kept him back; he stayed until the next morning, July 1, and visited cell 474 at Stadelheim prison one last time. 'You have forfeited your chance to life, Ernst,' he whispered in his old friend's ear.

'My Leader!' Röhm shrieked, as that stubby finger pulled the trigger twice and the already mutilated face took the bullets that removed his life.

Sometimes it was not enough to order a killing: it was necessary to be a killer oneself – to watch the fear in the eyes, then the mysterious vanishing of life as the soul flies out and leaves a crumpled piece of meat. Then calm comes.

He flew back to Berlin. The killings, which had been going on all night, the night which came to be known as the Night of the Long Knives, had deeply disturbed the old President. 'Is it true?

That you have had General von Schleicher and his wife shot?' he asked gruffly when his Chancellor came in to see him at midday.

H could feel the revolver, hard and strong in his pocket, an everlasting manhood that would not, like ephemeral manifestations of his prowess, rise and fall. The killing of Röhm, and the purge of the SA boys in Munich, and the knowledge that so many had died during the night in Berlin, had given him a preternatural burst of energy. 'It was necessary,' he said curtly to the old man.

'How so?'

'My General, I have brought you a telegram to sign. It is addressed,' he said with such rising excitement in his voice that he also yelped the words, 'it is addressed to myself . . .'

FROM THE REPORTS PLACED BEFORE ME I LEARN THAT YOU BY YOUR DETERMINED ACTION AND GALLANT PERSONAL INTERVENTION HAVE NIPPED TREASON IN THE BUD COMMA YOU HAVE SAVED THE GERMAN NATION FROM SEROUS DANGER FULL STOP FOR THIS I EXPRESS TO YOU MY MOST PROFOUND THANKS AND SINCERE APPRECIATION

'Can we go back a bit?' asked Tietjen. 'Titurel, we need a bit more emphasis on "Shall I ever look on the Grail and live – must I perish, unguided by my Saviour?"'

On 13 June we were sitting, Helga and I, in a bar just off Schüllerstrasse. We liked going there, it was the sort of place not patronized by the Festival Theatre lot and there were old men drinking beer quietly in the corner. We had a particular reason for choosing this place today, however, since we did not want to hear the broadcast of the Leader's speech from the Reichstag. In about three of the bars we'd been into, loudspeakers had been set up to make sure that no one missed the glorious words. Imagine, then, our disappointment and disgust when we got to this normally quiet little spot and found that even here a big wireless set had been placed on the bar, which was playing patriotic music.

Helga was making one of her usual political jokes: 'Reichstag! How many times has it been summoned in the last year? About twice. They have no parliamentary function whatsoever. In fact, all they do is file in, sit down, listen to his nibs talking nonsense and then they get up and sing "Deutschland, Deutschland über Alles". They aren't a parliament, they are the best-paid choral society in Germany.'

I liked these jokes, but I wished she wouldn't make them so fearlessly and publicly. Several of the old geezers who normally greeted us with friendly nods looked scandalized when they overheard, if not her exact words, then her tone and subject matter.

But now it was 'Pray silence for our Glorious Leader' and we heard that voice, so familiar to me from puppet shows and dinner talk, rasping out from the loudspeaker on the bar.

'If anyone reproaches me and asks why we did not call upon the regular courts for sentencing, my only answer is this: in that hour I was responsible for the fate of the German nation and was thus the Supreme Judiciary of the German people ... I gave the order to shoot those parties mainly responsible for this treason ... The nation should know that no one can threaten its existence – which is guaranteed by inner law and order – and escape unpunished. And every person should know for all time that if he raises his hand to strike out at the state, certain death will be his lot.'

'My God,' said Helga. She took my hand and held it very tight.

'Shut up, you.' An old man – a perfectly respectable old man, nearer eighty than seventy – was standing beside our table. 'I heard you – the whole bar heard you mocking our Leader, mocking our Reichstag. Can you see and understand nothing, you stupid little child? All the unemployed men getting back to work. Our country feeling pride in itself again.'

'Pride? At having a Chancellor who shoots people rather than putting them on trial?' she fired back.

'Leave it, Helga,' I pleaded, touching her hand.

'It's a few people. It will settle everything down,' said the old man. 'What do you want? Anarchy? To be ruled over by France for ever and ever?'

I saw an expression pass over Helga's face that was already familiar to me – it was indeed one of the reasons I had begun to fall for her. It was moved by an innate superiority complex. She was not merely cleverer than most people, she didn't mind showing them, even rubbing their noses in it. With a very scornful smile she seemed to be considering the old man's rhetorical question. 'I'd live with it,' she said, nodding and lighting a fag.

We left the bar almost immediately. I am probably rewriting history when I say that I already had a sense of foreboding, but I am sure I knew that such open talk as Helga had indulged in was dangerous now. Two days later, after I had checked the post in the office at the Festival Theatre, I ambled off down one of the innumerable subterranean corridors of the theatre to find her in one of the rehearsal rooms. We often took a mid-morning break like this nowadays and her colleagues had come to accept us as 'an item'.

When I flung open the door, however, I saw at once from the faces of her friends that something dreadful had happened.

'They've taken her,' said Erich, a clarinetist. 'They've taken her and about six other members of the orchestra – Eva Fraenkl, Rudolf Levi, Andreas Kaminski . . .'

'You mean the Jews in the orchestra? They've taken the Jews . . .'

I know in retrospect that following the Röhm murder and the Night of the Long Knives there was a huge 'culling' in Germany and that for several weeks afterwards those deemed by the government to be undesirables – Jews, Commies, anarchists, troublemakers of various kinds – were rounded up and arrested. My emotions on hearing that 'they' had 'taken' Helga were confused. I think at first I simply felt fear, dread that something was going to happen to her. Almost immediately I could imagine her impertinent tomboy manner not being quietened by some secret police bully-boy. I had a horrible vision of their maltreating her, beating her face.

'Where have they taken her?'

'No one seems to know,' said the clarinetist, 'but there is a rumour they've taken a lot of people from here to that camp outside Munich the newspapers are always raving about.'

It is true that when the Dachau concentration camp was started, the news was greeted with rapture by most of the conservative-minded newspapers and not simply by Nazi rags. Naturally, when this terrible place opened, no one had any inkling, probably not even the people who built it, how many would die there in the early 1940s. What shocks us all in retrospect, us Germans, is thinking how easily we turned a blind eye to the implications of building such a place in the first instance. The old man in the bar who was so angry with Helga was probably very typical: if the price for peace, stability, prosperity was to remove a very few people, well, why not? One could turn a blind eye to that. Here at last was a solution to all our national problems – lock 'em up!

'But this is . . . This isn't possible, this . . .' And I ran, I ran down the corridor until I could find Winnie.

At the end of the war, when the whole nightmare was over, Winnie herself was arrested, as is well known. By then, Helga and you and I had got out of Bayreuth, left behind us that scene of carnage and rubble and misery, and found some other one, some other pitted, burnt, wrecked hell-hole in which to live the next five or ten years of our lives. (We headed first for Leipzig, Wagner's birthplace, Bach's shrine. We had lost your cello. You were ill. Do you remember your thirteenth birthday in that hostel in Leipzig? We thought you would starve, your legs and arms were so thin.)

By that stage the Americans had taken over Bayreuth, and we were in a part of Germany that would eventually come under Soviet control, though everything was still pretty chaotic at that stage. Word reached me from someone we hardly knew – you remember Dietrich Hönisch, that kid who was an assistant stage manager trained up by Tietjen? He wrote to say Winnie had been arrested and was in danger of being hanged. All kinds of stories were going around.

The American troops had searched (the bombed and half-wrecked) Wahnfried actually expecting to find H in hiding there! The 'denazification' process began.

Here isn't the place to say what I think about that, though I will say in passing that by 'denazifying' Germany, with the best possible intentions, the Allies sucked out a vast amount of what made Germany so distinctive. Because the Nazis had appropriated so much German literature, music, religion and tradition for themselves, and pretended that Luther, Goethe etc. etc. were all proto-National Socialists, it became necessary to 'cleanse' much that was interesting, especially in the area of, to use a term very loosely, the Gothic in the German imagination. By that I mean both the genuine medieval Gothic, such as the incomparable carvings of the Wise and Foolish Virgins outside the St Sebaldus church in Nuremberg which so miraculously survived the bombings; or the eerie, etiolated Crucifixions of Cranach. Such as these have a tangible connection with the 'Gothic' or 'Romantic' strains in much later German art, with the fantasies of Novalis, or the troubled strange canvases, set in high rocky peaks, where a few evergreens or ruins or Calvarys jut against mad skies, of Caspar David Friedrich. This world, this Gothic German world, to which Richard Wagner gave the most incomparable expression was destroyed by denazification. And when the vacuum cleaner of good Western liberal democracy came and denazified us, they sucked out much else too – which must in part explain why life here has become so bloody boring and we in the East have nothing better to do than sit here half envying the prosperity of the Westerners and half despizing them for the moral compromises we believe they have made; and they are probably sitting there demonizing us and thinking we are all brainwashed Soviet agents. But that's my hobby-horse.

Fifteen years ago, at the end of the war, the denazification process was deemed not merely a polite bit of window dressing but an absolute necessity before our country could rejoin – God, the hypocrisy of these phrases! – the Family of Nations. And Winnie was part of that process. They had her up as a major offender: not surprising, since she was one of the first Germans to join the wretched Party, and she insisted throughout the hearings that she was a personal friend of H and would not deny that she still considered him, as a private individual, whatever evils he had done as a public figure, to be her friend. This was a distinction which many, many people (though not I) believed was in itself positively evil to make at this juncture of history. Helga did. Christ, the rows we had about that, with her shouting, weeping, screaming abuse at me, tears starting from her face, and you, from thirteen onwards staring reproachfully at both of us for our bad manners, not being able to stop ourselves having these rows in your presence.

When the worst of the criminals were actually put on trial in Nuremberg, Winnie's future still lay in the balance, though it was clear by then she would not actually be hanged. Some spoke of her being sentenced to ten years' hard labour. That was when I persuaded Helga to write a letter – believing it would do no good, but that justice required that we should write. I can't even remember now how we found out that there was an address to write to; but one brief letter from Winnie, sent years later – my last communication with her ever – suggested that our letter had not only got through but had been allowed as evidence. And several of the Jews she got out of Dachau after Helga's arrest actually came in person to testify on her behalf.

'What! Arrested!' I remember her face so clearly when I burst into her office that morning and told her that Helga had been arrested. Every member of the local Communist Party, not only in Bayreuth but in Franconia and in Nuremberg, had been rounded up over the space of that week and many had suffered the fate of Helga. She spent only about ten days in Dachau, many spent much longer, but Winnie did manage to get all the members of her orchestra and chorus out before the big productions that summer.

'You told me' – this the furious, the incandescently angry Helga had shouted when, in about 1950, I told her the full truth – 'you told me at the time that the Wagner family name had been enough to get us all out of that camp. That was what you *said*! Oh, can't you *see* how this makes me feel? I'd rather have stayed there, I'd rather have stayed . . . that I came out as a favour to *him*, I came out because he had authorized it, I came out so I could get back in time to play in fucking *Parsifal* for *him* . . .'

With her seemingly unshakeable belief that Wolf personally would never condone any of the atrocities of his own regime, Winnie had rung him up in a temper. Did he know that at the moment when rehearsals were reaching the most critical stage the local gauleiter had arrested various members of the orchestra? There had been quite a lot of shouting at him – not least because she was unable to believe that he had anything to do with the murder of Röhm and the others. 'I know that you would have insisted on a fair trial,' she told the telephone receiver.

When he told her that the bloodletting had been necessary for the greater good of Germany, she was silenced, puzzled; but even this admission did no more than strike her as hideously out of Wolf's normally decent and reasonable character.

The short spell Helga spent in Dachau had been horrible, but she described it all in a very matter-of-fact manner. They had not tortured her, merely treated all the inmates toughly – a great deal of exercise, enforced works; short commons, short sleeping hours; bullying guards. Some of the prisoners had been tortured, but not her, though she had, as I feared would be the case, been struck several times by a sergeant for insubordination.

Helga's arrest, and the whole Night of the Long Knives experience, opened my eyes finally and for ever to the nature of this regime. I saw that whatever veneer of order and prosperity the new government would bring to our country, these advantages had been bought at the expense of holding us in fear. The capacity of that old man in the bar to turn a blind eye, for the sake of the advantages which would come from such blindness, had not been lost on me. Without the clear faith of my brother or my parents or (in her different way) Helga, I could see clearly enough that one could no longer support or countenance what had happened – and this was very early days, compared with the horrors in store.

But what did I do to stop it? Did I join in resistance movements, like my brother, or speak out against the anti-Semitism, as both my parents and a handful of old ladies at their church were brave enough to do? Did I heck.

Winnie continued to behave as if the manifestations of the true nature of this regime – the arrests, the bullying – were aberrations. She continued to bother Wolf with her shopping lists of complaints and on the whole he was always ready to listen to her. The first lie, the first series of lies, I told Helga – lies by omission, lies which were not spoken, the suppression of what a large part Wolf played in all Winnie's decisions and activities – held back from her the fact that she had only received almost instantaneous discharge from Dachau at the personal diktat of the Leader.

I do not think she was ever able to come to terms with that, nor was she ever able wholly to forgive me. Of course that anger, perfectly justifiable, was only the beginning of our estrangement over this matter, which took place throughout your teens in the 1950s. The ultimate indignity – that Helga and I had been asked to adopt you because you were Winnie's and Wolf's daughter – that was something which was never, ever, spelt out between us. But I am sure that Helga had begun to suspect.

In one of our rows, when you were about fifteen, she said, 'You just never got that woman out of your hair, did you? You wanted me for sex – was that all it was?'

'Helga, you know that's not true . . .'

'Not even for that?'

'You know it was so much more than that – don't spoil it all.'

'Oh, so it's me spoiling it all.'

'I haven't finished – don't spoil even the past by pretending we never had anything together; we did and I'm for ever grateful that . . .'

'Oh, you're for ever grateful? You're for ever grateful – you patronizing bastard! Why not go to her – go back to Bayreuth where she's probably still sitting with her Nazi friends, chuckling at having got away with it all.'

'I'm sure, I'm convinced, she's put all that behind her,' I said, hoping more than believing that this was the case.*

'Are you sure you aren't little Senta's father?'

This shot, fired out in your presence I am afraid, was so confusing for you, wasn't it? Neither Helga nor I had hidden from you the fact that we adopted you, when you were nearly three years old, from the orphanage in Bayreuth. We did so because Winnie asked us to and we both, at that stage, felt pathetic, total gratitude to her for getting Helga so quickly released from the concentration camp. She told us merely that the child should never have been sent to an orphanage, that its parents had been unable to look after it themselves, but that they longed for it to have a happy family upbringing, to be normal. Winnie had spoken to us movingly about her own desolation in the English orphanage, and of her feelings of security and happiness when the Klindworths had brought her to Germany and set her free.

We brought you up very closely, very lovingly. It had become clear by then why Helga had not worried about taking precautions when we made love. She was much more experienced than I and she had already begun to fear, what medical examinations later made definite, that she was unable to conceive. She told me, excitedly, when the idea of adopting you first arose, that she wanted a kid more than anything – that she'd first started taking me seriously because although she wasn't sure of me as a bloke, she thought I'd do as a dad. (Fair, I hope you agree, on some levels.)

We smothered you with over-attention, probably. And I know it was hell for you when, not long after the war, our normally bickery, slightly combative relationship turned really sour. One aspect of

---

*N—— is probably writing a good decade before the five-hour-long television interviews given in 1975 by Winifred Wagner to Hans Jürgen Syberberg, in which she caused scandal by her impenitent expressions of personal fondness for H, exclaiming that if he walked through the door at that moment she would rejoice – 'The part of him that I know, shall we say, I value as highly today as I ever did. And the H that everyone utterly condemns does not exist in my mind, because that is not how I know him.'

our over-cautiousness with you was that we kept you innocent, much longer than I would think perhaps wise, about all aspects of sexual knowledge. Even after your first period – and we were still living in France then, I think – neither Helga nor I had really told you anything about the 'facts of life'. Hence the peculiar horror of the moment, yelled out when you were in your mid teens, about the possibility of my being your actual father. By then you knew, you must have known, how children are born into the world, but the complex business of who you were, and who your birth father had been, clearly a matter to obsess Helga, was now being tossed about as a cannon ball in our marital crossfire. I've never been able to ask what that did to you, hence this coward's way out of writing the whole thing down as a story, hoping that bits of the truth will emerge – for me if not for you.

Certainly, the love I felt for Winnie, the calf love or crush, was not something that ever went away. It hasn't gone away to this day. I recognize that she was and is a silly woman, but there was something about her which was magnificent, and magnanimous, and in every sense big. Helga began like someone who seemed as if she was capable of being big, but the experience of being married to me made her shrink, it embittered her, it limited all her emotional and intellectual possibilities, just as it did to me too. In taking on the responsibility of caring for you we somehow gave away more of ourselves than it was right to give. And the fact that we could not ask candid questions – of one another or of Winnie – about you meant that we lost the capacity to tell the truth at all. Respect went; love had gone long since; soon even vestigial liking, or the ability to be pleasant in one another's company, was impossible. And that was the poison gas you breathed in, day in day out, in our little flat, every bit as polluting as the belching acrid orange and charcoal-grey smoke from the artificial-fibre factory where most of our fellow townspeople work.

The awful thing is that I responded to Helga's accusation, that you were my love child made with Winnie, because I so wanted it to be true. I loved and love you as a father, and I would love you if you were not *his*. For some time afterwards perhaps you thought (hoped too?) that this was true. Of course, we could only communicate in half-sentences and silences and hints, so the matter was never aired even some years later, when Helga had moved out and you too were getting ready for university (Dresden).

The production was the last Richard Strauss conducted at Bayreuth, so it would have been memorable for this reason alone. Strauss had a Jewish daughter-in-law and he had moreover that summer written a letter to the writer Stefan Zweig, which was intercepted by the secret police. It made his position as President of the Reich Music Chamber untenable.

We were in a serious pickle at the Festival Theatre, in danger of losing all our star conductors. Fu was in disgrace and his dragon of a secretary-manager-agent-companion Berta Geissmar had left Germany – non-Aryan. Toscanini had made it clear he would not work in Nazi Germany and was now in America, keeping in touch by letter only with his favourite Wagner child, Friedelind. Winnie said to me several times before Strauss's last appearance that she wondered seriously whether the Festival would take place the next year. But they had been wondering that every year since they revived it ten years before ...

There was a paradox about Bayreuth, however, which enabled Tietjen to do some of the most innovative operatic work that had ever taken place in Germany. All theatres, opera houses and concert halls in the Reich now came under the control of Nosferatu, head of the Chamber of Culture, of which the Music Chamber was a sub-section. Winifred alone of all theatre directors in the Reich refused to join. And she alone in the Reich, because of her special relationship with Wolf, was allowed to get away with it. There developed the extraordinary paradox that her very closeness to Wolf enabled her to dare more than any other theatre in the country. She could continue to employ those who would have been forbidden to work anywhere else – Jews, political dissidents and so on. Many of these were the ones who came forward in 1945, when she was in danger of being imprisoned, or even hanged, and got her sentence commuted to a mere reprimand for her 'culpable stupidity' in having supported the Third Reich.

All this had a great effect upon us, on me and Helga. For although I agreed passionately with Helga by now that I ought to 'get away from all these people', and would have been happy to make a break and leave Bayreuth, it was, paradoxically, Helga who could not leave. Given her membership of the Communist Party, her short spell in a concentration camp and her record as a dissident, there was no possibility of her getting employment as a player in any of the orchestras controlled by the Reich Music Chamber. Only in Bayreuth, where we existed like vassals dependent upon the whims of a medieval king, was it possible to bend the rules, and for a Red like Helga or a 'non-Aryan' like Alice Strauss, the composer's daughter-in-law, to get employment.

I think that 1934 Festival was in some ways the strangest I ever witnessed. It happened like a dream, in the background of my obsessive concern about Helga. In Dachau, she had been made to do military drill and gymnastic exercises. The hours had been strict, the food and drink disgusting, and the conditions of some of the longer-term inmates clearly most alarming, with rumours of torture rife. Her poor father, a chest specialist at the biggest hospital in Munich, drove out to fetch her and bring her home. Helga loved her father and mother, and it seemed that, conservative and Catholic as they (and most of her siblings) were, they tolerated her political deviation. They did not like the atheistic tenor of Marxism, but they did not feel that it was, like National Socialism, an actual blasphemy against the Holy Spirit who is indwelling in every human soul.

I had Dr Gerlandt's telephone number in Munich and rang it obsessively. On the day of Helga's release she came to the receiver. Her voice had a slight tremble in it, but retained its usual tone of jokey irony. 'My gag about the Choral Society didn't amuse the old comrades in the bar.'

'You must be careful.'

'Any particular reason?'

'Because I have found I can't live without you.'

She came back to Bayreuth a couple of days later by train. She'd missed some of the *Ring* performances but was on hand to play her cor anglais parts in *Parsifal* and in all subsequent *Rings*. What I told her was true. I was waiting for the Munich train to come in to Bayreuth station. She could hardly have been thinner than before, but she looked if anything paler. Presumably with a view to pleasing her parents, whom she had just left in Munich, she was more than usually conventionally dressed, with a little cloche hat, a dark-blue linen coat and skirt and only the lightest hand luggage.

'Is that all you've brought?'

'For some reason they did not invite me to take ball gowns or a grand piano to the KZ.'

'I didn't mean ... I ...'

It was I who was more or less crying and she who was laughing, as I put her bag down and once again enfolded her in my arms. 'Marry me.'

'What, now?'

'Yes.'

'Maybe wait until the Festival's over – only three weeks?'

Which is what we did. The wedding has no part in this story, though it had its dramas. We were married by the registrar in Munich, in an office with a giant painting of H behind the man's head. And then we repaired – this was the tricky bit – to a Catholic church for a nuptial blessing by a priest. I was amazed that Helga consented to take part in this rigmarole, but she did so to please her family. My non-Catholicism was a very great stumbling block with both Dr and Frau Gerlandt. At the somewhat chilly wedding breakfast – the temperature outside was warm enough, it was the old parents on both sides who provided the refrigeration of atmosphere – Frau Gerlandt was heard to remark that no member of her family had ever, so far as she knew, married a Protestant. My brother, dear, friendly, open-faced Heinrich, chatted earnestly to one of Helga's brothers about the Pope,[*] and whether there was any sign of the Vatican strengthening its denunciations of the German regime.

[*]Pope Pius XI (Achille Ratti, a former Vatican Librarian) was a cautious but vehement critic of National Socialism. Some people believed he was murdered by the fascists in 1939.

'I liked what he said earlier this year – that we are all spiritual Semites,' Heinrich said.

'The Pope said that?'

'It was reported in the papers. It was a real disappointment to us in the Confessing Church that Pacelli* caved in over the abolition of the Catholic Party. Do you think he is just playing politics? We can't tell. Kaas† seems to think anything is better than Bolshevism, but some of us hope Pacelli is giving the Nazis enough rope to hang themselves with, in the hope that the Catholic Party can return. The anti-Nazi vote held up very well down here among all the Catholic Party faithful . . .'

My parents looked intensely embarrassed by the guilelessness of my brother's talk. It was undoubtedly bad manners on Heinrich's part to quiz my brother-in-law so innocently, having no idea what his own particular take on events might have been. I, as usual, misinterpreted my parents' anxious and disapproving silence on this occasion, having no idea at that stage how deeply they identified with Heinrich's position and how bravely they would express their opposition to the regime only a few years down the line.

My family life began during that summer. Deep, deep fondness for one another, Helga and I, somehow made the strange world of *Parsifal* little more than noises off, background music if you will.

It was, by any standards, a triumph for Winnie. Against the aunts, against the bank manager, against the Fates themselves, she had

---

*Eugenio Pacelli, as Papal Nuncio in Germany, agreed various Concordats with H in an attempt to preserve the freedom of Catholics to worship, and to educate their children, as they pleased, and to avoid a widespread persecution of the Church. As Pope Pius XII from 2 March 1939 onwards he was widely criticized for not speaking out more forcefully against Nazism.

†Monsignor Ludwig Kaas, leader of the Catholic Party, had been prepared to disband its ranks and accept the Concordats offered by H as a way of keeping Bolshevism at bay. 'It matters little who rules so long as order is maintained' was his view in 1933. Most Catholic bishops in Germany took a broadly similar view at this early stage of the regime, though the laity were divided and many would have agreed with Heinrich N——'s much more radical denunciation of the racialistic intolerance of the Nazi life view.

brought off this production. And though Tietjen and Roller had designed it, and though Richard Strauss conducted it, and though the choral director and the chorus and the orchestra and the stage managers played their usual tireless roles, there could be no doubt that this was in some senses a Winnie and Wolf production; their finest hour.

Wolf arrived for the opening night and his appearance at the Festival Theatre, in a swallow-tail coat and a stiff shirt and white tie, on Winnie's arm, could almost have been that of a crown prince and princess coming into their kingdom.

It was during the interval of that production that I happened to be beside him, and he repeated that gnomic remark which I have pondered on and off ever since. '*Parsifal* is your favourite of them all?' he asked.

'It's wonderful – this production is wonderful – but for me the true interest of Wagner will always be in the *Ring* cycle.'

'I thought that when I was your age,' he said with a genial smile. 'When you are older, you will understand that *Parsifal* is the masterpiece.'

I love *Parsifal* to this day and I suppose I always shall, though I think it is an incoherent masterpiece, which touches dark places in an unintended way – that, therefore, it is an imperfect work of art. But I have never made the transition Wolf predicted. I have never considered it a more interesting or more impressive thing than *The Ring*.

As we all sat there, on a very hot night in Bayreuth, crowded into the darkened amphitheatre of the Festival Theatre, and as the Grail Knights sang their peculiar Eucharistic devotions, the world outside was changing and, looking back upon it all, it seems to me that somewhere there in the darkness, Wolf stopped being Wolf altogether and simply became H. Winnie never noticed this, of course, or if she did, she was determined never to let on – since if he ceased to be Wolf, he ceased to be hers. The private self of her old friend was being subsumed into the mythological national hero; and this was very largely not because of a change taking place in himself – though that change had almost certainly been hastened by the Röhm murder and the Night of the Long Knives – it was events. While old Titurel lay in the grave, half dead but more alive than his wounded son, and growling at his Knights, the ancient hero of Germany, President von Hindenburg, was slowly sinking towards death in Berlin.

During the interval in which Wolf made his remark to me about *Parsifal* there were movements afoot. The Mad Gamekeeper arrived towards the end of that interval with a fleet of huge cars and out he climbed, wearing an extraordinary white tunic, half military, half the tuxedo of the wine waiter on a transatlantic liner, with a large peaked cap which could have been that of a self-important chauffeur. He came to warn H that a Nazi coup in Austria had been unsuccessful. The Austrian Chancellor, Dollfuss, had been assassinated, but the government had fought back. Many Nazis including young Ulrich Roller, son of our set designer, had been arrested. Von Papen, the Conservative Catholic Vice-Chancellor, arrived by the end of the opera to sound out H's position on the crisis.

Wolf seemed utterly indifferent to the international news, as it was brought and muttered to him at the back of the Wagners' family box. When he appeared on the loggias and balconies with Winnie, his face was lit up by that 'sublime' and trancelike expression which possessed him when listening to the music of the Master. It is impossible for me to say in retrospect whether he was genuinely transported by *Parsifal* (my own view) or whether he was acting a part of indifference, so that the world press, some of whose photographers were present outside the theatre, could never accuse him of having a hand in the failed Austrian coup. Accounts I have read since told me that when he got back to the Villa Wahnfried, he went into a tirade of fury with von Papen, shouting out the names of various Austrian politicians as if they were swear words. And he cut short his visit to the Festival, swooping back to Berlin at some moment in an aeroplane.

I was a witness to none of that. Helga and I were in her bedsit in Weissenburgerstrasse. Being very careful what jokes we made, we had eaten some spaghetti at a cheap Italian restaurant and headed for bed and the consolations of purely private affections. Only in the morning when, naked and Giacometti-thin, Helga sat up in bed to ignite her dawn cigarette did she talk of the assassination of Dollfuss – which had been on everyone's lips in the restaurant – and speculate with an unrealistic hopefulness about the chance of an anti-government coup here bringing low the 'criminals', as she often and rightly called them.

Wagner saw *Parsifal* as a renunciation of violence in favour of mystic love – love of animals, of the universe, of all things living – yet behind it there lurks a strange fascination with blood and the booming all-male choruses cannot be heard without feeling that they foreshadow the sinister orders of knights who kept us so painfully in order during the 1930s.

I can't conclude a chapter about that year of *Parsifal* without recalling the moment when, for me, H became a figure in his own opera and ceased to be a person upon whom I could easily focus as a private individual. It was the following year, in spring 1935, and Helga and I, who had been married about six months, had been to Freiburg to visit old university friends of mine, and to take our honeymoon in the Black Forest. The coming of spring never seemed more miraculous, the buds of the trees on our forest walks, coming into leaf, the sunlight filtered through pale green, the song of the birds. We were making love so often, in boarding house and hotel rooms as we journeyed about, that I was convinced that by the time we returned to Bayreuth, Helga would be pregnant. Sometimes, in our worst moments before we separated, over a decade later, we snarled such cruel sayings to one another – that we had never loved one another. And recollections would then return of those walks in the Black Forest in the spring of 1935, memories that stabbed me with guilt at my blasphemy against our love – for we were in love in the hope of spring and the alchemy of sexual joy, spiritual union, ecstatic happy fondness took us out, as a pair, from the horrors that were possessing our country and allowed us, for a week or so, to be indifferent.

We were in an artificial heaven of love. Though the world was beginning to go mad and Germany had perhaps been mad since the end of the war, nature continued its powerful, self-renewing journey through time, bringing deep messages of peace to us who loved. It was when we came back to Freiberg that a rival dream clashed with and invaded our own. It would be impossible to say that 'reality' intruded, for what we saw, and experienced, when we queued outside the cinema and watched the performance of Leni Riefenstahl's *Triumph of the Will* was an alternative to reality every bit as artificial and choreographed as a Wagner opera or a high mass.

I cannot even remember now why we went to see it – we weren't obliged to do so and before we entered the cinema we had been so happy. One or both of us had evidently concluded that we 'ought' to see this work by a rising young female photographer and director.

'No one who has personally seen the face of the Führer in *The Triumph of the Will* can ever forget it. It will stay with them day and night, and like a silent glittering flame it will burn into their soul' – so, Nosferatu.

I can more remember the sensation of seeing the film, and of Helga's reaction to it, than I can remember much of the actual footage, though of course it has become a classic of cinema. The torchlit processions; the numberless ranks of the faithful in the stadium by night and day; the workers marching with the tools of their trade to show that our country had thrown off the curse of unemployment; the youth innocently emerging from tents; the troops marching through the medieval streets of the loveliest old town in Europe; but at the centre of it all *him*, that figure whose facial muscles and hypnotic eyes had been so well known to me for a decade, now projected on to a huge cinema screen, working the enchanter's magic not only on the crowds in the film, but on the rows and rows of people, transfixed in their cinema seat and staring upwards. If I had not been in love with Helga, and if I had not been sitting beside her, I can easily envisage that this masterpiece of the black arts would have carried me away, at least for a time.

I forget now where I read, or heard, that Leni Riefenstahl who worked solidly on the film, from the time of the Nuremberg rally in September until its release the following spring, had an extra-ordinary effect on H. He had known, perhaps since his youth but certainly since the war, that he had the power to electrify audiences.

At meeting after meeting, in huge sports palaces, in the Reichstag, on national radio, H had demonstrated his power to bewitch the masses. Never until he became a character in Leni's lens, however, had his figure come into so sharp a focus, had the witchcraft been quite so polished, so fatal.

Years after the war – our war, not the First War – I must have read or heard somewhere Leni's claim that they had walked together, H and she, by the shores of the North Sea, and he had told her that he always spent Christmas, the time of his mother's death, alone. When she had stretched out to comfort him he had embraced her and then drawn back, saying words to the effect, 'I may not love a woman until my work is complete.'

The supposed scene (I might even have remembered it wrong) has the whiff of fiction about it, yet it is convincing for that very reason. Certainly I can remember how scornful Winnie was whenever Riefenstahl's name was mentioned in the later years of the 1930s. (A similar hostility existed between Riefenstahl and Nosferatu, since that particular evil puppet master obviously liked to think that he was pulling all the Leader's strings.)

The monkey or the organ grinder? The old question I had asked myself in the Chancellery. Riefenstahl, herself an organ grinder of genius, left audiences in no doubt that H was in an all but divine control. Whatever the truth or otherwise of his relations with her, she had invented a person, or found out a person, who was, like other demigods, above carnal relationships. His work must be completed before he could love again.

Outside the cinema in Freiburg the crowds were awestruck. It was like coming out of a great oratorio. The Saviour had come to earth. When we stood beside one another on the pavement, Helga took hold of the front of my shirt with her fists. It was a passionate, bitter gesture, which hurt me, because she had gathered up nipple, chest hair, shirt buttons so indiscriminately in her nicotine-stained fingers. She put her brow against my throat and I realized she was weeping, weeping bitterly.

Tristan und Isolde

The orphanage where you spent the first four years of your life is at number 14 Friedrichstrasse in Bayreuth. It is on the corner of Ludwigstrasse. From the Villa Wahnfried, if you cut through the Hofgarten and walk through the stable archway of the Neues Schloss, it is less than a ten-minute walk.

I had noticed once or twice that Winnie made visits there. Pedalling down the cobbled surface of Friedrichstrasse on my bike I had more than once seen her unmistakable form, now much bulkier than when first we met, entering the large rather forbidding eighteenth-century building which abuts upon the street. The sculpted relief in the pediment above the main door depicts young children reaching out to their mothers, something the inhabitants of that place, being incarcerated there, were almost by definition unable to do.

Winnie had no 'side'. She made no secret of the fact that she had been brought up in an orphanage. I assumed that she made periodic visits to the Bayreuth orphanage because she felt some empathy with the inhabitants. At any one time, she always had some 'lame ducks' to whom she was being especially kind, musicians whose finances or marriages were in crisis, widows, children. It was noticeable that this philanthropic side to her character was thrown into ever sharper relief as life, personal life, became more fraught. Being young, insensitive and myself embarking on a new life with Helga, I childishly took Winnie for granted. Only the lonely hours of reminiscence and memory I spend in this dump of a flat give me an insight into the sufferings she was then enduring. She was still – we are thinking of 1936 – a comparatively young woman, not yet forty. The four Wagner children were adolescent and giving her much cause for anxiety, the two boys at one another's throats, Friedelind an emotional chaotic.

All four hated Tietjen who was a tyrant at the Festival Theatre and a testy, charmless little domestic despot at Wahnfried. For, despite his refusal to give up mistresses in Berlin, he had clearly moved into a quasi-stepfatherly role in the Wagner family. Winnie, who could be hot-tempered enough herself, as anyone who worked at the Bayreuth Festivals could tell you, cowered before Tietjen's tongue lashings, often dissolving into tears when he launched on his tirades.

Towards the end of one particularly disastrous *Tristan*, the soprano Frida Leider had been almost inaudible. Her voice had been going for the whole evening and it was agonizing to hear its croaky failures to reach the more spectacular climaxes of the first two acts. By Act Three there were actual moments of silence as she mouthed, but could not sing at all and her final spectacular aria was entirely drowned by the orchestra.

'We beat her that time,' was Helga's jokey response when I saw her afterwards. Apart from any other considerations she always loved playing *Tristan* because of the prominence of the cor anglais parts. She would say that if it is properly conducted the combined notes of oboe and cor anglais should be heard through and even above the strings in their final poignant repetition of a theme that asserts the eternal sadness of things. You'll remember better than I do that Helga used to say that in *Tristan* the most important character is the orchestra, that attempts to explain the themes of the opera are all bollocks, that it's music, pure and simple – Wagner's greatest moment. On this night, though, her jokey wish that the singers should know their place and submit to the strivings, yearnings, hypnotic swayings of the strings and the persistent sadness of the woodwind repeating their notes of everlasting pessimism had gone further even than her expectations. The soprano was a choking, silent, nervous wreck.

Much had been going on in poor Frida's life to provoke such a collapse, not least the fact that she was probably fifty by then and far too old to be singing the part in the first place. Her husband Rudolf Deman was insistent that she take some rest and Winnie agreed with him. Tietjen exploded with wrath, asking them both where he was expected to find another Isolde at a moment's notice.

Deman walked out on him at that point and Winnie had then pleaded, pathetically, with Tietjen, who was a good half-metre shorter than she was, reminding him that Deman was 'non-Aryan', that Frida had been suffering torments about their safety and that what they needed was sympathy – understanding . . .

'Oh, I see – you who know so much about music. I need no sympathy, but this selfish cow – you gave her cigarettes this afternoon – croaks on me and you know better than I do.'

So he would rage. And Winnie would weep. (Deman went into exile not long after – to Switzerland.) Frida was forced by Tietjen, a stupid decision, to sing the role to the end of that season, wrecking the performance for the other players, the orchestra, the audience. Winnie tearfully implored him to try some of the understudies but this merely produced more rage. *What* understudies? The pushy young women who thought they could sing Isolde and who had been encouraged by Winnie to learn the role were *not*, in Tietjen's view, understudies and Winnie knew nothing. Got that? *Nothing*. Friedelind's attempts at intervention during these rows, to defend her mother, only made matters worse, since the mutual antipathy between Friedelind and Tietjen had deepened to poisonous loathing.

In the past, when Festival life or family life were a source of grief, Winnie at least had her relationship with Wolf to fall back upon. At the time I considered that this was still the case, since she maintained for the most part her breeziness, her heartiness, of manner. Only retrospect makes me ask what lay behind this carapace of cheeriness when 'Uncle Wolf' made one of his periodic and often unannounced visits to Wahnfried. He showered her children with presents – gold watches for the boys, gold bracelets for the girls. For Wieland's eighteenth birthday a Mercedes-Benz.

She came to wonder, surely, whether it was her or the children that Wolf loved. Once, when she was in Berlin staying with Tietjen at his flat, the telephone had rung: 'Winnie?'

'Wolf . . .'

'Do you feel like seeing your children?'

'Very much but – My Leader' – her cigaretty giggle at anything improbable – 'this would involve a rather long journey. You see, Wieland is at one of those insufferable camps which our new gauleiter insists he goes on – really, Wolf, if these hearty fellows only *knew* you they wouldn't insist on torturing poor youth in your name with gymnastics! Wolfgang's at a fearful school and the two girls are safely locked up in the convent, and miss them all *dearly* as I do, I'd have had no time to work unless they . . .'

'They are here.'

'In Berlin?'

'At the Chancellery.'

'What's happened? Has there been an accident?'

'I missed them too. I sent cars for them.'

'But the girls' convent is in Heiligengrabe –'

'Why else do you think I built the Autobahns?'

She had gone to lunch and of course she had made it all into an anecdote – of the irrepressible, fun-loving Führer sending cars all over Germany to give his favourite young people a treat. But how had she felt about this unilateral co-opting of her children without consulting her? A little excluded? And for his part, what? Unable to have the company of his actual child, to whom Winnie had given birth, he threw himself with ever greater enthusiasm into friendship with them, rather than trying to prise her away from her obsessively unhappy relationship with Tietjen?

To this phase of life belonged, when chance allowed, her most frequent visits to the Bayreuth orphanage, some of which I had started to notice.

On one particular occasion when, cycling along Friedrichstrasse, I saw her, my mind was filled with my brother Heinrich. He had been arrested and charged with preaching sedition. My parents were worried to distraction and without telling them of my intention, I thought I'd try discussing the matter with Winnie. This moment of finding her alone, on the pavement, was not to be passed by.

'N——,' she greeted me by name, using the familiar '*Du*' form.

'Frau Wagner, can I talk to you about something?' I always spoke to her formally, using the polite 'Sie' for 'you', confirming that our relationship was that of junior to senior.

I poured out my brother's story: an enthusiast, an idealist who wanted to help the poor and the young, one who made no secret of his feelings, who had thrown in his lot with the Confessing Church under the leadership of Pastor Niemöller.

'My friend Lange, Hans Joachim Lange – he used to come and play with me when I was living with the Klindworths in Berlin – has already asked me to put in a good word for Pastor Niemöller. The poor Führer says that he loses sleep at night from all these turbulent priests. Niemöller was a very good man no doubt – he was in the navy with my friend Lange and seemed sympathetic to the Cause – but now he's turned *against* Wolf and he fills that huge church of his in Berlin, denouncing the government . . . I've said to Lange, I'll ask Wolf to protect Niemöller from the Gestapo, but Wolf says he wouldn't need protecting from the Gestapo if he would just *shut up*.'

'I don't think Heinrich can shut up.'

'Which prison is he in? I'll see what I can do.'

How often she had made that promise, and she had more influence than most. It is easy now, in retrospect, surveying a landscape torn with fire and thunder, to see these few brave persecuted ones, Jews and Christians, as the forerunners or pioneers of the millions more who were to die before the drama sounded its last chords. At the time it did not feel like that. Because of loving Helga, because of loving my family though they drove me nuts, I was perhaps more conscious than many Germans of how the regime was viewed by the dissidents. To date, two of those I loved most, Helga and Heinrich, had ended up in prison, albeit for short periods.

(Heinrich was hanged eventually, but that was much later, during the war, when I was away in France. After repeated warnings he had spoken out once too often, and after my father's death in the concentration camp near Bayreuth he spoke with greater reckless-ness than ever.)

But these were the very distinct minority and I have to say that I could not see things *at the time* as they saw them. These brave and high-principled people were, as we now see, right: the regime was built upon murder and the suppression of the human spirit; from its first setting-forth the march, at whose vanguard strode our glorious Leader, led inexorably to an intended engulfment of massacre, to fire and destruction. All I can say is that in 1936 it did not feel like that to the great majority of Germans. Our country had changed, changed very swiftly and dramatically. Where once millions were unemployed there was now full employment. That sense of inhabiting a madhouse had gone. You might say, but surely the National Socialists have erected the greatest madhouse in European history, but it didn't feel like that. When H had still been struggling for power, and when he came to Wahnfried sunk in depression, following the death of his niece, our country was on the edge of civil war. There was now the most palpable feeling of happiness and calm. Jobs were safe. We felt secure from Communist oppression. (Insufferable I may sound, perhaps am, but I never took Helga's Communism seriously and I shared the view of all my other friends that a Marxist-Leninist Germany would lead to the loss of all freedom – and to a bloodbath.)

There isn't much freedom from where I am sitting in this foul little flat, but the amazing achievement of Wolf and friends is that they eventually created a hell beside which a repressive Marxist police state such as I have inhabited for the last fifteen years actually feels ... well, if not better in every way, at least more decent. In 1936, the year I'm thinking of, the euphoria and the national pride which we, most of us, had recovered, was to a large extent the result of deception. The economy had turned round because none of us knew, or none of us could quite face knowing, that it had become a war economy, with much of the 'regeneration of industry' being in reality the stockpiling of aggressive weaponry, which would eventually kill millions of people.

In 1936, the year of our greatest pride as a nation, it did not feel like this. My parents never spoke a word in praise of H or of his government. Even they, however, could not prevent their eyes sparkling and their mouths smiling when they heard the news that the Rhineland, so utterly unjustly taken from us by the Versailles

Treaty, had been reoccupied in March that year. All the generals and bigwigs and diplomatic experts told H that it was too risky, that the French would be bound to retaliate, and that Germany would suffer what was worse than actual military defeat – international humiliation as our men returned to the Fatherland with tails between legs. But not for nothing did he love the story of the fisherman and his wife, and he gambled. The 25,000 German troops who reoccupied what was German land were greeted, not by French field artillery but by cheering crowds, and by priests with incense burners blessing and welcoming them. Aachen, the burial place and capital of Charlemagne, German Emperor, was ours once again.

His boast, made more than once as Uncle Wolf at Winnie's table, was 'I have achieved a bloodless revolution. That makes me proud.'

If we ignored the brutal imprisonment of the troublemakers (which seemed to include most of my family except myself); if we ignored the bullying and harassment of the Jews (not at that stage much in the way of murder there, and certainly no genocide on the scale that would unfold beneath the black cloak of war); if we ignored the 1934 massacres following the murder of Röhm it was true. You can say, from your youthfulness and your exile in the 'free' West, that we should not have ignored these things, that they were all warning signals of how dangerous National Socialism was. I'm telling you that if you had known what it was to be half starving; to see Reds and SA fighting on the streets; to see your life savings reduced in a few months to two dollars; to see a quarter of the workforce unemployed and to see your country belittled and shamed at every diplomatic turn for years – my God, I'm telling you that in 1936 it felt good to be a German.

Helga, quite rightly, always contradicted anyone who said that National Socialism and Communism were two sides of the same coin, or that one form of absolutism was just like another. I have lived for the last fifteen years under Communism and I lived for six years under Nazism until the outbreak of war. There is no comparison. When I set out in the morning in this small town of ours, I hardly ever see a cheerful face. Oh, true, we all have a flat and we all have a job, but we are living under a fog of gloom here in the East and there is no obvious future release from it. I've actually come to like the gloom; it seems more fitting to life than the eternal optimism of those heady days in the 1930s. Perhaps political systems have to choose between the tyranny of doctrine and the despotism of a person. I do not attribute our daily sensations of depression to Ulb or Hon or the Sov-Soiuz.* Any system that tried to follow Marxist-Leninism would have resulted in this universal greyness, regardless of who was in control. Whereas 'a happy people under a strong king' was what H liked to say. Under the Leader there was a small proportion of people who were miserable, angry, morally shocked. But I am telling you, the huge majority were happy. The Rhineland was ours again. The world flocked to Berlin to see the Olympic Games in the summer, and they began to admire us, love us even. Old enemies like the British loved us.

Winnie, who had never previously made much of her British origins, was ecstatic about the new King of England. 'Very much one of us,' she had stated approvingly. 'Proud of his German roots and appreciative of what Our Leader has done for us. Why, look at them now in England – the same old men who have been running the country for years, doing nothing to help the poor. They even confiscate their property – did you know that? They send inspectors round, for a so-called "means test" and if some poor unemployed man with five children to feed has just one little heirloom, as it were a silver teapot, they will steal it, take it away. Their new King will put a stop to that. If only we could have a fascist government in England. Here in Germany the Leader has provided proper benefits for the very few workers remaining without work – and no theft of their treasures.'

So excited were Winnie and Wolf by the new English King that they felt they wanted to do something for him.

* N—— is referring to Walter Ulbricht (1893–1973), premier of the DDR, responsible for building the Berlin Wall in 1961, to his deputy and successor, Erich Honecker (1912–94), and to the Soviet Union (in Russian, Sovyetskii Soiuz), which exercised an iron control over East Germany at the time of writing.

It was Wolf who had the idea, after an especially glorious production of *Lohengrin* on the Green Hill. It was perhaps Tietjen's finest hour, that production. Old Roller was dead, but the sets designed by Tietjen's protégé Emil Preetorius were grander, more spare – the aesthetic of the aunts had been most definitely rejected. Furtwängler conducted – I doubt whether *Lohengrin* has ever been better played. The chief roles were sung to perfection by Max Lorenz, Maria Müller, Jaro Prohaska and Margarete Klose.

'Winnie, I have it! The present we were planning for our King, our friend the King of England!' he remarked, pop-eyed and sweaty-faced, during the interval. He was hyper-energetic that night, ecstatic with the pleasure of the music, but also rolling on the waves of his political and diplomatic successes of the previous year. 'We'll give this production of *Lohengrin* to King Edward as a present – to mark his Coronation!'

'How do you mean', asked Winnie, laughing, 'give it?'

'We'll send it over to London, it will be staged at the Royal Opera House Covent Garden – who is that conductor who is crazy about me, Sir Thomas Beecham, Ribbentrop says he is a Nazi.[*] We'll take Herr Preetorius's set. I'll come, Winnie, you can show me the treasures of London – the menagerie in the Tower, the lions who ate the poor little Princes, the great tombs in Westminster Monastery. I shall arrange for my plane to fly over to Tintagel and for us to see King Mark of Cornwall's castle together.'

The stage at the Festival Theatre in Bayreuth is apparently about four times the size of that at Covent Garden and it would have been impossible to move Preetorius's scenery into place there. Even if the orchestra at Covent Garden had been prepared to surrender to that of Bayreuth, and even if Furtwängler had surrendered his baton to Beecham, the logistics of the Leader's extravagant enterprise would have been considerably more difficult than reoccupying the Rhineland. They did, however, begin to negotiate the matter – even

---

[*] H was, as so often by his Ambassador in London, misinformed. Sir Thomas Beecham, though a Germanophile who did indeed conduct in the presence of the German Chancellor, was by no stretch of the imagination a political sympathizer.

I had to write some of the letters to the Director of the Opera House in London. In the end the thing foundered because the new King of England himself got to hear about it. No opera fan, he was more the sort of man whose musical tastes would be satisfied by sitting in a nightclub and tapping his co-respondent shoes to the rhythms of the latest American dance band number. When the scheme of German generosity reached his ears he had said that personally he had nothing against it, so long as he didn't have to go to 'the damn thing himself'.

But ... I have left Winnie in Friedrichstrasse and myself approaching upon the cobbles on my wobbly bicycle. She waved cheerily at me. Although the meeting was entirely a matter of chance, it was as if she had been waiting for me but, such was the beauty of a spring morning in Bayreuth, she was by no means impatient with me for being late.

Helga and I had been married for a little over eighteen months and we were still very much in love. The jokes were fantastic and so was the sex. Both of them made a protective cocoon, which enabled us to live as if outer circumstances only partially existed. We had in fact achieved that happy egotism which was the life ideal of our small town's only famous native-born philosopher, Max Stirner – he who despised Hegel and his systems, who put no trust in political systems, or the dogmas of religion as defined by other people and who believed that the attainment of wisdom was found when we recognized that the only reality is in our own ego, our bodily experiences, our trivial sensations, of taste, sound, sexual appreciation, bowel well-being. These are what constitute 'reality'. It is, of course, when life is sexually happy between two people, or when a non-sexual friendship is going especially well, possible for two people to share in some small part the egoistic pleasures of the other; but we are all ultimately alone in our egos and attempts to break these egos down, or to intrude upon them, will always ultimately fail.

Yet, although I had made myself late for work, and Helga late for a rehearsal, by cheerfully lingering in bed, savouring her smell and feel and touch, and although, as I pedalled along, I could still taste and smell her, and was in a dream of warm, physical pleasure, and although I was luxuriating in the happiness that her companionship brought to me, there still existed another, dreamier part of my ego which was decidedly mine and not Helga's, in which Winifred was, and always would be, a goddess.

If expressed in words, these matters would be hurtful to whomsoever believed herself at any one time to be important, or the most important person in our heart. (Do you remember? At school? Who is your best friend? Your third-best friend? Your tenth-best friend? And how important these gradations were to you, to all of us?) In my inner imagination, in the quiet private part of myself where I alone exist and where my dreams are all, there is something which I almost envisage as the reredos of a great church, adorned, as in some medieval chancel, by figures of those I have loved. In a medieval building the central place would be occupied by the Virgin and around her would be the particular saints to whom the building was dedicated. Next would come the Twelve. Then, there might be prophets, evangelists, or other figures of history or legend, stretching far up into the Gothic tracery. In my inmost soul such a screen is populated chiefly by women. My mother is there, and Helga is there, and of course you are there. Some of the figures in this fantasy screen carving would be amazed to know that they were there – they are 'crushes', waitresses, women who have served me in shops, faces regularly glimpsed on the tram. They are 'my' guardians, the tutelary angels of my inward self. They make life in this little flat endurable, especially when I close my eyes. But central to them all, like the great Madonna on a medieval choir screen, is Winnie. And as I write I see her on that spring morning in 1936, raising her arm to me. I see her fine aquiline nose, and the fresh moisture of her pink skin, and the thickness of her wavy Welsh hair piled on her head, and bound at the nape in a bun. Even then, even on that morning when every wobble of the bike reminded me of the previous passion night with Helga, Winifred waving constituted a vision of glory. She seemed then, and she still seems to me for all her 'punishable stupidity', to be one of the best human beings I have ever known.

'I'm going in here,' she said when I drew level with her and the large front door of the orphanage.

'How so?'

'I do visit the place quite a lot. Perhaps it is my orphanage childhood that explains this. Like to come in and look at the little perishers?'

Such an idea had never previously occurred to me. My tendency had been to scutter past this institution, almost as if it were a place of which to be ashamed. Perhaps I imagined it was a place where the children were ill-treated – I cannot, to myself, let alone to you, explain my feelings of diffidence about it.

We were admitted by a man in livery, a green frock-coat and yellow breeches, who could quite easily have been living in the time of the Margravine Wilhelmine who had founded this place, as she had founded so much else in our town. There was a cordial bow, as to a dignitary, and as to a regular visitor, and he announced that he would fetch the *Direktorin*. The woman in charge of the orphanage – rather oddly, her name escapes me – came to greet us. She was tallish, though not as tall as Winnie, and she had curly blonde hair cut quite short in the bob mode then fashionable. She wore a white shirt and a dark-blue skirt; whether or not this constituted a uniform I could not say.

'You're in time for cocoa and biscuits!' she said with a merry briskness.

We were led into a rather fine dining hall, with hammer beams, and three low-level refectory tables. There were, I should guess, about fifteen children at each table – and this constituted the entire population of the orphanage.

The children were at that moment filing into the hall. Some were little more than toddlers of two or three. None was older than ten. The boys wore blue knickerbockers, grey stockings and short grey coats of the traditional 'Bavarian' cut, which Fidi used to like wearing. The girls, many of whom had beautifully elaborate plaited hair, wore grey pinafore dresses over their immaculate white shirts.

They paused for a moment and all placed their hands together in prayer before the enormous portrait that hung over the chimney-piece. It was the only modern addition to the room, which was otherwise furnished traditionally and which contained no other painting. It was a giant picture of Wolf, wearing a brown shirt and swastika armband, and staring benignly into the middle distance.

> Oh Führer, Our Führer, sent by God's right hand,
> Guard us we pray, and guard our German land!
> Thank you, dear Führer, for our daily bread,
> Guide us from dawn of life until the grave's dark bed.
> Führer, oh Führer, our faith and our light
> Hail to thee, Führer, our saviour and our guide.

They chanted it in the rhythmical manner in which children always chant poetry or prayers collectively, their tinny combination of voices depriving the words of any meaning they might conceivably have had.

Their grace said, they proceeded to the hatch where a cook, abundantly greasy and red and fat, was distributing cocoa from a metal jug into enamelled mugs, each of which bore the arms of the House of Bayreuth-Brandenburg. Having taken their mug, they then passed another table where some home-made biscuits arose from the plates in mountains.

Winnie came forward, when they were all seated, and approached a small child at the end of one of the tables, her legs dangling from the grey smock dress but not yet long enough to reach the floor from the bench. 'Senta, this is my friend, Mr ——'

'Hello – Senta?' I was not sure that I had caught the name correctly and for a moment I wondered whether all the juvenile inhabitants of this establishment had been given names from Richard Wagner's operas.

It was our first meeting, yours and mine. I think of it now. I think of squatting down on my haunches and looking into your deep-blue eyes and thinking how pretty you were with your thick dark-blonde hair wound in plaits round your head. And even as I think of that first meeting I think of what will have been our last – my leaving you in Leipzig after the *Meistersinger* performance in 1960. And between those dates – from the mid 1930s to 1960 – there was our life together. And I suppose that image, of Winnie leaning over you in the orphanage, is what is central in my reredos.

Very characteristically, you did not say anything at all to me at that first meeting, though you chatted away to Winnie when she whispered to you. She asked you if you had been learning songs and whether you could play the triangle.

I suppose our visit took about ten minutes. Before we left, Winnie picked you up in her arms and hugged you and kissed your cheek, and rather than wriggling with awkwardness as any four-year-old would have done with a stranger, you were happy to be held in her arms – though the truth of your relationship did not occur to me on that day, nor indeed for years afterwards.

When we had left you in the orphanage, it was not of you but of her own childhood that Winnie spoke: 'The difference between Germany and England . . . if you had to explain it to somebody, you could not do better' – she said the words with her firm emphasis on every syllable – 'than to compare this place with the orphanage in East Grinstead. Naturally, there are rules here. Naturally, there are certain disciplines and if the children step out of line they are punished. Children need to know the parameters of their moral universe. But no one here is cruel. Of that I am convinced.' (It is three syllables in German and once more, her head moved from side to side in rhythm, almost like a clockwork figurine as she said *ü-ber-ʒeugt.*)

There was no self-pity in her memories, but she smiled with contempt as she told me about the Protestant nuns of East Grinstead. 'The whole place had been started by a hymn writer – he wrote a poem called "The Golden Jerusalem", which is very well-known, highly regarded, in the English Church. He had a fondness for the old Middle Ages and so he dressed up these young women, including his own daughter I may say, in these outlandish medieval robes and veils. And they thought of some outlandish medieval tortures, I can tell you. For everything we were whipped. If you cursed, you had to eat soap. If you said an angry word you had to hold a spoonful of mustard in your mouth – that was an especial favourite of Sister Ermenild, the hymn writer's daughter. Sister Geraldine Mary had a leather thong with which she chastized the bed-wetters. I do not believe they were atypical of the English, look at their so-called public schools, where the aristocracy and the upper classes send their children to be tortured. People complain about the few, the very few who are kept by our authorities in KZ – and who invented the KZ, I ask them? The English!'

There was no English accent in Winnie's speech, but she could not summon up her past in this way without reinforcing for me the sense of her as a stranger, at odds with the world, never truly at home in it – one of the chief things she had in common with Wolf.

She did not spring her idea upon me immediately that morning. It was later in the day that she asked me to tell Helga about our visit to the orphanage, and to wonder whether, next time, she would like to come too to visit little 'Senta'. 'I think it's a little chick, isn't it?'

And then, perhaps not on that occasion but in a couple of days: 'We can't think of the little chick spending its days in institutions, now can we? Where should I have been if I hadn't been rescued by the Klindworths? Working as a parlourmaid – that's what we were being trained up to do, you know.'

Helga was much quicker than I was to recognize just what it was that Winnie was proposing. Helga knew of my 'crush' on Winnie, as she sometimes called it; my 'Winnie-worship' being another term of semi-affectionate abuse. She did not approve of my loving Winnie and she certainly did not approve of Winnie, whose politics she completely abominated. But she did share my view, and never strayed from it, that Winifred Wagner was a good-hearted person. And in our present situation she was more than that; she was our lifeline. It was she who had rescued the KEH from Dachau of all God-awful places. And now that the ban existed throughout Germany on

Communist Party members working in German orchestras, there was nowhere, apart from the eccentrically organized Bayreuth, where Helga could have found work. She could probably have got a job teaching music in schools if she had been prepared to forswear her Communist allegiance, but this she resolutely refused to do. Her political commitment was deepening as the international situation changed. The rumours that our government was to send German planes – fighters and bombers – to help the rebel General Franco in his military revolt against the legal Republican government of Spain had reached the ears of the Communist Party faithful via the bush telegraph of the Popular Front, and it had merely confirmed all Helga's fears about the European parties of the right – in Spain, in Italy and at home.

She was in no way inclined to soft-pedal her objections to Winnie's politics. But nor was it a question of jettisoning her political convictions for the sake of a job in the orchestra. You knew Helga better than anyone and you know she would never have done that.

'What you can't get away from is that she' – that is, Winnie – 'is a decent person. How you explain her choice of friends – that's a mystery.'

It is indeed, and I am certainly no nearer solving it, fifteen years after I last saw Winnie, than during that spring.

What Winnie had intuited, and I had not plumbed, was Helga's longing for a child. Helga told me, some years after we had adopted you, that she had actually talked quite freely about this to Winifred Wagner. Unlike me, but like Winnie, Helga was a person of uncomplicated generosity of nature. If she saw someone in need, and she was in a position to satisfy that need, she would not hesitate, whereas I would always contrive to think of five good reasons why I should not force myself to perform a good deed. Helga did not have any problems with adopting a child. We had a (just about) big enough flat. We both wanted children. Here was a kid who wanted a home.

'But what about when – if – what if I have . . .' she had stammered to Winnie.

'You want a child of your own very much, don't you?'

I wasn't present during this conversation, but I can see it, that sheepish grin which lit up Helga's face when she was most serious.

'I have known so many people' – nod, nod, nod – 'who have adopted a child and almost immediately found that they could conceive.'

Helga apparently then replied to Winifred that she too had heard this, but what would happen if, having adopted Senta and had a child of her own, she found that she loved her own child and neglected the one we were arbitrarily proposing to rescue from the nursery.

'Look,' Winnie had said, 'life is full of mysterious emotional chances. You might have three or four children of your own and find that there is one whom you simply cannot love as you love the others. Or you might favour one and neglect the others. These things happen. Children learn to live with such problems. Do you think it would be better for little Senta to grow up in an institution or to have you as her mother?'

So the thing was settled, and soon after that you came to us and Helga bought you your first recorder, and your first triangle, and taught you your first exercises on the piano; and I read to you from *Struwwelpeter* and the fairy stories of the Brothers Grimm. And so our lives began.

Out of the primal, cloudless ether came a breath. It grew. As the movement of breathing swelled, so there grew a yearning cloud which, in its condensation, became our world. Being. So the process of yearning, apparent fulfilment and everlasting frustration is repeated, and repeated, an endless sad music filling all things. So – the origins of being. From cloudless infinity came being itself. From two yearning body-souls there came about the fusion which led to – you, me, all. Like all yearnings in a conscious being, they are doomed to be unsatisfied. For the two spirits and yearnings cannot escape their egotism, and for ever tug and strain. Out of an impersonal desire grew matter, moisture, the world. But in its later stages of evolution certain beings, endowed with consciousness and cursed to name their yearnings as hope and love, were doomed to an eternity of unhappiness until such desire could be numbed by acts of wisdom and of will. Only when we have so disciplined our minds as to be released from desire can we reach nirvana. Every instinct of nature teaches us the illusory opposite, never more so than when we fall in love, and it appears to our tormented and deceived souls that 'happiness' can be found with 'another'. The Lord Buddha taught that if we reverence all things, forswear violence and practice meditation, we might learn how to renounce the ego itself and prepare ourselves for a purification in our next rebirth. Bayreuth-Boy Stirner taught the corollary (do I mean opposite?). That we should learn to swim happily in our own egos, not hoping to escape them by the means of systems, politics, religions, even in the modern religion of personal relationships.

Winnie, with some perhaps Celtic instinctual wisdom, knew that the fusion of human souls was illusory, that the best we could hope for on this planet was good-humoured friendships and partnerships, but that we ultimately remain alone. She was not He. He was not She. You were not They. The fusion of will, desire, energy which practised its deception upon them both, your blood parents, during those unhappy days of November 1931 could lead to the emergence of yet another yearning, dissatisfied soul into the universe of suffering; but it could not lead to an eternal union between the agents who brought you into being.

The 'love story' of Tristan and Isolde, which began to occupy Richard Wagner in the middle of his long life's work, the composition of *The Ring*, was, among other things, a discovery of our eternal separations, our tragic loneliness. For over a decade, from his mid thirties to his mid forties, Wagner, in poverty and exile, laboured on a work he had little hope of ever seeing performed: *The Ring of the Nibelung*. By the year 1857 he had finished the first act of *Siegfried*. It would be years, twenty years, not until his marriage to Cosima, before he would see it to completion. Meanwhile, another music began to possess him, during this extraordinary time of creative fecundity mingled with gloom.

The whole world is tormented by words
And there is no one who does without words.
But insofar as one is free from words
Does one really understand words,

says Saraha's 'Treasury of Songs'.* To the daughter of Liszt's mistress, Marie Wittgenstein, he wrote that he had 'fallen into the *Tristan* subject ... For the moment, music without words.' It was the first of his stage works for which he wrote the music first, fashioning the words later.

Political hope, of a Social Democratic revolution and of a Socialist or Young Hegelian Germany, had long since vanished. So, too, had any hope of finding happiness with women. He knew that he had made Minna as miserable as she had made him with their ceaseless jealousies, squabbles, outright fights and infidelities. His adoration of Mathilde Wesendonck was a source of misery rather than joy, an obsession, a wound to whose scar he could not stop himself returning with agitated fingers, but which would have been better left alone. In addition to which the simple need to make some money was a recurrent and demeaning requirement. The Brazilian consul in Leipzig, Ernest Ferreira-Franca, had approached him to ask him to compose an opera for the Emperor Dom Pedro II in Rio de Janeiro and in the first instance he imagined that he might, from the old Celtic legend of Tristan and Isolde, fashion an 'accessible' Italian opera, almost another *Rienzi*, for the royal court there.

Only when one is free of words does one understand words. In this extraordinary furnace time of his creative life, none but the most prosaic biographer could imagine that his reading of Schopenhauer and Buddhist philosophy, or his unhappy relations with Mathilde, could be said to have 'explained' the miracle which was the Prelude to *Tristan*, from which all else follows with an intensity and an ingenuity unmatched. He can barely, quite, have known what it was himself that he was doing. Such turning points in the

* *Buddhist Scriptures*, selected and translated by Edward Conze (Penguin Books, Harmondsworth, 1959, p. 177).

world happen very rarely. You could as well speak of an angel coming to guide his pen over the score, as you could suggest that the external circumstances of his marriage, or his reading, or his debts, made *Tristan*. The breath came forth and was condensed into being.

Just before he left Switzerland – the situation with Mathilde having become too sad, too hopeless, too embarrassing – he had a waking vision. Lying alone in his bed, he saw Mathilde come into his room late at night. She kissed him and, with the kiss, she as it were sucked out his soul. She put her arms round him and he died. He heard a shriek and turned up the gas light beside the bed. He was alone. It was the hour when ghosts walk. His ghost? Hers?

He went to Venice, the city where, twenty-three years later, his soul was in reality to depart his body, and there in freezing cold, in a rented apartment in the Palazzo Giustiniani overlooking the Grand Canal, he wrote the second act of *Tristan*.

I never understood it until that hard, jokey Marxist, your adopted mother, gave me her curt commentary, one day in bed. We had had a good time and I murmured, 'Second Act of *Tristan*.'

Over a ciggy, she puffed and said, 'Only that's what's so brilliant about it. The music is all about fucking and the story is all about separation. They can get it together, but their dream of staying together, of fusion, that's all – twaddle.' (One of her favourite German words, *Quatsch*.)

'I'll go.'

'Where?'

'Thought I heard her stirring.'

This was in the early days of your arrival and every time we heard you stir, one or other of us would go to you, in the little bed we'd put up at the end of our sitting room. But of course I had not heard you. I had merely felt a sudden chill and sorrow at Helga's words. I had never felt for her the sort of yearning I felt in my calf love for Winnie, but I had so hoped she believed we were a sort of unit, a team. From her cold Marxist perspective, she suddenly seemed as detached as a Buddhist.

That is why, perhaps, despite the many volumes of interpretation of his work, the endless productions and recordings of *Tristan*, it is better not to try, except possibly in the most technically musicological detail, to expound his work, which nevertheless *speaks*. Anyone who has felt its power might, like Nietzsche or other lapsed Wagnerians, be ashamed of themselves for the extent to which they fell under his thrall. They might come to despise the narcotic of this music as unhealthy, as decadent, as pandering to all the negative sickness of Romanticism. Its bold redrawing of the history of music, leading to the atonal experiments of Schoenberg and Hindemith, to the Symbolist poets and the abstract painters, no doubt contributed to the dislocation between high culture and the popular imagination, which was one of the most sinister features of the twentieth century. Friedrich Nietzsche, himself no walking embodiment of the quality, looked for *Heiterkeit* in art and came to prefer Bizet's *Carmen*. But here, simply to use the word 'prefer' is to enter a farcical non-debate. In *Tristan* there came a new planet into the sky, a new way of expressing what could not be expressed. The incoherent *Ring* cycle, begun by a young Hegelian optimist and finished by an old Schopenhauerian pessimist, is an imperfect masterpiece, a flawed giant, a collection of magnificences which never completely, any more than do the scrappy and carelessly composed plays of Shakespeare, achieve completion. But *Tristan* is a perfect statement, a soul-wrenching greatness.

His night vision, in which Mathilde, otherwise known as the Muse, kissed him and took his soul, was an accurate one. His soul is contained in it. He is there, the essence of him, wholly untouched by the assaults which envy or biography have tried to hurl at him. In gelid Venice, which would reclaim his soul, he sat and laboured in loneliness and cold, looking wistfully, as he wrote to Mathilde, 'towards the land of Nirvana'.

In all the act which he so incomparably wrote out in that Venetian palazzo, nothing really happens. The lovers come together, the traitor Melot betrays them to King Marke, Melot wounds Tristan (fatally).

It was completed in the following year and it only had to wait six years before it was performed. Not an opera but '*eine Handlung*', a bit of drama.

It was a year after his own miracle had occurred and the young Ludwig II had rescued him. Despite the chaos of his emotional situation – *eine Handlung* indeed – here was his chance not merely to see one of his works performed but to direct it. (He invented theatrical direction in the modern sense of the word – before Wagner there were no directors.)

It was an occasion of delirious excitement. The not quite twenty-year-old King was in such a state of frenzy that Pfistermeister and the other royal ministers feared for his safety. The boy was besotted with the fifty-two-year old composer, bewitched by him, and the affection, in terms of verbal endearments and the times they spent in one another's company, appeared to be reciprocated. Wagner was his 'Beloved, his only Friend'. The King was, to the composer, 'The Dear Exalted One – *Lieber Erhabener!*' They were going to make beautiful music together and, much to the courtiers' horror, the King did not mind how much it cost. Already Wagner's enemies at court, and in the Munich newspapers, were saying that he was a Prussian spy, trying to bring down the kingdom of Bavaria, ruin its exchequer, send the already eccentric young monarch mad with his unhealthy and hypnotic musical emotionalism.

The King defied them all. Though Wagner was happy to stage his difficult masterpiece before a small audience, the little rococo theatre of the Residenz, Ludwig wanted it performed in the big Court Theatre, seating 2,000.

While the King pursued the love of Wagner, Wagner was deep in the beginnings of his love of Cosima, who gave birth to their first child, Isolde, on the day that the orchestral rehearsals began. The conductor was Hans von Bülow, Cosima's husband. Such was Hans's belief in Wagner that he felt guilt at the failure of his own marriage and did everything he could, until she wished to leave him, to support Cosima and protect her from the gossips – though quite to what extent he was aware of her infidelities at the time of the *Tristan* rehearsals it is difficult to say.

Tristan was an extraordinary shape, vast and full-bearded, but with the most magnificent of tenor voices – Ludwig Schnorr von Carolsfeld, he was a twenty-nine-year-old who had first enchanted his namesake the King with his interpretation of Lohengrin. His wife Malvina made the perfect Isolde. The audience had been drummed up from potentially sympathetic Wagnerians from around Europe. Wagner sensed that this was not a work of art with an immediate appeal to a wide public. Indeed, when von Bülow had asked for an extension of the orchestra pit, and been told that this would mean losing thirty seats out of the auditorium, Wagner, on a lighted stage during rehearsal, exclaimed, 'What on earth does it matter whether we have thirty more or less Schweinhunde in the place?' The remarks got written up in the next day's paper, fuelling the anti-Wagnerians' case at court. Very few, however appreciative, of the first audiences could have imagined that the '*Handlung*' stood a chance of being performed in a commercial theatre and attracting enough audience to pay its way. The King was happy – 'Unique One! Holy One! How glorious! Perfect! So full of rapture!' But the luck of Wagner, and of *Tristan und Isolde*, did not last long. Three months after his creation of the role, the gigantic young Tristan contracted rheumatic fever and was dead. And it was not long before Wagner, bitterly aggrieved at the machinations of the ministers against him, left Munich for Switzerland, accompanied by his servant Franz and his poor sick old friend Pohl. Perhaps only in the wordless love of dogs could the kind of yearning of which *Tristan* speaks ever hope, however briefly, to be satisfied.

I normally approached the house from the back, cycling up Ludwigstrasse, under the stable arch of the Neues Schloss and through the Hofgarten. It was a superb early morning. Helga and I had parted happily; I had left her, and you, sitting at the breakfast table, drinking chocolate and eating fresh rolls – for yes, even Helga had to admit, we Germans were now drinking real coffee again, real chocolate. There was pork in the sausages rather than cat's meat and we went to work with full bellies.

It was not yet eight in the morning as I rode through the Hofgarten. It was one of my days for doing correspondence in the office at

Wahnfried before I rode over to the Festival Theatre. Only dogs and their owners were about in the fresh summer air. It wasn't until I drew level with the garden gate, which led through the shrubbery to the graves of Russ, Wagner and Cosima, that I saw Sussi hunched on the greensward, completing her morning dump. The intense concentration visible in her eyes at the actual moment of evacuation made one have one of those moments of questioning about the whole business of consciousness, which so interests students of psychology and philosophy alike. Dog lovers probably think that their friends in such moments are 'thinking', or having mental processes comparable to our own. Others, myself in some moods, will suppose that the existence of some form of 'consciousness' in dogs, horses, mice, birds, so observable from their features and expressions, is something for which natural historians have formulated entirely functional explanations. What entitles us, then, to suppose that our 'thoughts' and 'ideas' are anything more than the vibrations of our mental faculties urging us on to eat, survive and avoid our predators? The arrangement of data in our brains might be more extensive and ingenious than that of dogs or honey-bees, but isn't that all we are doing? Who is to say we are 'thinking'? On some days such 'thoughts' lead down the old blind alleys of philosophy, for example, prompting me to pointless speculations about how my mind *knew* that it was contemplating itself thinking. On other days – this morning was one – I merely note the expressions in an animal's face and say to myself inwardly, 'This is having its doggy expression, its doggy thoughts, and I am having my man-thoughts and they could never meet.' This, of course, is precisely what dog lovers will never do.

'Ah! Now you feel better.'

Sussi's owner – master, companion, he would probably have preferred to say – stood there, typical dog lover, having her thoughts for her. 'Now you feel equal to the day, my Sussi.'

'Good morning,' I said.

I had not expected the Führer House to be occupied. It was the wing Winnie had rebuilt to accommodate the Chancellor whenever he chose to come to Bayreuth. Sometimes, even nowadays, he came alone, though this 'alone' meant merely that he was unaccompanied by any of his entourage; there were always SS guards everywhere. I spotted two of them standing beside the garden gate.

I had not exactly made a promise to Helga, but there was an unspoken understanding between us that, although we both worked for Winnie in different capacities and could no longer, for the time being, hope for work anywhere else (given Helga's political and prison record), I should give a wide berth to Winnie's 'friends' – we did not often name them, but it was perfectly clear whom she meant. Sometimes I had broken this rule, as when, at the bar of the theatre one lunchtime I had fallen into chat with Putzi Hanfstaengl, the tall American, who told me the story – recorded earlier in these pages – of coming to the theatre during the period of its closure with H and finding the cobwebby stage set of *The Flying Dutchman* still in its ghostly place. For the most part there was no difficulty in keeping my unspoken but clearly understood bargain with Helga; the Nazis did not come my way, nor did I wish them to. Winnie told me sometimes of her rows and tempests with the local gauleiter, a dreadful figure called Wächtler. (Schemm was dead. Wächtler, who made great play of having his baby son christened at the Spitalskirche, the most Nazi of the Lutheran churches in town, had a bit of a religious obsession, and made it his business to persecute and harry all the decent pastors and priests in the town.) It was at this stage that I began to realize that my own father, who received endless letters and visits from the wretched Wächtler, had become radicalized, though I did not realize until the fateful Crystal Night, already described, how far he was prepared to go in defence of his principles. Both my father and Helga would have been horrified to see me there in the Hofgarten, with my hands on the handlebars of the bike, hobnobbing with Sussi and Wolf.

Sussi, a predecessor of the more famous Blondi, was a highly intelligent-looking German Shepherd, with a magnificent healthy coat and eager, bright eyes.

'Look at you!' he exclaimed with utter love, as he knelt and kissed her. Then, as if she had spoken, he replied, 'Oh, all right then, one last run.'

She did appear to understand him, since she bounded with the speed of a wolf through the forest across the grass, with that particular spurt of energy dogs always display just after emptying their bowels.

'Darwin tells us of his own dog balancing a biscuit on her nose and eyeing his cat with wary suspicion,' said Wolf. 'It is obvious from his writings that he considered dogs far superior in their intelligence to the Negro. Indeed, he says in one of his books that the nigger is a different species from ourselves. Oh yes. Oh yes.'

I forbore to ask him in which of Darwin's writings these expressions of opinion are to be found.[*]

'It is wonderful to live in a scientific age and see that we follow natural laws. It increases, rather than diminishes, our sense of sympathy with animals. This, for me, is one of the messages of *Parsifal*. Vegetarianism becomes, not simply a fad but a moral necessity when you consider the chain of being that links all life together. The Reichsmarschall eats so much pork, I tell him his resemblance to a pig is hardly surprising.'

Wolf was in expansive good humour, as well might a man be who was now worshipped as a god by the majority of the population. I suppose I was seeing him, that morning, at the apogee of his achievement and personal happiness.

'I never read Darwin,' I said. 'I suppose I should.'

'The laws of nature, the *absolute* laws of nature. The strongest monkeys oust the weaker monkeys. The clever monkeys begin to stand. Always, always, it is strength, cleverness, which will single out the superior species from the herd. This is the very principle of nature itself. When nature reasserts itself, then comes calm. After the chaos of being ruled by nincompoops, weaklings and criminals,

[*] The observations about the dog eyeing the cat are to be found in his *The Expression of the Emotions in Man and Animals* (1873); in *The Descent of Man and Selection in Relation to Sex* (1871) Darwin did suggest that the Africans and the native inhabitants of South America (both 'savages') were a 'sub species', just as he states as a categorical fact that women are inferior to men, but he does not actually state that black and white people are a separate species as H imagined.

Germany knows that the strong hold the tiller. Sussi, girl, *Suss, Suss, Sussi*!'

The animal turned and looked at us, flirting with her master, pretending that she would run away further. He chuckled appreciatively.

I saw that he had a book under his arm – Karl May's *Der Pfahlmann*.

'It's a *very* good book,' he said, noting my eye movement. 'I have read it many times.'

'Really? I don't think I know that one.'

'Then you will remember the scene when the cowboy is alone in the desert, and he sees desert dogs and vultures hovering near an almost-dead figure in the sand? Oh, that is a masterly scene. Try telling me that some Slavic pacifist nobody such as Duke Tolstoy could write a scene like that and I am sorry, I shall not be convinced. Oh, when he dismounts and he waits for the prairie dogs to come for him. Up they come, trustingly . . . Suss, Suss, Suss!'

The dog was running towards us now.

'And he shoots – oh God! He shoots them and he drinks their blood, and then he fills a vessel with that dog blood and kneels to the half-dead figure in the sand. What a moment. "Water!" You remember that moment?'

It seemed superfluous to repeat that I had not read the book.

'Water! And the man drinks the blood and he is revived. Yes, revived' – he was saying this to Sussi, whose head he was fondly caressing and who had now returned full of pleasure after her run.

I let them go through the gate before me, wheeling my bike past into the little cemetery garden. Wolf removed his trilby hat as he came past the slabs. Then, at the grave of Richard Wagner, he turned to me and said, 'Germany was that exhausted man in the desert, lying a prey to the vultures. I was that cowboy who rescued him. And if it takes a glass of blood, which he believes is water, to revive him, then so be it.'

We went in, he to his austere breakfast and I to the morning's correspondence.

There had been speculation about whether he would attend that evening's performance of *Tristan*. What had become common knowledge by the time I reached the Festival Theatre was that several leading members of the government were to be there.

Winnie was in a particular state of tension and agitation throughout that day. She was not snappy with me, but there was a shortness bordering on unfriendliness as she chain-smoked. Normally, when she signed letters I had typed, she would make some good-humoured allusion to the correspondents or to the contents of the letter, but on this occasion she simply signed and signed, with a regal air, the ciggy dancing on her lips. I guessed she was having trouble with Tietjen, or with the children.

Suddenly, having signed the letters, she burst out, 'N——, what *am* I going to do about Friedelind?' Friedelind was a perpetual worry to her mother – her obesity, her burgeoning sexuality, her crush on Max Lorenz (flattering to him since, much to his wife's fury, he had been found *in flagrante* with a man in the chorus), her bad school reports . . .

'Anything in particular?' I asked.

'She's starting to say such terrible things about Wolf. And I am afraid she plans to say something to the Goebbelses when they come tonight.'

'They are coming?'

'We have Herr Speer, we have Dr and Frau Goebbels, we have Reichsmarschall and Frau Göring,' she reeled off a catalogue of murderers' names, but at that date in history they seemed, though a dislikeable bunch, not much more so than other politicians. 'I just don't want Friedelind to . . . well, to upset Wolf. And Goebbels is . . . between you and me I don't *like* Goebbels. He is so cruel – he lacks all Wolf's gentleness and sensitivity. I think he is a sadist really – his reason, I guess, he chose to marry a member of the persecuted people.'

'Frau Goebbels is Jewish?'

'All but. Technically not, but she had a Jewish stepfather. Her last lover was Jewish – shot in Palestine by Goebbels's men a couple of years after the little brute married her. Magda is in such trouble. She is in love with Hanke – you know, Goebbels's Number Two at the Propaganda Ministry? I don't know how far things have gone, but she has simply had enough of the Herr Doktor's philanderings and cruelties, and she has told the Führer so.'

'And what does Wolf ... what does the Führer say?'

'Naturally, he says that they must patch up their troubles for the sake of the Fatherland. I say they should have another baby. That always binds a couple.* Mind you, with men like little Goebbels you can't stop them – actresses, whores, they simply cluster to him.'

How strange it is to lie here in my flat a quarter of a century after that evening and to think of the passions of Isolde so urgently, but to my ear always forcedly, expressed by Frida Leider. How strange to think of Frida, of whom we saw a certain amount during our time in Paris† singing that last extraordinary aria – 'Mild und leise'. She did it perfectly well, but anyone who has heard Kirsten Flagstad sing will never think that any other Isolde quite rises to the part. But there, at the end, is Isolde's voice. King Mark blesses her and the dead Tristan, but the other figures on the stage are mere ciphers. The thing has resolved itself into a dialogue between Isolde's voice and the orchestra; and, coming through the strings at the very end, that spine-tingling combination of oboes and cor anglais. Played that night by Helga. So, on the stage Isolde. From the orchestra pit my wife. And in the Wagners' box (so Winnie told me later) an inconsolable Magda Goebbels, sobbing at times so loudly that they considered taking her out. During the intervals they got her out of sight of the crowds and put her in a small drawing room where she continued to sob, while Wolf and Dr Nosferatu worked the crowds from the balcony. Every impression of life, every viewpoint, shifts with time – perspectives, altering like a townscape seen from a

---

* The Goebbels children were Helga, Hilda, Helmut, Holde, Hedda and Heide, all destined to be killed by their mother in H's bunker in April 1945.

† Again, a reference to N—— and possibly his wife, having been in France, presumably during the German occupation. The text throws no light on this and much about his war years will remain shadowy.

moving car or train – towers which were once in the foreground now shrinking and buildings which appeared side by side now hidden one by another. Listening to Frida's Isolde my dominant expression was that she was singing of 'us' – of me and Helga who were getting on so well – of an eternity of love, a love which transcended death.

For Wolf, whose obsession with the 'Liebestod' motif in the opera was a sort of addiction, and who would play it over and over on his gramophone, the opera can hardly have spoken of any love except that perhaps of his mother dying in pain in a poverty-stricken kitchen with a Christmas tree at her side – a *Liebestod* of a different sort. Now in my solitude I see the opera as I have already written, as being not so much about consummation as about separation. But for Wagner, who wrote it in despondent mood and who saw its first performance in the emotional chaos of Cosima van Bülow bearing his child, an unforeseen and highly 'unWagnerian' future was destined. That is, in spite of illness and money worries, the deep happiness and the domestic bond he had with Cosima.

The only advantage of the crisis in the Goebbels family marriage, as far as Winnie was concerned, was that the unhappy pair were far too absorbed in their misery to allow any chance for Friedelind to come up to Nosferatu to denounce him. Poor Winnie. With Friedelind's burgeoning anti-Nazi sympathies, her mother must have felt as devout Christians do – my parents say – when a child ostentatiously loses his or her faith.

You? Would you come to share your mother's Marxist faith, or your father's no-faith? I was working my way forward to my creed, which was 'No philosophy of life, not even the philosophy of having no philosophy of life'. Your (surprising?) life of Lutheranism was as yet hidden from me. Aged four, you were at home in our small flat. My mother, who doted upon you, had come to babysit and sing to you, folk songs and hymns, as you sank into innocent sleep.

Götterdämmerung

On 14 April 1945 my mother would have been sixty-four years old. On 11 April, however, a young man from Boise, Idaho, killed her. He did not know this beautiful, vague, musical woman with her white hair everlastingly about to escape from its clips and combs, with her excitable dark eyes and pink cheeks, who had consistently disliked National Socialism and who had lost a husband and one son in concentration camps, and another, quarter of a century before, on the battlefields of Northern France. She did not know her killer either and nor do I, and perhaps he came from Portland, Oregon, or Denver, Colorado, or from Salt Lake City. I have sometimes spent whole days looking at the map of the United States wondering where this young man lived who killed my mother, the woman you called Granny.

Usually, in my imagination he is a clean-living, amiable, unimaginative hulk of a boy, perhaps a little over twenty, proud to be flying with the US 18th Air Force in the closing stages of the Second World War. He has been sent to drop bombs on Bayreuth and one of the bombs he dropped happened to fall on the house of the Fräulein Boberach, two of the old ladies who, with my parents, demonstrated in front of the synagogue on Crystal Night in 1938. My mother had been living with the Boberachs since my father's arrest and their necessary departure from the clergy house. One of these old ladies was already dead, but the raid of 11 April killed the surviving sister, Brigitte, as well as my mother. It also flattened my father's old church, reduced to rubble the baroque carved pulpit, the gallery adorned with the armorial bearings of all the original patrons of the church, the superb painted altarpiece and the organ that had pealed forth, in its time, almost every note of music ever written by Johann

Sebastian Bach, as well as hymns and chorales without number from other composers. During that raid, and the two of the previous weeks on 5 and 8 April, a storm of fire descended upon our little town, destroying the railway station and all surrounding streets, the whole of the northern side of the Market Place, the Old Palace – though not, mysteriously, King Maximilian II, whose statue proudly survived outside his former residence amid its rubble. Most of Richard Wagnerstrasse got hit, and Wahnfried, their chief target, was bombed, though not utterly destroyed.

The reason my mother was killed, and the reason the US 18th Air Force wished to destroy a gentle eighteenth-century town beautified for and by the Margravine Wilhelmine (they managed to bomb her Eremitage, though not utterly to destroy it as they would have wished) was simple. This small Franconian town, with its eighteenth-century palaces, opera house and churches, its small pottery industry, its Colosseum Factory (Fabrik-Kolloseum) manufacturing cloth scarcely posed a military threat to the Allies, whose victory over Germany was in any case by that date totally assured. (Wolf, sick unto death and all but mad, was in his Berlin bunker, preparing for suicide.) The bombs were a message to Winnie. They were a punishment bombing because Winnie had loved Wolf and Wolf had loved Richard Wagner. More than this, the bombers whose preferred music was Glenn Miller and who might well not have heard of Wagner, were punishing the memory of this composer because of the supposed evil, not only of his admirers, but of his very music which was, over the years after the Second World War particularly esteemed to have contained within it some of the poison that would destroy our country. So our poor little town was reduced to rubble for the sake of a philistine, clodhopping musicological theory, and my mother – did she die instantly or was she imprisoned for hours beneath the rubble? – was killed because she happened to live in a town where a nineteenth-century composer had taken up residence in the hope, one day, of performing his cycle of all but unstageable musical dramas, *The Ring of the Nibelung*. A war which, begun because Germany had broken a treaty and crossed the Polish border, ended in a chaos of fire and revenge in which the aristocratic British and Communist Russians joined forces against us and – in the case of our unfortunate town – the Americans bombed us for liking the wrong kind of music. Thank Wotan, Christ and all the gods you were not staying that night with my mother. She loved having you to stay. It was the air raids on 5 April that made her move you to the safety of Winnie's chalet in the Fichtelgebirge. Little as she liked Winnie, or approved of her, my mother overcame her aversion for Wagnerism on this occasion and so saved your life.

It was the Margrave's opera house that first drew Wagner to our town, as he searched Germany for a place where he might conceivably stage the drama he had been devising and composing for quarter of a century. As anyone knows who has seen this beautiful little rococo theatre, in which every trumpeting putto, every sprouting column and fluted architrave is carved out of wood and brightly painted and gilded, there could be few less suitable settings for a Wagnerian music drama. By a series of accidents, however, not least his befriending the local bank manager, Herr Feustel (reading of Wagner befriending bankers makes one almost sorry for them: it's like reading of a friendship between a fox and a plump chicken), the little town saw the commercial potential of an annual music festival, were Wagner prepared to build a new theatre on the Green Hill just out of town with money from his insane royal patron. Rather as the little Pyrennean village of Lourdes could hear the cash registers jingling almost as soon, in 1858, as the Virgin Mary had appeared to a local peasant called Bernadette Soubirous, even so did the burghers of Bayreuth see, and rightly see, that the creation of a Wagnerian festival in their town would attract pilgrims by the thousand, all of them in need of hotels, restaurants, shops, their equivalent of rosary beads and illuminated Madonnas – miniature busts of the Master, musical scores and prints of the masterpieces.

So in April 1872 they arrived from Tribschen, the Wagners, living at first in the aptly named Hotel Fantaisie in Donndorf, a village nearby, until Wahnfried was completed to their extravagant requirements – Cosima aged thirty-five, Wagner aged fifty-nine, and their children, Fidi, three, Isolde, seven, Eva, five. (Daniela von Bülow was twelve and her sister Blandine nine.) The Royal Family of Bayreuth, as Friedelind called them in a needlessly sour book about her life experience.

The move to Bayreuth coincided with, and caused, the rift between Professor Nietzsche and his old hero. There is no doubt that Wagner behaved deplorably to Nietzsche, as he did to most people in the end, except Cosima and the children. He wrote to Nietzsche's doctor, Otto Eiser, an ardent Wagner fan resident in Frankfurt, to question the pathological abnormality of the young man's apparently celibate state and to suggest to the doctor that the reason the wretched philosopher was almost blind before his thirty-fifty birthday was that he was a masturbator, a judgement with which the doctor, and contemporary medical wisdom, concurred. Not content to share the 'knowledge' with his doctor, Wagner spread the rumour so that Nietzsche, when he came to Bayreuth, was openly sniggered at in public places. This, combined with an unrequited and Platonic love for Cosima – parallel, I have often thought, to my own for Winnie in the twentieth century – may be deemed to have contributed to Nietzsche's disillusionment with Wagner, his belief that he was a disease, not a man, that when it came down to it, Wagner was nothing but an actor.[*]

True, shamelessly true; human, too human. Nietzsche, with his intense inverted religiosity, his hatred of God for being dead as his Lutheran-pastor father had too early died, had in his nature all the fastidiousness of the clergy house – his detestation of alcohol, his obsessive cleanliness, his shyness with women – how I empathize with them all. Blowzy boozy Wagner had grown up with the smell of greasepaint. His mother, his stepfather, his sisters were all in the theatre. His father's serious brother, Adolf, had disapproved of them all and tried to persuade his nephew Richard to be serious, to read books. There was always a certain dichotomy in Richard Wagner's nature. When he finally finished *The Twilight of the Gods* he saw

---

[*] *Auch in Entwerfen der Handlung ist Wagner vor allem Schauspieler* (from *Der Fall Wagner*).

it as a great German masterwork, immortal as Goethe, and he exclaimed, 'If only Uncle Adolf knew!' But the truth is that as soon as he had had the Festival Theatre built, to his own exact specifications, he was at his happiest, not in theorizing, but in the sheer fun of the theatre.

He wanted the new Festival Theatre to have as many as possible of the splendid technical effects he'd seen at the pantomimes and Vaudeville theatres in London. The Rhinemaidens, for the opening scene of *The Ring of the Nibelung*, the first drama in the cycle, swayed in a Big Dipper which made the girls vomit during rehearsals. The mists of the magical Rhine were to be recreated by a twelve-centimetre pipe from a little boiler house fifty metres from the stage, with two old locomotive boilers. The lighting was initially gas, though they were early pioneers at the theatre of electricity. For the dragon to be slain by Siegfried, Wagner once again turned to the English pantomime stagers and employed Richard Keene of Wandsworth, south London. When the dreadful thing with papier-mâché hooves arrived from England Wagner was in despair: 'Get rid of it! Into the junk room.'

But these disasters, together with all the excitement of working with overwrought, egoistic, highly sexed thespians, was such a world away from Nietzsche's experience that he could not begin to understand it – any more than he ever really, in spite of their deep friendship, caught the measure of Wagner's throwaway humour.

'Can anyone remind me what the hell *The Ring* is supposed to be all about?' he asked in an early rehearsal as he stood at the podium. (Parallel to his chuckle before a rehearsal of *Parsifal* – 'And now for our Black Mass!' – or his remark to Cosima, piously setting out to the Stadtkirche for a Good Friday Service: 'Give my regards to Our Redeemer'.)

Nietzsche the professor attempted in his writings to throw over all constraints of 'morality', 'religion' or the Socratic method in philosophy, but deep down he could not stop himself being local and serious. It was the older man, Wagner, man of the theatre, who was really much more of an anarchist, yet ultimately, and so unfairly, a deeper creator. Nietzsche wondered how it was possible for a drama conceived in terms of almost Marxian optimism in the 1840s to make sense when recast as a mystic Schopenhauerian work of renunciation. *The Ring* Mark One suggests that the old order – the *ancien régime* financed by the Industrial Revolution – is to be overthrown by a new liberated humanity. Brünnhilde is a new emancipated woman, Siegfried with the self-forged sword smashes the old wand of throne and altar. This is the Wagner who appeals to the comrades here in the East, of course.

But then along came Schopenhauer, or that's what Wagner wants us to believe, and when Wagner had read that gloomy pessimist the drama became a story of the illusoriness of power, the futility of human yearning.

Nietzsche, like many – perhaps nearly all – of the Wagner scholars since, is taking Wagner too much at his own word.

Wagner once told Cosima that he was not an artist who could think in *wholes* – he was a details man. He'd just been orchestrating a little scene from the beginning of *Siegfried* and he said, 'You know, the weird thing about the way I set about my Art – I look on *every detail as an entirety*. When I'm concentrating on it, that's all I think about, I never stop to say hang on, if we do this now that means I'll have to change *that* earlier back in the play.' The result is, of course, an incoherence in *The Ring of the Nibelung* as it now appears on stage, and however you try to disguise it. For example – to take something rather crucial – the Ring of Power itself. It has been stolen from the Rhinemaidens by the wicked dwarf Alberich. Nothing will go right until it is given back to them. The gods trick Alberich; the one surviving Giant, transformed into a dragon, gets the ring as a ransom. Siegfried kills the dragon and gives the ring back to Brünnhilde who in turn gives it back to the Rhine. The older order should therefore have been restored – but it isn't. The gods still fall.

The last of the operas, *The Twilight of the Gods*, is the most puzzling thing of all since most of its story has nothing to do with the gods, or with the passing away of the old order of things. It is a straightforward Shakespearean comedy. Man – Siegfried – leaves girl – Brünnhilde – is beguiled by a love potion into loving another girl, Gutrune: her brother Gunther disguises himself as Siegfried to trick Brünnhilde into sleeping with him. In May 1874, as the Festival Theatre neared completion, Richard and Cosima continued to read to one another each evening, as often as not from Shakespeare. They were reading *The Two Gentlemen of Verona* as they moved into Wahnfried, the sort of silly stagecraft which Shakespeare made to *work* in the theatre – *Two Gentlemen* being the same story of broken vows and improbable disguises as the so-called *Götterdämmerung*.

For some years after coming to the East I underwent a Nietzschean sense of revulsion against Wagner. I did not think of him as responsible for the Nazis, any more than I blamed Nietzsche for the Nazis. (Unlike my contemporaries, I was never fooled into thinking that the Nazi text known as *The Will to Power* was really by Nietzsche: we now know it was cobbled together by his hateful old sister Elizabeth, partly to make money and partly to ingratiate herself with the new regime.)

Just as Nietzsche in his reviling of his dead God is one of the great original Christians – with Kierkegaard and Dostoevsky part of the immortal trio who rescued the Christian soul in the nineteenth century from Nibelheim – so Nietzsche in his attacks on Wagner is really the greatest Wagnerian. One says this not out of a love of paradox but because of the evidence in Nietzsche's own writings. There is no more tender hymn to Jesus and his pity for humanity than in Nietzsche's *Antichrist* and his Wagner denunciations, which breathe such profound disappointment in his hero's failings, are peppered with admissions that his friendship with them both, Cosima and Richard, was the high point of his life and that the music, maddeningly, is wonderful, even when you have pulled it all to bits and laid bare its crude appeals to the emotions, the sickness of its late Romanticism.

The truth is that Shakespeare was far more important to Wagner than Schopenhauer. Wagner once told Cosima he was a mixture of Don Quixote and Hamlet. (It would have been truer to say he was half Falstaff, half Osric.) *Hamlet* is not only one of the greatest plays ever written – it is also one of the most incoherent. The man musing on death as 'that undiscover'd country from whose bourn no traveller returns' has just seen a ghost.

We draw so much out of Wagner's *Ring* cycle, and it continues to fascinate audiences around the world, partly because it is stupendous musically, but also precisely because it is so incoherent. It does more than touch us, it stabs us with all the deepest preoccupations of which we as human beings are capable. It is 'about' the crisis and storm cloud of capitalism, sure. It is, too, a drama of beings who do not know who they are, who, in pursuit of lovers, are also looking for lost parents. In discarding the gods, it enters ever deeper into the spiritual basis of religious life. The old northern mythologies, as found in the Prose Edda, have the Earth-tree Yggdrasil gnawed by the Wolf, Fenris, who brings the whole existing order into ruin. In the end, the Wolf has dominion and devours even Odin/Wotan, father of the gods, and darkness descends over the world. The three Norns at the beginning of *Götterdämmerung* make allusion to all these terrible things, but when their rope of destiny snaps they are no longer able to see into the future. Wagner, with his mastery of detail and his indifference, from scene to scene, of the big picture, ends with Brünnhilde's song of triumphant love. As Valhalla goes up in flames she turns a brave horse towards the fire, shrieking of eternal love.

Bayreuth – I think of you every day; I think of you as my childhood idyll; I think of you as the backdrop against which Winnie's destiny touched my own, until the Wolf gnawed at the tree and all fell to ruin and flame. What are you now? The Festival still continues, I believe, with Winnie's sons presenting stylized versions of the Master's works and, while they quarrel among themselves with the intensity of the gods at the beginning of the *Ring* cycle, they no doubt, in that hypocritical shithole which is the West, have contrived to forget that there ever was such a person as Uncle Wolf who gave them fast cars and paid for the Festival to survive.

It's funny, I knew those boys so well as children – and I do not write this in bitterness because Wieland snubbed me, that last evening with you – but neither of them returns to my mind with the vividness of their grandparents, old Cosima, whom I knew only as an old lady and Richard, who lives for ever in the mysterious immortality of his music.

'What's the matter, don't you love me any more now you're married?'

'Oh, hello, Friedelind.' I had stopped calling her 'Mausi'.

'Like a fuck?'

'Not just at the moment.'

'Like a coffee?'

'I hesitate to say, but in both cases just had one, thanks.'

'Please. I'm serious – not about the fucking – about wanting to ask you something.'

'Oh, all right then.'

The little girl who had thought I was a policeman in 1925, on the trail of her beloved Uncle Wolf, had become an altogether different being at a gargantuan twenty-one. There was an air of swaggering self-congratulation about this obese young woman, which failed to beguile me. By now she was spending most of her time in Paris and Switzerland. When war eventually broke out she refused to return to Germany. Later she wrote a book in which she claimed Winnie had come to Zurich in 1940 and threatened her with kidnap, or even murder, if she did not stop her denunciations of the regime.

That Mausi and Winnie had been enemies, as mothers and daughters often are, for a number of years, really since the outset of her teens, there could be no doubt. I do not know what to believe about her book. It was written in English, published in New York at the end of the war.[*] I never read it or even knowingly saw a copy, but everyone knows what it says, but . . . I don't know. The story of Winnie going to Switzerland and threatening Mausi that Himmler would have her bumped off if she didn't shut up doesn't ring true to me. However, war had broken out and war drives people to behave in a manner which in peacetime would be considered insane.

[*]Friedelind Wagner, *The Royal Family of Bayreuth*, Eyre and Spottiswoode (London, 1948).

'N——'

'Yes.'

We were in the cafeteria and Friedelind was leaning forward in a conspiratorial way. 'Helga hates them, your family hates them. Why are you so bloody . . . wishy-washy?'

'Hates the . . . ?'

'You know who I mean. You know Mother insisted on taking me along to dinner at the Chancellery and Goebbels told this story: "Oh, my boys are thoroughly enjoying themselves," he said. It was a foul story about some of his thugs stopping a Jew in the street and demanding to see his wallet – they found 300 marks in his pocketbook and insisted on seeing the proof that he owned this money. They took the cash, of course, and the man was arrested. I asked the good Doctor what had happened to him and he said the Jew had been sent to a concentration camp. N——, Mother was just sitting there. She did not utter one word of protest. "What had that man done wrong?" I asked and, quick as a flash, Frau Goebbels called down the table to me, "Just look at the child – she's gone pale. You must not pity, girl. *Never feel pity*."

'She said that. Mother just sat. She was *agog* for what the Führer was going to say next – some crap about German art which the Goebbels thing had interrupted. I decided there and then I've got to get out of this madhouse. Doesn't Helga feel the same? Don't you want to get the kid out?'

The answer to these questions was *No*. Anyone today, in the early 1960s, who knew that I had been so often in the same room as the architects of the Second World War would be inclined to ask whether I ever felt tempted, for example, to assassinate Wolf. The truth is that the idea never crossed my mind. His entourage of thugs and gangster-weirdoes was obviously uncongenial. He himself, it must be said, was never anything but courteous to me and I saw him, even in the late thirties when he had become the most famous man in the world, as primarily Winnie's friend. This may seem ludicrous or even shameful, but insofar as I thought of a bigger picture, well, yes, I was what Friedelind called a wishy-washy. Our country had been in complete chaos in 1933. Six years later we appeared to be the most powerful country in Western Europe. The British negotiators had cowered before H at Munich. There was great anxiety among all of us Germans, all that I met at any rate, about the coming of war, but we all hoped it might be averted. Just as he had achieved a revolution which, if not bloodless, was more or less so compared to the Russian experience, so H had managed to reoccupy the Rhineland, and to annex the German parts of Czechoslovakia and Austria without any fighting. The Austrians were rapturous, yearning not merely for absorption into a Greater Germany, as every plebiscite since 1919 had revealed, but also enthusiastic for National Socialism. God knows, we regretted horrible incidents like the arrest of a wretched Jewish man with his pocket full of cash, and only fanatics would have gone along with Frau Goebbels's 'Never feel pity'. But the street violence of this kind did not make any of us foresee – how could *anyone* have foreseen? – the fate of the six million Jews who were exterminated three, four, five years later.

Did I want to get you out of Germany? I see now clearly enough that it would have been for the best . . .

'Look, N——, Papa Toscanini is going to get me a passport – to the Argentine. From there I can sail to New York. He liked you – he'd do the same for you . . .'

I did not know, absolutely *know*, though I had begun to suspect, who you were. I had no idea how the next six years would pan out. I believed that H had performed a miracle. I had forgotten the fisherman and his wife. I believed he shared the vision of the huge majority of Germans: namely that something like martial law and an autocratic government were necessary as a short-term solution to the problems we all faced in 1933. We were approaching the time, surely, when after a brief period of necessary autocracy things would get back to . . . what was normal in Germany? The dear old monarchy and aristocratic hierarchies of nineteenth-century Bavaria, Mummy would have said. A modern liberal democracy such as was attempted after the defeat of 1919 would have been my brother's answer. For my father who, next to Hegel and Bach – and Harnack, of course

– loved Goethe more than any other German, the answer was federalism. Germany for him was most itself when each locality had autonomy. In the conversations with Eckermann Goethe says that the Germans are more cultivated in general than the French because they aren't centralized, they don't have a Paris by comparison with which every other town is provincial. Instead, every little duchy and principality in Germany has its own theatre, opera house, university.

I thought, in 1939, maybe one day we'll come back to that – for the time being H has brought us prosperity, strength and peace.

So that was why I rejected, almost hotly, Mausi's suggestion that she help get us three out of Germany at that juncture. She sat opposite me in the coffee room of the Festival Theatre. Under the table our knees met and across the table her large fleshy face almost touched mine. I could feel and smell moist coffee-flavoured breath on my face – no trace of halitosis. I thought of all the moments when this young woman and I, since her girlhood, had been alone together. I thought of how I had always been aware of her physicality, her plumpness and moistness. Although she had never seriously propositioned me I had always felt it was on the cards.

As schoolboys, totally ignorant of sex and the emotional life as one is at that age, we'd muttered to one another about nymphomaniacs, girls or young women who were desperate or who would do it with anyone. A lot of smutty talk in which we swaggeringly indulged involved fantasies about nymphos or crudely cast out suggestions that a friend's sister (mother even) might come into the category. I had no desire to be Joseph before Potiphar's wife. You might have supposed that for an intensely shy boy like me the thought of my first 'experience' with a woman being accomplished in so uncomplicated a way would have its attractions. But I was intensely fastidious and dreaded it – for quite specific physical reasons which I need not set down here. They had to do with smell. I wrongly supposed that Elsa, our housemaid until Crystal Night, smelled of *it* – though wider experience of life has told me that it was from her armpits that the odour emanated. No doubt my overt fear of this smell putting me off my stride was in fact a useful cloak, an excuse for a much deeper fear, which probably remains with me to this day, of women – and not only of women but of people – of commitment, of the loss of self involved in any relationship. Certainly, although you fill my head day and night – wherever you may be: New York? – and although I think much of Winnie, I am never lonely. It would be torture to make me share this little flat with anyone else and my only fear of prison related to *the others*.

I mention these, perhaps distasteful, details about myself as a way of trying to explain to you my state of mind in the late summer of 1939. You must after all have asked yourself, given what was happening to my father and brother and to those Church ministers who opposed the regime, why did I not join the resistance or get out of our country until it had come to its senses. Such talk is very easy with hindsight, and hindsight is the one gift – forgive the absurdity of this tautology – you don't possess at the time. Even with the precious gift of hindsight, I do not know whether either Helga or myself would have wished to follow Mausi into exile. You see, the only real reason I'd have had for doing so was to ensure your safekeeping, your anonymity. Your identity was something I only began to guess in that crisis month, August 1939, just before the outbreak of war. It was indeed the crisis which made me have the suspicion. There is one other factor, historically all but unimaginable, which you have to bear in mind about Helga. That is her fundamental and doctrinaire Communism.

Until that August I had, insofar as I tried to understand her political views, assumed that she had joined the Party as the most effective way of fighting fascism and the Nazi ideology. I knew that at certain moments during their struggle for power, the Nazis, largely at the instigation of Nosferatu, had joined forces with the Reds in organizing strikes against the Social Democratic coalitions of the Weimar era – for example, over rents and housing. I don't *think* (to this day I don't know) such alliances occurred in Munich where Helga was a student and where she joined the Party. I think the Red –Nazi coalitions happened in Berlin and the northern cities. I don't remember and it doesn't matter. As you can imagine, we hardly saw anything of the Reds in our conservative little town and as you will have gathered my political interest is all but nil.

Cursed or blessed by the inability to believe, or at any rate to believe in, large catch-all metaphysical systems such as Wolf's social Darwinism or Helga's Marxist-Leninism, I am unimaginative when meeting absolutism in other human minds. I think, 'You can't *really* think that; you are telling yourself you think that because it is a system at present useful for your purposes' – rather as a scientist, in order to make any sort of progress with an experiment, has to start with an hypothesis that can then be discarded. (So Helga's perfectly intelligent parents stayed with Catholicism – so I told myself – because they were tribally programmed to share its value systems, because at that date in history it was lonely to be on your own, because, because . . . but not because they 'really believed' in the mythology about the Archangel Gabriel or the Virgin Mary.) Apart from being patronizing, this attitude of mine is quite simply wrong. Absolutists *do* believe what they say they believe. How else can we account for their preparedness to die, and to kill, for their beliefs?

Helga believed in Marx with the simplicity and fervour that enlivened my brother's belief in Christ and Wolf's in Darwin. Extra-ordinary journeys are travelled by those who believe. In August 1939 Joachim von Ribbentrop persuaded Stalin to sign a non-aggression pact with the National Socialist government of Germany. From that moment – until Wolf's decision to invade Russia in 1941 – millions of Communists throughout the world instantaneously lost their hostility to the Nazis. It was rather as if for a serious and literal-minded (what's the point of being any other sort of minded?) Roman Catholic, Rome had spoken. Although the Reds and the Nazis had fought to the death on our German streets, this new alliance, no doubt seen on both sides as temporary, was part of the scheme to further World Revolution.

I assumed – rather like assuming that the Catholics can't 'really believe' that the wafer becomes Christ's Body – that Helga could not have changed overnight. But she had. Naturally she remained a decent person. She would still, I have no doubt, have stood up to a thug bullying a Jewish old lady on a bus as she had done at our first meeting. Her attitude to H himself, however, appeared to have changed instantaneously. And the sign of this was her preparedness to let you, my dear, be presented to him at the Festival Theatre when he came to hear a performance of *Götterdämmerung*.

We met in 1933, we'd been together six years now, married for four. I never tried to defend Wolf to Helga, but what I did try to defend, and what I hope these pages have been able to describe, if not exactly speaking to explain, is Winnie's attitude to him. Outsiders saw it at the time and see it even more so with hindsight, as grossly irresponsible that she offered Wolf not merely her friendship, but the endorsement of the Wagner family name and by extension the Festival itself. People the world over who loved Wagner's music now knew that Germany's revolutionary leader had the endorsement, the love, of one of our country's prime cultural shrines, as of its High Priestess.

Do I think her culpable for this? My attitude to that is: everyone else is busy blaming her. I'd rather sit here in my flat, knowing I'll never see Winnie again, and leave the blaming to others. For instance, I could leave it to those who were enthusiastic supporters of the Third Reich while it lasted and who then, as leaders of industry or as politicians in the post-war era in the West, turned out to have been dedicated democrats after all. It's amazing how few Nazis there were found in West Germany after 1945 – not enough to fill one small village hall, let alone the whole stadium at Nuremberg or the Sports Palace in Berlin. No doubt all those cheering crowds were illusions, not really there – magic by Dr Nosferatu. Winnie's truthful refusal to deny her friendship with Wolf might be shocking, but it is less shocking to me than the nauseating humbug of West Germany.

I've been thinking about these things, largely in silence, for the last fifteen years, and I'm more and more convinced that you lay at the centre of Winnie's attitude to her Wolf. He for his part knew that almost any other woman in the Western world would have somehow or other wanted to exploit the fact that she had borne his child. Had she been that kind of woman, there can be no doubt that you would have been killed – so would she, probably. Even if the man who authorized the Night of the Long Knives had stayed his hand, his murderous entourage would never have wanted their divine Leader to be open to blackmail. And so the secret was kept, and you were rescued from the orphanage and became *our* child, Helga's and mine, much loved, the centre of our lives, the excuse we both used, after a little while, for hiding from ourselves that we had nothing whatsoever in common.

After you'd gone to university, as you know, Helga and I split up. I don't think you wanted to discuss it all in great detail with either of us. Perhaps you've wondered, since, what conversations we had about you. Here was one – I suppose it was about six months before we finally parted: it would therefore have been in the late 1940s just after I got my first teaching job.

'You *knew*, when you were first taken to the orphanage?' said Helga. 'You went with her – she told you . . .'

'Winnie – Frau Wagner – told me *nothing*. Don't you see that if I'd suspected *then* what you suspect *now* we couldn't have adopted Senti – don't you see her safety depended on our *not* knowing who she was?'

'But you did know – you *said* so.'

'No I *didn't* – don't distort my words. Why can't we speak to one another without either mishearing or deliberately distorting –'

Furious as I was with her I chucked a packet of cigarettes in her direction. She lit up. I was smoking more or less continuously in those days, as I still do.

'You admitted you knew –'

'Helga – I said I think I now understand why Winnie trusted us. She knew we were too intelligent to ask questions.'

'So you were prepared to put me in that position, make me the stepmother of *his* child. With all that implies. You loved me – or I thought you loved me – and you were prepared to do *that*.'

'Helga, I . . .'

'You were so soppily devoted to her – so don't try and defend yourself. By Christ, the boring evenings I've had to spend with you hearing about that *Bloody* family – Frau Wagner this, Herr Wagner always said that, little Prince Wolfgang did the other . . . You should have heard yourself. If you wanted to spend your life licking Winifred's arse, why marry me? Why get me mixed up in this . . . in this . . . why make me love that bloody' – she was speaking more and more jerkily as the tears came – 'child as if she was *mine* . . . No – don't come near me.'

I'd reached out to hold a hand. It was years since we had made love.

As you know, this isn't a country where you lightly or casually commit thoughts to paper. I do not think that the Stasi had any inkling of our secret, but if they did have, the flat would have been bugged. I wanted to write Helga a letter – and as well as being an overdue explanation to you, perhaps these pages constitute the letter I never could write to Helga, who already had cancer when we had that row and who died three years after we separated. If I had tried to write Helga a letter while you were still at university, and if that document had been found, what would your life have been? Now you have emigrated, and I am hoping to get this story parcelled up and mailed to you in the United States before I myself die.*

When we were having rows, I knew there was something undignified about nabbing the last word. But on this occasion, when Helga was accusing me of having adopted you and kept your identity a secret simply because of some arse-licking sycophantic attitude to the Wagner family, I could not let her words pass without a reply. I remembered the whole weirdness of the Soviet–Nazi axis.

It was August 1939 and we knew that H would be attending the performance of *Götterdämmerung*. We did not know it would be his last visit to Bayreuth and I suppose no one knew for certain, perhaps

---

* Herr N——, from internal evidence, would seem to be writing his book during the 1960s. Although believing himself to be near death, he seems to have concealed his manuscript at least until the early 1980s when he managed to mail it, or otherwise get it transported, to Senta, later Winifred Hiedler, in Seattle.

not even he, that within a few weeks, Europe would have been plunged into war.

Helga was rehearsing most days. You were being cared for by my mother. I was involved in the variety of humdrum tasks that fell to my lot in the Festival Theatre. It was one evening, when we were all together in the flat – you, me and Helga – that Helga quite casually let fall that Winnie had approached her. Would it be possible, when the Leader came to the theatre, for little Senti to present him with a bouquet of flowers?

To give her her due, Helga was quite crestfallen and awkward when she made this announcement. When I looked up at her with blank astonishment at the suggestion, she gave a sheepish grin that was trying to be ironical. But it could not, in such circumstances, entirely succeed. This was a woman who until a few days earlier had regarded H as the enemy of mankind. Because he had signed a treaty with Stalin, another mass murderer – indeed, one who at that date had killed innumerably more people than Uncle Wolf – she was prepared to let her own child go up to the Monster and give him a bunch of flowers. I had spent the last fourteen years watching children fawn on Uncle Wolf and him doting on them. For me, there was nothing especially surprising about the idea. What made me speechless with astonishment was the volte-face by the KEH.

We did not have a quarrel about it, but a strange silence descended on the little flat after you had gone to bed. It was agreed that you would be kitted out with a new hat, a new pair of shoes and that you would learn a little sentence off pat – some twaddle of the sort children are taught to say to visiting dignitaries everywhere.

'It was you who got Senti to present him with a bouquet.' That was the sentence I came out with eight years or so after the event, when Helga and I had entered the phase of total hostility.

It was true, but she had her guns pounding continually: 'It was your friend who asked me. Winnie. And we know why, don't we?'

I flashed a look at Helga. I knew she was capable, in her rage, of blurting out the truth and this was a burden with which it would simply have been unfair to weigh you down. 'No – no, Helga. Don't say that.'

With a glimpse of you – you, aged sixteen, were buried in a book, trying not to notice that this unseemly conversation was taking place – Helga retreated: 'OK.'

But in this incoherent exchange was buried a depth of meaning you were quite intelligent enough to discern; which is why, I suspect, the story contained in this parcel, if you ever get to read it, won't come as a surprise to you? Maybe there are things we know, without knowing we know them. From the moment I saw your eyes in the orphanage, there had been recognition; but my knowledge was only really confirmed when I heard of Winnie's plan – to engineer a meeting between you and Uncle Wolf on that night of *The Twilight of the Gods* – that the obvious truth began to click inside my brain. Winnie, with her natural wisdom, must have known that we were near to war and that war would separate her from Wolf for a very long time. Perhaps deep instinct told her that she would never actually see him again. She wanted this last encounter to involve you – their child. She did not ask me. Very properly, she went to your 'mother', Helga, for she knew that if she got Helga's assent there would be no gainsaying it.

It was a time of extraordinary tension. Sir Nevile Henderson, the British Ambassador, had come to Bayreuth, nominally to hear Wagner's operas, but in fact to see if it would be possible to meet the Chancellor and try a last-minute effort to make peace. Tietjen, I seem to remember, had a lot to do with inviting Henderson, who stayed at the Golden Anchor. (Uncle Wolf was being accommodated in the Siegfried House, the wing of Wahnfried that was now kept for his occupation whenever he needed it.) Tietjen believed that if Winnie could only arrange for Henderson to cross the threshold, if the two men could just meet one another, the catastrophe of war could be averted. By now, Czechoslovakia had fallen into German control – the British had cravenly given it to us, thereby increasing both Wolf's high opinion of himself and his contempt for the cowardice of the Englishmen who attended the Munich conference.

The next stage of the game would be for Wolf and Stalin to carve up Poland between them. But it was a gamble, as the man knew, who had so boldly enacted the demands of the fisherman's wife. And if the gamble failed, the worm-like British conservatives – Neville Chamberlain, Lord Dunglass, Lord Halifax and the rest – might finally stir themselves to fight a war to save the Poles. If that occurred France, our old enemy, would amass its huge armies against us and the dreadful carnage of 1914–18 would happen all over again.

None of us Germans wanted war – none I ever met. We had been lulled by the fisherman's wife into supposing that the 'conquests' of the previous few years – Austria, the Sudetenland and so on – had come about because the German-speaking peoples of these lands actually wanted a Greater Germany. There had been no loss of blood. But Poland was a different story. As I buzzed about, at Tietjen's and Winnie's request, delivering notes to Sir Nevile at the Anchor, I too had come to share their superstitious ardour – their belief that if only the very pro-German English diplomat could be persuaded to meet our Leader, the two men would somehow be able to patch up a compromise.

Wolf continued to refuse to meet Henderson. Winnie brought the British Ambassador to a performance of *Die Walküre*, but he was not admitted to the box where the Leader sat with his entourage. Afterwards I heard from Wieland Wagner that it was the only time he saw Uncle Wolf truly snub his mother.

'Please, Wolf, I beg you – as a *friend* – for the peace of the world,' she had pleaded.

His reply was curt: 'The German Chancellor will not be compromised by such an unscheduled meeting.' He did not have one of his famous explosions but Wieland said it looked like a close-run thing.

Poor old Henderson went back to Berlin the next day. He had done his best.

It was the following afternoon, at the beginning of *The Twilight of the Gods*, that you were to have your moment. The presentation was to happen just before the performance began. Wolf was dressed as a civilian. Military uniform had been set aside in favour of the simplicities of a tuxedo and a black bow tie. Rather incongruously – but then he never did anything entirely by the rule book, in spite of the years of training in the social niceties Frau Bechstein had given him – he was clutching a Bavarian trilby hat with a feather stuck in its side.

You were meant to say, 'My Leader – I present you with these flowers as a token of the love which we all feel for you in Bayreuth.' Or some such nonsense. Helga denied having briefed you to say anything else. Given the fact that you had a pretty headstrong attitude to the world, especially to the world of grown-ups, and also the identity of your natural parents, it would have been surprising if you had not been a tough-minded person with ideas of your own, even aged seven.

The Führer arrived, with Winnie on his arm. If there had been *froideur* the previous evening, when she tried to preserve the peace of the world, such coolness was now, for the sake of public appearances, laid to one side. He seemed to be all affability. We were waiting, the three of us, on the sidelines at the main entrance to the Festival Theatre. You were clutching a bunch of roses. In your white summer hat, your pale-blue coat, your white socks and sandals, you looked not unlike the newsreel pictures of the little English Princesses.

As almost invariably happened when confronted with a child, Wolf seemed to be quite genuinely delighted by your appearance.

'This is Senta,' said Winnie. 'She's got something for you, Wolf.'

'So I *see*!'

It was really strange to watch Helga, quite formally dressed in a hat and a coat and skirt, coming forward with you to make your presentation.

Wolf asked you a number of questions about where you lived and where you went to school. It was routine stuff, only for me an occasion of overpowering emotion. I found myself in tears as I witnessed it. Many would have supposed this was a simple patriotic love of the Leader, which was felt by so many Germans at that time. But by then I had lost whatever affection or admiration I might have had for him and had learnt to see him through the sane eyes of the KEH before her party line made her think otherwise; I had learnt to see him as my parents and my brother saw him, though I could not share their faith.

'We must meet again,' Wolf was saying . . . to you . . . to his child . . . This was when the reality of the situation fully dawned on me and this was why I wept – Winnie at the orphanage, Winnie's utter self-sacrifice (on one level) to this man, and on another level her extraordinary confidence, which led to her being the only woman in Germany who had done what, presumably, so many would have been so proud to do: borne his child.

Wolf took the bouquet from you and when a flunkey tried to take it from him he said, 'No, no, this is a present from my friend Senta. I shall hold on to it. And if I can ever give a present to you . . .' He bowed down to you and crouched on his haunches so that his face was level with yours. 'What can I give you, my girl?'

'Please – is there going to be a war?'

His smiling face was instantly clouded. You could see his suspicious nature calculating who had planted this question on the child's lips – in fact, I think there was no such prompting. Then the cloud passed and he was all smiles again. 'I can give you my promise, little Senta,' said this man three weeks before the invasion of Poland, 'there will be no war. Trust me – there will be no war.' He then stared silently at you for some time, with an expression of great tenderness, before asking gently, 'Do I get a kiss?'

'If you promise there will be no war.'

'I promise.'

You put one arm round his neck and bestowed a little kiss on his apple cheek. Then, with the smile of a child who had just sung a solo at a concert, you were visited by nerves, and with a blush and a giggle you ran back to Helga.

We were in Munich with Helga's parents when the raid on Bayreuth began. Her mother had appendicitis and for a short time this family

350

crisis had overshadowed all others, including the fate of our country. We did not think it was safe to travel from Bayreuth to Munich with you. The war had reached the stage when any German city was vulnerable to attack. The Russians had surrounded Berlin and the last terrible battle was being fought – so unnecessarily and with such loss of life, all to satisfy the crazed ego of the Man in the Bunker.

In the south, Munich was suffering, still, from aerial bombardment, though what strategic purpose the Allies thought it served God knows. It seemed safer to leave you, then a child of thirteen, with Granny (that is, with my mother) in Bayreuth. Since there was no reason on earth why the RAF or the American Air Force should want to bomb our beautiful small town, Helga and I agreed you would be safer there.

But then – we were in Munich, Helga's mother had made a good recovery from her operation – the calamitous news came: the US 18th Air Force had started to bomb Bayreuth. Telephones were down, but somehow or other we found out that the station and all surrounding railway lines had been bombarded, so there was no possibility of getting home by train. My father-in-law immediately gave us his car. As a doctor, he had a more generous petrol allowance than most, so there was just about a full tank in his distinguished old Mercedes. We knew that there was next to no chance of our being able to buy any petrol en route, but despair makes human beings act impulsively. We drove off. The journey is in the region of 200 kilometres and it was the most extraordinary car journey of my life. The outskirts of Munich were pitted with smoking rubble and ruined houses. All along the road we passed refugees, hobbling along with their belongings on their backs, and as we approached Nuremberg we could have been driving into hell. The whole city seemed to have been destroyed. We were driving through soot and flames. At one point we lost the road altogether and appeared to be driving across a smoking plain of burnt-out rubber tyres, wrecked vehicles and gutted buildings, so scorched and so totally pulverized that it was impossible to guess whether they had once been garden huts or Gothic cathedrals. The allies of freedom had managed to wreck the finest

Gothic city in Europe, while leaving untouched the sinister great stadium built on the outskirts of town by the National Socialists for their rallies, and these were the first intact buildings we saw as we careered through Nuremberg and left it behind as fast as we could.

The longer we drove the more anxious we became, sometimes telling one another that you would be safe at my mother's house, sometimes unable to believe that we should ever survive the journey, and sometimes in a daze of fear, unbelief, anger at what we saw all around us. I do not know, actually, what guardian angel led us round the outskirts of Nuremberg. Driving through it, or round its ring road would not have been possible, since it was a ruinous, sulphurous mass of smoke and flame. At every roadside were despondent, destitute people, children, women, the old, some standing like scarecrows, others making pointless movements, though to what purpose and in what direction it would have been hard to guess. Beyond Nuremberg the road cleared, and for twenty kilometres we were cruelly deluded into thinking that we had left all scenes of desolation behind us. The placid, rolling Franconian landscape lulled us into thinking that this gentle bucolic place knew nothing of the war. Then we came across a checkpoint, where the Americans had set up a roadblock. A GI who spoke no German, or none that was intelligible to Helga or to myself, told us that we could not advance any further. This was just beyond a small town called Trockau. Helga spoke English. I did not, though I could make out what was being discussed. She had 'that look' on her face – the look of defiance which had come over her that evening in the café when she started making jokes about the Führer and ended up spending two weeks in Dachau. I just hoped she wasn't going to get up the GI's nose.

She was explaining that we had a child in Bayreuth and that we needed to get home. The man chewed gum and seemed unimpressed. I thought he was a bastard. People in the West talk about those months as the Liberation. I never met any Germans during that time who felt they were being 'liberated' by these people. However glad we might feel to see the back of the Nazis, none of us welcomed the bombs and none of us welcomed these invaders. Helga was trying to be reasonable. She was gesturing with her hands a lot.

Then the bastard offered her a cigarette. Maybe a bit less of a bastard than I thought? She laughed at something he said.

'What was that? What was that joke?' I asked.

'He said they are American cigarettes – better than I'd been used to. True,' she said, as the smoke blew out in straight lines on her laughter, and as she handed me the ignited fag for a puff.

'Let your husband have one, please,' said the GI.

So I too had some of his excellent Virginia tobacco and the conversation went on. I realized that the two syllables I'd heard so often on his lips during this talk – 'Ber-ruth' – were his way of saying Bayreuth.

Helga began to translate for me: 'He says there has been heavy bombing in Bayreuth; it wouldn't be safe to drive there. He forbids us to drive. What do you think?'

'The look' had turned to pure mischief and my eye gave a quick glance towards the machine-gun the American boy had slung over his shoulder. Would he use it on us if we did what, so evidently, Helga was going to do?

'So,' she said in English, 'you don't recommend us to drive on.'

'That's right, ma'am.'

'I'd better just – what? – turn the car round?'

We got back into the car without looking at one another. Helga was at the wheel and started the ignition. The checkpoint did not cover the entire width of the road and it was possible, by mounting the pavement, to squeeze past the small kiosk the soldiers had erected for themselves.

'Hey-eh-eh, lady!' was what they appeared to be shouting.

But Helga's foot was down and we were driving out of town like the wind.

We had no further trouble until we approached the outskirts of Bayreuth.

It was midday on 12 April 1945. As we drove over the brow of the hill the familiar skyline of our dear little town was completely altered. The twin towers of the Stadtkirche were still standing, but amid clouds of smoke. As we came into the town it quickly became necessary to abandon the car, since all roads were blocked with rubble and ruins. Houses from whose fronts the walls had been wrenched out displayed the tattered destruction of life – here some sticks of furniture, bizarrely still intact on the top floor of a building whose staircase was ash; there a fireplace or some wallpaper in an otherwise gutted set of rooms. They looked like dolls' houses destroyed by a malignant child. Many buildings, especially as we got near the centre of town, had been reduced to mountains of rubble. The attic eaves of top storeys lay at angles across piled-up girders and piles of debris. Some buildings tottered with half-life, their metal girders or wooden joists stretching out like despondent limbs. Huge blocks, torn from pediments, had been hurled across the streets like pebbles. There was a terrible stench – of burning and of drains, all combined.

Though I grew up in Bayreuth and would reckon on knowing my way about the town blindfolded, I had several moments, as we stood beside yet another pile of rubble, of not knowing where we were.

Eventually, however, I recognized the small shop at the corner of my father's old street. We looked towards his church, hoping for the reassuring sight of its tower and cupola, but also, with the Pavlovian instinct, as a way of seeing what the time was, since I had always followed the passage of the hours from the sundial clock on the side of this tower. The church was flattened. The cruel sky beyond it showed a jagged profile of wrecked houses and roof beams stretching at desperate angles.

Instinct made us run. We ran to the corner of the street and down the cobbles towards the house where you, and my mother, would have been lodging the previous night with the elderly spinster, Fräulein Boberach.

If you go down a very familiar street that has just been bombed, it is impossible to take in, at first, what you are seeing. The bombs rearrange the buildings. Where the eye is accustomed to see a high wall it sees open sky and wrecked cars, burnt sticks of furniture; dust and piles of bricks, stones and masonry lie completely at random, so that the shape of the street itself is altered. You clamber, making your way as best you can, but no longer following the line of the road. And when you reach the spot you have been seeking, you so very much don't want to read the signals that it is giving you that you go on scrambling until you are lost.

We had walked, or climbed, or tripped, about four times round the ruins of Fräulein Boberach's house before its message penetrated my skull: it had been destroyed by enemy action. That meant that the inhabitants had probably been killed. That meant Fräulein Boberach was dead – a sweet old lady and I was sorry about that. It meant my mother was dead – and that's something to take in, the death of a mother. I certainly did not take it in there and then. And it meant you were dead – our adored adopted daughter, the centre of our life together over the last decade.

Time, sound, space, all the settings in which we assume we move during 'normal' experiences become suspended. How long it took us to recognize that we were in the ruin of a house, that its inhabitants were almost surely dead, I do not know. It could have been hours, we were wandering about like that, it could have been only a few minutes. At some point Helga came over to me and hugged me, and we stood there among the ruins, simply moaning and hugging one another, and then moaning some more.

Then someone was shouting to us.

We went over to him. It was a fireman. He told us it wasn't safe to be so near the buildings, there was a danger of falling masonry.

And one of us, either Helga or I – for at that moment we had become one consciousness, one bewildered shared grief – began calling out your name and saying my mother's name, Frau N——.

And he looked at me, the fireman, and – we are a small community in Bayreuth and most of us know one another by sight – he said, 'The minister's wife, a good lady. A very good lady.'

'My *mother*!' I was howling.

'And our child – our child – what happened to the kid?' Helga was bellowing.

Everyone was yelling, or talking, or making noises all at once. We were not asking for information, or receiving it, in the balanced to-and-fro of rational enquiry or discourse. The pain and confusion had made our exchanges an opera of sound.

Somehow or other, at some point someone – perhaps the fireman, perhaps someone else – told us what had happened. The two old ladies were dead. They had carried the old ladies out from the rubble – my mother and the Fräulein Boberach.

But the child, the child, the child?

Where were you?

You had gone missing. No one had found you.

'Winnie?' Helga was saying to me. 'Winnie has her?'

'But why? We left her . . . we left her with *Mutti*,' I was saying.

But we weren't standing in the ruins of the Boberach house any more, we were running through the town, or what was left of it.

Bayreuth, as well as being the subject of air raids, had also become a spot of convergence for refugees. Where were they all from? There were some Austrians and Czechs among them, as we found in subsequent days. The end of a war finds millions of persons displaced, their homes uprooted or destroyed, their chief needs being food and warmth.

It was a raw April, with a high wind, and many of these ragamuffins had arrived in our town without any resources. They had fallen on the Festival Theatre like scavengers and, in their desperation for warm coverings, they had raided the opera costumes, which they continued to wear for several weeks until more normal attire was supplied by the International Red Cross. So it was, as Helga and I made our painful pilgrimage across the remains of the city centre, that we passed fur-clad Siegfrieds and Siegmunds; Grail Knights in pale-grey cloaks adorned with scarlet crosses; medieval Nurembergers clad for a song contest; pilgrims coming from Rome to tell Tannhäuser that he was redeemed. The opera costumes, worn on wrecked street corners alongside American soldiers and helmeted airmen, added to the surreal timelessness of the scene. Wagner, who had come here to stage his dream dramas, now watched as they escaped the theatre and spilled over into a ruined world. Most of us keep our dreams, hopes, fantasies, unrealized inside our skulls. It is given to a very few – film directors, dramatists and opera composers

– to see these dreams embodied, but contained, on stage or cellu-
loid. What we appeared to be seeing, as we watched two Norns help
fur-clad Burgundian knights across the precarious road and avoid
the huge chasms made by the bombardments, were the fantasies of
Richard Wagner escaped and at large – figures who for thirty years
could not escape his head and who were at length staged on our
Green Hill at Bayreuth, were now free. The great doom of our
world, Ragnarok, the end of all things, seemed to be enacted. The
gods had sunk in their twilight. The wolf gnawed at the great Ash
Tree of the World. Chaos and despair ruled.

I do not know whether Helga had an aim in view as we continued
to run, but instinct was taking me to where it all began – to the
house where Richard Wagner and his wife had settled and brought
to our sedate little town their disturbing messages from the world
of passion: Wahnfried, Peace after Passion.

We found it as we had feared. Actually, the sight of the house
after the bombing was rather worse than anything I could have
feared, but since our primary thought, at that stage, was for your
safety, the wreckage of Wagner's house seemed but the appropriate
background of our despair rather than its primary cause.

Like Brünnhilde before her awakening, Wahnfried was surrounded
by fire. Most of the fires had been put out by the time we arrived,
but in the gardens and the adjacent Hofgarten heaps of ash and
rubble still smouldered. Enormous craters had made the Hofgarten
a volcanic landscape, black and smoking.

The main façade of the house was intact, and the inscription
placed there by Richard Wagner could still be read:

Hier wo mein Wähnen Frieden fand –
Wahnfried – sei dieses Haus von mir benannt.

Here where my passions found in peace their frame
May Wahnfried be my chosen house's name.[*]

[*] Literally, Here, where my passions found peace, may this house be named by me
– Wahnfried.

These survivals demonstrated their own doughty defiance, perhaps aptly, since Richard Wagner possessed in abundance the qualities of the survivor and would demonstrate after the war, despite the disastrous association of his name with Uncle Wolf, that he would rise up again to haunt the human consciousness. His house, however, had not exactly survived. The whole of the wing known as the Siegfried Haus – where Uncle Wolf had been wont to stay – was now in ruins. The top storeys of the house had been burnt out. The nursery, with the toys, had been blown to smithereens.

'What are you *doing*?' Helga's crossness, an habitual reaction to almost everything from now onwards in our lives together, was here no doubt a useful corrective against hysteria or grief.

I had crouched down in the ashy rubble and was holding on to a small wooden hand. Gentle dusting of the cinders and flakes of fallen masonry revealed Mr Punch in a remarkably good state of repair. I could not see Judy, or the policeman, though it was possible that some of the charcoal remains, crunched beneath our feet, were the puppet's old companions. Either the passage of time, since he enacted the role of the Jew in the thornbush, or a scorching, or his Icarus-like descent from the nursery floor had removed the papier-mâché nose, or most of it, from his wooden one.

'Put it *down*,' said Helga furiously.

'By God, that's Wolfgang,' I replied.

At a distance of some fifty yards, standing in the ruins and staring through bare joists and girders to the relentless grey sky, stood Winnie's younger son. When he recognized us he smiled, a big toothy grin, which was a welcome rather than a token of mirth.

'Wieland is still in Berlin,' he said.[*] 'Mummy has taken Ellen to the country. She hasn't had the baby yet.' He was talking of his young, heavily pregnant wife.

'Senta – Senta –' Helga was saying your name like a mantra. At that moment we had no hope that you were alive. We were both in shock. My mother was dead. Since we had left you in her

[*] Wieland was in fact on his way by car.

company, it was natural to conclude that you were dead. The house where you had been staying was a bombsite; Wahnfried, too, was in ruins.

'We will rebuild this place,' said Wolfgang. 'I am determined to rebuild this place.'

'Your mother?' I asked.

'Mummy's gone to the cottage. It's all right. Your kid – Senta – she's taken her there. She took her to get out of the raid. Your own mother . . . ?'

While I gestured speechlessly, tears streaming from my eyes, I would not have been able to know whence they flowed – from grief at so much loss, or from relief that you survived.

I have no idea how we found the car again, Dr Gerlandt's Mercedes. We did so, however, and this time Helga was at the wheel. I sat in the passenger seat, lighting cigarettes, which I passed to her lips and then took back for a puff of my own, while nursing Mr Punch on my lap.

I had been to Winnie's weekend retreat in the Fichtelgebirge on a number of occasions and we managed, by using small country routes, to avoid the American roadblocks. As we approached the cottage garden we saw you hanging out washing on a line, with a beautiful peasant woman who, with clothes pegs between her lips, was doing the same.

'For God's sake' – Helga's response to my tears – 'she's *alive*. Take a grip on yourself.'

You put the unpegged shirt, drawers, bodices back in the basket and ran to greet us. Your resemblance to the peasant woman at the washing line was uncanny, the same polished weather-beaten cheek-bones, the same thick dark-blonde Celtic hair. Only the deep midnight-blue eyes were different. How often, in your childhood and adolescence, would strangers, or those meeting you for the first time, remark upon those eyes. Of course, once my suspicions about your identity had formed themselves into a certainty these comments made me bridle. Did they know? Could they see?

The peasant woman finished pegging a sheet, waved to us and

came forward: Winnie in all her beauty, all her gutsiness, all her absurdity, her culpable absurdity. 'How are things in town?'

'We've seen Wolfgang,' I said.

Helga said, 'N——'s mother. Darling' – she took your hand – 'Granny . . .'

Winnie said, 'Oh, I'm so sorry. So very sorry.'

You reacted immediately. You burst into tears while Helga enfolded you in her arms.

I do not know how long this moment lasted. It was a timeless tableau. It could well have been an hour, or several hours, later that Winnie defiantly asked, 'Any news from Berlin?'

'I gather Wieland is coming. Wolfgang thought he might have escaped.'

For a moment her sons seemed of no importance to her. 'The last proper news we heard on the wireless was that the Führer has given orders that we should fight on. Of course, the Americans have taken over the radio stations down here now, so it is impossible to get any news.'

'I wish they'd stop this nonsense – it's obscene,' said Helga. 'The Russians have taken Berlin. I wish they'd just stop the killing.'

Winnie drew herself up to her full height and there was a deep intake of breath. 'I have no doubt *whatever*,' she said firmly and she began to nod her head rhythmically to emphasize each syllable, 'that the Führer's policy will be vindicated, that he is probably *even as we speak* mobilizing our divisions. He will drive the Russians out of Berlin. He will drive the Americans out of Bayreuth.'

I so well recall where we were all standing when she said this – on the lawns of her cottage. I could see the spring sky behind her proud head. She looked very confident, almost happy. Helga was shaking her head in disbelief, in the way you might if someone had taken leave of their senses. But she wasn't mad, Winnie – unless you think it is mad to live exclusively in a world of your own and to insist on life being understood exclusively on your terms.

We had not planned to stay, and we were not invited to stay, with Winnie in her cottage. We did not part with her on bad terms, we did not quarrel with her conviction, as hundreds of thousands of Germans died and our cities went up in flames, that Wolf would once again perform a miracle. But it became clear we should move on. A row was smouldering, and in the car it escalated, between me and Helga about whether we should drive the Merc back to Munich – my idea – or pursue her proposal that we go to Leipzig, the birthplace of Bach, Wagner and music. In making this decision, for Leipzig, we unwittingly became East Germans, and the rest of your upbringing and education was destined to be in a Communist state. Here you stayed – until your chance to escape came, some time after that *Meistersinger* in 1960.

None of us in the Mercedes knew what the future held. You sat in the back, with some apples, some cheese, some bread and some sausage, which Winnie had given us. It must have been so boring for you when your 'parents' began their warm-up routines for one of their rows. Even as Helga reversed the Merc, she was advancing the case for Leipzig and I was asking, 'Don't you think your father would like his car back?'

'Oh, I see, so you know more about what my father wants than I do?'

You'd turned your profile, identical to that of dear Win, and you were waving to her – it was the last glimpse you had of her, as she stood there, in her white apron, a broad, confident smile lighting up her face and her arm raised, either in valediction or salute.

THE POWER OF READING

Visit the Random House website and get connected with information on all our books and authors

EXTRACTS from our recently published books and selected backlist titles

COMPETITIONS AND PRIZE DRAWS Win signed books, audiobooks and more

AUTHOR EVENTS Find out which of our authors are on tour and where you can meet them

LATEST NEWS on bestsellers, awards and new publications

MINISITES with exclusive special features dedicated to our authors and their titles

READING GROUPS Reading guides, special features and all the information you need for your reading group

LISTEN to extracts from the latest audiobook publications

WATCH video clips of interviews and readings with our authors

RANDOM HOUSE INFORMATION including advice for writers, job vacancies and all your general queries answered

Come home to Random House

www.rbooks.co.uk